One Woman,
One Spirit, One Nature

One Woman, One Spirit, One Nature

The Bernadette Engstrom Story

Second Edition

Era Lewis

This is a work of fiction. Names, characters, places, and incidents are products of the author's imagination or are used fictitiously and are not to be construed as real.

The diagrams in the book are to help the reader understand the story. They are not representations of real locations.

Any resemblance to actual events, locales, organizations, government entities, or persons, living or dead, is entirely coincidental.

This book contains mature situations and adult themes. Please review the book and determine if it is acceptable for your child.

ISBN 9798218229184

Dedicated to My Father
Frank R. Lewis

And

My Spiritual Master
Paramahansa Yogananda

The Genre:

One Woman, One Spirit, One Nature is an action–environmental thriller. Some parts in the book approach the fringes of farcical humor, because truly, the human ego can drive people into the farcical realm in many situations, on any given day. If you detect a bit of spoofery in the story, you might be right. Because love can be such a beautiful thing, there is romance in the book; both human and spiritual love are to be found. Nature and her spirit are big characters in this book. The truth is, we can't live without nature.

Joy to you and happy reading.

Thank you:

A special thanks to Bob Henderson for helping me with the cover of the book. I would also like to thank Greg with the Lebanon Senior Center Book Club for reviewing the book and giving me materials for a sequel, even though I haven't thought about a sequel just yet.

Their support means a tremendous amount to me.

Era Lewis

Table of Contents

Part I

Chapter 1
Bernadette's Introduction to Earth

(January 9, 1962)

Up to this Sunday, Roger's days held purpose, but his life's foreordained purpose had been in standby.

A heavy sheen of perspiration glistened on Dr. Roger O'Rafferty's face as he skillfully reacted to the slipping motion of his truck, ceasing the fishtail with slight steering and acceleration adjustments. For Roger, there were no over-adjustments, no correcting an over-correction. He modelled efficiency and that made him a healer for the infirm and a slayer for the villainous.

Loosening the first few buttons of his heavy wool coat with his left hand, he then turned the heater switch down a notch with his right, mentally noting that his elevated temperature was contradictory to the biting ten degrees Fahrenheit outside, but in keeping with his elevated levels of adrenaline. His powerful hands returned to the steering wheel while his mind spun through a lengthy list of considerations relevant to the day.

Seeking to settle his heart rate, he decided to create a new aphorism, a soothing activity he routinely performed when the hornet's nest of life was stirred up. His aphorisms always encompassed the deeper teachings imparted to him as a young Irish lad; teachings that were both his light and his guide. Always. He existed within those teachings, and for them.

Roger, a man of crowning mental and physical form, drove the Northern Lights Highway at an irritatingly slow speed on his way to the Anchorage Community Hospital. The highway conditions this Sunday were treacherous; a layer cake comprised of high humidity snow on the bottom, followed by a thick center of ice, and since 7 a.m., an additional top layer of crunchy needle-crystalline snow had been falling. It would take a superhuman, whose reflexes mimicked a sour bear defending her cub, to effectively maneuver a vehicle over the combination of sheering ice and billions of mini crystalline ball bearings, should they dare drive above twenty miles per hour.

The aphorism came to him just as the intermolecular forces composing the ice and snow erratically altered under the moving weight of the truck, causing the rear of the truck to slip toward the ditch, then bounce back.

> Bountiful fortuitous events would be graciously appreciated but for the lens of scarcity.

The aphorism sent a chill of caution though him. Stripping any lens of scarcity from his view, he mentally bowed before the gracious bestowal granted to him this morning.

Opening another two buttons on his coat, as his perspiration rate was continuing to climb, Roger once again checked the rear-view mirror, then glanced deeper into the trees on his right and left. Based on what happened earlier this morning, he was anticipating someone would be following him, or waiting for him as he drove along an isolated section of the highway. He hoped it was the former and not the latter, because the road conditions would make it very difficult for him to evade an ambush from the front or side. He had the comfort of both a rifle and pistol, one propped on the passenger floor and the other snugged tight to his side with a shoulder holster, but they didn't improve his lack of speed and extensive exposure.

Regardless of the road conditions not being in his favor today, Roger took a moment to be thankful for the survival enhancing qualities he did possess. There were three qualities, just three, which propelled his life down a path of positive events instead of hardship: an exacting, analytical and feeling mind, superior hand-eye coordination, and the rare ability to assess a person's character shortcomings and the health effects resulting from those shortcomings.

Roger's mind, even when used in what might be considered the commonplace exercise of home buying, excelled at concrete and intuitive reasoning. When he bought his house eighteen miles outside of Anchorage, he clearly understood needs from wants from imperatives, weighing the importance of each. The hazardous winter weather conditions found in Alaska and the obvious difficulty of quickly driving to his work at Anchorage Community Hospital on the desolate roads near his home, were of lesser importance than his necessity for privacy. Colleagues had badgered him to live in town, providing him with harrowing details of winter driving. He was not to be swayed and this made sense, because Roger was the only person who had all the information to make the decision. His life demanded a constant level of obscurity, and the ever-prying eyes and disruption within towns made privacy and security impossible. He reasoned that being outside of town would allow him to better assess any problems or threats.

That pragmatic line of thinking became truth today when Roger stepped outside into the civil twilight, which in January was mid-morning. Binoculars in one coat pocket and rifle slung over his back, he found every step to be a rejuvenation of life, the only rejuvenation he got lately. The quiet, purity of smells, and complex beauty only found in the great wilderness soothed his empty restlessness, the ever-gnawing tension alerting him that something of importance was to come. He waited for that moment to come, had been waiting. The waiting was maddening.

Mildred, an exuberant Newfoundland dog and a gift from one of his frail and ailing patients, had drawn his attention to the ominous evidence with several yips. A measly two hundred yards from his woodshed there were uninvited snowshoe tracks. Immediately, Roger understood their owner to be the cause of Mildred's barking in the wee dark hours this morning. He was grateful for the sturdy indoor shutters he had installed, for they would have block anyone from seeing within the house, even Roger or Mildred's silhouette when the lights were briefly turned on in his bedroom and living room. The style of snowshoe and the depth of depression, now lightly obscured by the falling snow, indicated the person was most certainly a man of over two hundred muscular pounds.

Knowing the vulnerabilities of his position, Roger whistled for Mildred, a sound that would be mistaken for grey jay by all but Mildred, as he ran several hundred feet, ducking into a stand of birch offering them a sprinkling of protection. Rifle chamber loaded, he viewed an opponent's possible vantage points with his binoculars. Within the span of a minute, his realization of the security in his surroundings increased. As with any animal under the threat of predation, Roger was automatically, both consciously and subconsciously, gathering and assessing all the information from his senses: the calls of the birds were normal and held no urgency; the animals living beneath the snow still stirred; and the charge in the air held excitement, but no menace. Most telling, Mildred was unconcerned, the long guard hairs around her neck and down her back which stood erect when danger was near, were relaxed.

He took that temporary subsidence of the threat to head back toward the house, holding the rifle in both hands, ready to sight in any danger should conditions change. He walked with the swagger of a man of confidence and exceptional physical build. He knew, if anyone was ever able to get a shot off toward him, they had better make sure their first shot was the only shot they needed, because Roger's second exceptional quality, his exacting hand-eye coordination, gave him the advantage over any gun toting mob in Alaska. His colleagues in medical school often joked that Roger's hands and eyes were actually the same organ. From scalpel to sutures, the smaller the detail, the more beautiful his work became. The larger the wound, Roger's keen eyes could repair the jagged fragments into a healed pink blush, absent of the large annoying pucker so often found with such serious wounds. This skill served other areas of his life. Whether driving a truck on slick roads or flying his bush plane in harrowingly windy conditions in remote parts of Alaska, he could outmaneuver most forces that would render other people sorry puppets of fate. And, with shallow effort, he was an admirable crack shot. Actually, he was best.

The threat today was gone for now, but the questions sizzled within him. *Why did the person come near his home and just leave? When would be their next uninvited visit? What was their goal?* Things had been heating up for the last six months and this was a definite indication that the formerly smoldering log of threats was now rolling down the hill, ablaze from the oxygen rushing past the fuel.

The call from the hospital came in shortly after Roger withdrew inside the defensible sanctuary of his home. The lead nurse, Nancy, explained that Dr. Lewis, who was scheduled to work this Sunday, had suffered several lacerations to his head and legs following a minor altercation with a moose in his front yard. Roger shook his head in silent disgust. Everyone in Alaska knew that "shooing" a moose from one's yard was risky business. Nancy assured Roger that Dr. Lewis would be in later that evening, but as of right now they had admitted a woman, Mrs. Jan Engstrom, in the early stages of labor and he was asked to come posthaste.

After hanging up the telephone, Roger contemplated the use of the word "posthaste" by Nancy. Tucking the peculiarity of speech aside for later analysis, he thought about the woman in labor. She had never visited the hospital, which meant he wouldn't know prior health conditions which might lead to problems during childbirth, a situation which could prove troublesome.

However, Roger did know her husband, Bill Engstrom, and quite well, although Jan and most of Anchorage wouldn't be aware of their friendship. Neither Roger nor Bill Engstrom, and actually a broader group of men around Anchorage, would ever publicly acknowledge their comradery. They were Alaska's stealth, the brave men who were prepared to stay behind and feed information to the U.S. military if and after a Soviet Union invasion, an invasion considered imminent by many Alaskans during the antagonistic Cold War. Although the direct funding for this secret operation, code named "Washtub", had been curtailed in 1959, the funds were metered in through other backdoor governmental methods. The Washtub program, three years since its superficial demise, was stouter and better equipped than ever. The men, a variety of trappers, miners, train operators, bush pilots, doctors, electricians, geologists, and fishermen, were highly trained and ready to survive what many considered would be a death sentence during an invasion by Alaska's power-hungry neighbor, the Soviet Union.

It was this diverse group of men working within the Washtub program who had a much better understanding of the Soviet threat than those ignorant government officials residing in the Lower 48. They knew the threat of the Soviet Union (SU) wasn't a result of some intermediate level SU military official who had come and gone, or a featherbrained future concept, but an ongoing infiltration of SU spies into Alaska for the last decade. Washtub men were readily used to eliminate high target and weapon proficient spies penetrating Alaska's wilderness and society. There were no arrests nor any write-ups in the paper and certainly no reports made to the federal government. The commie problems were fixed locally, quietly, and with finality.

The Alaskans working in the Washtub program began noticing, since early last summer, more overt aggression from the newly arrived SU spies. The actions of attempted retaliation following the elimination of a comrade became more prevalent and more intense. There was a growing concern that these ordinary Alaskan men and their families would be impacted by the commies' growing anger, yet none of the benefits from being in an official U.S. military group would be available to any of those wounded or killed while defending the new state of Alaska. Dissatisfaction over this situation was beginning to permeate the Washtub program.

As Roger continued his drive to the hospital, he pondered the phone conversation with Nancy. He decided that the use of "posthaste" didn't convey a medical emergency, rather a mental emergency. What further concerned him was Nancy's tone of voice and the unusual spaces of static silence. There was an uneasiness in her voice, telling him something was amiss. Roger did his best to dismiss this annoying, nagging idea, for the was little he could do about it right now. He wondered if the uneasy feelings were just a reasonable outcome of someone intruding onto his land and the constant Cold War hype.

Most unfortunately, Roger didn't get to see the other end of the phone conversation. After getting off the phone with Roger, Nancy stood with her hands on her hips and her lips pressed tightly closed in an effort to contain the primal screech of rage she felt thundering up from her torso. Jan Engstrom had already managed to insult her and the rest of the staff in the hospital within a record breaking few minutes of her cursed arrival. Nancy had not given Roger all the details of the patient in labor because the phone she used was not in a private location and at that moment, someone was probably within hearing range. What she had really wanted to tell Roger was the only way to survive this patient would be to properly gag her. Picking up a sedative vial and twirling it wickedly, Nancy then eyed the recently laundered linens on the table in front of her, a more archaic but time proven silencing device. Taking one of compatible size, she intently folded the behavioral remedy, stashing it with the vial and a needle into the pocket of her crisp nurses' uniform. With a small smile of satisfaction, Nancy turned and marched back down the hall toward the room from which emanated an uninterrupted series of complaints and discord.

Had Roger known what he was about to encounter the most complex adult person he would ever meet in the healthcare setting or in his life, he would have been mentally preparing for it during the drive. Instead, the harrowing road conditions and possibility of ambush, were now accompanied by another point of focus, an unusual abundance of wildlife just within the tree line. After traveling seven miles from his home, he realized this was a parade of animals, only he was the entire parade, and all the animals were the spectators. Moose were around in droves, a regular sight for the Anchorage area. But there were over twenty snow hares, eight red foxes, a big male Yukon wolf, a black bear that should be hibernating, numerous species of birds, and three domestic dogs that looked to be well kept. Was January 9th auspicious in some way? By the time he was at the hospital he had also passed a number of minks, ermines, and several wolverines. *Completely strange!* Roger thought to himself. None had been in the road, but they all were watching his car. Roger knew this because when he passed an animal and looked in the rearview mirror, the animal has turned its head in the direction of his truck. None of the animals tried to flee from his presence. They stood by comfortably and with interest.

Finally at the hospital, Roger briskly neared Mrs. Engstrom's maternity-ward room, still distracted by the glorious display of animals along the road. Glancing down at the chart, trying settle his thoughts, he became more aware of an annoyance, an irritating tone, and his mental fascination with seeing the animals was jarred into a less pleasing state.

"I don't need any of your help or any of this useless fluffing of pillows. Just give me some medication so I don't have to think. I know I am having a worthless girl, a stupid brat. I feel it. Had to carry this thing I don't even like and for months on end! I already have a nice little girl. I wanted a boy, a boy I could cherish. A boy who will take care of me when I am old. A boy I can be proud of. Boys have value." Nancy, who stood with a pillow in hand, took several steps back from Mrs. Engstrom's bed attempting to avoid the spewing venom. Her hand involuntarily hugged the pocket containing the possible remedy for the situation.

Walking in the room, Roger glanced up from the chart in his hands. Noticing a flicker of movement near the curtain, he cleared his throat in surprise, but gave only a passing glance to the five back-capped chickadees precariously situated on the narrow window ledge looking toward the room. Tucking the additional animal oddities away in his mind, he looked kindly at Nancy, favoring her an unexpectedly sexy wink to put her at ease, before taking a deep breath and shifting his attention to Mrs. Engstrom. Nancy took several more steps away from the bed and toward the pleasant demeanor of Dr. Roger O'Rafferty. For the last two weeks she hadn't been on shift when he was in the hospital, and from what she could tell, he grew more enticing by the week. To say he was good looking wasn't very accurate; such a shallow statement just didn't give enough credit to his Adonis build; a five-foot eleven-inch frame, unruly rich brown hair, and a mouth that looked to be created by Leonardo DaVinci. His nose was ever so slightly to one side and had a bump on it, as if he had been in a fight and broken it. But it added a look of intensity to his eyes. He wasn't model gorgeous, but rather manly gorgeous. He had winked at her! Oh, the other girls would be so jealous.

Inwardly, Roger sighed as he looked at Mrs. Engstrom. Roger's third phenomenal quality, assessing character short comings and their impact to health, switched on.

"I am Dr. O'Rafferty, and you are a soon to be not so pregnant Mrs. Engstrom? It is a pleasure to meet you." Reaching out, he lightly placed his gentle hand over Mrs. Engstrom's cold hand as she lay in the bed. Underneath the white coat and stethoscope, Roger was seething. He asked himself, *why couldn't people just be happy with a child? Instead, they want a maid, butler, or some type of servant to help them in twenty years for the following twenty or thirty years.* Frowning, Roger wondered if freedom was a complete fallacy in many households.

Mrs. Engstrom, a pretty brunette with a very distinctive British look, smiled, but what struck Roger was the woman's eyes held no hint of motherly contentment, only a calculating assessment and an insatiable neediness. Then, as if a black veil had fallen from the ceiling and shrouded the bed in maliciousness, Mrs. Engstrom's countenance entirely darkened. Her sugared voice was a repulsive contrast to a face painted with loathing. "If you are in the mood to help here, all I need would be some pain medication. I can't take pain. Just put me out."

Quickly changing her expression to that of a feeble-minded nitwit, her face dominated by a slack jaw and unfocused crossed eyes, she said in a perfect imitation of Roger's diminutive Irish accent, "Where you from, you with the funny accent?"

Nancy gasped.

Roger thought, *so that is how it is going to be, eh? You want to lower me down to your level of agony by suggesting my accent is a sign of stupidity.*

Roger focused on his breathing and waited several heartbeats as the anger flowed out with each exhale. Mrs. Engstrom's mercurial behavior assailed his senses, elevating his wariness, and increasing his concern for the child to be born. He felt himself break out in another wave of sweat and not the glands for cooling but the glands that operate under stress. Roger did the only thing he could at that moment, the only acceptable reaction, prioritize and categorize. All things fell away from his conscious thought except the need to successfully deliver the baby.

Turning to Mrs. Engstrom, he looked into her eyes, which was not hard to do because she was giving him a defiant stare. Warring emotions ebbed and flowed within her, and then, he understood. She unequivocally *hated* herself. She swam in a lower pool of agony, coming up to the surface when she chose to find love, only to dive back under to douse herself in sickly hatred. He understood her mental suffering would lead to degenerative conditions of her heart and further chemical imbalances in her system, leading to a vicious cycle of personal torment.

Mrs. Engstrom's face contorted in pain from a contraction. She had been concealing her discomfort up to this moment under a bushel of wasteful emotions, but Nancy and Roger were well aware of the baby's progression.

Shaking his head, Roger mentally adjusted his position from a giving healer to one of self-preservation helper; this wasn't his war to fight, not today.

Roger politely explained, "First of all, I need you to push the baby out, so you can't be "out of it". If you are "out of it", you most certainly will need my help. Second," and he thickened his Irish accent, "I spent a considerable amount of time in Ireland when I was growing up. It isn't funny, just an accent that is different from yours Mrs. Engstrom. Or different from yours when you're not rancorously imitating someone else."

Nancy, deciding the best way for any of the hospital staff to deal with Mrs. Engstrom was in shorter spans of time, a proven method to limit the transmission of emotional disease, came back into the conversation at this point. "Dr. O'Rafferty, this is probably a good time for me to get Mrs. Enstrom in a comfortable position. We shan't take too long." Raising her right eyebrow, she gave Roger a knowing look; *the sooner we get on with this, the sooner we will be done with this.*

Thankful for the reprieve, Roger nodded and headed for the door. He was almost out the door when the tirade began again.

"My husband did this to me. He wanted this. As soon as this thing is born, I want all that pain taken away and I want to be in oblivion. Why couldn't I have a boy." The immature whining was causing Roger to grind his teeth.

As his protective instincts grew for the child to be born and his loathing increased for a woman of despicable character, Roger decided to give Mrs. Engstrom something real to worry about. Sticking his head back in the door, he said, "Oh, and Nancy, would you be sure to have the large scalpel out in the event Mrs. Engstrom needs a <u>major</u> episiotomy?" Brilliant toothy grins spread across the faces of both Roger and Nancy. Then he was gone from the room again and the only sound came from his foot falls on the hallway linoleum.

Deciding Bill Enstrom was a patient worthy of his comfort, for Roger couldn't imagine what Bill had to endure daily, he headed to the waiting room to visit with him. He thought about why a man, who had a decent amount going for him - pleasant features, strong build, and amicable character - would marry a woman who appeared to provide so little. During his short walk, he came to one conclusion: loneliness. Bill was a loner of sorts. Loneliness could not only encourage but cement the unhealthiest relationship. Anchorage was filled with independent loners, and loners were accepted here, so the only pressure to alleviate loneliness was the internal one.

Bill stood and warmly shook Roger's hand. His respect for Dr. O'Rafferty was complete. This doctor could have avoided danger by hiding behind his important credentials, but instead he risked his life with the Washtub group, a group that had little clout and even less gratitude from officials in Washington.

Bill confirmed that his wife was most irrational about pain. "A splinter almost requires immediate surgery, days of rest, and medication," he said with a nervous grin. Then, looking at Roger with a lost expression, he said, "She wasn't like this before our first child. After Julie was born, everything changed." Bill shook his head showing his dismay and continued, "I don't know. Maybe I did something wrong. Sometimes it gets better, then she goes into one of her episodes. I keep thinking I can make it better, better for everyone."

Roger doubted Mrs. Engstrom would get better unless she wanted to change; change her thoughts, her emotions, and her ideas of control. Since the human condition was always filled with surprises, he decided that further consideration might lead him to a manner of healing for Jan. Given it was important to focus on the delivery of the new child, the beauty of such an event, addressing the wife's issues at a later time was logical. "Why don't we talk about her health next week, when we won't be interrupted by a new baby?" He clasped Bill's shoulder in a manner of reassurance.

Bill looked relieved at the thought of help with an issue that confused him. "I would appreciate that."

Checking that no one was outside the waiting room door, Bill then lowered his voice before he continued, "Heard how you and Norm ousted those two commies up on Big Lake last week. You do some excellent flying with that Cessna 180. Pushed that ol' engine like a hawk riding the storm, I'd say. Think you rounded them all up?"

Easing themselves into the waiting room chairs, Roger matched Bill's low tone, "Nope, I know there were three, could have been four or five. I think two took the hit to save the others. We should have stayed up there another few hours, but with the new storm coming in everyone wanted to get home. The commies are getting fed up with their losses and I think they will take more aggressive measures to avenge their departed comrades. We have got to keep our guard up." Looking Bill in the eye Roger added, "I had a visitor at my place last night, so you keep an eye out too. Just because you are in town doesn't mean you aren't at risk. You get the word out to everyone you see."

Bill looked startled. "You had someone at your place?"

Roger just nodded in an affirmative manner.

Bill said, "I am not sure I should have gotten mixed up in this thing. It looked rather harmless in the beginning. I never thought Alaska would get invaded and I didn't think those idiots would continue to send agents into our territory after they lost a few. On top of that, we are a part of the United States now and the military should be dealing with any foreign aggression. Because of family responsibilities, you know… my wife isn't well with all the short days up here and a new baby makes her darn unreasonable, I have been exploring my options to move to Oregon. I have a job offer down there at a lumber mill. Thinking it might be better for all of us with this new baby."

Roger wanted to comment about Jan's health, but Nancy appeared in the door, giving a nod. Roger rose. "Think it is getting to be about time. I should return with a new baby for you."

Roger found Mrs. Engstrom's room was blessedly quiet. He raised his eyebrows to Nancy. Sue, the nursing assistant, was also in the room, and they both smiled at the change in Mrs. Engstrom's demeanor. Mrs. Engstrom averted her gaze and made a minimal amount of noise during the entire birth. Within his mind, Roger deadened all other stimuli in the room, bringing his attention to the baby whose head was being pushed through the birth canal.

The delivery was quick, and Roger didn't remember much of it, that is the mechanics. What he did remember was the emotion, the gentle perturbation of the air as he held the baby's head, waiting for the rest to appear. A tenderness, so sweet in purity, washed over him, causing him to bite down on his tongue to stifle the feeling. *How strange would this emergency call get?* he wondered. When the newborn had slipped entirely into his hands, he eased her over on her back, his large hands encasing her in warmth and strength, and looked closely at all of her. Turning her backwards and forwards, he scanned and rescanned the wiggling baby.

He wanted to roar.

My goodness, he thought, *this couldn't be!*

Although many wouldn't recognize the birthmarks on this baby for what they were, as the birthmarks didn't have the precision and definition of a tattoo, Roger knew exactly what they were, for as a young boy his mother had explained them to him, and he comprehended their significance at this moment.

A mark, almost like a small burn from grabbing a hot frying pan, laid powerfully under her left breast. It began with a point, decreasing in width till it ended bluntly. It was a sword, sign of the courageous warrior she could become.

Being under her left breast was significant, for it meant no matter the struggle, she would be triumphant in her journey.

What looked to be an odd series of dots and swirls on her left shoulder blade was a triskele.

She would be positioned to explore a higher calling, the protection of nature.

There, on the top of her left foot was an ailm,  signifying her spiritual journey and pureness in energy exhibited in this lifetime.

All of these combined meant she was a defender of nature and the spiritual essence of nature; she could bring healing to nature if she so desired and she could lead others on that same path.

The sword and triskele were café-au-lait in color. The ailm was a remarkable port-wine stain, which Roger considered beautiful. Anyone of those birthmarks would have been remarkable; all three together were extraordinary.

Nancy, noticing something was wrong, came to Dr. O'Rafferty's side and assisted with the umbilical cord. She looked into his astonished eyes, then turned and asked Sue, to see to Mrs. Engstrom's comfort.

This fantastic event seared his mind with a sense of privilege. Given his training as a youth in Ireland, he understood the significance of what he saw before him. For he held not just a baby girl, but a designated daughter of Anu, the Celtic Goddess of Ireland, a baby who would become a warrior for spirit and nature should she so choose to follow her path.

Roger sat quietly, caressing the quiet but responsive infant, marveling at the true birthmarks. Nancy nudged him again when the silence and lack of activity became too expansive, getting the normal routine flowing once again, then removing herself from the room to return to the nurse's station once the basics were completed. Transferring his gaze from the rich ringlets of hair, an auburn glory streaked with mahogany embellishment, he again evaluated the baby girl's health, looking at all her limbs, checking that her senses were functioning, and listening to her internal organs. Sue assisted in wrapping the baby in a warm blanket. Usually, Sue would hand the child to the mother, given that baby was healthy and in no need of additional care. Instead, Dr. O'Rafferty cradled the baby several extended minutes with a look of concern. Finally standing, he turned toward the bed to place the cooing infant with Mrs. Engstrom.

Mrs. Engstrom was filled with jealously, for Dr. O'Rafferty care with the child had not gone unnoticed. "I would like some strong medication now. Take her to the nursery. I am too tired to deal with a squirming, crying girl-brat. Then with a calculating eye, she pierced Roger with unabashed fury, "You name her, since you care so much about that thing."

Roger observed Mrs. Engstrom with censorship. She was not only mean but had some smarts about her. She had quickly assessed his loving emotions toward the baby and took that as an opening for attack. One could often overlook mean and ignorant as perhaps an unfortunate combination. But smart people had no real good excuse for meanness, in Roger's view.

Turning his back on Mrs. Engstrom, instinctively sheltering the baby from a mealy-mouthed mother spewing hatred that would last a childhood, he sweetly smiled as the brown baby eyes widened, looking at him in wonder and love. Then joy spread across her face, a toothless type of smile dominated Roger's vision, not an infant reflex smile, a conscious smile with true understanding of happiness. *Impossible!* he thought again. There was a virtue within her, different from what he saw in any newborn, and certainly most people he knew. Cradling the baby to his chest while walking briskly out the door, he escaped Hades, moving on towards the nurse's station. With an afterthought he called back to Sue, saying she was most qualified to finish up with Mrs. Engstrom.

His thoughts were swirling while his strides took him away from the emotionally toxic waste dump. Glancing out a hall window, he slid to a stop, shocked by the three huge moose standing in the parking lot just twenty feet away, all looking at him. He amended that thought. *No, they were looking at Her.* A warrior who could choose to fight for nature and the spirit within nature. In a moment of thought luminosity, a name spontaneously came to him. *Bernadette.*

Gently giving the baby to Nancy, Roger decided on a course of action. "Her name is Bernadette Engstrom. You should check with the father on a middle name. I'm headed to the shower, unless there is something else right now."

Nancy thought, *yes, there is something else. If you aren't busy this afternoon, want to get married?* Stammering while thinking of the honeymoon she said, "Ah, hummmm. We are glad to have you this afternoon. Would it be possible for you to somehow change Mrs. Engstrom so she isn't such a witch?"

Roger frowned. "That is a task I don't think can be accomplished while on earth."

Nancy watched the perfect twin cheeks walk toward the shower room while her finger softly touched the right, rosy cheek of Bernadette. Nancy wondered if Dr. O'Rafferty ever noticed that she was an attractive young woman.

Once under the shower spray, Roger felt secure enough to pound the wall a few times. He pondered why fate would find it necessary to put a warrior for the Goddess Anu in a stew pot with a mother who would never care about her. His thoughts then turned to why the government didn't do something useful to curb inappropriate people from having children. The application and training to have a baby should, at a minimum, be the same requirements for being a doctor to deliver the baby. He couldn't get Bernadette's actions out of his mind, for the little girl had reached for him while he examined her. Did she already understand that her mother didn't want her?

Of course, she did.

Roger checked on the few other patients in the hospital after his shower, until Nancy cornered him. "Dr. O'Rafferty, would you come and check those odd marks on Bernadette? Mr. Engstrom is visiting his wife right now. But since he saw those strange marks, he has been hounding me every chance he gets. And Bernadette doesn't blink much. Just looks at everyone with those big brown eyes."

Going to the nursery was both the first and last thing he wanted to do. He would protect Bernadette with his life, if necessary. He understood Bernadette's future in ways unimaginable; her love and confusion, her strength and her pain, her resolve and her loses. But he didn't want to think of Bernadette's future with a hateful mother, the lifelong impact it would have. He couldn't imagine such a splendid human being growing up with such a demented person. "Did Mrs. Engstrom see her yet?"

Nancy gave Roger a frown, to which he replied, "Careful, you will crease the epidermis in no time at all. Let's get some formula together and I'll feed her. I think she is fine but will observe her for a few more minutes."

Nancy, a master at hiding emotions during surprising or traumatic situations, did not reveal how shocked she was. A doctor would never feed a newborn; those menial tasks were always the nurses' job. She couldn't think of any situation which would cause a doctor to idle his time away with such a task. Glancing askew at Dr. O'Rafferty, Nancy teased curiously, "Finally found a love?"

Roger's eyes lit with delight. "Perhaps."

Bernadette was more interested in holding onto Roger's finger. After some struggle, she finally took the bottle, but only if she could grip his finger. When Nancy took the empty bottle away, Roger still sat with her. "Do you think I would get in trouble if I stole her?" Roger gave a pained smile.

Nancy marveled at this turn of events. Here was the best-looking doctor in Anchorage with the sexiest accent and the only girl to turn his head was just born and wouldn't be dating for years. All of the women who had paraded around in front of him, from the physically beautiful to the mentally brilliant, had failed to spark any interest. Now she knew that the rumors seeking to explain his immunity to women, a constant topic of discussion amongst women of Anchorage, were just plain wrong. Nancy realized he probably had noticed the women but had chosen to keep himself separate.

Nancy's new insight into this mysterious doctor led her to a conclusion: only a secret, a big secret, would have kept him aloft from the multitude of engaging and willing women. That was the only plausible reason for his behavior. The one to get into his heart, the only one it was safe to let into his heart, was a baby girl. Nancy said, "I won't tell if you steal her, and I am sure the mom will do cartwheels at the thought, but the dad might wonder."

When Bill walked up and saw Dr. O'Rafferty with Bernadette in his arms, he immediately asked. "Is she alright? I am concerned about those, ah, marks. They look odd. Do you think they are some type of skin cancer? Jan's mother died from cancer just two years ago. Should we have them removed before she gets too old?" With some regret he said, "I told Jan about them and she is already convinced the child will die."

Roger looked at the concerned father and internally sighed. He needed to reassure Bill, because otherwise Jan would keep the family in a constant state of turmoil. More than likely, she would find a way to convince Bill that it would be best if the baby was adopted out. Bill needed to know, needed to know who this child was and could become. "I would like to talk with you privately Bill. Let's find an empty room for this discussion.

By the time they got to a room, Bill was sure there was something very wrong with his new daughter. "Okay, don't try to give it to me slowly. I want the truth about this baby. You don't need to worry; I can handle it."

Roger unwrapped Bernadette and pointed to the three marks as he said, "Bill, these marks are birthmarks. They will not affect Bernadette's health in the least. However, they have a great deal of importance based on their location and form. They have great significance in Ireland. So just listen for a minute, and then I will answer your questions."

Roger took time to explain each birthmark, what it was and what it meant. "Your new daughter is a warrior for the Goddess Anu. Anu is the mother Goddess of Ireland. Anu is one with nature and the spiritual essence of nature. Your daughter is a chosen defender of nature and the spiritual essence of nature, should she decide to take that direction in her life. Your daughter has great honor to be born this way."

If Bill hadn't respected Dr. O'Rafferty as an incredibly talented doctor and skilled flier, he would have thought the man was delusional. The birthmarks were odd, one would have to squint and use their imagination to see the marks as anything but random, consequently the story sounded too far-fetched. He stood shaking his head. "So, you are saying my daughter will be some Joan of Arc for nature, riding around on horses slaying those who hurt the forest and the wild animals? Will she cast spells to protect the spirit of nature? Will she live like Tarzan in the jungle?" Turning, he looked Dr. O'Rafferty in the eye, "What - Are - You - Talking - About?"

Roger replied, "First, she will have a choice as to if and when she becomes a warrior. She can choose to defend nature and that can occur on many different levels, some more obscure, some more predominant. She doesn't have to be famous to fulfill the role for which she was born. She has free will. Her path and the height of her path will be her choice. Should she choose to pursue her calling, she will have the talents and skills to fulfill her goals."

"Roger, I think a lot of you as a doctor and a person, but this sounds like a bunch of malarky. I have enough problems without some freak daughter. How would you know these things?" Looking Dr. O'Rafferty up and down, "I know you are not a daughter of some Goddess Anu."

Roger, let out an exasperated breath and stood, "No, I am not a daughter of Anu. I am a son. I have the exact same birthmarks as Bernadette." With that, Roger removed his doctor's jacket, leisure jacket, shirt and tie, shoulder holster, and t-shirt. Bill noted the pistol, but given their earlier conversation, he wasn't surprised.

Bill remained sitting and could easily see the sword and triskele. Sitting back down Roger removed his shoe and sock, exposing the ailm. There was no sound in the room, other than the breathing of both men.

Bill looked at the superbly fit man before him. *What did he know about family life?* He thought. *What was he to do with such a daughter given the state of his wife?* "This… stuff…doesn't matter. I don't dare mention this to Jan. With her bouts of jealousy and ill health, hell, I don't know what she would do to this child. I could never say or do anything to suggest that Bernadette was special."

As Roger dressed, he said, "Let's think on it. Nothing has to be done now, other than assure Mrs. Engstrom that the birthmarks are not a cancer or a problem. We should just assure her they are nothing."

Neither spoke as they walked down the hall toward Mrs. Engstrom's room, with Nancy quietly joining them just before they entered. The trust in Bernadette's eyes started to wane and she grasped Roger's finger a little bit tighter as he followed Bill and Nancy into the somber room. The curtains in the room had been opened to dispel the air of negativity, for the brilliance of the new snow was a sure force against Mrs. Engstrom's irrationality. Bill and Nancy came to stand by Mrs. Engstrom's bed, on the far side. Roger stood by the side closest to the door. Bernadette began to squirm, and Roger held her a little tighter.

Bill spoke first, "Jan, I have been consulting with Dr. O'Rafferty about the few birthmarks that Bernadette has. He has assured us it is nothing to worry about. We have a wonderfully healthy baby." Leaning over, he placed a kiss on his wife's cheek as she pursed her lips.

Jan said, "Will I need to avoid taking her out in public? Is she going to look a spectacle in a swimsuit? How will I get her out of the house and married off if she has disfiguring marks all over her?"

"Mrs. Engstrom, they are hardly noticeable." Nancy said with a pleasant smile.

Roger began to lean forward to lay Bernadette near her mother's side. While trying to pry the small fingers off his index finger, she arched her back, causing her head to slip out of the crook of Roger's arm. Roger bent down a bit further to hold her tight against his body while he readjusted her position.

A huge ***boom*** exploded in the room. At that moment, the window had shattered, and a rifle bullet imbedded itself in the wall, just above Roger's head. Roger dropped to the floor, encasing Bernadette in his arms to protect her, just as a second bullet struck a foot lower into the wall. Bill had grabbed Nancy by the shoulder, dragging them both to the floor.

Mrs. Engstrom was screaming and thrashing about in the bed but made no move to get up. "Somebody help me! Help me!" she cried.

Roger looked at Bill and Nancy, as they lay on the floor. "Go under the bed and get out of the room, now!"

Roger, holding Bernadette to his chest with one hand, scuttled on the other hand and his knees out the door, with Bill and Nancy close behind."

Outside in the hall, crouching on the floor, he handed Bernadette to Nancy. "You and Bill take her to my office. Nancy, you lock yourself and Bernadette in the back medical records room off my office. There are no windows in there. Bill or I will come and get you when it is safe. Stay low, close to the floor on your way, don't show yourself above any of the windows."

Directing his attention to Bill, he said, "You can make phone calls from my office."

Taking off his white doctor's coat he tossed it on the floor. He then opened his leisure jacket and ripped his shirt open, allowing him to retrieve his pistol from its holster.

Bill looked at the pistol. "A pistol won't help against <u>that</u> rifle."

"I have a rifle stashed in the truck, but I have to get to the truck first. My guess is, whomever shot at us, is already gone. But I will check around." Roger then got on his feet, still in a crouched over position and ran down the hallway, heading for the side door.

Jan was still screaming in the room.

Nancy stared at Bill. Her voice was shaking, "Do you think the shooter is gone too, or are other staff at risk?'

"Nancy, I think they are gone, or they would have kept shooting. Let's get you and Bernadette to that room and then I will work with the other staff to keep them safe until the police arrive."

An hour later, Roger and Bill spent time with the police to ensure a proper story would be in the Anchorage Times the next morning. Everyone responding agreed that the headline should read something like this:

Stray Bullet Hits Hospital – Police Encourage Gun Safety

-

Two hours later, Bill sat down next to Roger, who was holding Bernadette at the nurse's station. The hospital and surrounding area were quiet now.

"I already told Jan that we are going to move to Oregon. I have two daughters now; I can't have revengeful Commies shooting at me. I am going to hire someone to help with Bernadette, as I don't think Jan is well enough to care for her right now, after this shooting and all."

Roger was thinking that Jan would never be well enough to care for Bernadette, under any circumstance. He looked down at the sleeping baby in his arms. *Purpose. Love. Honor. Loyalty.* Those were a few words that came to his mind.

"I agree. It appears that Washtub has gone from an intermediate exercise to an all-out war. Due to the snowshoe prints near my place this morning, my guess is, they were shooting at me. How about I come with you? I can help care for Bernadette and that will give Jan time to convalesce. I have an excellent housekeeper, Laura, who can care for Bernadette at my home while we are in Anchorage. I will call her and see if she can move into my place tomorrow. We can figure out a long-term plan once in Oregon."

The men looked at each other and understood what hadn't been said. Bill had the sinking feeling that perhaps the shooting had something to do with his uniquely birthmarked daughter. Incredulous, he asked, "Do you think they were shooting at my *baby*? Someone needs a high- powered hunting rifle to kill a newborn baby? What the in the hell is going on?"

Roger repositioned Bernadette, then stared at nothing. "There are always good and evil forces in the world. It would be possible that Bernadette's path of goodness is a threat to evil. The attack on you or I could have served as an opportunity to get to her."

Bill stood, walking several feet away, he then turned with his hands on his hips. "How did you get to this age, without being killed?"

"My parents were very protective of me. It isn't like an assassin was after me. It just meant that I wasn't put in situations that were unduly dangerous, where the dangerous actions could be exploited to a meet a greater evil."

Bill frowned, "With your flying, you put yourself in dangerous situations all the time. So, you should have been dead several years ago, right?"

"No, I am an adult now and I have skills that help me. But as an infant and toddler, I was at risk because then I was dependent on the skills of others." Roger's voice, was even, calm, and kind to Bill. "Let me help you. You are in a tough spot. I have some skills that can help."

"Roger, this sounds over the top "far out". But this Cold War is rather "far out" too, and nuclear wars are really "far out". I think if you want to come to Oregon, then you do that. How soon can you leave Anchorage?"

Looking a Bernadette, Roger's mind revolved around two words: *Foreordained Purpose.*

"When Bernadette leaves, I will leave too."

After Bill left to check on Jan, Roger spoke to Bernadette. "It is too bad, but I fear I won't be able to entirely protect you from your mother. I will do my best, but I know damage will be done."

In that moment, he sent up a prayer.

Heavenly Father, give me a chance to help Bernadette when she is a grown woman. Let me help her in some way, to make up for the childhood I can't protect her from.

Chapter 2
Growing Up Pains in Oregon

(Spring 1967)

Bernadette learned to be independent, even at five years old. She spent considerable time outside with the dog, horses, cows, and sheep. Since Bill was at work five days a week, and Jan was often "distracted", her favorite term to explain her lack of parental supervision, Bill had to fervently hope that Butter, the border collie/collie mix dog, and smarter than many people, would keep Bernadette safe. Unknown to Bill, Roger was often nearby when Bernadette was at risk. He remained in the background, rarely interfering with her activities, but close enough to intervene if necessary.

Unfortunately, Bill and Roger weren't the only men in the neighborhood who knew Bernadette was outside without a visible, supervising parent.

This Saturday, Bernadette woke early, when her mother entered her room to put something in her dresser, then leaving without a word. There were no words of motherly endearment. No loving whispers or gentle hand to the brow. Nothing. Bernadette had learned to remain quiet when her mother did quirky things, for no response to the maternal void kept her mother's temper hidden.

Bernadette didn't have the elaborate words to describe her family life, but she knew what made her sad, uncomfortable, and what gave her a deep sense of unease. The one place in the house that presented the most unease was the kitchen.

The Engstrom kitchen should have been a warm, homey place. It looked out over the backyard where the filbert orchard supported a healthy blue jay population. Bill had worked hard to remodel the house and the kitchen had all the latest perks: a walk-in pantry, lots of counter space, double oven, and new pine cabinets. Yet, the kitchen seemed out of sync and never was really a place where love was baked to fullness. Mistakes didn't steam out but lurked like a dangerous mold in the corners. A person could spend time in the kitchen, but not remember it. When Bill stood in the center of the beautiful kitchen, something he had saved money for, thinking it would bring the family together, he felt a cancerous frustration. Jan had told him this remodel was needed. She had lied. She wanted the kitchen to impress her friends and neighbors, and that was not a need.

Over the last year, dark secrets took up residence in the kitchen. Once Jan learned of Bernadette's disinterest in meat, she used that knowledge to weaponize the kitchen. It was a calculated tactic of revenge; Jan angrily noticed the sweet love Bill and Roger bestowed on Bernadette and she detested their care for the innocent girl. So, when Bill wasn't around, and Jan could corner Bernadette in the kitchen, Jan's monologue went like this:

"Oh, we are having ground-up, pretty Herford cow for dinner. Moooo."

"Cute pink piggy will be on the plate this morning. Hope it didn't suffer too much in its death."

"You better stop mourning the death of cows because then we might think you are a cow. Oh, you do look like cow."

"Bah, bah black sheep, here is the kitchen. Yes sir, yes sir, let's get out the knives."

"Oh, that is my big eared Bernadette, not a sheep."

Bernadette had cried the first few times her mother had behaved like a demented savage. Her tears had led to more sinister laughter. Quiet was best. And, avoid the kitchen.

Now awake after mother's intrusion, Bernadette thought about the excessive amount of sausage her mother took from the freezer last night. She didn't want to be around her mom this morning. Bernadette waited to hear her mother go down the stairs and back to bed. Why her mother would wake her, then go back to her own bed for more sleep, was a question Bernadette would not ask herself until much older.

Slipping out of her small cozy bed, she put on her worn jeans, some clean socks, and a soft sweatshirt. The stairs to the lower level creaked, but Bernadette had discovered that if she kept to the left side, she could get to the mudroom without disturbing her parents. The hardest part was getting her jacket off the peg, for the coat rack was too high on the wall for Bernadette. She figured out how to use the broom handle to lift the jacket and drop it to the floor. With jacket and boots put on, she was careful to open the door slowly, keeping Butter calm by scratching behind his ears. Once off the porch, they ran like the wind for the field.

At 7:30 a.m., Jan had served up oatmeal, potatoes, and sausage, this cool but clear Saturday morning.

Bill was working in his study on an important problem from the mill, a breakdown affecting production, when Jan called to him, "Breakfast is ready. We are having your favorite sausage."

Oh, timing! Bill thought to himself. Bill was pleased to hear Jan sounding so happy, yet the problem plaguing him would interfere with his enjoyment of breakfast. "Just a few more minutes. I have a blasted problem from work I need to understand right now. I am going to have to go into work early this afternoon to address it, so I have got to decipher this drawing done by someone who hit the bottle a little too much. I'll be right there."

A few more minutes turned into thirty-five more minutes. He finally left the study confident with his solution. Sitting at the dining table, he found Jan serving him food she had kept warm in the oven. Regardless of all the family pleasantries and Roger's desire for such a homey scene, he immediately stared at the empty chair and clean plate, knowing full well Jan might erupt if he showed even a normal level of concern for Bernadette's absence.

The more Bill tried to get Jan to love Bernadette and care about her, the more Jan ignored the little girl. Bill was getting fed up with the balancing act. In the last 3 months he had started wondering how he could "unknowingly" turn his wife into the child protective services for endangerment without it affecting their marriage, or perhaps it was more accurate to say without turning the marriage into solitary confinement for Bill. The opportunity hadn't presented itself. He wanted this family, and he enjoyed Jan when she was well, but her incessant lack of caring for Bernadette was a problem he just wanted to go away. The entire situation nagged his conscience and hounded his sense of duty.

Roger, living just a half of a mile away from the Engstrom's, rose before Bernadette did. Because of his concern and love for her, he had a heightened sense of awareness about her, especially when she was at risk. With his binoculars, he saw Bernadette and her dog Butter tromping out in the field before the full light of morning. He quickly dressed and went outside, leaving Mildred at home. Standing across the road from the Engstrom field and partially concealed by several large oak trees, he watched as Bernadette settled in with the large matron cow who was lying down, chewing her cud. Bernadette's head of curls rested on the cow's belly and one small arm tucked around a front leg. At times the sweetness and purity of this child staggered him. Butter rested his head on his front paws, just a few feet away in the grass. Roger rarely smoked, but he brought out his pipe to enjoy the enriching smells along with the calm. The other cows bed down nearby them.

All was quiet and serene until an old beater car went by, slowed, stopped, backed up, then pulled off the road. The male driver who got out had obviously seen Bernadette in her pink parka and had probably seen her roaming the Enstrom farm before this day. Roger assessed that this man hadn't bathed in weeks; his hair so greasy it would sustain maggot growth and his filthy clothes hung slovenly from the drug ravaged body. When the drug addict laboriously climbed the fence, Roger was right behind him, silently jumping the fence without touching it. Butter sat up, watching, yet making no sound.

Roger spoke menacingly to the man, "Can I help you? Or you just looking for a place to bathe?" Most normal people would have heard this as a threatening introduction and hastily retreated from the property. At the same time, three of the cows stood up, looking agitated.

The greasy hair flew as the man spun around. "Who are you? I have been looking for my daughter and just spotted her. You get the hell away from her." The stench from the man's breath was so repugnant, Roger backed up a few steps.

Roger's anger was increasing. "You're the girl's father? How odd, since I am her uncle and I have never met you before. Why don't you take your sorry self back to your car and get out of here?"

The drug shriveled brain cells didn't understand reality; all they contemplated was the opportunity to satisfy a sadistic craving and maybe even make a bundle of money when the girl was "rescued and returned", by him, alive. The druggie had seen Roger back up and associate the action with fear. He took several steps toward Roger and swung, an ineffective right hook that Roger easily dodged. Roger unleashed his fury with a front kick, knocking the man down, right smack in a cow-pie.

The man, winded and weak, could mount no defense as Roger firmly placed his boot on the filthy right hand, squishing it into the sod.

A pleading voice rose up from the ground, "You can't do this. Get away from me."

Roger rolled his eyes at the pathetic worm, "If I ever see you again, I'll take your sorry arse and turn into something like Swiss Cheese. No one will ever find your body because the coyotes and vultures will have picked it clean. You got that? You tell all your friends about it too. I can get over a hundred men from around here and all of us would like nothing more than to help you understand the error in your pathetically sick thoughts. Now get."

Roger pushed the man on his side with his boot, grabbed the man's belt at the back and dragged him toward the fence as the man crawled along on his hands and knees, wheezing and near vomiting. "Get out of here before I finish you off or sic the mad dog and cows on you."

Roger pushed the man over the fence, as he was now too weak to accomplish such an easy task on his own. There was the sound of shredding clothes and blood oozed from the filthy frail skin as the barbed wire completed its job. Then the car was gone, and Roger returned to the oak trees to wonder about humanity and some of its disgusting inhabitants.

Back in the Engstrom home, Bill sat back and crossed his arms, giving both Jan and Julie a look of disgust.

Jan, behaving as if this was the first moment she realized Bernadette wasn't at the table, said, "Julie, would you go upstairs and wake up your sister. Let her know that she will be grounded again."

Bill wondered how any mother could further punish a five-year-old girl who was already deprived of maternal love and treated worse than the dog by her mother. Wasn't that enough punishment?

Julie returned a few minutes later, too young to understand the why's of this dysfunctional family game and renewed her focus on the sausage. With her mouth full, she said. "Bernadette isn't there."

Jan looked at Bill, pursing her mouth in a way that told Bill there wouldn't be any intimate relations for the next six months because his misbehaving daughter caused too many headaches. "I don't think I have the patience for this behavior. Would you go look for her?"

Bill scrambled from the chair, heavily scraping the legs along the wood floor. An accident, but had he given it any thought, it would have been sweet revenge so Jan couldn't brag about the perfect floor from this morning forward. After searching the upstairs and then the main floor, Bill headed to the basement.

Coming back into the dining area he asked, "Did either of you unlock the mudroom door this morning?" Because Bernadette's jacket was also gone, Bill felt he knew the answer, but asked the question regardless.

Julie, mouth still full, rolled her eyes and tossed her hair while sending out her garbled message. "I don't like going into the mudroom and wouldn't go outside this early." Bill inwardly sighed at this snobbish announcement. Where Bernadette spent every moment out in the yard and on the farm, Julie spent every moment in her bedroom or craft room because she believed an attractive girl didn't get her hands dirty or fingernails chipped.

"If that child gets herself lost, I don't know what I will do," Jan said, all the while looking at her plate.

Bill didn't know if he could stomach much more this morning. *Yes*, he thought, *how true; it would be a terrible balancing act to show concern when you don't feel it at all. If the neighbors caught a wind of this farce, what would they think then about your elite ideas?*

Bill was stuck. How do you keep a family together when a mother hates a daughter? He headed for the back door. He already had a plan. Butter, the border collie, and favorite friend of Bernadette's, would know where she was. But Butter wasn't on the back porch or anywhere in the backyard. Bill started whistling for him. After several minutes, Butter arrived on the back porch, dancing around Bill in urgency. "Butter, show me where Bernadette is. Go get her."

Butter was down five of the stairs with one leap, with Bill right on his tail. Butter cleared the four and half foot-high gate out to the east pasture, forcing Bill to call him back, as he had to open the gate and didn't want to lose sight of Butter. Once in the field, the herding dog circled several cows. Alertly watching, Butter picked a spot and laid down in the grass.

Getting close to the Herefords, Bill finally saw the pink of Bernadette's jacket. There she was, curled up next to the belly of a cow. Bill was a rugged man. He had a rough childhood and had seen active war duty as a young man. Means were sparse when he first arrived in Alaska and it had taken long hours to accomplish his goals. He endured the mental illness of a wife but kept his marriage vows. But it would have taken the blackest of hearts not to feel immense compassion for this little girl. Bernadette so desperately wanted love, she sought out companionship from a bunch of cows. *Hell, maybe it was the best thing for her,* Bill acknowledged. *At least they cuddled with her; something her mother never tried to do.* He figured the only thing he could do to compensate for Jan's behavior was show Bernadette more love. The ramifications of that action would be a death spiral with an eminent nose plant into the ground for the marriage. But then, what was the point of this marriage anyway?

Bill was running his hands through his hair when he heard Roger call for him. Turning, he watched as Roger easily jumped the fence. "Don't teach my cows to do that, okay?"

Bill bowed his head and stared at the ground as he spoke, "Roger, tell me, how could marriage go from being a kite to a vice during one nine-month pregnancy? How can love be limited and doled out like rations during WWII? I chastise myself for not seeing the warning signs of a woman who wanted but didn't understand love and of most importance, didn't want to give it freely."

Roger placed a warm hand on Bill's back to show empathy and comradery. "Bill, I have some serious news for you." Roger explained how people must have notice Bernadette by herself on the farm and the greasy head man this morning was just one person of perhaps several, who would attempt to abduct Bernadette given the chance. "I have an idea and I hope it is a good solution for you. Why not let Bernadette come live for me for the next two to three years? It may not be too long before I am requested to return to Europe. I need to teach Bernadette many skills: how to survive in this world, how to live in harmony with nature, and how to hear the voice of spirit. I need to teach her about who she is and I may not have forever to do that. I can protect her now, until she can protect herself. What do you think?"

Bill stood shaking his head, showing his resignation with the situation. He was disgusted with himself. "I am a failure as a father."

Roger was quick to reply, "No, no you are not. You were chosen to be her father. You have another daughter and a very, very mentally ill wife. You are in an impossible situation. Let me help, while I can. I have already told my housekeeper, Laura, that Bernadette might live with us sometime. She is thrilled with the idea. She can take care of Bernadette, get her to school, and back home when I am at work. The grandmother's house behind my place is fixed up. I can live there while Laura and Bernadette have the house if that would make you more at ease.

Bill frowned, completely astounded. "That is not my concern. Ever. I don't care what people around here think. But Jan will never go for it. It would make her looked like a failure to her friends and family and that would be intolerable for her." Bill looked Roger in the eye, "Jan will call you a pervert, say you have mental issues, and that is why you want to do this."

Roger stood with his hands on his hips and said, "No, she won't, because I have the ace card. I have caught Jan trying to "accidentally" kill your daughter so many times, I have lost count. Jan knows I understand her *modus operandi*. You haven't been aware of all the times I have stopped by the house under the guise to see if Jan needed any help. There would be Jan, feeding Bernadette huge hard candy, hoping she would choke. She would leave out big plastic bags for Bernadette to play in, hoping she would suffocate. I have been picking up plastic bags and throwing out hard candy for years at your place. This morning your wife was up very early. I know this because the light was briefly on in your front craft room. My guess is, she woke up Bernadette early this morning, then went back to bed. She wakes her up early so Bernadette will leave the house out of confusion and leave house all by herself. Let me ask you, how many mysterious frayed electrical cords have you found? How about the stove being left on? How about tools or appliances mysteriously plugged in and left out?"

Bills expression went from unhappiness, to confused, to furious.

Roger continued, "She won't blame you either. Let me talk with her alone. This conversation has been in the making for a long time and it needs to happen now."

Roger saw the war within Bill. He had so much compassion for this man. "Let me help Bill. I can be the bad guy here with Jan, and I can help Bernadette. I won't always be in the States to help. Let me do this now."

Bill walked over and picked up Bernadette. Turning back to Roger, he said, "Okay. Let's get back to the house and do this before I lose my nerve. You talk with Jan. I will come visit all of you whenever I can. Three years is the most. I wish I could come live with you too, but I have another daughter."

The men walked silently back to the house.

Once on the back porch, Bill said, "I think it is best if I take Bernadette and Julie out to the barn for a few minutes. Let me get Julie." When Bill returned, he walked away with both girls to brush the horses.

Roger found Jan in the craft room. The yelling and threats from Jan started quickly.

At the barn, Julie asked, "Dad, why is mom yelling?"

Bill smiled. "Well, she is about to get a lesson. Let's keep brushing the horses."

After fifteen minutes, it was quiet. Roger laid down the law. Jan either worked at getting better in the next three years or he would see to it that she ended up in a state mental institution. At any time, he would be more than happy to approach the police and child protective services about Jan's mental illnesses, her instability as a person, and her willingness to kill her daughter. She had three years to figure it out, while Bernadette stayed with Uncle Roger.

Roger called Laura and she came over with the truck. The truck was loaded with Bernadette's things as Jan watched from the craft room window, her face filled with rage. In contrast, Bernadette's face was a study of joy and peace as she sat in the truck waiting to leave. When the truck was loaded with Bernadette's things, she kissed and hugged her dad goodbye. Then Bernadette, Roger, and Laura drove down the road.

Bill knew he had done the right thing, but it still hurt like hell.

Chapter 3
The Learning Curve

(1967-1973)

Roger spent six years teaching Bernadette skills and intellectual knowledge she required for meeting the challenges to come. The training wasn't limited to the ways of living harmoniously with nature, understanding Irish lore of Anu, and the deeper spiritual laws of nature and soul. It also included a long list of skills utilized by Native Americans or the modern American: wilderness survival, hand to hand combat, body conditioning, meditation, spiritual study, mechanics, home repair, animal husbandry, gardening, and the list went on. Both Roger and Bill were amazed at her ability to focus for long hours and her willingness to study.

Bill often stopped by to chat or for fun outings such as a hike, picnic, or horseback riding. Jan and Julie never once visited. Bernadette never asked about her mother but did talk to her sister when they interacted at school or on the school bus. Neighbors only spoke within their respective families about the situation, speculating in whispers as to why Uncle Roger was raising Bernadette.

Roger worked to ensured Bernadette had a well-rounded social life. There were team sports, play dates with other kids, summer camps and slumber parties. He encouraged her to develop close friendships with all grandmothers in the area, as he felt they might be a source of comfort for her when he left.

Then the day came when Roger received an ominous but expected envelope. He had delayed his return to Europe for a long as possible. Once he saw the envelope, he knew he wouldn't be able to put off his departure again. He was torn with agony. He had come to love the roll of father to Bernadette. Being with her, Bill and Laura, had filled his heart with a comfort and familial satisfaction. He loved Bernadette beyond what most would imagine. From his perspective, she was a superior warrior daughter of Anu, she was destined to be taught by a son of Anu, and his life's purpose was to train, support, and love this girl who would grow to become a warrior for nature and spirit in ways unimaginable.

He spent most of the day in his study and both Laura and Bernadette sensed something was wrong. Later that afternoon he called Bernadette to his side.

"Bernadette, I must give you some news. I have been summoned to return to Europe."

Not understanding what this meant, Bernadette replied, "How long will you be gone?"

"I won't be returning here Bernadette. You will have to go back and live with your mother, father and sister."

The words were beginning to slowly sink in. Bernadette looked at Roger with huge eyes. Frowning she asked, "Will you call or write? Will you be back in a year to visit?"

Roger's stomach was starting to churn. "I don't think I will be able to write or call. I won't be able to visit either."

Bernadette's bewilderment was palatable. "What? Why are you saying this? What is wrong? How could you leave here? Don't you care?"

Tears stood in Roger's eyes. "I love you as a daughter, Bernadette. You are the most special daughter to me. But I also have obligations in Europe. You are ready to move on in your life. You are strong and smart, and courageous. You understand nature in ways that surpass me. Part of learning is understanding your strength and how to be on your own. You will have to stand on your own many, many times. To do that, I must fade into the background. It isn't my wish, but it is my role. If I am always here, I would hold you back."

Her pain and confusion ripped at his heart as her face became redder than her hair. "I don't want to be around my mother! How can you do this to me? I love you." At this point, Bernadette was screaming.

"I know. I love you too. Your mother has been to treatment. I believe she is better now."

Roger hugged her, then set her back from him. Placing his hand over her heart, "Hold me here Bernadette, in your heart. I will always be there to guide. I promise."

Bernadette ran to her room and refused to come out for dinner. Roger sat up all night. The next week was one of tears, angry looks, and few words.

Roger understood why this summons arrived. Bernadette must never believe her success came from outside of herself. She needed to know that she had the power within her and that understanding would come through being on her own.

Two weeks later, Bernadette moved back home. A month later, Roger had sold his home, helped Laura buy a new place to live, and moved back to Europe. As he stood to catch his plane, Bernadette stared grimly at him and said, "I will find you some day."

Roger held his hand to his heart, and said, "I hope you do."

Bernadette came with one trait above all others, resilience. Before Roger left, he spoke to her at length about how to cope with loss and to move on when she was ready. Her grades suffered temporarily, but summer came, and she accepted the new routine with few verbal complaints.

Months later, Bill still worried about such a huge loss for Bernadette. She spent time with her friends and yet she spoke little. She did chores with him, and they went horseback riding, yet her smile didn't touch her eyes. Her laughter was empty.

As the next school year sped forward, Bill watched as she focused on studies, sports, and her animals. He hoped it was enough. It had to be.

Chapter 4
The Kiss of the Antler

(Summer 1976)

Bill Engstrom did his best not to worry about Bernadette. He recognized that his red-haired daughter wasn't like many other children, but understanding how to navigate those differences with encouragement proved to be difficult in a world of whimsical ideas and parental views that shifted with the wind. As other kids were finding countless ways to aggravate their parents, Bernadette utilized the wisdom acquired under Roger's training, thereby leading her on an exciting but secluded journey. She did well in school, did her chores, tried to cook a meal if asked, and loved helping on the farm. Contrastingly, she was detached and uninterested in many of the things that were considered normal kid behavior. She didn't like watching TV, she didn't want to go shopping, she shunned gossip, she avoided cliques, and she didn't appear interested in boys. There was an unusual innocence about her.

Bill believed that the reclusive element so fundamental to Bernadette could only find true relief by being in nature. Bernadette bonded with all of nature in a way that most people never would. She didn't just take experiences from nature, but she gave back to the plants and animals in a loving, gentle way. She was always feeding animals, brushing them, petting them, scratching them and noticing if something was wrong with them. She cared about all wild animals and worried if they were injured or sick. Bill had learned that if Bernadette told him something was wrong with an animal, it was true, and he best look into it.

The cause for worry would escalate, Bill knew, when the innocent girl became a young woman; she would encounter a world of unsavory events and people. Would she come to know the characteristics of people and all their flaws as well as she understood animals? He doubted it. And that was the concern.

The summer before Bernadette entered 9th grade, the beginning of high school, would be one of her best childhood summers since Roger had left the U.S. Jan traveled to Montana the first of June to spend the summer with her brother, sister-in-law, and their two boys at a summer home in Kalispell. Bill didn't divulge to Bernadette or Julie that their mother had suffered a number of serious mental health breakdowns in the last six months, events more debilitating than her baseline state of misery, which resulted in her physician prescribing a change of scenery.

These episodes had left Bill exhausted. He was finished with attempting to placate his wife. He tried every avenue he could think of to bring happiness to Jan's life. None it worked. His feeling on the matter was straightforward today; she could visit Montana and figure out for herself what would lead to happiness. Julie, now in high school, asked to attend a summer long college preparatory camp for girls. Since her best friend was going and he liked the influence she had on Julie, he consented.

These changes at home left Bernadette alone during the long summer hours while Bill was at his job. Due to his family situation this summer, the human resources department and his boss worked together to find Bill a more accommodating work schedule, 3 a.m. till 3 p.m. four days a week. Bill set rules for Bernadette on the days he was at work, confident that she would follow them: she wasn't to leave the house until after 7:30 am, she was to stay on the farm property, and she was not to ride a horse when he was gone. The first three weeks of his new schedule, Bill drove his old Ford farm truck home with of the speed of a panicky rabbit, envisioning Bernadette in the midst of some blood-soaked tragedy with Butter watching helplessly nearby. None of the neighbors noticed his excessive speed beyond a casual consideration, thinking to call Bill with an offer to help on the obviously sticky gas pedal. The neighbors had long developed feelings of empathy for Bill and his kids. They did their best to help in unobtrusive and nonjudgmental ways.

After the first month, Bill's concern dissipated while he watched his daughter flourish in an atmosphere of ease, laughter, and love, strikingly similar to a rose garden coming into full bloom. A situational catalyst of peace appeared on the farm, transforming the often emotionally remote daughter into a radiant beauty, progressively noticed by more than a few neighborhood boys. Bernadette was always doing something to help around the farm. She would have a dinner in the fridge or baking in the oven, the effort beautifully seasoning the meal even if it was an off-flavor cooking attempt. The garden, under Bernadette's attention, became the envy of all the neighbors with its abundance and had the unanticipated effect of alleviating Bill's chronic constipation. The animals were always fed and watered to the fullest. Happy contented animals greeted Bill every afternoon when he checked on the farm.

During the first week in July, something monumental happened when Bill got home. Bernadette ran to him as he jumped down from the truck, threw her arms around him in a squeezing hug, and excitedly described the newly sprouted pumpkin seeds. From that day forward, and for the remainder of Jan's absence, Bernadette displayed a physical affection that was capable of thawing many a hardened heart. Bill wondered if he could ask Jan to stay in

Montana forever, but that probably wouldn't have been nice, nor did it meet with his commitment to family.

After the hay had been harvested in mid-July and garden maintenance consisted mainly of watering, Bernadette found herself with more time for exploration. The Calkins, one of the Engstrom's closest neighbors, owned a section of land still supporting the remnants of a long-forgotten homestead: a falling down tiny house, a barn that no longer could keep out any weathering elements, and a meadow frequented by all the critters searching for food. Bernadette loved to visit the area; her imagination of the animals who found homes in the dilapidated structures gave her a sense of wondrous joy. This particular day her father was off work, a Friday, so she set out to ask his permission to leave the farm. Not finding him around the barns, she finally ventured back in the house to come upon him deep in thought, reading a letter in the study.

"Dad, is it ok if I take Butter and go up to Calkin's old homestead? You know, the meadow up there."

Bill abruptly set the letter on his desk, with the type face down.

Bernadette eyed the letter warily. "Is that from Mom? Is she coming back soon?"

Bill replied, "It is from your Uncle Jimmy. Your mother doesn't appear to be enjoying herself at the summer Montana home, so they will be returning to Billings earlier than expected. They are hoping some city life will be enjoyable for her. It is nothing to worry about."

Bill smiled to set his daughter at ease. He said, "Now, for your request. Yes, you may go to the meadow. And…take the backpack I put together for you."

Bill had worried that Bernadette would get lost sometime or perhaps hurt during one of her roaming adventures, so he had prepared an emergency backpack. It had the basics which included protection from the weather, water, food, survival tools, a very tiny first aid kit, and items to assist in being found, such as mirror and whistle. Frankly, he doubted Bernadette would ever get lost, as Butter was most loyal to Bernadette and he would always know how to get home. Watching her develop a frown he added, "Yes, I know it bounces on your back when you run. You will just have to take up speed walking to avoid that."

"Speed walkers look funny Dad. They move their hips like the barn door left open in a windstorm." Then, she brightened, "I'll take it and be back before dark." Bernadette sprinted toward the mudroom. All he heard was "later" and the door slammed shut.

To get to the Calkin's meadow, Bernadette had to walk for a quarter mile on the paved road, then walk down Calkin's long gravel driveway, and finally cut through another's neighbor's forest which had a well-kept logging road leading directly up the hill to the meadow. While on the public road, Butter was kept on a leash for safety, resisting such a constraint by pulling

Bernadette along. Once they reached the Calkin driveway, Butter was off his leash. At the start of the neighbor's logging road, Bernadette pulled up a loose section of fence for her and Butter to scramble under.

Now their trek entered into a world of moist smells and muted noises. Bernadette marveled at the moss and lichens ruling the shadows and the fir treetops supporting the thrones for majestic birds. She watched for snakes bathing in a bit of sun, not because she feared them, but rather to give a full account of the species and size to her dad, knowing he enjoyed reptiles and discussing them. Stopping to pick a few flowers to take home, Bernadette was brought out of her reverie by the barking of Butter. She called and called for him, walking more quickly up the logging road, for she could hear he was ahead of her, closer to the meadow. After a good five minutes of calling, Butter returned to Bernadette. Quickly snapping the leash back on the dog and petting him, Bernadette said, "What is it, Butter? Go get it," while the dog was already leaping forward.

The logging road petered out several hundred feet before the old homestead, making the entrance a deeply rutted mess with a high center of grass and weeds, sure to suck even a tractor into it rough trap. As they approached what was once a gate into the old homestead, Bernadette heard an odd noise. Butter started to growl. Cautiously approaching the gate, now a shamble of old boards held together by newer woven wire fencing, Bernadette listened intently. The woven wire was stapled to the large end posts on each side of the driveway. The posts were actually stumps from massive old fir trees; their diameter at least three feet and over twelve feet above the ground. Wire fencing extended east and west from these posts, an ugly contrast to the beauty of the materials used years ago. Bernadette noticed that the wire fence to the east shook, then stopped, then shook again. Following the fence for several hundred feet into the woods, Bernadette stopped as she took stock of what was before her. A bull elk, with enormous antlers decorated with strips of fuzz, was pushing on some saplings near the fence causing the wire to shake. Bernadette marveled at his majestic size, but wouldn't have known he weighed in at a whopping twelve hundred pounds, probably the largest and oldest bull elk in hundreds of miles. His rack was almost nine feet across, from furthest tine to tine. When standing, his top tine reached eleven feet high. His antlers had grown in early, maturing almost a month before any other males, showing just how powerful he was.

Butter, lunging on the leash, spooked the elk, causing it to thrash about but not run away. Bernadette, quick to realize something was wrong, took Butter back to a big post and secured him to the fence. She didn't like the idea of tying him to the fence, but she couldn't have him spooking the elk. If something went wrong, it was the best place for him to be found by her dad.

Returning, she made a wide arc around the elk, allowing her to figure out what the problem was. A section of woven wire fence had been rolled up and left behind, probably because it was somehow damaged and had been replaced. Young alder saplings growing within the wire bundle were protected from the grazing deer and elk, allowing a thick and healthy stand of saplings to grow up through tangled wire mess. All was fine, until the bull elk decided to work the felt off his rack on these young trees, an excellent manner for proving one's strength with a display of swaying and snapping. Then, in the height of his masculine display, the rack moved too low, becoming entangled in the wire. It appeared that the more he fought it, the more he managed to enmesh his antler into the unnoticeable wire killer.

She thought about going back to the house and asking her father to help, but it was clear they would have to get up close to the elk's rack to cut the wire. Her father would say it was too dangerous, she knew that. If he couldn't come up with a way to release the elk, she worried he would just want to shoot the bull to prevent its misery, something she couldn't stand to think of. This elk was statelier than any animal she had ever seen, even her lovely appaloosa horse, Stormy. She toyed with the idea of going to the house and getting wire snips, but sneaking in and out of the basement was an unlikely success, as her dad would be listening for her return. Going to the Calkin's house for help presented the same set of problems.

Taking off her backpack, she kneeled and unzipped the burden, which normally represented too much parental worry, but now offered a possible solution. Opening the main zipper she found an emergency blankets, a lightweight raincoat, several granola bars, some dog treats and a flask of water. There was a leather pouch that was her father's, smelling like his aftershave. Inside she was pleased to see a whistle, signaling mirror, waterproof matches, some fire-starter with a note not to use in summer, a small first aid kit, and a Leatherman multipurpose tool. It took her five minutes to understand all the functions on the Leatherman. One tool was a small, but sturdy pair of scissors, able to cut much more than just paper or string.

Putting everything back in except the Leatherman, she left the backpack on the ground and approached the bull from his left side. After getting fairly close, she realized she would have more room between the bull and small alders if she was on the right side of him. Making a wide arc, she approached his head slowly, each step a measure of kindness, noiseless as possible, and her eyes down in what she hoped was a show of submission. All was calm until she had narrowed the distance to thirty feet; the bull suddenly tried to escape. The dark hair on his muscular neck shook in waves as the huge muscles arched, corded muscles along his back legs rippled under his skin as the legs shot out then came back down with a huge whoomph. He continued to twist and turn his antlers, ramming the wire with all his might using impressive hind legs like thrusting pistons.

Bernadette stumbled back in fear, tumbling over a log, and landing with a thud as her head smacked the ground. Moaning, she crawled back up, looking at the massive beast now watching her. "Ouch!" Bernadette stood holding her throbbing head for several minutes. She was not deterred, for if she didn't get him out, he would die.

This time she approached more slowly. The bull remained calm, even when she tentatively reached out to touch the wire holding the stately antlers. She later thought back on why the bull didn't fight again. Perhaps showing her underbelly was such a submissive reaction that the bull's fear was appeased, or maybe any animal that fell over a little log wasn't a worthy opponent. In her mind of gentleness, she hoped she reminded him more of a fawn then a predator, for Bernadette often wished to be a fawn running free in the woods, especially when her mother became mean and nasty toward her.

The elk watched, his breathing deep, at times snorting, or making a deep guttural noise. The Leatherman tool was small and didn't have enough force to match the capabilities found in long handled tools. The wire was dented with the first cut. Then she had to work it back and forth with her hands to further weaken that spot until she was finally able to sever the wire with one final cut. After the severing the fifth wire, her hands started to bleed, not only from working the metal, but the force she had to apply to the Leatherman. She pulled her sweatshirt cuffs over her hands to cushion them from the metal. With each wire cut, she moved further between the bull's head and the alder stand, giving herself a death sentence should the bull decide to charge again. Painstakingly, she cut the wire, with the bull snorting down her back a few times.

With only two more cuts left, she had to walk back around the bull to get to the wire on the left side of his rack. He was becoming more restless, pawing at the ground with his front legs and causing the wire to flex more with his movements.

After the final cut, Bernadette tried to pull the wire bundle off his antlers, but it didn't budge because some of the wire fencing needed to move up to get over a tine and at the same time, the fencing needed to be pulled down to get past a tine. Pulling and grunting, she finally slipped, falling back and once again, hitting her head. The fall startled the bull and as he twisted his head while rearing back, his rack now easily came out of the human wire cage.

He jumped, then ran fifty feet out, before stopping, snorting, and pawing the forest floor. He smelt more fresh blood, increasing his instinct to run, yet he stayed. Turning, there was nothing but the brush, the deadly metal that had held him, and the moaning of the human. Cautiously, he stepped forward till he could see all of her, laying prostrate.

Bernadette's head was killing her and it was bleeding. This was the second time she had fallen on it today, and the pain was bad. Her stomach curled, knotted up, and she feared she would throw-up. Instinctively, she tried to sit up, but the pain increased, so she continued to rest on the cool ground. Opening her eyes, she saw the bull only a few feet away, the fathomless depths of his eyes brought her a sense of comfort and the pain eased. The bull, knowing that things on the ground were as good as dead, prodded her legs carefully with the antlers. Bernadette's love for him expanded as his weapons for fighting became a connection of one species to another.

Any adult human would have found this sequence of events unreal; Bernadette did not. Her innocence and love of animals often blurred the lines between this world and others, this plane of existence and those nearby.

Tucking her legs under her, she shakily stood up. The bull backed off, then stood at full height sniffing the air. He looked at her again and she started to cry, silently, the tears dripping down her checks, falling from her jaw to be soaked into the summer earth. In that moment, when her heart spilled forth admiration for him, an awe for his immense beauty and grace, she loved him with purity, as one might love their grandparents, and he felt that love and purity she so freely gave.

In return for her gifts to him, two things happened. Somewhere in his essence, what would instantly become a part of his DNA, although scientist and biologist cannot identify the area where instinct is stored, some tiny bit of energy was altered and permanently recorded. In that moment his makeup was changed, such that his offspring and his offspring's offspring, all of his progeny, would always have the instinct to protect and help Bernadette. It was based on her unique smell, her unique essence. This wonderous connection was only for her.

A second exceptional event occurred, of equal importance for Bernadette. Just as a human handshake or looking someone in the eye causes a transfer of energy, the bull elk gave to Bernadette, in his unfathomable glance, a part of his spirit which had made him the splendor of nature. He gave to Bernadette something she would need for her lifetime, a cunning bravery, which had been undeveloped and underutilized within her, allowing her to overcome many mental and physical obstacles.

Through the tears, she smiled at him. "Go, go be free. Go on." She waved her hand, shooing him on. Then he spun around and was gone. But not from Bernadette's inner mind. She held that vision close to her for a lifetime, here and beyond.

In truth, the bull elk would come back to these parts and would see her at times, for several more years. Always from afar, he would watch her in the summer, before the hunters came. He would head back to the hills as fall and hunting season approached.

Aware that Bernadette had been gone longer than Bill expected, he got up to greet her when he heard her opening the porch door and walking into the mudroom. She was washing her hands in the mudroom sink when he came to stand in the doorway.

Remaining calm as he watched bloody water run into the drain, he asked, "What happened to your hands?" Noticing her matted hair he added, "And your head?"

Bernadette jumped, then refocused her attention on her palms. She realized the blood was just another sign that she was different from most everyone. "It's nothing. They just got a little scratched up." She looked up at her father, the sorrow in her eyes something Bill hadn't seen since Jan had left. "Are you going to ground me? Can I still eat dinner and dessert?"

Bill refocused his attention on the filbert orchard seen through the mudroom window as he tried to tamp down his immediate disdain for his wife's behavior. "Why don't you change clothes and come to the kitchen while I make a nice dinner. If you want to talk about what happened, we can do that. Just be sure to keep your hands clean, wear gloves more often this week, till they heal up."

As a quick after thought, "Let me look at your head to be sure you don't need stiches."

Bill found a nice bump and a scrape in Bernadette's scalp, but nothing too serious. "I don't think we need to go to the hospital today. Hurry up and get clean so we can get on with dinner." Bill smiled at his beautiful daughter and then headed to the kitchen while Bernadette watched him go.

Some words in the Engstrom house were banned from speech, not because they weren't felt, but because of Jan's idiosyncratic joyously. But today, the words broke free from Bernadette, "I love you dad. I'll be right back down for dinner." She sprinted toward the stairs leading to her room.

Bill called after her, his voice strained with emotion, for "love" was a word that the farmhouse had lacked since they moved in, "I love you too Bernadette."

As Bill laid in bed that night, he thought over the conversation he had with Bernadette in the kitchen. She had spoken about wanting to go to college and if she could earn some money to save up for it. As he said the words, *I'll be working and can help pay for it*, a sorrow opened up in his heart, and he knew the words weren't true. He had a feeling that he needed a backup plan ready for the girls, should he not be able to work during their college years.

The next Monday, when the human resources staff arrived at work, Bill made a point to go see the helpful women about special life insurance policies so both of his girls could attend and complete five years of college, if something should happen to him. They worked with him on options to ensure that the funds could not be used by another relative. He did not mention Jan and they didn't ask.

Bill passed away from a deadly bacterial infection following an accident at work just two weeks before Bernadette graduated from high school. The grieving hole left in Bernadette was humungous. She cried at night, wondering why people she loved would leave her. She didn't understand why she was so unlucky or as others said, unfortunate. She didn't know what she had done wrong, why this entity called God would continue to punish her. She believed that all the people who understood her uniqueness were gone, and she was alone.

Although consumed with despair, she continued with her plans to attend university and she was able to attend because her father had planned for her. The university helped Bernadette not only to utilize her mind, but it proved to develop her emotional health and maturity in ways Bill never would have guessed.

40

Part II

Chapter 5
A Morning Swim

(The Year of 1984)

While trying to adjust her legs around her backpack, a mighty boulder in weight and form, Bernadette glanced at her German vocabulary notes, again. She contemplated how it was possible that she could read and reread these words, only to have nothing stick in her brain, when in sharp contrast she could eat a cookie and have it immediately take-up permanent residency in her thigh's adipose tissue. Barely getting a solid B in the class, she wasn't able to find fault in the university instructor's ability to pass on information. The UCSD (University of California, San Diego) professor came from Germany, could easily explain the nuances of his native language, was remarkably fair in his grading, and kept everyone awake in the early morning hour with a sense of humor. In a quick mental exploration, she determined she couldn't blame her high school German teacher either; he was just as good as the university instructor, plus more approachable. With no additional time for such thoughts, she laid blame at those pesky umlauts and rolling r's, for they were just like a little rusty nail; all three looked quite harmless yet were capable of fowling up the entire system, either by poor enunciation or tetanus. There was always more below the simplistic surface.

At exactly 0830, the German professor, attired in his usual starched white shirt and creased navy-blue trousers, directed the students to take out a sheet of blank paper. He would give them ten German vocabulary words and all Bernadette had to do was write ten little German sentences, each sentence using one of the German vocabulary words. For just ten minutes she needed her brain to function at an optimal speed in a foreign language, without her synaptic needle skipping around on the conversion turntable.

In exactly ten minutes, the sharp eyed and stray scrap paper leery professor called out, "Put your pencils down."

The tests were immediately passed to the isle row, a chair she was currently occupying. Bernadette thought about sneaking out of class early for the blessed oblivion in her small dorm room bed. The professor took the quizzes from Bernadette's hand, then continued down the five rows in front of her to the bottom of the classroom. Bernadette softly started to pull up the tiny writing table currently laying above her lap, intent on moving it without a squeak, when the professor turned, expectantly waiting for Bernadette to meet his eyes, then announced, "We have a special speaker here from Orange Coast College to talk with you about a work-study program in Germany." Then his expression softened, the sternness he had every day washed away, replaced with a tinge of mirth appearing at the creases bracketing his lips. "It is an excellent opportunity to immerse yourself in the language and cement in those nuances of sentence structure, language inflection, and... it can be a cultural awakening for anyone ready to experience such a transformation."

Bernadette radiated a smiled at him, pleased that the professor had actually noticed her in the huge class. She was always shocked when a professor or another student specifically communicated with her, for she often felt her quietness made her worse than invisible, an entity present but not worthy of interest. Slightly inclining his head in her direction, he then turned and took a seat as a woman at the podium, adjusting blank applications and fliers, looked up and began to tell the class about an opportunity that sounded too good to be true for a college student. There were college credits to be had, "free" room and board for her submersion in the culture, and all she had to do was work in a convalescent hospital with people who would need her.

Those were the standard reasons one could recite to friends and family when explaining the need for a trip abroad. There was a deeper reason for Bernadette to go. A reason that she didn't often examine as it was kept in the locked darkened closet filled with sorrow and pain stemming from her current family, a family absent her father and Uncle Roger. Her reason, her greatest hope, was to find some place that felt like home, a place where she might belong. *Could a faraway country be the miracle location?* she wondered in anticipation. She was willing to try.

In the coming weeks, she put her mind to the travel opportunity and the door opened. Several months later, in June, Bernadette found herself on a flight to Germany.

-

Mastering the German language was Bernadette's top desire when she arrived in Offenburg, Germany, a typical German city on the edge of the Black Forest and close to France. She settled into the job routine and loved the people she helped. Her bungling of the language only served as a source of entertainment for her patients; the resulting laughter, hers included, radiated down the halls. Bonding closely with a few of the elderly women, Bernadette was amazed when she realized those relationships were solidly built on nonverbal communication. There were no words to adequately convey the emotional pain and loneliness of illness and Bernadette responded with actions of sincere caring that words can only minimize. Her lovely newfound friends would remain in her heart and mind for decades to come, for she would pull out those feelings of mutual love and joy in times of uncertainty and hurt.

During her first exciting week in Offenburg, unusual beer, elaborate pastries, and dark heavy breads were the after work and evening interest. Each evening, with a new snack in hand, she explored the city, marveling at the feel of history. The stability in buildings that <u>hadn't</u> been slapped together in the last century, expected to be replace in the next century, were evidence of humanity's profound duration in Europe. Her first Friday evening in Germany, dressed in the one of her unfashionable, down-to-the-shin skirts, Bernadette ventured further away from the city center, north of the clanking and clattering train station, and past the fancy tennis club. Wondering through a park designed to accommodate the fall Octoberfest and butting up to the local cemetery, she came upon a pavilion, several gazebos, three large fountains and plenty of stone benches. There, by the fountain with the anatomically correct sculpture of Adonis, all her thoughts of elaborate pastries were abandoned in an instant. Bernadette encountered a group of young German men in sexy leather pants and jackets. And that wasn't all. There were colored mohawks and bare chests.

For the next week, Bernadette developed a pattern of first visiting the cemetery, with notebook in hand, as if she was conducting some mapping or genealogy study, or she hoped it looked that way. Then, pretending fatigue, she plopped down on a stone bench to eat and read, or perhaps document her findings from within the cemetery. The chosen bench always allowed her an intimate view of the fascinating German guys jostling and lounging at the Adonis fountain. From this vantage point, she longed to be a different woman. She didn't understand what these men could talk and laugh about for hours and therefore, she felt she would never be "cool" enough to communicate with them. There was punching and shoving, which was always accompanied by laughing and more talking. The longer she watched them, the more envious she grew.

A few times, one or two of the men, most often the one with a purple mohawk, would glance her direction, but she could easily pretend immense interest in her book, as if she didn't notice them. Bernadette used her flowing hair to shield herself from them. She didn't feel guilty or weird for watching them, as her intent wasn't malicious, and certainly, she convinced herself, that if they didn't want an awkward introverted woman gawking them, then they would be some place other than in a public park. On warmer evenings, their jackets came off and Bernadette was sure to break out in a sweat with them. The contrast of a soft cotton shirt, if they wore one, to the leather pants spoke of tenderness within all the muscle. This was a package she could understand, as it reminded her of the spirited appaloosa horse on the farm; a tender gentle nose attached to a body of muscle capable of inflicting great injury. The men's most fascinating attire was their boots. She couldn't imagine why men in the city, no manure for miles, would need such sturdy, elaborate black leather boots lacing up to mid shin. They looked heavy and hot.

Every evening for four weeks, except on Sundays when the guys weren't around, in all the weather systems Germany had to offer, Bernadette sat, a quiet spectator of the rambunctious men.

It isn't known what biomolecular transformation occurred within Bernadette that fourth Saturday evening, as the metamorphosis within her was certainly undocumented in any medical journal. The instantaneous impatient yearning from within, a squashed essence stuffed under the layer upon layer of her mother's emotional oppression, awoke with the ferocity normally found in the externally dawdling but internally seething volcanos making up the Pacific ring of fire. As she sat on her usual bench watching the men's muscles flex and relax in the pheromonal leather lures, they ignited the invisible heartbeats of soul magnetism, a mix of anguished emotions and demanding desires all focused on imperative goal; to find her friend and lover.

Bernadette's desire for a special love, a sensual love, was awakening and becoming a battering ram to her exoskeleton of unworthiness. Her specific seductive melody streaming across the infinite waves of humanity's thoughts and ideas was far from generic. Not any man with a job and kind heart would do. A loyal companion, understanding confidante, and emotionally strong advocate would be the only soul mate who could compliment the complexities of this developing woman and everything she would become. She knew that as fact.

Her song of longing was heard instantly in the ether, as all songs of yearning are.

She did not return to her bench after that transformative Saturday or for the remainder of her stay in Germany, nor ever view the fountain of Adonis in Offenburg again.

That following Monday, the ladies under Bernadette's care, who suffered from physical maladies but were of sound mental constitution, had the motherly understanding that Bernadette was not experiencing a bout of gas from rich German food consumed on the weekend. The powerfully cheerful countenance of their foreign caregiver had turned distracted and broody, affecting all the residents. Long faces, transposed on the normally comfortable patients, were spreading like skipping dust bunnies as the days turned into a week, then more. When the cancer ridden woman in Room 17, always optimistic and normally providing an endless litany of jokes for the entire hospital, had developed a permanent scowl to match Bernadette's, the nurses secretly congregated on a Wednesday in the supply room. It was time to develop a plan and hopefully remedy the spreading malaise, for the nurses were seeing effects on the patients' health.

At the Thursday morning break, the nurses pounced, conspiring to change Bernadette's world. Due to an upcoming Offenburg holiday, vaguely described by the staff with lots of German terms Bernadette couldn't understand; a sudden surge in summer help, of which Bernadette saw no evidence; and some type of German mental health rule for staff suffering from an anguishing heart, Bernadette was told she might enjoy an extra week off to travel around Europe.

Everyone smiled encouragingly while Bernadette considered her options. Funds were always an issue, but she figured she could manage with day outings and further conserve funds by sleeping on the trains for longer trips. Perking up at the thought, Bernadette found herself practically pushed out of the hospital door at noon, encouraged to take an extra week discovering Germany and perhaps France too.

Turning around she called, "I will see you next Thursday!" just as the double doors slammed shut.

Standing outside the heavily closed doors of the hospital, Bernadette found her promiscuous emotions coalescing into tears. The close relationships with her patients were of such a new and grounding experience for her, Bernadette realized she would desperately miss any time away from these dear soul friends. *Why hadn't this occurred to her inside the building?* she wondered. And she only had a summer to be with them.

Love for her known patients or a quest for an unknown lover? She wondered what a woman of heart afflictions was to do. Should she already be taking a vacation from a job she worked at for a mere five or so weeks? It was here, at this hospital, she had a feeling of belonging that she never felt in the States. But everyone was so sure that she needed a "personal" week, so perhaps taking a minivacation was acceptable.

Her vision obscured through her indecisive tears, Bernadette turned and began walking back to her dorm room. *Wham!* Bernadette suddenly found herself ferociously smacked to the ground without time to break her fall, her head making a loud thump as it bounced off the worn bricks. As she lay on her back, exasperated by all the times she had hit her head in her short lifespan, she gingerly used her fingertips to examine her head for flowing blood. Feeling nothing slimy, she carefully attempted to get up, only to have a gentle hand slowly ease her back down.

A concerned older man knelt by her and speaking in German he said. "Are you alright? Just lay here a minute. I heard your head smack the sidewalk. I am so very sorry. My car door keeps sticking and I was shoving at it with all my might, when it suddenly flew open."

He was speaking very quickly, but Bernadette could understand enough to know he was concerned for her.

People were beginning to crowd around her. Mortified to be laying on the sidewalk and the center of attention, she placed a hand over her face and said the first German sentence that came to mind, "Ich bin ein schmetterling." (Translation: I am a *butterfly*.)

Realizing what she had said, she moved her fingers, creating a V between her third and fourth finger, so she could stare at the man in complete bewilderment. *Where did that come from?* she wondered. *Couldn't she think of anything else? Apparently, even five weeks immersed in the German language couldn't prevent her precarious German language knowledge base from bouncing out of her head and rolling down the street.*

The kindly German man smiled, then placed one hand behind her back to help her sit up. In perfect English he told her, "I adore butterflies. Please call me Johan. Now that we have that introduction out of the way, let's see if you can stand." Johan worked with many foreigners, but never had one called herself a butterfly. He found himself fascinated with this bashful woman.

Bernadette stood fine but the back of her head ached, and she felt disoriented. Looking at the sidewalk because it prevented the buildings from spinning, she said. "Thank you, I am fine. I can always go back in there," she pointed to the large doors of the hospital, "and sit if I need to. I work there."

With no response forthcoming, she had to raise her eyebrows to sneak a look at Johan. His eyes twinkled with joy and Bernadette began giggling. She said "I love the word schmetterling. It really is the best German word."

Johan's hand slightly placed on Bernadette's back, he guided her back into the hospital. "My mother lives here and we have both heard how kind you are. Let's go sit in her room for a bit and ensure you don't need to see a doctor."

As Bernadette sat with Johan and his mother, tea in hand, several nurses pawed through her hair, feeling the developing bump. Johan's eye's widened with interest when he was told Bernadette was taking a week off to travel, starting now.

"Did you have plans for the week, Bernadette?" Johan asked.

"I'd love to explore Germany, but I already planned to travel around Germany and France the last week I am here." Hesitantly, she added, "For this unexpected trip, I would like to see Scotland, if I can get there. I just thought of it a little bit ago and I don't know anything about visiting Scotland," She was really thinking about money. She doubted she would have enough money even for the youth hostels, but she would at least check costs in her youth hostel book.

The mother and Johan shared a knowing glance.

Johan put his hand on Bernadette's knee, "Say no more. I am in the travel industry and I can get you a round trip plane ticket in a blink of an eye. Or perhaps faster than a smack to the head. And we have coupons for use at certain hostels or hotels, eating establishments and transportation. I will return in an hour."

Johan saw Bernadette's concern and knew she would decline the gift, so he quickly continued on, "And it won't cost me or you a thing. We do favors all the time for very rich people without a thought. Trust me, they expect freebees, and they don't blink an eye when using free coupons. You should not give any thought to it. It is the least I can do for causing you injury. I will get you set up. I insist." With that he was gone.

After half an hour to think, Bernadette began to worry about what Johan might schedule for her. She was well aware that the travel industry could make one's life wonderful, in an idyllic setting, or a living hell, like being stuck at an airport with lost luggage never to be found. *Was this the time to go so far outside of Germany by herself?* she wondered.

She thought of Roger's teachings from years ago and two great truths relevant to the travel industry: First, spiritual growth occurs as a person patiently works toward an outcome with the understanding that control of a specific outcome and its timing was ultimately in the hands of the divine. Second, that a life of beauty begins and ends with internal control of one's self, a mindfulness control.

She was unsure as events quickly unfolded around her. With an open mind, if not a pounding one, she resolved herself to enjoy the next week, come what may.

Bernadette's mind now at ease, she smiled at this turn in events. Apparently, the health care system, with all its uncertainty of outcome and timing, was in collusion with the travel industry. What a powerful pair they were.

The next morning, Friday, just after dawn, Bernadette awoke in a comfortable Scottish bed in the city of Stirling, making her exceptionally thankful for Johan's hotel coupons. Having flown into Glasgow, she traveled on to Stirling early in the night. Although exhausted, she wanted to make every minute of this trip count and waking up in Stirling would give her the advantage to begin exploring this city known as "the gateway to the highlands" without delay. A smaller city rich with history was perfect for her pensive mood.

While indulging in extra dark coffee and pastries at a local bakery with restaurant, she mapped out an itinerary for the day. Her tentative plan was to start out early with a nature walk along River Forth. When the tourist sites finally opened, she would cut south to Cambuskenneth Abby, Stirling Castle, and finally Stirling Smith Museum. Later in the day she could hop a bus over to the other side of town and see the National Wallace Monument and Mill Trail Visitor Center. Popping some aspirin with the last of coffee, Bernadette slung her backpack on, tossing her riot of red curls off to one side to avoid entanglement in the straps. It was not surprising that Bernadette completely failed to notice the admiring gazes of all five men in the shop across the street. The U.S. treated her red hair like an easily transmittable disease, a sharp contrast to not only her acceptance here in Scotland, but men's open admiration of her radiant hair.

It was a morning to revive any stale poet's hand. Along River Forth the air was crispy clear, the mood absent of humanity's commotion, and the satisfaction flowed from all the splendor nature can achieve. Feeling like God had created this morning just for her enjoyment, she sent up gracious thanks for the brilliance in the trees, strength in the river, and the critters who chatted over the wealth of food.

Having lost touch with time as she soaked up the Scottish essence that roamed this city, Bernadette finally realized she had walked beyond the turn off for Cambuskenneth Abby. Stopping, she stood undecided, contemplating if she should go back or if she should get out her map and tourist book to revise the days plans.

In this moment of indecision, the happy morning melody of the birds grew silent and the grating interruption of a car approaching, long before she saw it, started to pique Bernadette's focus. Whether genetics or from growing up in the country, she had excellent hearing, especially the higher pitched noises. Based on the tone, she knew it was a high-performance car, for even though it was screaming through the gear changes, the engine hummed with satisfaction borne of money. The tires' slipless grip squealed in perfect synch with the hair pin turns of which River Forth drew fame. RPMs topped at each gear, telling Bernadette about a driver of elite training and an intense motivation to capture the very essence of this engineering marvel.

Jumping a ditch, she moved well off the road into a nearby field. Although the black BMW hurled by with speed, maneuvering the last thirty degrees of the turn as it passed her, the car was well centered in the lane. It was hard for Bernadette not to admire the beauty of the aerodynamic design as it went momentarily air borne from a slight rolling bump found within the next two hundred yards of straight away. The brake lights went on, as she expected, before the next turn which led to a narrow bridge crossing a fresh creek serving to replenish the ever-thirsty needs of River Forth. This curve would be easy to navigate compared to the last one, but Bernadette recognized that the BMW was going to either entirely miss the curve or roll, as its swiftness exceeded the curve's insufficient banking. Worse, the BMW never slowed and in stunned confusion, Bernadette watched as it appeared to be speeding up. Making a quick decision, she threw her backpack in the brush, jumped the ditch in one deer-like bound and sprinted for the car before it even left the road.

There was the crunching of gravel, the snapping of tree limbs, the screech of metal deforming and then an odd silence containing only the hum of the engine as the car soared beyond the trees, looking like some freakish kite. The touchdown on River Forth sent water shooting in all directions, the splash disturbing the ducks from their hiding places in the normally quiet eddies along the bank, their wings flapping madly to escape the mistaken threat of a voracious predator.

Bernadette started stripping off her clothes as she ran. First her jacket and lightweight scarf came off. She was unzipping her denim pants and pulling her shirt out of the waistband while skidding down the riverbank.

The BMW had not flown far from the road, the tree limbs having slowed it kinetic jump, and looked to be in less than two feet of water. The trunk was floating but the front where the engine weighed it down, was touching the river bottom. Already breathing hard, Bernadette frantically untied her shoes and kicked them off so she could get out of the denim pants. From her experience as a kid on the farm, she knew that denim in water was the equivalent to swimming while swaddled in a canvas bag; just better to get the pants off. It was the same farm experience that helped her to hesitate a fraction of a thought; she slipped her shoes back on, tying them securely, and jogged into the water.

Most damage to the car was in the front, the radiator pushed up under the crumpled hood and the fenders were mangled. The driver's side roof was bent in, probably from some very strong limbs. Both the front windshield and driver's window were heavily cracked, but still in place. Overall, the damage was minimal given the speed of the car and the elopement distance.

Trying the driver door handle proved that this escapade was not going to be an instant slot machine win, as her effort did nothing. She tried several times just to be sure, and the passenger door behind it. There were no other options, she had to get the door open quickly as the car was being dragged into deeper water by the current. Shuffling her feet in search of the perfect tool to use on the driver's window, Bernadette felt a frantic surge of energy. Feeling her balance go unsteady, she sensed what she needed. Diving her hands, arms and torso below the water, she retrieved the rock, the size of a football, with the delight that one might find an emerald.

Holding on to the door handle with one hand, Bernadette repeatedly smashed the rock against the window. The window wasn't giving up easily and the water was reaching up to Bernadette's mid-thigh with swifter current upsetting her balance. In desperation, Bernadette smashed the rock again, yelling in frustration as the car kept up its suicidal submarine decent.

Breathing deeply, Bernadette knew what would work. It had to work. It was a trait that everyone claimed was bad and lead to nothing positive. But she doubted that idea, because she had used this trait to not only survive but succeed. Get mad. Using that welling tide of anger, she had managed to overcome lifting, pulling, pushing, and holding obstacles during past events. She was so close to helping this person or persons; she couldn't let this person die, wouldn't let them die. Levering her arm back, she swung her arm like the batter with bases loaded. Bernadette opened her eyes after the resounding thud, to finally see the window crumbling away. Using the rock, she did her best to clear the glass, especially at the bottom of the window.

The water was making everything impossible. A man was leaning against the seat, with his seatbelt on. He was the only one in the car. Putting her right arm down in the car, she found the buckle release in the mirky water, obtaining her first cut on the shattered window. She shook him, his eyes remained shut but he sighed. Finding the door latch on the inside she was only able to open the door a few inches. She just couldn't get good leverage to really pull the door open.

She was out of time. The current, although placid on the surface, was strong and sure. It was only a few more minutes until the car sunk and he'd drown. Finally, cringing with knowledge of the impending pain from the glass, she sunk her finger into his leather jacket and started to pull him out though the window, her forearms painfully soaking up the rough edges. The car further tilted toward this extra weight, making the decent faster. Perhaps from the force on the door, it swung fully open, knocking Bernadette off her feet. Grabbing the window frame, she pushed the man's head back through the window. Finally, she dragged his body out of the car, just able to touch the river floor with her tip toes, as the car made a final bob, then dipped and vanished.

Bernadette was glad she had taken lifeguard training in high school. She secured her already tired right arm past his neck, across his chest and tightened her hand around a bunch of slippery leather near his opposite arm pit. He was such a large man; it was impossible for her to reach under the opposite arm pit.

Out of breath, she floated with the current for a bit as she supported them.

Once her breathing wasn't coming in gasps, Bernadette began the slow process of swimming the side stroke toward shore. He weighed a good two hundred pounds and several times she had to just rest in the current to recover her breath. The fact that she didn't go swimming every day made her muscles burn and cramp. In what felt like a long time in the water, she was finally able to stand up. Extending her arms under his back, she clutched at the jacket and pulled him toward a sandy gravel bar. Her shoes were long gone; rocks further bruised and hindered her progress. Glancing around, she realized how far she had traveled, the bridge and curve were out of sight.

Securing her arms under his arm pits and grasping the opposite sides of the jacket, she pulled him out of the water. He was so heavy, and Bernadette was exhausted, she was unable to get his legs all the way out of the river. Laying back on the sand, she tried to relax through the screaming of her muscles. The man was breathing quickly and very shallow, with intermittent deep moans. As Bernadette tried to get her breath, she gently touched his head, sliding her fingers through the thick shaggy hair near his forehead and temples. She felt the beginning of a bump on his right temple. Carefully, she explored further. There was another bump lower and further back, behind his right ear. Bernadette figured he hit his head several times against the window.

She knelt by his head. "Sir, can you wake up? Can you hear me."

Rearing back, she was startled as his eyes opened, focused in on her, then closed with a moan.

Looking up, she wondered how she was going to find her clothes and backpack. She needed to get help for this man, but good grief, how could she try to stop a car on the road for help when she was only in underwear and a camisole. She briefly thought about floating down the river to find help, but quickly dismissed the idea as she had no idea if the river flowed through a populous part of Sterling. There weren't any good options. She would have to walk back along the bank to where she could see the road and get help.

Taking a few steps away from the man, she heard him moan again. She turned back, torn over leaving him to get help or comforting him. Kneeling she touched his chest with one hand and placed the other on his brow. "Don't worry, I will be right back with help. Just hang in there a little longer."

His eyes opened and he said, "I'm cold."

She smiled. It was a good sign he was talking. "I am too." She was shivering at this point but had decided not to focus on that problem. She relaxed while looking at the intelligent green eyes.

Bernadette felt rather than heard someone behind her. Under normal circumstances, she would have heard a person approaching through the brush, then along the sand bar. But stress and exhaustion had muddled her senses. With a sense of relief that someone had already found them, she started to look back to see who had arrived, when Bernadette found her head being stuffed in cloth. Everything went black and a panic erupted in her mind.

Bernadette went completely off the rails. Roger had taught her well. Even though she couldn't see, anyone who touched her became an immediate recipient of her training. The person trying to keep the hood on was kicked, clawed, head butted and punch. She grabbed frantically at the hood, tiring to pull it off, but it was finally tied in place and all the pulling was only choking her. Someone tried to pull her hands behind her back. They were immediately thrown over her shoulder and landed on the sand with a smacking thud. Then thick arms snaked around her chest holding her savage fists in place. Her kicks were on target; more grunting and cursing erupted from her attackers. Bernadette's arms and feet were finally tied after she was thrown to the ground, knocking the wind out of her. She heard a language she didn't understand. Then her thoughts dissolved into nothing.

-

It was stifling dark, gigantic goose bump cold, and muscle stabbing uncomfortable. Bernadette awoke to these feelings. She was on her side with her hands tied behind her back, her ankles bound, blackness covered her face, and a soft but ineffective blanket haphazardly laid over her body. Something had woken her. She tried to keep her breathing even, slow, steady, hoping that she would figure out what to do if her captors still thought she was sleeping.

There was at least one person in the room, their footsteps soft as they approached her.

Carney had been watching Bernadette for over forty-five minutes before she awoke. Her shallow panicked breaths, upon first awaking, quickly changed to a regular deep breathing, alerting him to her calculating awareness.

He had been analyzing how a simple morning drive, which often cleared his head, had resulted in a major head adjustment, maybe even a parting of the river, so to speak. Wherever his thoughts went, they circled back to this woman before him. In Carney's world, trust was always tested, held up to the feedback mirror to see if the reflection matched the initial picture. It was uncommon to find himself trusting so quickly, but then the feedback mirror was currently a tender spot on the side of his head.

Now that Bernadette was awake, he hesitated in his approach toward the bed on which Bernadette had been deposited some hours ago. He just didn't know what to expect from this woman. To clarify, he did know from the numerous injuries inflicted on his associates that Bernadette could kick like a mule, punch with the force of a wild boar, and claw like a Scottish wildcat; overall she was a worthy opponent even if she had a sack over her head.

But that was far from her complete story; Carney suspected there was amazing depth in this woman. Her actions reinforced the unusual truth that Bernadette was a very strong woman, physically and emotionally. Carney didn't underestimate that his clothes had added a sizeable drag to his formidable six-foot one-inch bulk. He was a muscular man and how this one-hundred-and-thirty-pound woman had found the strength to get into that car, get him out of the car and then swim them both to shore, spoke of a rare determination not seen in billions of people.

Puzzling over the best approach, Carney decided to use what he would have wanted, direct and succinct. He had to assume that her courage would trump fear, leaving her able to reason.

"Bernadette, I am going to remove the hood and the bindings on your wrists and ankles. I need you to remain calm. I can help you only if you remain calm."

His accent sounded warm, comforting. *No*, she thought, *best realize now, it is manipulative.*

Getting the hood off sounded like a win to Bernadette. It was hard to keep the panic at bay with the hood a constant symbol of suffocation. "Okay."

Carney smiled. Her comment wasn't a firm agreement to the conditions he stipulated, but she wouldn't deceive him with treachery either. Nice. He appreciated that and so, he was on guard.

The tie at the back of her neck was loosened and lifting her head a fraction, the hood eased off her head. She blinked several times at the bright glare, only to find it was more comfortable to keep her eyes closed. The bindings were removed, with a knife, the tip cold on her freezing skin.

"I am leaving your backpack and some warm sweats for you. There is a bathroom to the left. I will return in fifteen minutes. There isn't a way out, so don't waste your energy ... or mine. Besides, some of us are sore from either a car wreck or encountering a Tasmanian devil, so keep in mind our pistols just might be fond keepers of the peace."

Hearing the door shut and lock, she tried her eyes once more. As much as her eyes hurt in the light, she wanted warm water and dry clothes. There wasn't a shower in the bathroom, but there was hot water, a sink, and soap. If she was going to get out of this alive, she had to be in better condition and that meant moving though her screaming cold muscles.

Bernadette sat by the window ten minutes later in sweatpants and shirt. She had already sized up the room and her options for escape. Not only was she upstairs, but two men stood about 500 feet from the window. She would wait.

She felt the vibration of someone approaching before hearing the footsteps. Two, two sets of feet. Was she to be tortured? Some sadistic game? Happened all the time in the news. Perhaps someone to hold her and the other to kill her. Her heart pounded and she felt a scream coming on. She clamped her teeth shut and waited.

The door was unlocked, and the knob turned, but the door didn't open immediately. She watched, doing her best to get ahold of her heart. She couldn't fight effectively if she was panicked, she knew that. The man she had saved walked into the room with a tray of drinks and food. If she hadn't recognized him, she would have deduced it was him as he was sporting a lovely purple and yellow bruise over his entire right temple. He was a tough looking man and when you put the package of his parts together, the effect was arresting. His nose was a little wide, his large lips looked almost too feminine in their shape, his jaw was overly square, green eyes were so dark as to look almost brown, and high forehead was lost in an unruly swirl of thick black hair sporting a center cowlick. He didn't look very deadly with all that bruising. It would be this minor state of his perceived vulnerability that took Bernadette from fear to anger.

"I thought we could discuss our situation over some food." He managed a smile.

Bernadette frowned. She had lived a long time with a mean mother who had manipulated situations; "I" statements became "we" statements to bend truth and reality, and she certainly didn't have patience for it right now. "Our situation? I saved your sorry ass because you can't drive worth beans. Then I am treated like a gunny sack of corn and am now a hostage like a cow at its last feedlot. I would say this has become my problem and not much of yours. How is it that you look all refreshed, like you have been to a nice day spa; you were just in a major car wreck and obtained a serious concussion." Bernadette's temper grew fiercer, "Like the saying, no good deed goes unpunished."

"I am sorry about the gunny sack treatment, but you were..."

Bernadette interrupted him with a searing look. She began yelling, "Don't you dare go there and blame this on me. I know that kind of mind warp all too well. My mother specialized in it. Your... your people or somebody, threw a hood over my head. All they had to do was ask me if I wanted a ride to get my clothes and I would have gone willingly back to wherever. You idiots are all the same. You don't see the obviously nice way to behave because you're so busy tweaking reality to be a fight."

Carney blew out an exasperated breath. No doubt about it, Bernadette was a hell-cat. And he was refreshed and invigorated by it. As of late, he had become so tired of the masses of people who spent exorbitant amounts of time whining, couldn't speak for themselves bravely, failed to use their backbone, and wanted life to whisk them along on some fluffy duvet cover of cushiness.

"Do you think we could start over? Hello, my name is Carney, and you must be Bernadette. It is nice to meet you. Thank you for saving my buttocks. How about something to drink and a bite to eat?"

Bernadette didn't say anything, just sat there. Her cheeks had become bright red and he could have sworn that her hair was becoming redder, like a flame beginning to feed off of furious fuel vapors. He half expected it to stand on end, a soon to be fire tornado on her head.

Patiently, Carney started again, "Bernadette, this is my problem. I realize that you risked your life to help me. I now need to protect you. If you don't talk with me and work with me on this, it will be tougher on both of us."

Here it was, the real problem for Carney, looking as innocent as barbed wire wrapped around the axel and under immense tension, ready to come unleashed and whip the hell out of a person. Inwardly, Carney was unsure if he could protect Bernadette. It was clear that he couldn't protect himself, but he hadn't expected that his killer would come from within the organization. Now he knew there was a serious "staffing" problem, but it didn't help because he wasn't sure who he could trust. For all the people who had pledged loyalty to Carney, none had been at River Forth when he needed them. The only person who was there was this high spirited, tenacious woman. He didn't know much about her, the phone conversations regarding her had been brief, yet he trusted her. Her eyes had an ancient, and honest awareness about them. On some very deep, basic level he felt he needed her, and Carney had made it a point not to need many people. This was a day of shocking surprises, not the least of which was what he learned while on the phone with Bernadette's passport in hand.

Setting the food down on a table, Carney picked up a folding chair and approached Bernadette slowly, never taking his eyes off her. He sat down, with his knees touching hers.

She looked up, then quickly looking back down, as if embarrassed. "Who are you protecting me from? I don't understand that."

"Because you saw my face and could identify me if you were to report the accident, my, ah, staff, thinks it is best that you are encouraged to be quiet about this event."

Looking up, Bernadette sat back in the chair, crossed her arms and began speaking as if Carney was missing a few key parts of grey matter. "Okay, how about I agree not to tell anyone. You take me back to my hotel and I go on my merry way. Wouldn't that be easier than all this other stuff going on?" Her eyes narrowed, "Somehow I am getting the impression that you people don't trust anyone unless that person is six feet under and creating compost."

Carney laughed, a deep rich belly laugh, which was also as infrequent as his trust. "Compost? No, your word is not good enough right now. Others might know about this accident and sort of encourage you to talk about it, talk about me, even if you are back in Germany. The only way I can protect you Bernadette is if you become a close member of our group." Now it was Carney's turn to sit back and cross his arms, mirroring Bernadette's protective posture.

"What group is this? Is this going to be like the Patty Hearst thing? Which, by the way, it was so stupid that she went to jail. For goodness sakes, she was a hostage. When you're abducted and you are trying to survive, your life and views change a bit. Only a completely befuddled jury and judge would sentence that woman. It figures. That is how we treat women, to maximum extent of some man's law, right? That was a complete failure of the justice system." Shaking her head, Bernadette was really getting herself worked up.

Admiration continued to blossom within Carney for the woman sitting across from him. No crying, no hysterics. He could see she was scared, but she used her anger well, to help keep it together when she needed to. Most people would be begging for their lives, and she was blabbering on about Patty Hearst. She thought about issues, in depth. What a refreshing, novel, and well overdue trait to see. She wouldn't judge things just because she was told how to think, she would take her time and look at all the smaller nuances. He realized she would have an initial opinion, but later, she would think. He was in awe that he was attracted to this woman's mind so completely and he knew this unique mind would be a spring of sprouting adventures, with wit, strength, and caring.

"I said you will become a close member of our group. I didn't say that you would be involved in our day-to-day activities."

Carney was silent a long time. Bernadette quickly looked at his brilliant green eyes, one half swollen with bruising. She thought, *oh here it comes. This is going to be a real fur ball, all splat on the carpet.* The air between them was charged with contemplation and assessment.

He waited. Carney had to understand her as a woman before moving forward. Finally, a fraction of a second, just a little, not much, Carney saw her willingness. There was no loathing or repulsion directed toward him. A wanting to be on good terms was there and that was all he needed.

Most days, Carney's view of the world was jaded, but this woman gave him something; a fresh desire for life. Not one to make rash decisions, Carney just didn't have the time to dally around the woman without getting them both killed. A close confidante had not only suggested the idea but recommended it as their only option. So, he did what needed to be done and he did it with the honor his father had taught him. He had to hope it was the right thing to do for both of them.

"Bernadette, I need to marry you. It is the only way I can assure others that you will be quiet. It is the only way I can ensure others won't act against you. I will arrange everything, and we will need to leave within several hours. There is a chapel some distance from here where we can be married later tonight. I am sorry, but no more discussion about it."

Mentally dismissing the shock he saw in Bernadette, he bounced out of the room, feeling confident of the decision. If he had gotten any sense that she was a mole, he would have excused himself and thought about other ways to deal with the problem. But she was the only woman who didn't know him, but had protected him. He had looked at other women in the group and wondered about marriage. They had worked to seduce him and he found to be sought after but never seeking, was a bore. Every other woman wanted him for something; status, ease of living, importance, sex, or perhaps children. This redhead didn't want him for anything. Her independence streak stood out like banners in the wind on the coastal jetty. With each passing heartbeat in her presence, he became more convinced that she would be loyal and faithful to him in a world filled with many false reasons not to be those very things.

As he pulled the door shut, he gave Bernadette a bit more to think on. "Some ladies will be in shortly to help you prepare for the wedding and bandage up those cuts in your arms. Don't dawdle."

Once the door closed and latched, Bernadette put her head in both hands and began to cry. She couldn't see how a marriage would do anything other than put a bigger, brighter bullseye on her tush. The only thing she could do was go along for the ride and hope to find a safe off ramp soon.

-

More than two hours later, two beautiful dark-haired women entered the room. Bernadette had been thinking about all her options, as yet, even with the door open, escape didn't look promising.

The women looked mad, both of them. They stood in the doorway with their arms full of garment bags. Bernadette put on her best fierce scowl and returned the look.

The shorter woman took control. "Little missy, anyone of us would have given our right, ah, our right something, to marry Carney. You don't even know how lucky you are. You are to come with us. Keep in mind, push us too much and we will make sure you look like a freak for your wedding." Both women laughed hysterically at that idea.

Bernadette didn't look like she was going to budge. Her white knuckles were clasping the chair arms, as if the chair could save her.

Now the taller woman felt obliged to chime in. "You can either come with us down the hall to a room with a shower, where we can, much to our distain, get you beautiful for your wedding, or we will just get a couple of guys to throw you in the shower. I have no sympathy for you. I have been eyeing Carney for a number of years now, hoping everyday he would look my way. I have tried every seducing number I know. Nothing has worked. All you had to do was go swimming with him."

Bernadette didn't move, the knuckles were whiter, and even her lips had disappeared into a frosty line.

The women stepped back from the door and closed it. There was some mumbling and footsteps going back down the hall.

It wasn't five minutes later that the door opened again. Bernadette stared at the floor. Her mouth set in a hard line; her teeth were clinched so hard it hurt. She felt people looking at her, but her intuition told her that one person, a man, wasn't just looking at her but evaluating her physical strengths and weaknesses. Evaluating her looks. Bernadette wasn't a beautiful woman in the way of blonde barbie. She was arresting with her red riot of curls, high cheek bones, beautiful lips, and eyes of antiquity. He couldn't see the eyes, but he was told how they held the beauty of any gem. He was excited at the thought of dressing down this wench, and Bernadette could smell his excitement. His name was Sindbad.

It was a palatable stench of violence that oozed out into the room. Bernadette's felt a sweat break out all over and her scraped up arms started to throb.

Bernadette, still looking at the floor, got to her feet. "I am coming."

The women stood guard while Bernadette showered. Given the river and hood thing, a shower was wonderful and taking as much time as possible gave her more time to delay and think. That was, until the ladies threatened to get Sindbad to help rout her out of the shower. Confident that the women would make good on their threat, Bernadette finished and wrapped herself up in several towels.

The women started working on her hair and make-up. And frankly, when Bernadette finally saw the results, she was impressed. Her hair had been dried, curled, then put up with some headband thing. The ladies did a nice job on her lashes, which were already long, but naturally light in color. They added a nice brown eyeshadow and a soft red lipstick.

As they opened up the garment bags, one woman explained, "We are sorry, but there just aren't many wedding dresses around. We found a lovely full-length navy-blue skirt and this beautiful long sleeve blouse, which should hide the bandages on your arms. We were able to find some simple blue clogs that match the skirt. We wanted you to wear a burlap sack under all of this, but Carney threatened us with horse-stall chores, so we have this stretchy lace negligée thing and some pink nylons." The negligée was tossed to her. "We got some additional clothes for you to have after your wedding. And I swear, if you complain, all of this finery gets wine spilled all over in some unforeseen accident."

Bernadette's mantra had become, *BUY TIME.*

So, she dressed, quietly and slowly.

When done, the ladies quickly ushered Bernadette down the stairs and toward a waiting black BMW, looking identical to the one that went in the river. Bernadette hesitated when they stopped a good fifty feet from the car, motioning her to go forward. Bernadette stumbled, hanging in limbo. She looked back at the women, whose expressions had softened considerably. For a moment she stood gazing all around her, wondering how this had happened. How had a work-study program turned into a marriage? Maybe they were identical, but she hadn't realized it till today.

The back passenger door was opened from the inside. Carney in the back seat and two other men in the front watched Bernadette resume her hostage shuffle. She looked beautiful, except for her face, which was furious. The driver slapped the steering wheel several times while laughing and said, "Oh, this is going to be a perfect honeymoon." The guy in the front passenger seat threw back his head and hooted.

Carney said, "Shut up, guys. You won't make this easier by laughing."

The idling car engine revved.

Getting close to the BMW, Bernadette bent at the waist and looked in the open door. Carney was breathtaking in a midnight blue suit. He looked rather smug and that pushed Bernadette's defenses further into orange alert. Best not be some mushy, doe eyed woman; in all likelihood, he got such sappy adoration the time. Bernadette resented anyone who expected her to act like all the other fawning women. She figured it was time to tip the scales back on an even keel.

Bernadette let loose. "I am not getting into this BMW. You don't take care of your cars or maintain the brakes and I don't feel like saving anymore asses today. I mean, how men can I marry in one day?" She turned away from the car, stood ramrod straight, and crossed her arms in a major show of defiance.

Carney had been stunned by how beautiful Bernadette looked in her blouse and skirt, but it wasn't the outside that continued to put him in awe. Her wit and her internal strength were something he had never seen before. Bernadette's red hair was ablaze. Carney fell hard for Bernadette at that moment, and he would have begged her to marry him had this been another lifetime. It was going to take all his bravado to pull this off.

Getting out of the car, Carney held up a hand so no one else would force her into the car. Walking around the car, he then took her hand and pulled her a good one hundred feet from everyone, so they could talk privately, "You have no choice in this. You need to get in the car."

"No. I don't know what you are doing or why, but no."

Carney felt corned. It was time to tell her. "Bernadette, your Uncle Roger is going to marry us, and he expects you to arrive in one piece."

The blood drained from Bernadette's face, and she gasped. "How could you...?" Confusion pushed her eyebrows and the corner of her lips down. In a few seconds there was a dawning realization, "It was the birthmarks. Does everyone in Ireland and Scotland know about them? How could you know about them and who to call?"

Carney said, "They are Irish lore. I am familiar with it."

"You got Roger mixed up in this mess. How could you do that? He is a good man and now he could be killed too!" Bernadette took several steps back from Carney and looked ready to flee.

Snaking out to grab her hand again, he said, "Regardless of what you might think, men are independent thinking creatures too. Roger didn't do anything he didn't want to do. Get in the car and let's go talk with him."

Carney watched the war in Bernadette's eyes. She was assessing and waiting. He was going to have to watch her like a hawk. She took the information about Roger with strength, never letting it weaken her in a soup of memories and emotions. Then, with the caginess of an angry lion, she went into stalking mode. She made instant decisions as conditions changed.

"I guess I will get into one of your cars, hoping this one gets more maintenance."

Bernadette marched back to the car, sat and then elegantly folded her legs and the lovey skirt into the car, allowing Carney to shut the door behind her. Once Carney was in, he reached over and buckled her seatbelt. Leaning close to her ear, Carney's lips almost touched Bernadette's sensitive skin. "I do maintain my cars. Someone unmaintained the other one for me." He fastened his own seatbelt and leaned back, wondering how this information would affect her.

Her eyes opened larger, helping Carney to see the various shades of brown and some green in her expressive irises. She didn't say anything, but he could almost hear the synapse working frantically in her head. She then focused her attention on the men in the driver's seat and front passenger seat. Several times, the guy in the front passenger seat turned his head slightly, sharing a knowing but unspoken word with Carney. When it occurred for the fourth time in the span of a few minutes, Bernadette looked at Carney, eyebrows raised.

He met her eyes with regret. "Bernadette, I am sorry, but I need to put the hood back on your head until we get to the church."

They had already pulled away from the house but were not on a main road yet. She wanted to see Roger, yearned to see him, and therefore, she would have considered any request. This demand wasn't what she wanted, but something she wasn't going to fight. "Well, I think it will look just smashing with my blouse, huh." The searing look in Bernadette's eye told Carney just what he could do with the hood.

Not taking his eyes from Bernadette, his hand closed over the darkness offered from the front seat. He didn't lean toward her, sending the message that she had to be willing in this game they found themselves. He was asking her to have some trust even if she felt none.

Her overwhelmed emotional state peaked from the anticipation of seeing Roger after so many years and consequently, her nerves began to fray, behaving like a run in some shiny tight pantyhose. Bernadette leaned her head sideways and Carney easily slipped the hood on. To her immense shame, she started to shake. The shaking became worse, migrating up her arms and legs to her torso. Or perhaps it started at her core and then migrated out. She didn't know.

Carney's hand moved to her shoulder. "Bernadette, you are going to make yourself sick. Everything is alright."

She didn't want to cry, she didn't want to be weak, and absolutely didn't want to mess up her make-up. If she was really going to be getting married and seeing Roger after all these years, she wanted to look nice. But how do you trust people who are behaving like gangsters? Bernadette started sobbing. Her head bowed and it started to shake like a bobby dog from the dime store. Her breathing was becoming difficult with all her sobbing.

First, loosening her seat belt, Carney's arm snaked behind her back and pulled her toward him. "Bernadette, listen to me. This is all going to be fine. We are going to be fine. In a few days you will be back on a plane to Germany."

In between broken sobs Bernadette ground out, "Why did I have to go and save you. I should have gone to the nearest house and let them know a stupid car was at the bottom of a river. Good thing you aren't driving today or I would have had to put on a helmet and scuba gear, under this stupid hood of course. I hope you are going to take driving lessons. I need a tissue." There was a hiccup and a forced laugh. In a moment of broken tension, Carney laughed with her. Even the guys in the front seat were chuckling.

Handing her a handkerchief he said, "I don't think we will need the scuba gear today, but I will keep it in mind for future driving adventures." Carney kept his tone light to match Bernadette's levity. Inwardly the ramification of the crash was very serious for Carney. The joke was a welcome release of tension, but a very temporary state of relief. He would need to come up with a strategy to find the newly budding mis-mechanic in the group.

Carney had his arm around Bernadette, massaging her right arm and shoulder. "Like I said, the car was rigged. Once I was in fourth gear that last time, everything stuck at full throttle. I couldn't get it out of gear and the brakes didn't work."

Bernadette put a hand inside her confinement and wiped her nose. She had to get a handle on this fear. She had to mentally emphasize that she was very lucky to be worried, as a small tweak in in any circumstance probably would have led to her death.

The men in the front of the car began talking about weather and nondescript fishing adventures, she figured to put her at ease.

Bernadette could tell when they were on some sort of highway, not a back road any longer. The motion of the warm car started to make her drowsy. She was exhausted, tired from all the swimming and all the adrenaline. The last she remembered was Carney placing her head on his chest. Then the calm of sleep finally took over.

Chapter 6
The Wedding

(Summer 1984)
Friday

The front passenger got back in and slammed the car door shut, after opening and closing another gate they had to pass through.

"Why does it smell like cows? Are we getting married in a barn?" Bernadette asked. After all that had happened today, and then being stuck in this hood for hours, Bernadette's temper and tongue were going from silent recess to boisterous refresh. She had also taken the drive time to think more on her fate and she felt slightly confident that Carney's goal did not include the rape and murder of her.

The men in the car laughed. Carney said, "The chapel we are going to is on a private estate, some of it farmland. We are at the chapel, so you can take off that hood now, if you wish."

Pulling the offending thing off her head, Bernadette scowled at Carney, "Right, if I wish."

Bernadette saw a small stone building illuminated by one tiny outdoor light. It looked to be a lone survivor of some long-ago war. "I hope it is modern enough to have a bathroom, or I am going to have a take an excursion around the back of the cow barn."

The driver quipped, "Spoken like a farm gel."

"No, spoken like a practical woman who has been abducted."

That comment shut everyone down. Carney grinned and sat back, refreshed by Bernadette's sparing.

As they pulled up in front of the steps, Bernadette removed her seat belt and had her hand on the door latch. She was so excited to see Roger. She couldn't believe this turn of good fortune. She had waited for this moment for <u>years</u>!

No one moved, but the doors unlocked. Carney said, "Go ahead. Roger is waiting for you inside. We will remain out here while you two talk for a bit."

Bernadette launched herself out of the car, ran up the steps, flung the chapel door open and looked wildly around. "Roger, are you here?"

He appeared out of a side door, his arms open. She ran to him and wrapped her arms around his torso. "It is you. I have wanted to see you for so long. How are you?" Bernadette looked up at Roger. Her face was beaming in joy.

He had hugged her, but his grip relaxed quickly, and he stepped back, then holding her shoulders. "Look at how beautiful you have become. And I heard you are a fine independent woman now."

Bernadette felt the push of distance from Roger. She could already sense a disconnect between them; confusion and disappointment started cracking her relief and joy in this moment. He then dropped his hands, while rubbing them together he said, "It feels a bit cool tonight. These chapels are often so drafty."

She stared at him in shock. His hair was streaked with grey, and he looked thinner, yet more puffy in places. The lines around his eyes sagged in weariness borne of continuous stress. Instead of a loving family reunion, this meeting was taking on the tone of a court reciting the final divorce decree.

Roger eyed Bernadette's expression solemnly. He said, "Bernadette, I want to assure you that Carney is a good man. He will do the right thing for you. Your discretion is of most importance here. Carney and I can only be of so much help. Do you understand what I am saying?"

Bernadette stood rigidly straight before giving her curt reply. "Yep, got that."

"Good. Then why don't you step outside and call Carney in. We should get this wedding underway."

In every imagining Bernadette had about a reunion with Roger, she never saw it as a falling-out filled with emotional squalor. She had nothing to lose, and she had learned early in her life that loving words kept locked in one's heart could not be known, regardless of future words spoken. She leapt, "I may not understand much here Roger, but I know that I love you, and always will. No matter what the situation or the secret."

As she walked back to the front door, Roger said, "I know, and I love you too." When she turned back to face him, he was already walking toward the front of the chapel. He looked so defeated. It was difficult for Bernadette to feel outrage.

Roger O'Rafferty performed the service quickly. Bernadette's exhaustion caused her to sway while the vows were exchanged; she wouldn't remain much longer on her feet. They signed the church register and as they were leaving, Roger quickly put his arm around her shoulders in a half embrace. Then they were back in the car and traveling.

"Bernadette, I know you are exhausted. The cabin where we are staying is another hour of driving."

Bernadette grudgingly put the hood on and learned her head against Carney.

–

During the final leg of this journey, Carney's mind raced through the events of the day. He felt pleasure at being a married man. Yet, the doubts about Bernadette's possible dangerously hidden motives couldn't be ignored. He tried to ignore them, but he kept coming back to several important conclusions that got him nowhere:

- Not even the best case officer could have planted Bernadette as a junior insider, or underling mole, to save him from downing in that BMW. Her battle with the water, current, car, cold, and timing was not something normally asked of an underling or sleeper.
- The fact that Roger not only knew her, but had raised Bernadette, was too coincidental; the only plausible explanation was a mole had just been planted by his side.
- Yet, her loving Roger as a father, and Carney had seen how she looked at Roger with a deep love and trust, assured Carney that she would never talk about their marriage, relationship, or the accident. Therefore, her benefits as a mole for any organization was very limited and near worthless.
- Her training by Roger, and he knew she had been well trained because the injuries inflicted during the sandbar fiasco, made her an excellent candidate for a mole. A mole for which adversary was unknown.
- The birthmarks and their significance for nature, the spirit of nature, meant Bernadette couldn't be a mole. Her destiny and fight were in another arena.
- Roger had advocated that Bernadette was Carney's chosen mate. He emphasized that Carney was to help and protect, but not coddle her. Her mission had nothing to do with any of them and everything to do with nature. That didn't sound like a mole but could be a darn good cover.
- He had seen the birthmarks on her foot and shoulder blade. They were definitely not tattoos. Therefore, she wasn't, couldn't be, a mole.
- Roger told him much about Bernadette's childhood, her pain and suffering. He also recited a very long list her unique qualities. No one ever bothered to give a mole such an in-depth history. Why would someone trouble with such details? Didn't sound like a mole.

Carney decided his train of thought was a symptom of going nuts. Then he thought of other marriages he knew and realized they might all be similar in complications. He decided to set the thoughts aside for now, as his concussion was causing a darn good headache.

-

The vehicle finally stopped, making a sharp left turn onto a gravel drive, which was blocked by an immense iron gate. Carney removed Bernadette's hood. The driver rolled down the window to speak with two men dressed completely in black, both holding the leads of very huge Irish wolfhounds. Bernadette was impressed, not with the men, but the gigantically beautiful dogs. They sniffed the air then settled on looking at her. Their interest and lack of menace was not lost to Carney.

Not long after the iron gate, the road split in a Y. They took the left drive, which was increasingly pitted with ruts and potholes. It was another quarter mile till the headlights shown on several buildings. Once at the cabin, Bernadette noticed there were no neighbors, no outdoor lights. She wondered if there would be power and was relieved when the front door was opened and lights were turned on.

The driver and other passenger placed their luggage in a room then drove off. Bernadette quickly explored the interior seeped in Scottish heritage. It was a beautiful cabin showcasing logs and artistically stained wood boards. Rustic yet elegant. A large fireplace was ready to be lit. Set up much like a one-bedroom apartment, there was a living room area divided from the kitchen by four-foot wall. A hallway, filled with more paneling and cabinets, led to a huge bathroom, probably updated in the last decade, with a shower and a separate tub. A door further down the hall led to a bedroom. There was only one bed in this cabin.

Bernadette's stomach did a flop. Carney walked into the bedroom and dropped their luggage. He stood looking at her in question, one eyebrow raised.

He knew, Bernadette had to decide what this early morning hour would hold. He already had thought about the complications of their situation. If he was firm in the decision they would make love this early morning, then she could feel forced into it. If he said they weren't going to make love, then she would feel unattractive and think he would have sex with her out of some weird obligation. He had seen her shy and insecure glances. He found Bernadette completely attractive mentally and physically, but she needed to learn of his feelings through experience, not words. So, he waited for her to make the first move.

Finally, she said, "Carney, do you mind if we just go to sleep? I don't think I can take much more in a twenty-four-hour period. It has nothing to do with you. I am at the unzipping point, really."

"We will do as you wish. I will use the bathroom and get on some pajama bottoms."

Bernadette watched him walk out. She scrambled to find and put on her old flannel nightgown, the one she used when traveling. All the bridal finery was hung in the closet.

Hearing Bernadette in the kitchen when he returned to the bedroom, he got under the covers and waited. Bernadette didn't take long in the bathroom. Her soft footsteps entered the bedroom and she quietly slide under the covers, on the other side of the bed. Carney's arm snaked out, pulling her up to him and her head into the crook of his arm. He felt her tears rather than heard her distress.

"It's alright Bernadette. We will get through this."

After a moment she replied, "I was thinking of Roger. I had hoped for a loving reunion. He looked ill and on edge. Nothing like my Uncle Roger. He was almost a stranger."

Carney said, "What reality holds at the moment has a way of eclipsing the emotions we might hope for in a reunion. But that doesn't mean the relationship was anything less than originally thought. It is just different now."

With those words, they drifted off to sleep.

North ↑
Note: Not a real map!
Cape Wrath
Ocean
Loch Laxford
Laxford Bridge
Loch Stack
Loch More
Loch Merkland
Loch Shin
North Minch
Lairg
Scotland
High lands
Tain
Inverness

Chapter 7
Riding the Waves

(Summer 1984)
Saturday - Sunday

Bernadette awoke disoriented. Her head rested on Carney's shoulder and her arm across his chest kept her tight to his side. Not wanting to wake him, she slowly inched away.

"If you are trying to run away, best know that I am awake."

Supporting her torso on one bent arm, she looked down on him and asked, "Where would I run? How would I outrun those Irish wolfhounds? I just need to go to the bathroom. What time is it?"

Looking at his Rolex, "Half past eight. Should we have breakfast now?"

Bernadette looked at his six o'clock shadow and the erotic chest hair showing above the sheet and comforter resting at his waist. His shoulder and chest were sculptured with muscles, flexing, beckoning when he even moved a smidgen. The raw growth of beard accented his square jawline, framing his inviting lips. *He was WAY too good looking for her,* she thought. Getting some food sounded much safer than worrying about how he might laugh at her during sex.

She said, "Breakfast sounds good." She went to jump from the bed, but Carney latched onto her forearm. He had seen her desire, and watched her doubt come in and annihilate it.

Carney said, "Wait a minute. I am willing to make you a proper Scottish breakfast if you give me a good morning kiss, on the lips." His gave it his best smile. Not cocky or seductive, a smile for enticing the timid.

She immediately retreated into herself. Carney worried she might not kiss him and if she didn't, the direction today would continue to be awkward and strained. She looked unsure of him, the bed, and mostly her own sex appeal. Making an instant decision, he pushed her head to the pillow and sought out her lips, especially the fuller lower lip that had been invading his dreams. He worked it, the best he could. Fifteen minutes later he broke the kiss.

"When you want to go beyond kisses, you will need to let me know. For those kisses, I will make you breakfast." Carney pull Bernadette out of bed with him. "You get the bathroom first."

When Bernadette exited the bathroom a several minutes later, there was no Carney: not in the kitchen, not in the bedroom. After fifteen minutes she put on some clothes and checked around outside the cabin and nearby shed. She didn't hear or see any person or even the dogs.

After entering the cabin, she shut the door, and stood at the threshold. *Holy moly! If something happened to Carney, she was as good as dead. It was so isolated here. What would she do now? The only thing to do now was wait. That made sense for the time being.* She walked into kitchen and looked for knives. Only several small paring and steak knives were to be found. Selecting a sturdy paring knife, she went into the most secure room, the bathroom, sat on the edge of the tub, and waited.

It must have been twenty minutes later when Bernadette heard voices and then footsteps on the front porch. She clutched her stomach. *What a trip from hell!* Only one person entered the cabin, and then stopped walking. Her heart was hammering, but she tried not to breath because when she was breathing in huffs and puffs, she couldn't hear as well. She was hungry and now felt faint. The stress of this vacation was really getting to her.

"Bernadette?" It was Carney's voice, deep and friendly.

Perhaps nothing was wrong she thought. "Yah"

Footsteps proceeded to the bathroom and the door inched opened.

What Carney saw was not what he expected. Bernadette sat on the edge of the tub, one hand behind her back and one hand shaking in her lap. Her face was a pasty grey.

She said, "When I found you gone, I was afraid something happened to you." Bernadette voice was cracking.

Carney sat down next to Bernadette. He took the knife and laid it on the floor, then put his arms around her. "I am so sorry. I didn't think. I am so used to being on my own. Well, I have never been married before so I never thought how this might look to you given our situation. I won't do it again. I promise. I really am very sorry."

"Not to worry. Just another few years off my life." Bernadette had a grin on her face, but it was a grin of anxiety.

Carney didn't want to dwell on their situation right now. He wanted a honeymoon. He only wanted to get married once and therefore, this relationship needed a trajectory toward love and passion. He said, "I have a surprise for you. Let's eat and make a picnic lunch. Come on." When Bernadette stood, he picked her up and carried her to the kitchen. Depositing her on the counter, he stood between her legs. "Am I forgiven?"

"Only if you feed me soon. I am starving." She winked at him, an unspoken assurance that the day would improve, and slid off the counter. "Let's get busy."

They worked together on breakfast. Within a half hour their stomachs found fulfillment, although other hungers remained unsatisfied.

Putting his hands on her cheeks, Carney said, "I have something you are really going to enjoy, so you better get ready fast."

Walking to a hall cabinet, Carney handed Bernadette a couple bags which were brought in with the luggage the prior night. They looked to contain new clothes and shoes. "How do you get this stuff so fast?"

"Once it was decided we would become husband and wife," Carney stressed the husband-and-wife part, so it sounded seductive, "I knew I wanted to make this time as special as possible for you. That probably sounds ridiculous given our circumstances. Anyways, I tried to come up with a few interesting day activities and a few gifts you might enjoy." At that moment Carney looked embarrassed and a trifle emotionally exposed. He continued, "Scotland isn't that large of a county. It is possible to find most clothes you need without driving too far."

Bernadette dutifully marched into the bathroom to change. The first bag held brown riding breeches and black shiny riding boots. She almost screamed with delight. She never had such sleek riding gear. The boots would take two socks, as they were a bit large, but she didn't care. In the second bag there was a starched white shirt and a green button-down sweater, such a dark forest green it almost looked black. She exited the bathroom, hugged Carney quickly, and proceeded to say, "Thank you. These are beautiful. Thank you for being kind to me."

"We are going to ride horses down by the ocean. I thought you might enjoy this riding gear." Carney was thinking that he was definitely, most absolutely, going to enjoy the riding pants on her. Holding out his hand, Bernadette took it, and they left the cabin with their picnic lunches in a backpack Carney wore.

-

Bernadette was in awe as she watched all the frilly thick horsehair flying in the wind. There were three Gypsy Vanners: one all black, one a piebald with more black than white, and the other a skewbald, with more white than brown. The fourth horse, a draft horse cross, sported stunning dapples within a blue roan, contrasting with three black socks and a white one. Two horses were still in the corral while the piebald and skewbald were at the hitching post, saddled and ready to go. Bernadette marveled at their bulky size, but it was the grooming that made these horses stand out. Each one looked like an entire salon of beauticians from Edinburgh showed up every morning and did a major blow-out on the tails, manes, and feet feather. She wasn't an equine expert, but common sense told her these horses were very expensive. Taking one of the horses from the hitching post, Carney held the reins, looking expectantly at Bernadette, he gestured in a come-hither manner.

In that moment, unease washed over Bernadette. She didn't understand the source of her discomfiture. Was it this man? Were the horses unsafe? Was the situation dangerous? Why would this good-looking man treat her well? Was he just playing a game of deceit? In the past, good-looking men had not been kind to her. At best they ignored her and at worst they insulted her. Feeling awkward and unsure, and she decided it was best to be aware and move forward.

Carney wondered what he had done wrong. He saw the emotions of insecurity and confusion as her forehead creased in a frown. He waited.

Bernadette took at large breath, looked up at him, squared her shoulders and moved forward. After she slipped her left foot in the stirrup, threw her right leg over the saddle and settled her seat, she asked, "You're not worried that I will run off with the horse?"

Carney gave a quick replay, "I gave you the lame horse for a reason."

"Is this horse really lame?"

"That is what the guys said. They didn't think it would be an issue as long as you didn't run her."

That simple statement caused the hackles on the back of Bernadette's neck to feel further abraded. The source of trepidation felt close. Bernadette watched as Carney mounted his horse, then made a decision, before turning back wasn't possible. Getting off her horse, she began feeling its legs, both sides. Carney watched her touch the horse with lightness, then an insistent prodding. He began to wonder if he needed to fake lameness to get such treatment. Tying the horse back up, she carefully picked up each hoof, inspecting the frog and hoof wall by using a stick to break away any impacted dirt. When that was done, she led it around in a tight figure eight, watching its gate and changing of its lead leg. The horse was lame, but the source of injury wasn't obvious to her.

Carney sat comfortably on his horse watching Bernadette, admiring her as a woman. Her red hair swirled around in the breeze and its color contrasted generously with the green sweater. She was on the thin side, but the riding pants made the most of her curves. Thinking about her athletic body had Carney daydreaming.

He started a bit when Bernadette turned and asked him, "Did you grow up around horses?"

Curious to see where this would go, Carney kept his explanation short. "No"

"So, you started riding later in life?"

"Yes." he replied.

After a moment, Bernadette said, "But you grew up working around cars, right?"

"Yes."

Sighing, Bernadette scowled at Carney. "What is this? Are we reduced to one-word responses? For goodness sakes, we were just married, and you act like a man hen pecked for over forty years."

Carney continued to tease. "I am hoping we get to go riding." She had sass and Carney did everything he could to look serious and not fall off his horse laughing.

"Carney, I don't think I should ride a lame horse. Riding a lame horse and saying it is okay because it can walk but not run, is like driving a car with a flat tire and saying it is okay because you won't be going over 15 mph or 10 km/h, whatever units you use here. She tied up her horse and walked over to his. Can we ride the ones in the coral?"

"I was told the blue roan bucks and the black Gypsy Vanner is barn-sour."

Putting her fingers in her hair and rubbing her palms on her forehead, Bernadette appeared to be doing some heavy thinking. Taking a deep breath, she dropped her hands.

"Something doesn't add up. How can the black horse be barn-sour when it doesn't live here? I would understand if this was the horse's home. I am not a horse trainer, but doesn't barn-sour imply a desire to return to a familiar barn where the horse has a routine and buddies?"

Carney asked, "How do you know it doesn't live here?"

"Simple. There isn't a huge pile of horse manure. I don't see a fenced paddock nearby. So, they are fed in this barn and roam in the corral, from what I do see. Given that, there should be a pile of poop from them being here all the time. If the black horse doesn't live here, it probably won't be barn-sour. Why don't we saddle up the other horses and see if we can't get in a good ride? If they are a headache, we will bring them back and we can walk somewhere. But I am not riding a lame horse."

Carney realized she was right. There wasn't a big pile of horse manure or evidence where a pile had been prior to being removed. "I think you have a point. Let's switch them out."

It took about twenty minutes for them to find the correct bridles and saddles to make the switch. Carney, having placed a pad on the bucking blue roan, was ready to toss on the saddle when Bernadette met him on the other side.

"Carney, I think it is better that I ride this horse."

Carney's expression darkened and his grip on the saddle tightened.

"Look, we are not going to have our first marital fight over a horse we don't even own. However, I have some very good reasons for suggesting this. First, your track record for driving accidents is much higher than mine right now. Second, it won't serve me well if you are hurt when you get thrown by this horse." Softening her tone, she appealed to his understanding of her inescapable vulnerability. "We both know that if I am left here alone to fend for myself, it won't go well for me. I don't even know where I am. I have no idea where to go for help and I don't know who I am fighting."

Carney doubted that Bernadette would be at a complete loss in any situation, but if something should happen to him, it would make for an incredibly difficult predicament for which Bernadette's chances of survival would be extremely low.

Allowing her to finish saddling the blue roan, he headed over to the black Gypsy Vanner.

Bernadette mounted with no problems. The blue roan was very much a gentleman as she rode him through a trot and canter, just so they were accustomed to each other. She wondered if the bucking problem was made up or based on a cruel rider.

Carney mounted his horse. "The coastline here is rather rugged, so we will be following a trail down to the shore. During high tide a person can get trapped down there, so we need to keep track of the time and get back before the tide starts to come in."

With all other thoughts evaporating in this minute, Bernadette was impressed with the man before her. "You look very dashing on that horse. I hope I don't have to protect you from a gaggle of women fans."

Carney grunted and said, "Don't concern yourself. It is just the horse they would be interested in."

Bernadette doubted that. The horse was beautiful, but the man was superb.

They had to travel single file because the trail was narrow. Carney led the way, which was fine for Bernadette. She wanted to get her fill of looking at him. The view of the ocean as they descended was breathtaking. The deep blue of the choppy water enhanced the whiteness of the rocks and sand. Rocky cliffs exposed to the battering storm surges reflected harsh times and a stalwart people. There were no trees, giving the entire area a feel of expansiveness.

Looking back at her, he said, "We won't be on this path very long."

They were at the sea's edge in about fifteen minutes. The beach wasn't very wide, but it stretched on for what looked to be several miles. Bernadette closed her eyes and let the surf's rhythmic sound wash over her. The salt in the air clung to everything. It was nice to be alive for this. She breathed deeply. She tried to relax from her head down, but the perseverant apprehension continued to crawl from her gut back up. Bernadette knew this feeling, for it had often led her to be cautious, and thus, saved her from harm. At that thought, she opened her eyes to find Carney right next to her.

Carney was looking at Bernadette's sensuous lips. They weren't overdone with make-up, just a healthy natural red. To his amazement, when she opened her eyes, she reached out her hand, and taking his strong hand, pulled him toward her, toward her lips. Watching, he didn't close his eyes yet, but focus on the warmth of her smile. She extended further from her saddle, her lips reaching his. It was just a light brush, a whisper kiss, then another at the corner of his mouth, and another on his cheek. She moved up to his ear, planting kisses all the way.

"Carney, do you have people watching us?"

That brought Carney from his hormonal haze to adrenaline alert.

Bernadette continued, "I have been apprehensive since I saw the horses. When I closed my eyes, I got the feeling someone else is here. I know it sounds strange; I just have this feeling." She continued to nuzzle his ear a few more moments, finally sitting back in her saddle.

Carney felt a frustration welling up in him. At one time, he had been very intuitive. It was in part, what made him a great leader. But recently, especially with the car episode, he never had an inkling anything was wrong until it was too late and the danger was on top of him. The two men who had been in the car with Carney and Bernadette were at the property, staying in another cabin. They were instructed to keep a watch, but to allow the newlyweds some privacy.

That nagging feeling came back again. Was there something out there, or was Bernadette a traitor of some type, trying to gain his trust for some reason? His doubts about her motives surfaced at times of irregularity and resubmerged quickly thereafter. Carney decided the best thing to do was to play along and see how she reacted.

"It is probably one of my guys. I asked them to give us privacy, but they might get close to us at times."

Bernadette looked confused. Well, that would explain why he wasn't concerned about anyone following them. Perhaps she was just on hyper alert. This trip would scramble the most stately mind. Sorting intuition from irrationality today was probably beyond expectations.

That was when the first shot rang out. There was a SNAP followed by a CRACK. Bernadette's horse reared back and squealed. She dug her heals into his flank, encouraging him to move forward which would require his front legs to come back down to the sand. Once on all four hooves again, she pulled his head around toward her leg. She made cooing noises to try to calm the horse as it trotted in an agitated circle.

Carney understood one machine better than all others, guns. He had spent much of his life with a gun. He knew the sounds of particular guns and he knew how they sounded in many environments. He had shot guns lying on the ground, from a car cornering on two wheels, holding on to a boat mast while firing with the other hand, and from a small plane as it skimmed treetops. Today, he understood the eco; the reverberation of the blast as it moved off the cliffs. Someone was out beyond the surf shooting at them. Four more shots rang out. Caney would not see any boat past the breakers, which meant, they probably couldn't see him for any length of time. The additional shots could be a strategy to scare them into a position where they would be easy targets.

Carney brought his Gypsy Vanner up close to Bernadette's roan and grabbed one of her reigns. He yelled while they tried to manage the roan. "There has to be a boat out beyond the surf. They can't possibly get a good shot in this rough water if we stay close to the breakers. If we try to go back up the trail, we will be an easy target. Run for the bend up the beach. The boat doesn't dare take on the dangerous cross currents by the bend so we should be able to lose them there. Can you handle him?"

"Yes! Let's go." The second he released Bernadette's reign, he tightened his legs and loudly clicked his horse into a speeding gallop, with Bernadette and the roan just off his Gypsy Vanner's right flank. He maneuvered his horse closer to the ocean, where the waves had already crashed and were just now just a few inches deep spreading across the sand. Bernadette and Carney were not accustomed to riding as such speeds, so their full focus was on staying in the saddle and maneuvering the horses away from piles of rock and large driftwood. The blue roan overtook the Gypsy Vanner easily, putting his all into the run.

If Carney hadn't been so focused on the horses and looking for flashes of light in the ocean revealing the presence of a boat, he could have enjoyed the view of Bernadette's backside. The way she rode had everything to do with a muscular core.

Bernadette was scared and exhilarated. The only positive aspect was both horses had amazing strides and stamina; the bend would be an easy run for them.

As Carney thought, once around the bend, a savage wind out of the north hit them and the ocean. The waves went from choppy to sizable swells and white capped. The wind and cross currents would make safe boating near the bend almost impossible and probably suicidal. Carney brought them to the beginning of a trail which looked to be much steeper than the one they had come down. All of them were breathing hard.

Carney said, "We are offered some protection here because of the choppy waters; they can't get the boat too close to shore. Let's get up these switchbacks quickly. Once we are up the bank, no talking until we are in the cabin. There isn't any sizable cover, and our voices might carry. Follow me."

During the walk back, Carney's mind pondered the source of this problem. If he knew who it was, then he knew the why. But the answers were silent and perhaps that was what made these attempts on his life so raw. His temper on this matter approached the raging zone.

They tended to the horses in silence. Quietly they rubbed the horses down, finally letting them eat and drink as they locked up the barn for the night. They were heading to the cabin when one of Carney's guys showed up. They walked a distance away from Bernadette; a tense conversation ensued. Once the discussion had abated, Carney, with a looked of fury on his face, walked back, took Bernadette's hand and they went straight to the cabin.

When the cabin door was closed, Carney slung the backpack off, methodically closed all the blinds and curtains, and then took both of Bernadette's hands while he kissed her passionately. After a good twenty minutes he held her close and said, "I guess today didn't go so well. But you are amazing Bernadette. If you had panicked, it might have gotten all of us killed. I am very thankful to have you as a wife. I can't say how sorry I am about this situation. What a mess." Looking uncomfortable, Carney added,

"How about you get a shower, and I will eat my lunch. We will switch when you get out."

After Carney got in the shower, Bernadette quickly ate. She had a plan to change the tense mood. She began searching the phonograph records (LPs) on one of the bookshelves. Pulling a bundle from the shelve, she began sorting them into three piles: music she didn't know, albums most likely without any dance music, and finally LPs that she knew had at least one possible dance song. Most of the music was Scottish or Irish, so it had to go in the pile of albums she didn't know. There were a few modern artists she knew. Looking up, she saw an album that had been stashed up against the wall, behind the other albums. Perfect. It had just the dance song she needed. She put on the stretchy lace negligée thing with the bathrobe over it.

When Carney emerged from the bathroom, clean and fresh, he looked more relax. She stood in the white robe smiling at him. "Just stay there, okay?"

Turning on the record player, she put the needle on the second song, Let's Dance, by David Bowie. Bernadette wasn't a great dancer, but the ladies at university told her she had a good groove. She hoped this would be the ice breaker needed for them. She started dancing with the beginning instrumental music, letting her robe come open. As the vocals began, *Let's dance. Put on your red shoes and...* Bernadette looked at Carney and could tell something was wrong. Very wrong. Carney eyes narrowed in anger and his jaw tightened.

Blowing out a breath of exasperation, Bernadette walked back to the turntable, removed the needle, and turned it off. Turning around she put her hands on her hips. "Okay, what is wrong now?"

"Where did you get that music?" Carney asked.

"Look, I am sorry this song doesn't reflect the culture and heritage here. It was right over there with the rest of the vinyl records. I didn't have time to listen to all the other music to figure out what did or did not have a good dance rhythm. This was a song I knew."

Bernadette thought to herself, *what a major disaster.* She tried to do something fun and now he is mad.

Carney placed his index finger on Bernadette's lips, silencing her.

"Show me where."

She walked over to the shelf. "It was right here. It actually wasn't with the other records. I found it up against the wall behind all of these records."

He took the LP's cover and sat on the couch. The cover had a sticker on it, *Edinburgh, 1983 Serious Moonlight Tour.* Bernadette saw, from his concentration and an expression of understanding on his face, that he had found a missing piece of something.

Carney thought back to the murder of Douglas, his best friend in the group, someone he could always count on. It had been a huge loss. Douglas was conducting surveillance on a member of the Scottish Football League. The person under surveillance went to a David Bowie concert at Murrayfield

Stadium in Edinburgh. Douglas never left the concert in his car; he was found dead three days later, his tortured body dumped just outside of Dornoch, almost two hundred miles away from Edinburgh. Carney did discrete and extensive checking to see who had been at the concert. Although Carney was told Keith was inside the venue, Keith said he never went to Murrayfield Stadium on June 28, 1983, and Keith's wife backed his story. Now the problem. This was Keith's cabin. Chances were high that the album was purchased the night of the concert and the sticker on it proved it came from that concert. There were other ways for the album to be in Keith's possession; it could have been a gift from someone. But then, why was it behind the other albums? Carney didn't believe it fell back there, but rather the album was hidden back there.

Carney felt a figurative noose tighten around his neck. If Keith was at the concert and he lied about it, did he know about Douglas' murder or did he participate in it?

Ten minutes later Carney finally broke his concentration, holding the LP cover in one hand, he squeezed Bernadette's hand with the other.

"Are you back to earth?" She smiled with her lips and eyes, hoping to lighten the dark countenance on his face.

"Bernadette, you are my good luck. You saved my life and have helped me to understand a riddle that has been plaguing me. Let's put this album back exactly as you found it right now."

Once they had the album back in its original location, Carney turned to Bernadette and suggested, "How about I go back in the bathroom and brush my teeth. You can put on another song and when I come out, you can show me those sexy dance moves."

Bernadette balked. She had grown up with much ridicule and calloused coldness. Now that the moment was gone and she had time to think, she figured Carney found her actions stupid. "Oh, it was probably just a dumb thing to do. Let's forget it."

Taking Bernadette's hand, he led them back to the couch and pulled her on his lap. One handheld her close, the other stroked her hair.

"Bernadette, I was just startled by the music. Because you found that album, you helped me to possibly understand, possibly, who killed a good friend of mine, Douglas. Yes, this has been a difficult transition for both of us. But right now…things are different. You are the best thing that has come into my life, ever. And I want to be your best friend and a lover you won't ever forget. Please, for me. Let's see those sexy moves, and I promise this time the only thing I will be thinking about is how to get this bathrobe off you."

In a soft whisper she said, "No, it was just dumb."

Carney had an instant flash of insight. "Fine. Let's look through those albums and I will dance for you. What other dance groups or American artists did you see?"

Bernadette laughed. "You want to dance for me? Really? There was heavy metal and some hard rock, which I didn't think would work. And I saw The Partridge Family album. Can you believe that? How did that get here? I know we aren't dancing to The Partridge Family."

"We aren't? They have a perfect song. I used to dance to The Partridge Family with my sisters. Actually, they forced me into it, but it was good practice. Show me where it is."

Once Carney had The Partridge Family album, he shooed Bernadette into the bathroom. "I just need about ten minutes. Will call you out when I am ready."

Carney slid on his wedding slacks and white shirt, but left the shirt unbuttoned. He decided to forego any shoes. After turning the lighting down, he put the needle on the song <u>I Can Feel Your Heartbeat</u>, and called Bernadette out of the bathroom.

Bernadette watched as Carney put his fantastic physique on display. He had a great deal of upper body strength which he moved to the rhythm.

The lyrics begin:

I can feel your heartbeat, and you didn't even say a word
I can feel your heartbeat, but you didn't even say a word
Oh, I know pretty women that your love can be heard

When the lyric said, *You can feel my heartbeat too, I can tell you're feelin' me*, Bernadette couldn't resist and began dancing with him. There was laughter and bumping and grinding. In total they restarted that song fifteen times. By the eighth time, Carney was just in slacks and Bernadette's bathrobe was somewhere by the couch.

After the fifteenth time, Carney turned off the turntable. To his surprise, Bernadette came to him, gave him a very clingy hug, hitching her legs up around his waist. Bernadette had decided that any man who was willing to dance to The Partridge Family with her probably wouldn't laugh at her in bed. What they had just done was so fun, sexy, and silly, her guard couldn't remain up any longer.

Bernadette asked, "Can we go to bed?"

"Does that mean you want to make love to me?"

Bernadette looked him in the eye and said, "Most definitely."

They got to the bed, but Carney never got the slacks all the way off. They had become drugged with hormones and Carney wasn't taking any chances that the shy woman might reappear, putting the kibosh on this. If she was willing to love him, he wasn't wasting a moment.

The second time they made love, they had slid off the bed and were on the floor. After they had made love four times, Carney looked at Bernadette seriously. He said, "I can't offer you a lot of time Bernadette, but I can try to give you some good loving memories. I know it will be better than one of those touristy snow globes."

She laughed. "You are my snow globe."

They dove back under the covers and were awake until four in the morning, when they finally slept from exhaustion.

They both understood they would need some amount of rest for the days to come.

Chapter 8
Castle Treasures

(Summer 1984)
Sunday

Bernadette was sprawled across the bed, her head cradled in her left palm, giving her elbow the work of supporting her rapturous gaze. Her checks, reflecting a healthy glow, revealed her feelings as she watched Carney sleep. Not wanting to forget this special time, ever, she tried to study his relaxed features, memorizing them for the months and years of separation to come. It was a beautiful moment, where the artful hand of the creator expunged the pressures of their lives.

Stretching, then opening his eyes, Carney was surprised to find comfort and trust with Bernadette in an extraordinarily short amount of time. Reaching out, she threaded her fingers through his wavey hair. The gentle massage to his scalp felt luxurious.

He waited for a familiar morning weight to weave its way into his consciousness, setting up an onerous camp. It happened this way every morning since actions within the group had become perilously complicated. After a minute, when it felt as if angst had taken a rare day off, he glided Bernadette into the crook of his arm, molding her to his side. Glancing at her from the corner of his eye, he found her smile to be the powerful antioxidant to the radicals of battle.

Bernadette sighed with deep comfort and decided to broach the subject of today's activities. "What are we doing today? Hiding out in the cabin or venturing out into vast vistas of adversarial surprises?" Bernadette added a teasing tone to her whisper voice.

Scooting his hand under Bernadette's hip, he pushed her on top of him, then taking her face in both hands, he caressed her temples with his thumbs. He asked, "Are you willing to venture out? After yesterday's gallop, I would completely understand if you wanted to stay inside."

"Are we more at risk outside? If someone wanted to, couldn't they just break in here?"

Carney's hands moved from her temples to the six buttons on her flannel nightgown. He got the first one undone, but the second one wasn't budging.

"How and when did this nightgown get back on you?" Knowing how shy Bernadette was, he just smiled, not expecting any answer. When she didn't look at him, he added "I will never tire of taking your clothes off, so put them on if you wish."

He spent the next hour showing her how much pleasure he received in the disrobing activity.

Over breakfast, Carney got back on track. He said, "So, about today… I wanted to ask you what you were going to do the morning you saved me in River Forth?"

Bernadette said, "I was going to explore Stirling. Stirling Castle sounded fascinating. There is such history here in Scotland."

Glancing up from his eggs, Carney sat back in his chair. He said, "I think you might enjoy a trip to the remnants of a castle here on the property. There isn't much left. You can see a swale where the moat was once filled with water and the crumbling remains of the outer bailey are quite visible. Part of the keep and barbican have held up over the years. If we ride the horses, then we can spend our time exploring what is left of this property's history. Rory and Brian, the men you met in the car, can go with us to help sight out problems today."

"Great, but Rory and Brian can't stop flying bullets. You want to venture out?"

"Bernadette, I like your practical nature. Here is my theory about how much exposure we would have outside, and this is all based on a few facts with a considerable amount of gut feeling. I think the attacks on me are an attempt to make my demise look like an accident or caused by an outside source. The reality is more likely this; some person or persons within this group have an agenda which is in conflict with me. I don't know if this person just doesn't like my leadership or if someone is a mole actively seeking to irreparably damage the group. This situation is complicated for a faction or mole, because they don't want to be identified by the rest of our group for obvious reasons.

If I am murdered in such a way that the killer just lazily waltzed past the people who are here to protect us, it would draw unwanted attention to people who knew my schedule and whereabouts. Such an event would draw attention to the mole, and they won't want to take that risk. Shooting at us from the ocean made it look like an outside source was the culprit. It was a rather sloppy job, and I don't think they will want to take another risk of drawing attention to themselves, unless they absolutely must. The car malfunction was unlucky for them, but very lucky for me because you were there. There are two courses of action for this deceiving entity right now. They will either become more careful to avoid detection or they will become more desperate to finish the job because they believe the longer this goes on, the more attention will be drawn to their incompetence. So, with Rory and

Brian nearby, not like yesterday where they weren't in sight, I think the person behind the attacks will want to be more careful."

Bernadette asked, "Siccing those huge dogs on us isn't going to happen then, right? Because it would be obvious who did it within the group."

"They won't sic them on us, because those are my dogs, and they would only attack on my command."

Bernadette looked shocked. "What? If those dogs are yours, why aren't they here with us?"

Carney replied, "Actually, men and women who should be able to handle those dogs, won't work with them. They are exceptionally large Irish Wolfhounds; their aloof demeanor combined with a staring eye and curling lip increases the fear factor. I like the fact that those dogs don't want to sit in your lap. I was worried that you would be uncomfortable with them."

"If you like the dogs, I will do my best to be at ease with them. Dogs sense a lot of things that we as people don't. My guess is, we are better with them than without. My farm dog, Butter, was my best friend, my surrogate mother, and my protection."

Bernadette mentioning her mother forced Carney to look out the window; he didn't want Bernadette to see the anger in his eyes. He wondered how many beautiful people have experienced family pain which was passed down from one generation to the next because hurt begot more hurt. He waited for the need to punch Bernadette's mother to pass. Needing air, he stood up and grabbed his coat. "I'll be back in twenty minutes with the dogs. I will get Brian and Rory working on the horses." Giving Bernadette a full body hug and deep kiss, he went out the door.

Not one to miss an opportunity to investigate the area around the cabin, Bernadette got dressed and went out to explore. She wondered around the creek flowing past the cabin, picking flowers, and sought out all the nearby sheds to see if their doors would open. All were locked. With a few tiny flowers to put in a glass, she returned several minutes before Carney said he would be back. The sweet bouquet was placed on the bedroom nightstand. When Carney wasn't back in twenty minutes, she set her sights on exploring all the nooks of the cabin.

It was a total of forty-five minutes for Carney's steps, accompanied by the click of dog nails and thumping tails, to return on the porch. Hearing the sit and stay commands, she knew the dogs wouldn't be coming in the cabin just yet. Bernadette had put on the riding breaches, boots, and a purple shirt with matching purple sweater; all purchased under Carney's instruction after he decided to marry her.

Carney was looking back at the dogs as he crossed the threshold, promising them fun and treats today. Hooking the door with his foot, he pushed it closed while shrugging off the leather coat and throwing it on the coat cook with an uncanny accuracy. Turning, he almost stumbled back into the door as he was assaulted with the personage of a goddess who reflected the power of mahogany red and high court purple. His conscience speared his heart with pain for what this woman had endured in his presence.

He blurted out, "Bernadette, you are the most amazing and beautiful woman. I apologize for what has been inflicted on you in my presence. I can't imagine how you must be feeling. How you must be wondering when this nightmare can be over. I have tried to do the right thing to protect you, but still, I am so sorry that I am putting you though all this rubbish in my life. I forget that my life is completely strange from most normal people."

Bernadette laughed as she walked up to him and took both his hands in hers. "My life has never been normal. I was shot at before I was even a day old. I wasn't born for normal. What are you worried about? You give me a sense of belonging and that is so important to me. Now, should we make our picnic lunch?"

Pulling Bernadette close, Carney said, "I am going to come see you in the U.S. every chance I get. Don't you forget that. And yes, let's make our lunches."

As they exited the cabin, Carney introduced Bernadette to the Irish wolfhounds. Both were female; Sophie was the typical dark grey with shaggy white eyebrows and Sasha was larger with tan and black markings, almost like a German shepherd. Bernadette fell in love with both, giving them lots of scratches behind the ears and belly rubs.

Carney stood back and watched. Sophie and Sasha never gave Bernadette a chill stare, never walked away from her showing disinterest in her affection, never showed any dislike in how she touched them. *Why hadn't he thought more about her birthmarks?* he wondered. She interacted beautifully with the horses, and today with the dogs was no different. She related to the animals as most people could not.

Carney and Bernadette took the same horses as yesterday, the blue roan and the black Gypsy Vanner, while Rory and Brian took the piebald and skewbald. Instead of going west toward the ocean, they headed northeast, on an old narrow road, long overgrown, and maintained only by grazing sheep.

Bernadette couldn't imagine a more beautiful day as they began their assent though several birchwoods separated by a huge grass filled meadow. Leaving all the trees behind, they entered an extensive heath filled with heather and blaeberry. The rocks sticking out of the hillside looked barren, yet the entire area teamed with life. For Bernadette, it smelled and felt like home. Everything was living this day,

Bernadette said to Carney, "I think heaven and earth meet here. It is so beautiful."

Carney replied, "I think heaven and earth meet wherever you are."

Rory and Brian were up ahead of them, so Bernadette decided to broach another tabu subject. She asked, "Can you tell me where we are?"

"We are in the Highlands."

Throwing her head back, Bernadette's smile was a beam back to the heavens. Her laugh gaining momentum, she fell forward to rest her head on the mane of the horse, an uncontrollable belly laugh took over. Finally sitting up and wiping tears away with her hands, she gave it right back to Carney.

"Thanks for narrowing it down for me. Let me guess, the closest large city is Inverness."

Digging his heals into his horse's sides, Carney and his horse took a massive leap toward Bernadette. Her horse stood calmly.

Taking Bernadette's chin in his thumb and forefinger, Carney raised his eyebrow in a remanding look. "I, my lady, am just trying to keep you as far from harm as possible."

Shaking her head and giving Carney a haughty stare as he took his hand back to his reins, she replied. "No, you are trying to keep me from finding you again. You don't want me to know where to start looking, should I ever get a notion to do that. Do your best at this because I am a formidable opponent. I have a very good sense of direction. As a little kid, I spent much of my time in the forests by myself, never getting lost.

In addition to that, I have never felt so at ease with anyone as I do with you. I would sense you anytime you are near, whether I can see you or not. And you can do nothing about that."

Bernadette goaded her horse forward, past Carney, continuing up though the heath.

As Carney followed, he pondered Bernadette's upbringing; if she had grown up with any other mother, would she still be the same? Somehow, a mom of hatred had forged a woman of tremendous fighting aptitude and towering guts; attributes normally reserved for situations of war. Perhaps it had been inevitable, like formation of a sun based on swirling gases, temperature, and pressure; Bernadette's traits were put in the presence of animosity, an emotional pressure, and presto, the bright blazes of strength formed.

The shrunken road continued, weaving its way along the mountainside and there, nestled between two outcroppings, were the remains of a home long past. The dogs had bounded ahead, as if scenting out the lives and livestock that should have been living in this picturesque land.

The dogs' enthusiasm infected Carney and Bernadette, for they spurred the horses into gallops. Carney arrived first at the barbican. Jumping off the horse, he greeted Bernadette with a bow and sweeping arm gesture. Holding up both hands he said, "Come to me my lady." A shiver went through Bernadette. Had she done this before? Another life, another time long ago?

Setting up their picnic lunch and sharing champagne transmuted into a forty-five-minute blur of present and past. Everything Carney did felt more familiar than the moment just before it. When Carney laid back on the blanket, resting, Bernadette sought to add some reality to the moment.

"Can I take Sasha and explore the keep for a bit?"

Looking very content on the blanket, Carney asked, "Do you want me to come with you?"

"You look so comfortable. Why not stay here with Sophie? We will be within a few feet of you."

Carney was at ease and found watching Bernadette highly enjoyable, so he remained on the blanket.

There wasn't much left of the keep. There were still four walls, but they varied in degree of height and deposit of rock at their base. Bernadette didn't go inside, but Sasha slipped in though the crumbling remains of what had been an old door and began digging though rubble. Not wanting the sagging floor above or stones from the wall to tumble on them, Bernadette called Sasha, but she refused to come. As she peeked her head inside the door, she saw it. She saw what Sasha was digging at. Bernadette, not wanting to alarm Carney by calling to him or alert Rory or Brian that something was amiss, crawled inside the door to grab Sasha's collar, getting a better look at what was of interest to the dog. It appeared to be a type of leather holster, and the grip of a pistol was visible. Feeling alarm, she grabbed the collar, pulling herself and the dog out.

Calling the dog several times, she kept Sasha close to her as they headed back to the blanket. Dropping to her knees, she held the dog close while reaching for Carney's hand. Noting her change complexion, from hectic pink to ashen white, he knew something was amiss.

Sitting up, he kissed her temple. Whispering, he asked, "What is the matter?"

"Sasha dug up a leather case with a handgun in it. It was in the rubble close to that decrepit door."

Carney asked, "How old is it?"

"Leather isn't discolored, still a rich tan, so I would say not more than a few years old. It is a bit sheltered by the portion of the floor still left above."

Carney laid back down, pulling Bernadette with him. He gave thought to the situation for several minutes. Whispering into her hair, she wasn't sure if he was giving instructions or a caress, perhaps it was both. "Rory and Brian are watching us and watching out for us. We shouldn't let on to the fact you found something of interest. We need them to become disinterested in us. We can do that in two ways. First, let's get all lovey. I asked them for privacy at times. If we are "cutesy" physical, they will probably find it disgusting. Follow my lead there. Lots of teasing and giggling on your part. Then, after ten minutes of that, comes part two. We should play a stupid lover's game, so it doesn't look like we are intentionally going to the keep to get something. Grab my sunglasses off my head and run off teasing me. I will catch you. You giggle and laugh, we kiss, then you grab them again and we start chasing each other again until you hid inside that door with my glasses. I will lean in, check the gun is secure, and hand it to you. Keep it under your sweater. Then I will pull you out with hugs and kisses, pick you up, and take you to the blanket. Keep it by your waist We will make out some more while you pretend to want to get things back in the backpacks. Put the gun in one backpack, discretely, during our lover's tussle. We will pack up the rest of the stuff and leave. You need to act like an immature young lover. Rory and Brian will be so disgusted with our antics, as I assure you, I would be if I were the one spying, they will not want to watch us. We will look at the gun when we get back to the cabin."

Bernadette asked, "Why do I have to play the part of an immature idiot?"

Carney replied, "Because they know me well enough to know how I behave. But they don't know you. If you play into their idea of a stereotype, a silly, in-love woman, they won't be suspicious with our behavior. I play to a stereotype at times when I need to accomplish something. Use those times to your advantage."

"This is disgusting." Bernadette, leaned up on her arms and began giving Carney pecking kisses to his face, mimicking a chicken pecking at the seeds on the ground, all the while giggling. Carney intimately tickled her sides, causing more giggling and lip smacking.

Further up on the hill, eyes started to roll.

Carney carefully moved the sunglasses from his nose, sliding them up to the top of his head. More teasing and giggling went on and Bernadette wasn't sure how much longer she could keep up this nauseating behavior.

His eyes smiled in invitation. Bernadette sat up and removed the glasses from his head. With one hand on his chest, she swung the glasses in the other hand above his head. Then with the agility of a cat, she spun around, popping to her feet. One eyebrow up and her hair hanging over one eye, she clearly sent the message that if Carney wanted the still twirling glasses, he was going to have to work for them.

Sasha jumped at Bernadette's side, clearly ready to play. Motioning for Sasha to sit, she didn't want her to interfere in the high stakes game.

For added affect, Bernadette pushed her riding pants down low on her hip and added a wiggle.

Rory and Brian looked at each other. Brian said, "Good grief. This is worse than the sitcoms on T.V." They set down the binoculars and took a swig of the brandy Rory had stashed in his inner jacket pocket. Looking at his watch, Brian said, "Let's give them thirty minutes to tire of this. Newlyweds are such vile happy creatures."

The extra eyes avoided the lovers' game of chase, an intimate tussle in the keep doorway, and Carney carrying Bernadette back to the blanket for a pulling and tugging touchy-feely session. Brian and Rory were surprised at their next observation. Most of the picnic was packed up, and the horses were getting saddled. Evidently the lovers were done for the day, at this location.

When they left the castle, Carney said a few words to Rory and Brian, causing them to remain behind Carney and Bernadette, but always within sight. Carney remained quiet during the ride to the corral. Stopping occasionally to give Bernadette a smooch as their horses came side by side, he would then quickly gallop ahead and lead the way. Even when Sasha and Sophie ran off barking toward a ridge, Carney called them back with a minimal one-word command. Bernadette felt sorrow for this man, whom she found so trustworthy, surrounded by untrustworthiness. At the corral, Rory and Brian insisted on rubbing down the horses and feeding them for the afternoon. They also wanted the dogs, to help keep watch. Carney nodded his assent. Turning, he put his arm around Bernadette's shoulders, and they headed back to the cabin.

Carney started a fire, shut the drapes, and then headed to take a shower. The backpack had been casually placed in the bathroom earlier, once it had been emptied of picnic supplies. With the water running, he slightly opened the door, calling to Bernadette. "Bernadette? Come take a shower with me, you silly woman."

She hesitated. Of course, the shy woman would balk. "Bernadette, we don't have many days left here. Get in the shower with me."

When she got close to the bathroom door, Carney's muscular arm whipped out and pulled her in. Whispering he said, "Take a shower while I look at this, in the event we are being watched or worse, bugged. I doubt we are bugged, yet we need to take care."

She said, "Really? Alright. No looking."

He shook his head and closed his eyes while Bernadette quickly undressed and got in the shower. It was five minutes before he joined her. Having her hair in a lather on top of her head, she looked wide eyed as he pulled open the shower door and walked in. Fully aroused, he pulled them both under the spray and kissed her passionately."

Stepping back, he whispered, "Remember my reaction when I heard the David Bowie song? I told you that a friend of mine, Douglas, had been killed."

"Sure do. Go on."

"It is a long story and most of it I can't tell you. The sticker on the album was from that David Bowie concert and Douglas was last seen at the concert. He was doing some surveillance. His car was found in the concert parking lot. His tortured body was discovered several days later outside Dornoch, which is a two-hour drive from here. The flap on the gun holster you found has the initials DGH. Those are the initials of Douglas. He carried this same model of gun, so I am confident it was his gun and holster. My guess is, he was here after the concert and died here. Perhaps he was tortured in the keep as some type of sadistic joke. Who knows?

"I am so sorry Bernadette, because there are serious implications for us, given what you found today. Since it looks like Douglas died here, it means we need to get out of this place, and I don't know how we will do that. We are going to have to escape past my own men. I don't know that they are part of the plot to kill me, but we should assume they are. They can't have any notice we are leaving. We have to just go and get away from them."

Carney watched Bernadette carefully. He was prepared for her to crack under this new twist in events.

"Let me get this shampoo out of my hair. It is getting in my eyes. Just a minute."

Carney kept falling harder for Bernadette and this was another one of those moments. No panic from her. No despair. Just the facts and action. He said, "I am glad you are practical. Let me help rinse you off." And he did. Although, somehow in the process his hair and body got thoroughly washed by Bernadette.

When Bernadette was done helping Carney shower, she said, "I think Rory and Brian are originally from Germany or have German ties."

Carney looked astounded. He asked, "Why would you think that?"

Shrugging, Bernadette sheepishly replied, "Because I have so much trouble with those German umlauts and rolling r's, I notice when others use them. Your men don't talk much around me, but when they do, I hear those sounds every now and then, as if they can't avoid them."

Carney needed time to think about this new and complicating information. "I am going to get dinner going for us. You my dear, have given me lots to think about."

Carney dried off, tucked the case and gun in his robe, and left the bathroom.

As the warm water sluiced over Bernadette's back, she began to think about what she had seen earlier today, when she had explored the sheds and the cabin. The person who said curiosity killed the cat was very wrong. The curious cat was a survivor.

Chapter 9
A True United Force

(Summer 1984)
Sunday

Carney had learned from Bernadette that she was expected to be back at work on Thursday. Since it was Sunday, they had Monday and Tuesday to get her to Inverness so she could make her flight back to Germany early Wednesday morning. He felt confident that if she could get on that flight, the remainder of the stay in Europe would be without threats.

He wondered what mental state Bernadette would be in when she came out of the bathroom. So far, she had held up better than any other person, man or woman, he knew. Breaking points, however, had a way of inserting themselves in a person's life, and if one did show up for Bernadette at this time, it would complicate their ability to escape and survive.

The bathroom door opened and Bernadette, wrapped in a towel, ran to the bedroom. Grabbing some clothes, she headed back to the bathroom, only to stop suddenly. She said, "What smells so good? Are we eating early?"

"My mom taught me to cook. Said it was a way to woo a woman." Carney smiled and winked at Bernadette. "We are having mutton, tatties and neeps seasoned with juniper berries, vetch root, and a little scotch whisky. Hurry, it is almost done."

When Bernadette emerged from the bathroom a second time, in a short stretchy black skirt and long white blouse, another purchase directed by Caney, he was tempted to put everything in the fridge for later, much later.

Holding out a chair for her, Bernadette sat down. Carney seated himself and Bernadette reached out a hand. Holding hands, they said grace. As Carney was ready to dig in, Bernadette did not release his hand.

"I just want to say thank you for making this the best vacation a woman could ever ask for." Giving his hand a reassuring squeeze, she then released it and speared some tatties. With a look of expectancy, she popped them in her mouth. "Oh, my gosh, this is so good. The flavors are so exotic."

"No, you my dear are the only exotic flavor."

Glancing down, Bernadette smiled at her plate in embarrassment. Carney ate, waiting for her to look back up. She said, "You are a nice man to say that Carney."

Carney's hand slammed down on the table. WACK! The plates and silverware rattled while Bernadette jumped in her chair.

Carney said, "Whoever told you all the lies - how you aren't enough - how you are nothing - was jealous of you. All this rubbish you were told was a bunch of lies! People don't want you to know how beautiful you are because they are jealous petty people. Don't ever go back home to live because they will beat you down. They don't know all that you are, but they are too afraid to find out how great you are. When people are mean to you, know this: it isn't about you. It is about a bunch of ignorant people."

Bernadette, wide eyed, watched the wrath in Carney's eyes. She felt tears coming on. It was wonderful to feel loved.

Carney stood up. "We will finish dinner in a half hour."

Sliding Bernadette's chair out, he picked her up and carried her to the bed. Tossing her in the middle, he stood, his chest heaving.

"I want you to know, I will honor our marriage vows every day of my life. There isn't another woman like you. There will never be anyone who can kiss like you or love like you. I never met a woman where I wanted to know the workings of her mind, her thoughts, and ideas. No one could ever compare to how strong you are. You are the only woman I know who wouldn't shy away from any of this mess. For goodness sakes, you just thanked me for a disaster I brought on your head. And, you don't recognize it. Just being in your presence Bernadette makes me a better person."

With that, Carney tore off his shirt, ripped open his pants and leapt on top of Bernadette.

Bernadette could think of only one thing - this vacation just kept getting better…and better.

-

Twenty minutes later they were resting in the comforting spooning fashion, with one important difference, Bernadette's front faced Carney's back. She had told him to roll over and when he rolled to face her, she smiled, and stated he needed to go the other way. Then she slipped up to him, snaked an arm around his waist, and rested her forehead next to his shoulder blade. Carney laced their finger together and thought how this woman had his back in so many ways. His mind was racing, thinking about how they could leave, when Bernadette spoke. "Can we talk about how we will get out of here?"

Carey turned to face Bernadette and said, "First, I want you to understand something. You are in a rather unique and positive position because you are an American, and a student on a work-study program. There isn't a group, of which I interact, within fifteen hundred kilometers who would want to be involved in your "in plain sight" murder and the discovery of your body by authorities. A murder of an American student in Scotland brings in the swarming press for who knows how many months or years, the diplomatic nightmares, the local and foreign under-pressure investigation teams, and the souring of local tourism. Murder puts a big spotlight on the known and imagined warring entities in various countries and only certain terrorist groups with an agenda will invite that debacle. It doesn't mean that you wouldn't be killed, it just means that no one wants a public display of it, and they will want to avoid it. A "missing" American student is one thing, a body floating around and photographed by the press would cause a complete kerfuffle. Keep that in mind as I walk through our options and remember, it is best for you to avoid being taken hostage under all circumstances, because then you can conveniently end up missing. It is best to remain in a public setting, be that on the road, in a river, on a train, and so forth.

"On to our biggest issue right now. Obviously, transportation is the weak link. First, let's look at driving a vehicle. There are two cars here. We don't dare get in a car and try to make a run with it because I don't believe we would be successful. It would be immediately known that we understand more than we should. My guess is that the cars are already rigged in some way that we can't just start them and drive off. If someone can rig my car so it won't brake properly, certainly they can rig a car, so it is difficult to start or doesn't operate for very long.

"Second, is bipedal motion. Walking through the countryside to get away is not a good option. It is too slow. I would become an easy target, then you would be left on your own to deal with whomever. We can't outrun a horse or motorcycle. We would be exposed to the elements. How far would we get before we are caught? Probably not far.

"Third, there is the equine locomotion. Horses are very easy to track: they have big feet that flatten foliage, their hooves leave impressions in the soft ground, and they tear up the ground if they are trotting or galloping. Anyone with a motorcycle would put an end to that jaunt. But it is better than nothing and we have horses here. We know they can gallop.

"Forth, there are no train stations nearby. There are bus stops, but a bus is easy to pull over and then escort us off of it. End of story there.

"Fifth, we could try to flag down a car or motorcycle and highjack it. Unfortunately, that complicates our lives and you become a criminal. That option is off the table.

"A close relative to that prior idea is we go to the road and try to flag down a ride. Risky. I am not sure who I am running from. There are other criminals in the world who might say they will give us a ride and then we get an unpleasant surprise. If we get innocent people involved in this mess, that is poor form.

"Sixth option is aviation. I have no knowledge of a small plane and runway in the area. Neither of us have a pilot's license. It might be possible to find a local pilot, but we don't have the time or resources here to get that option off the ground. That was the best joke I have for today.

"Seventh possibility would include aquatic options. We are surrounded by rivers, lochs, and the ocean. Swimming is not a pleasant possibility given the distances we need to go. We would succumb to exhaustion and hypothermia in no time. Boats are a great option depending on their size, but we would need to get to the marina to the north or south of us."

Bernadette interrupted, "May I interject here?"

"I am going to forget what option I am on, but go ahead."

Bernadette began, "It pays to be the hostage bride because then someone goes snooping around. As a kid I snooped all over the place Snooping was a natural thing to do here at the cabin given my situation.

"First, addressing the hypothermia problem, you should be made aware that there are two wet suits stashed up on the top shelf in the bathroom cupboard. They are in the very back of it. I didn't look closely at them, so I don't know their sizes.

"Second, there are two boats and two outboard motors in the locked green shed. One boat is aluminum and looks to be over ten feet long, from what I could see. The other is some type of inflatable boat that I am not familiar with."

Carney developed a huge frown. Getting up, he walked into the bathroom, shut the door. Bernadette herd the toilet flush, then the cupboards creaking. Holding on to the upper cupboard door, he stood on the second shelf to look at the back of the top shelf. He pulled out one of the wet suits. It was several years old but still in good condition. Sliding it back in, he turned off the light, and returned to bed.

Carney asked Bernadette, "Why would a wetsuit be here?"

"Well, I would guess the owner likes the ocean but doesn't want to get cold."

Carney thought back on the owner, Keith, and his proclaimed dislike of anything water. "That is the confusing part. He doesn't like swimming or so he says. He would never body surf." At that moment Carney decided that what he thought he knew about Keith was probably untruths or half-truths.

They laid in silence for a few minutes before Carney asked Bernadette, "How do you know about the boats?"

Bernadette said, "A knot fell out of the wood in the shed door and I looked through it. I wouldn't have noticed the boats if the light coming in, from a few missing roof shingles, hadn't been at just the right angle."

Carney sighed and said, "Really? You didn't need to pick the lock or use any high-tech surveillance equipment? Didn't need a team of spies or a team to dig an elaborate system of tunnels. You just look through the hole in the boards. And when did you do that?"

Bernadette caught Carney's sarcasm and laughed. She said, "When you went to get the dogs, of course. I did while I was picking flowers, so I don't think anyone noticed."

Carney glanced at the flowers. "I was going to ask you about those several times, but I am usually distracted in the bedroom. Thank you. They are lovely, like you."

Getting out of bed, Carney began to get dressed. "I want to take a quick look at those boats and motors. We will need petrol and I want to be sure there is some in the shed. I also want to get all the halters and bridles for the horses and bring them here, in the event we need the horses."

"How will you get in the shed?" Bernadette asked.

"I am very good at picking locks. From what I understand, you are too. Roger told me that. I should only be gone about a half hour."

Bernadette said nothing as Carney opened the bedroom window, took out the screen, and exited the cabin though the window.

Twenty minutes later Bernadette was in cleaning up the kitchen when Carney walked out of the bedroom, no shirt, no slacks, just underwear. Bernadette looked up and said, "Ah, we forgot that option. You can hitchhike out of here in your underwear. There will probably be a traffic jam and fight over who gets to pick you up.".

"Very funny. Come back to bed with me?"

Bernadette stripped down to her underwear. Carney lifted the covers, inviting her in. Once she was comfortable, he said, "Bernadette, the horses are gone. All the gear is gone. Rory and Brian must have planned it. That is why they wanted to rub down the horses. The horses weren't a good option, but it was always an option, until now.

"I looked in the shed. There is a fourteen-foot aluminum flat bottom boat. It is in good shape. I put the bigger of the two motors, a 25 HP, on the boat and filled it with petrol. It should carry us and our gear very well. It won't go like a speed boat in the movies, so we need the element of surprise on our side."

"We leave as soon as we can. We get on those wet suits, take the aluminum boat, and go for it. This is our moment. It stays light till almost eleven so we will have time to get a good distance away. The dark might help us, but it can also make our water journey very dangerous. If there is moonlight, we might proceed, or we might have to camp out on a bank. Let me get a map."

Carney got out of bed, went into the living room, and returned with a map. He opened the map in front of Bernadette and began to explain. "We are not going out into the ocean. It is far too risky. No matter what happens, we don't go to the ocean. Our only option is to go east. We are in the north Highlands, north of Eddrachillis Bay and the town of Scourie. The creek by the green shed flows into Loch Laxford. From there we can follow River Laxford which opens up into Loch Stack. There are problems with navigating the river: rapids, rocks and certainly shallow areas. We may need to drag the boat out and around some obstacles. After that, we will need to navigate a smaller river to Loch More. At the entrance to Loch More, I will take a few minutes to scout out for a buddy who hangs at Achfary. He should be able to get us to Inverness. If we can't get help at Achfary, then we will continue through Loch Merkland and Loch Shin. At the southern end of Loch Shin there is the Lairg train station. It is probably only two hours from Lairg to Inverness by train.

"Our biggest risks are at the beginning of this journey. Lock Laxford will narrow down until we have to pass under the Laxford Bridge. Anyone on the bridge or bank will have an easy shot at us. After that, the road runs right along River Laxford. We can easily be seen from a car. We really need a rifle. I have two semi-automatic pistols, but I need more distance."

Carney scowled at Bernadette. He thought to himself, *if she found a rifle in this cabin, I am going to pound my head against the wall.*

Bernadette looking up from the map and said, "There is a fake panel in the broom closet and a rifle with ammunition is hidden here. I think it is a powerful rifle - will do a lot of damage to something."

Carney sighed. "I knew it! How did you find that?" he asked with more exasperation than he intended to show.

"Roger spent years teaching me all kinds of things. He taught me how to build hidden compartments in walls to hide stuff. Under that nice rug near the kitchen entrance is a trap door. It opens up to a food and provision storage area."

Carney replied, "You know, if you keep this up, I might end up with a damaged ego. You should go easy on me."

Bernadette snorted. "What? Most of the time I am in my own little fantasy world looking for hidden stuff that doesn't exist. For once in my life, it paid off. Trust me, my fantasy world does not provide any benefit to anyone most of the time."

While putting on a bathrobe, Bernadette said, "Let's go look at the rifle."

Bernadette was in the broom closet moving around when Carney approached. As she moved aside, he could see a panel, just three feet by six inches, had been removed. The compartment behind was larger, to hold the length of the rifle.

Picking up the rifle, he whistled. "You're correct. We are in luck. This is a nice caliber Winchester. Can be used on some big game. We should start putting everything we need in one place. I think the tub is the best place to conceal our actions until we are ready to go."

"I like the plan, but how do we get the boat in the creek and leave without someone noticing. Can we try the motor now to see if it works?" Bernadette asked.

"There is a good spot right by the shed to slide to boat in the creek. We can't risk the noise from starting the motor. We have to hope it works. Let's make a list of things we need to take. Everything should be put in garbage bags to keep it as dry as possible. I hope you saw sleeping bags in that provisional storage because we will be camping out one and possibly two nights."

"Yep, there is camping gear in there. Lots of it."

"Let's get going. Let's start with clothes we will need."

Carey and Bernadette worked efficiently together. There was minimal talking. He was impressed with how focused she could be and how quickly she worked. He thought, *farm girl, resourceful, strong, and fun.*

Interrupting his thoughts, Bernadette asked, "What about Sasha and Sophie? Can we get them out of here?"

"As we make a boating run for it, they will probably be out in the fracas. I have a command so they will go into the hills and wait for me, but I might need them to attack Rory and Brian if we are being shot at."

Looking sad, Bernadette said, "I know this will sound odd, but I don't think we should sacrifice the dogs in this. I think we can escape without them. If we sacrifice them, if it isn't absolutely necessary, then that energy will hurt us. I like to work with nature. Let's try to protect the dogs, if we can."

Threading his hands though Bernadette's hair, Carney said, "I will do my best to protect them, but not at your expense."

As an afterthought, Bernadette added, "Do you have anything we can use to plug bullet holes? What if the boat gets shot?"

"I was thinking of that too. There are some old innertubes in the shed. We can take a piece of one and needle nose pliers to try and slow a leak. It is the best we will have."

Forty-five minutes later Bernadette and Carney were ready to go. Carney loaded the boat while Bernadette handed him the stuff from the bedroom window. Once finished, Carney got into one of the wet suits. Impatient to get going, Carney took several huge strides to the bedroom, only to stop short. Bernadette stood fingering her wedding skirt and blouse, hanging from the closet door frame.

Walking up behind her, Carney slipped his hand behind her hair, caressing her neck with his fingertips and said, "Why don't we find a place to hide this. Once I am out of danger, I will retrieve it. When I come to the states, I will bring it to you." Kissing her cheek, he then turned her head and looked her in the eye. "I am sorry it hasn't been an ideal wedding, not even an ideal trip to Scotland."

Grinning, she turned and wrapped her arms around him. "Your right, it hasn't been ideal. But it has been better than ideal. I have so enjoyed getting to know you, to have the honor to share your wedding bed, being your wife will always be the best part of me. It goes to show, if you are going to do something, it pays to do it right. And I did that by marrying you." Stepping out of the embrace she continued, "Let me get into my wetsuit. Don't worry about the skirt and blouse. I would always have to hide it, or it will lead to all kinds of questions from friends that I couldn't bear to answer."

The one wetsuit was large for Bernadette, so they used duct tape to tighten up areas. Looking seriously at Carney and the pistol in a holster, she said, "I need a pistol."

"Ready for that. I have one in the boat with your name on it. I was hoping you would ask for it before I had to ask you to wear it."

Carney held the rifle as they exited though the bedroom widow After closing the window and replacing the screen they ran to the boat.

Carney said, "Wait by the bank. I can manage the boat."

The boat slid easily across the grass as Carney pushed it down toward the creek and eased it in the water. Once they were both in, he pushed it further away from the bank with an oar. Giving Bernadette quick kiss, he then pulled the starter.

It took three tries and the motor came to life. The creek flowed past the second cabin on the property, where Rory and Brian were staying. The boat had only gotten about three hundred feet past the second cabin, when Carney glanced back and saw both Brian and Rory running along the bank, each holding a pistol. The trees, brush, and the distance offered the boat some protection. Carney opted against using a gun at this moment given the bounce of the boat and obstruction of brush, he figured it was a waste of precious ammunition. Bernadette and Carney watched as the dogs ran haphazardly, for they were confused by the angry shouts and commotion. Brian took a hard fall over Sophie when she ran in front of him. Brian yelled, "Carney, I am going to kill your dogs, you bastard!"

Bernadette gave Carney a knowing glance. She pleaded with him, using her eyes. He didn't think either of the men could get off a good shot at the boat, only a lucky one, but those dogs could ensure their lives were safe right now. Then, one thing Roger told him came into his mind. *You are going to have to trust her judgement at times, even if it doesn't make sense to you, or when it doesn't make sense to you.* He inhaled deeply and let loose three loud whistles, one long and two short, telling the dogs to escape capture and run for the hills. He immediately looked ahead and open the motor up to half throttle. The deep part of the creek was narrow and he could only hope that they didn't hit a sunken snag or rock. On a positive note, he figured Brian and Rory would quickly give up the foot chase and get a vehicle.

The distance to Lock Laxford was less than half of a mile. The stream deepened as they got closer to the Lock, but was still narrow. Only once did Carney have to stop, as a long branch blocked the surface of the creek. He made quick work of it with a saw they brought.

Once Carney could see the Lock Laxford ahead, he cut the motor, using the paddle to get closer to the entrance. Seeing no evidence of another boat, he said to Bernadette, "From here on I may need you to drive while I fire off shots. Are you ready to drive the boat?"

"I can drive it. I am also a good shot, especially with a rifle."

Carney found it difficult to trust another's competence when so much was at stake. Since operating the boat and shooting a rifle at the same time wasn't an option, he had to choose. "You use the rifle. I will operate the boat." Bernadette gave him a thumbs up and put the rifle on her lap.

Carney started the boat and opened up the throttle, sending the boat lurching forward at a good clip. The Laxford Bridge would come up quickly, as it was only a mile, maybe mile and one quarter, away. Brian and Rory in a car could easily beat them to the bridge.

His eyes continually scanned the banks and behind them. He couldn't help but stare a few times at Bernadette. Her riot of curls flew in all directions; it had a life of its own. He realized that this woman of burning spirit would never be far from his thoughts. She had never shirked from his ideas, this escapade or his wild love making. But he couldn't keep her here. Later, he would scream at the moon and the ocean and everything in between.

The Lock narrowed and became River Laxford. It wouldn't be long until they came to the bridge. Carney eased back on the throttle and stopped the boat.

"Bernadette, this approach is too dangerous. It took too long to get here. The creek wasn't like a lake where we could fly the boat. We lost too much time. Once we see the bridge, they will be able to see us, but I won't be able to tell where they are. We won't stand a chance."

Bernadette thought a minute. "Be quiet while I call for help, and don't move much."

Carney was about to ask her what she was babbling on about, when she opened her mouth and screeched bloody murder. "ik…ik…..ik,ik,IK,IK,IK."

He couldn't believe it. She sounded like an osprey. After several minutes, he noticed there were three ospreys in the air above them. She changed her tone to one of distress. "IIk, IIk, IIIIk."

Bernadette said, "Alright, lets paddle toward the bridge."

Once a corner of the bridge came into view, Bernadette continued with more osprey distress calls. The birds circled the old rock archway of the bridge.

Brian was at the south end of the bridge, Rory on the north. Both had rifles and the scopes were directed to the west. They knew Carney had one way out of Loch Laxford; he wouldn't take the boat in the ocean unless suicidal. They were ready to kill him here. Then, as they waited for the boat, a terrible screeching started. After about five minutes, ospreys began to divebomb Rory and Brian. They were pooped on and tormented, repeatedly. Rory was the first to decided he had enough and tried to get back across the bridge. One osprey put a crater in his scalp with a razor-sharp talon; he screamed in pain. Both men ran to the car, jumping in.

Rory yelled, "Keith can kill Carney himself. My head is bleeding. I have osprey shit all over the action. I am going to end up in hospital with some infection that can't be cured! You know how much bacteria are on those talons and in that poop?"

"What the hell happened? Brian asked. "I can't even see out of the scope; there is so much bird crap on it. I have osprey crap in my hair, on my clothes, and all over my gloves. I think you are right. Keith can figure this out. Let's get out of here. I need a shower."

Carney heard the car start and dive away. He looked up in the sky. No ospreys to be seen. He turned and stared at Bernadette.

She asked him, "Can we go now or are we going to sit here till they come back?"

Slapping his knee several times, Carney hooted in laughter. Then his face quickly changed expression. "You aren't going to shapeshift on me, are you?"

"If we don't get moving soon, I might have to change into the Loch Ness Monster and push us along." She smiled sweetly at Carney.

Carney replied, "Right. Remember we will be traveling a section of the river that is near the road, so be ready."

Once past the bridge, Carney and Bernadette continued to travel at a decent clip given the conditions of River Laxford. As they approached a curve, knowing that the road would be in sight soon, Carney cut the engine.

"Bernadette, I doubt that Brian and Rory will be back right now, but I bet that Keith is nearby. I am going to get out and investigate around the road. Should take me twenty minutes to half hour. If I am not back in an hour, you continue on without me."

With the paddle, Carney moved them to the southeast bank. Picking up the rifle, he slipped from the boat and moved off into the brush.

Only ten minutes had elapsed when the crack of a rifle broke the peace of the countryside, followed by another a few minutes later. There was an exchange of gun fire for almost five minutes. After that, silence ruled the late afternoon once again.

Paddling back toward the bridge a good hundred yards, Bernadette pulled the boat up on a sandbar and into some tall grass. She sat in the heavy brush, concealed from anyone looking in her direction. She heard Carney breathing before she saw him; he had been running. His eyes looked wild as he visually searched for her and the boat.

Standing, she said, "Coast clear?"

"Let's go. Quickly. We need to use as much daylight as we can to get away from here. We should try to make it to the east end of Loch Stack."

River Laxford continued to present problems for them; several times they had to get out and pull the boat through shallow or rocky water. Once in Loch Stack, Bernadette sat looking at nothing. She wondered if conflict would become a way of life for her. Like the first drink of the alcoholic or the first rush from a needle, was this the first chase in a life of adrenaline highs found in the narrow bands of life and death struggles? Was this more in a life of shoot or be shot? It definitely felt like the little snowball was taking on more material and building up speed as it descended down the snowy hill. What would the bottom look like?

Carney brought the boat up to a bank and cut the motor. The sun had gone down, but it was surprising light from the moon and stars. "How about we get on some dry clothes, have something to eat, and get in a sleeping bag?"

Working together quietly, they enjoyed the silence of the night. When they had finished eating, they used two sleeping bags to cozy up together.

They laid quietly for a long time enjoying the stars and the soft sounds. Bernadette finally broke the quiet, "I am sorry about Keith. To trust and loose that trust is always hard."

"Something big, I mean an outside source of some type, must have affected him. I don't think I will try to find my buddy at Achfary tomorrow. I don't want to take any chances when we are close to having you on a safe flight out of Scotland. I think we might steal some of his petrol and be gone. I will leave him some money for it, but we aren't asking, and we won't stay around to chat. We should be in Lairg by afternoon. It could be earlier, but I am giving us lots of time to get around shallow areas in the river. Once we are in Lairg, we can find out when the next train is to Inverness. I would like to get a hotel room in Inverness tomorrow night. We will get you to the airport early Wednesday." Pulling Bernadette on top of him, he said, "Right now, I would like to explore those birthmarks you have. I believe there is much more to you than I have understood, or perhaps anyone has understood."

Bernadette replied, "I would like that."

Monday and Tuesday were filled with highs and lows for Carney and Bernadette. It was easy physically and they got to Laird without interruption, but it was difficult emotionally for both of them. Once in Inverness, they ate out and Carney bought Bernadette a special outfit to wear home.

Wednesday, at four in the morning, they were in their Inverness hotel room, making love in the shower. Bernadette held it together, until they crawled into bed. When she thought Carney was asleep, she let the tears mark tracks of pain down her face. Reaching his arm out, he snugged her up next to his side, talking with her about all the ways he would love her in the States. It didn't help. She started throwing up at four forty-five; the pain of leaving him was too much.

A little later in the morning, Carney said, "Bernadette, it will attract too much attention if you looked a disaster at the airport. Customs and all the agents will perk up and wonder what you have been doing that is causing such trauma. You have to blend in, look fine." Propping her up, he gave her several shots of whiskey. Then he put her in a warm shower, helped her dry her hair and get dressed. Bernadette started to feel wonderfully fuzzy and relaxed.

"Remember, look chic, relaxed, and blend in. This outfit will work well; it is very European looking. I want you to smile and flirt a little. But don't flirt too much. Here is pack of gum. Get another drink at the airport. No tears until you are back at your room in Germany. You can't."

At thirty minutes past seven, Carney was kissing Bernadette, putting everything he had into the kiss. They were two blocks from the airport. He finally stopped and said, "I'll be watching you walk into the airport. I will be watching when your plane leaves the ground. You will be fine. Buy a book. Eat something. Get mad at me. But do not attract attention to yourself."

Bernadette nodded. "I got this now. Be safe."

She walked away and Carney wondered how he was going to hold it together.

Bernadette remembered very little of the airport, the plane flight, getting back to her room. In fact, the next month went by like those too hot summer days, endlessly numbing. The only thing good about the nighttime was fantasizing about Carney and the only good thing about the days was the fact that another night was on the horizon.

Bernadette didn't realize that she had been walking around in a stupor until she had returned to college and went to her first class. Finally, she had something else to think about. She took twenty credits just to make sure she had no time to think about anything, other than school.

Unfortunately, university is filled with young men and Bernadette's girlfriends wanted to know why she wasn't interested in any men. She was forced into a few parties and dances, but the guys only made her annoyed with their drivel and boringness. There were no horses, no boat chases, and no weddings out in the middle of nowhere. She had to admit, no one could measure up. To keep her friends off her back, she told everyone she was running low on money; she needed to finish up college as soon as possible by taking as many credits as she could. She did finish up early.

With university over and a chemistry degree in hand, Bernadette headed out into the career world. She was strong, independent, smart, had depth of character, and becoming more beautiful each day.

Chapter 10
Tender Learnings

(1987 – 1991)

After a few laboratory jobs, Bernadette decided to continued her education with University of Washington, Seattle. She was again able to partake in a work-study abroad, this time at University College London. Although Carney's life was still shrouded in mystery and complexity, his personal relations had stabilized. It was a time for Bernadette and Carney to explore and solidify their relationship. Once her studies were completed, she returned to Seattle, Washington and began working as a subcontractor for the U.S. Environmental Protection Agency, Region 10.

Chapter 11
Janus-Faced: Reality and Dreams

(July 1994)

Bernadette contemplated her life this particular Sunday afternoon, coming to the conclusion her reality and dreams were equivalent to the polarized ends of a magnet. The segments of her life that fell in line with societal norms comprised reality and the segments of her life which were secretive fell to the nebulous dream side. This categorization sounded very simple until, inevitably, the polarization would flip-flop. Then, secretive dreams became reality and the mundane normal stuff, like a job, took on qualities of a dream. The end result was massive confusion for Bernadette, not unlike what would occur if earth's poles were reversed today, in a minute.

Her distraction and disorientation this Sunday were acute; she didn't think getting in her car and driving would be safe. She knew the cause of her distress and it stood about six feet one inch and weighed in at two hundred some pounds. Carney had appeared in her life on Friday and magically vanished again this morning.

For the last two years, Bernadette had begun to feel more and more dissatisfied with their marriage arrangement. The part which really chaffed Bernadette was the fact that Mr. Good Looking Carney always got to choose the times for coming and going. There was never a calendar showing arrival and departure dates. Sometimes, depending on what Carney wanted to do, there would be a small notice that he would arrive soon. But nothing like a normal calendar existed where Bernadette could plan an upcoming event such as Christmas, birthday, or anniversary. Bernadette's irritation was increasing because she never got a say in when they got together, yet, was supposed to behave all sea-lion-lovey-eyed for Carney when he arrived. And, when he left, she was expected to just go on like nothing ever happened.

His arrival two days ago, Friday, was very bad timing because Bernadette was not in the mood for catering to a whimsical coming and going relationship.

It was end of the work week and Bernadette had been thinking about going out to the new bar called B52s with the girls. She had brought a change of clothes: short black skirt with a nice swirly flair, a pretty white sailor blouse, and brooding black leather jacket. As she stood looking at the women's restroom mirror at work, she had an overwhelming feeling of loneliness. Bone deep lonely. She wasn't completely married but she wasn't single. What the heck was she supposed to do, she reflected? Deciding she was too out of sorts for a fun evening, Bernadette bid the ladies good night, switched from heals to tennis shoes, threw her backpack over her shoulder, and headed for the bus stop.

As Bernadette stood waiting for express bus 15, her attention was on a couple of guys with bikes arguing in front of the bike shop, just a few shops down the street. She had met both of them when she was in the bike store, as one was the owner and the other was his son. As the argument between father and son got more heated, they raised their bikes up on the back wheels and were comparing something about the gear systems.

Bernadette was mildly distracted with the bicycle argument when a black Mercedes pulled up at the bus stop. A rear back passenger door opened and out stepped this gorgeous guy in a dark suit with aviator sunglasses. All the woman at the bus stop practically fainted. He held the back door open and extended his hand to Bernadette.

Two women at the stop jealously eyed Bernadette. Several others were supportive and said, "Go for that one girl! You got it go-ing-on honey."

She imagined screaming at the women. *Oh brother, it is just a dream that will become reality for a few days, then come to a screeching halt all too soon, so don't get too excited about this dude.*

Carney arrived like a super egotistical rock star and Bernadette found the charade a vexation. She was feeling like the dog left at the kennel all the time while someone went off and took a splendid vacation. In an instant, she decided it was time to undermine his position of power.

While a plan was hatching in her head, Bernadette pasted on her best fake smile for Carney. A beautiful brunette woman took that moment to interceded herself between Carney and Bernadette, attempting to gain the attention of this prime male specimen. That was all the distraction Bernadette needed. Frantically rummaging through the backpack for her wallet, she grabbed her driver's license and a credit card. Throwing her backpack in the back of the Mercedes and winking at the driver, she jogged over to the arguing cycle store owner, who was now fascinated with the events at the bus stop. Carney, who was mildly trying to disentangle himself from the brunette, had no idea what was about to happen.

Slapping the cards into the owner's hand, Bernadette said, "I need to borrow the smaller bike. I should have it back later today or tomorrow. Would that be okay?"

The owner chuckled and handed her the bike handles. "Take all the time you need to teach that boy a lesson."

Bernadette asked, "Is he looking?"

Her new coconspirator understood the question. "No, the brunette babe is proving to be as clingy as the algae on a piling." Placing his hand on the shifter, he said, "Push here to go up in gear and push down for lower gears."

Swinging her leg over the bike, she gripped the handlebars, testing the brakes. Bernadette pushed off.

The minute Bernadette's leg swung over the bike Carney's attention refocused, completely aware of her actions. Brushing the brunette aside, he took a huge leap to run after Bernadette, only to find himself sailing through the air. Carney was an excellent fighter and part of fighting was knowing how to regain ones balance. From airborne he went into a cartwheel, then landed on both feet, what in gymnastics is known as a round-off.

Carney was immediately in fight mode. He scanned the crowd in rage, his sights coming back to the brunette. She stood tapping her left foot, arms crossed. She had tripped him. Carney had never been tripped by a woman. He was instantly assessing her weaknesses and triggers.

The bravado the brunette felt began melting as she no long saw a good-looking man, but a man enraged. He took a step toward her and she took a step back. Instantly he had her by the front of her checkered dress.

Whispering, Carney said, "Don't ever do that to a man again. In another place or another day, you might look like hamburger after you trip someone." It wasn't until Carney had let her go, slammed the door of the Mercedes shut, and was sprinting toward the bike store, that the brunette realized her three hundred-seventy-five-dollar dress had been slit open from neck to hemline, without even nicking her.

The bike store owner calmly waited as Carney skidded up to him. He didn't say a thing. Rather, he held out one hand, palm open, and the other held the handle of the second bike. After fishing in his inside jacket pocket, Carney shoved a wad of bills at the owner, who was now smiling.

Carney recognized the importance of going after Bernadette. During his last few visits to the States, he had seen Bernadette's mood sour. She oscillated between boredom and irritation. Carney understood her frustration. He drew many of the lines defining their relationship, and thus, there were times he had to show that he could abide by her wishes, he would honor her desires in the relationship. Since he was cognizant of her need to feel love and of value, he would go to great lengths to ensure she felt and saw his depth of devotion. If a bike chase was the means to her heart, then he would give the chase everything he had and more.

Bicycles have the advantage in the often gridlocked downtown Seattle, but they still have to follow traffic laws. Carney was counting on traffic and traffic laws to help him catch up with Bernadette. Bernadette had several serious advantages in this chase: she knew Seattle, knew ways to avoid traffic, and she knew the ways to get Carney tangled up in traffic or pedestrians or both.

After only one red traffic light, Carney was figuring this chase would be short-lived as he was a minor half-block away from the woman that everyone on the road was watching. The black skirt flared out behind her like the plume of a graceful ostrich. Her red hair swirled and flew right then left as she pumped the peddles.

Glancing back to see where he was, she leapt off the bike, maneuvering it into a building. Carney sped up. Sliding up to the glass doors of the building he watched as Bernadette and the bike vanish into an elevator. Then he realized her trick. Because much of downtown Seattle is situated on a west facing hillside, many a building have a higher entrance on the east side and lower-level entrance on the westerly side. Carney decided to avoid the time of using the elevator, and skirted the building, hopefully catching Bernadette at the level below. Waiting at the corner, he watched a group of people, presumably who got off the elevator, exit the building. No Bernadette. It wasn't until the downhill light changed to green that he saw Bernadette exit from the parking garage a block away from him, heading downhill again. With a north-south block between them, Carney set off to the south, passing cars in an effort to catch up with her. She only had one more block to go before they arrived at the Puget Sound. She would have to slow down and go either north or south.

But she did neither; she didn't slow down or turn. She sped up the last block. There was a wharf, a railing, and a guardrail ahead. Carney didn't see how Bernadette was going to pull this off until he saw the gap between the railing and the guardrail. Folks used the narrow space to skirt down a steep bank to the Sound. Bernadette perfectly executed a jump into the Puget Sound, avoiding cars and pedestrians. When she was in the air, she pushed the bike away but remained holding on to one handlebar, to the surprise of all on the wharf. Carney followed suit.

The water wasn't very deep where they landed, maximum ten feet. Dragging his bike along, he swam up to Bernadette. "Could I have a kiss?" Carney asked with a smile, as if they were standing back at the bus stop instead of swimming around in Puget Sound, which was cold even on a warm summer evening.

"I guess so," Bernadette said with reluctance.

Carney got his kiss but underneath, he felt the discontent. The Mercedes picked them up. Saturday was a blur for Bernadette. Carney got the bikes back to the shop and took her to fun touristy places in Seattle. He did his best to dote on Bernadette. At times she was there with him, other times he felt the wall she had been erecting.

Sunday morning, when Carney went into the kitchen and never came back to the bedroom, Bernadette just felt numb. She walked into the kitchen and stood looking at the cup of coffee he was going to bring her. She took the mug, walked to the front door, and threw it out into the street.

That was a start to feeling better. Watching the coffee mug shatter helped her feel different, somehow. Come Monday morning, Bernadette called in sick to work. She couldn't decide if working a professional job was real or having an elusive marriage with Carney was the true sad reality. This Monday, working a job felt like a farce, so she stayed home to sleep off her disappointed and frayed nerves.

A week after Carney vanished from her house, Bernadette was still in a funk. She couldn't decide if she should be thankful for the time together or hate him for the time apart. The week of moping around at work hadn't brought any enlightenment to the situation,

Early Sunday morning, while curled up on the couch with her cat, Bernadette had a heart-to-heart talk with Heavenly Father. She asked if God wouldn't fix this mess. She wanted a companion with her as she navigated the sea of life, not once every six months, or once every fourteen months, or once every sixteen months or whatever time outer space threw at her. She needed a solid relationship; someone she could come home to each night.

She begged and pleaded and hoped. *Would God just help out here, a little?* She sat quietly for several hours. There was no booming voice from the clouds, just peaceful quiet.

After lunch, feeling the need for some action, Bernadette drove to her favorite bookstore in the northern part of Seattle. After selecting several books, she meandered to the cashier. In a rack on the post next to the checkout station, Bernadette took a third long glance at a book she had seen before. Unlike other days, today she looked at the face on the cover, really studied the face and the deeply moving eyes.

Holding the book, *Autobiography of a Yogi*, with indecision, she asked the cashier, "Have you read this book?"

The cashier's face beamed warmheartedly. She said, "Oh, this book is my very most favorite book. You will love it."

Late that night, as she sat reading *Autobiography of a Yogi*, Bernadette realized it took four minor steps to make one monumental change in her life.

Part one - she made a prayer.

Part two - she bought a book in a Seattle bookstore based on an intuitive feeling.

Part three - she took it home and began reading it.

Part four - she let the words touch her heart, she let it speak to her soul, and she opened her mind.

Here, in this book were answers to questions she so often asked. Help and guidance presented itself in ways she never expected.

Several months later, Bernadette became a disciple of Paramahansa Yogananda, the author of the book. It was the beginning of an eternal relationship with a spiritual master who would help Bernadette to know Heavenly Father, to know truth, to know true joy. With his help she began to unravel the confusion over reality and dreams.

It was only a year later, she realized how God had answered her prayer that Sunday past. Carney was a man who could offer what the world allowed. Her spiritual master was with her always and would always love her. Finally, the tapestry of her married life, her feelings of worthiness, and her faith in her personal quest, could not only be mended but held the potential to be woven in joy, depending on Bernadette's choices.

Chapter 12
Homeward Bound

(January 1995)

As priorities for Bernadette shifted from "excitement in the city" to "contemplation of life", she decided to return to Oregon in January of 1995. Seattle was fun and full of activities that no longer held an allure. She also missed a few of the old high school friendships which had more depth to them because of a shared history. Friendships in Seattle were often more transitory, and Bernadette had trouble finding a common ground with some of her acquaintances.

Because her mother was alone on the farm outside of Lebanon, Oregon, and getting older, Bernadette hoped that by living closer to her mother she could become a source of assistance and foster a better relationship. Unfortunately, those attempts at improved relations were often futile, and there were times when Bernadette's self-preservation prompted her to sever communication, as her mom continued to take delight in denigrating Bernadette.

A chance encounter with a vice president of a manufacturing company in Madison, Oregon, lead to Bernadette beginning a new job in March 1995. Bernadette was thrilled to move into a new arena, manufacturing, and use her chemistry skills to assist the company with compliance in environmental laws. She was optimistic that this new career would lead to a lasting sense of fulfillment.

Part III

Chapter 13
Noise of the Ghosts

(January 1997)

Dr. David Bernstein stepped out of his pickup into the almost freezing rain, exposing his senses to a swarm of forces.

His father's best friend, Cutlas "Cutter" Altree, had called him at work earlier in the day, asking him to stop by the dairy farm this afternoon, before dark. David understood Cutter's sense of urgency, because if the situation at the dairy didn't change soon, Chapter 11 bankruptcy would come marching up to Cutter's land. David came to the farm to help.

As an assistant professor on the tenure-track at Oregon Polytechnic Institute (OPI) in Corvallis, Oregon, David's commitment to his research in the microbiology department demanded every moment, conscious or subconscious. Yet, David never gave Cutter's request a second thought. David grew up in rural Lebanon, Oregon, and those origins grounded him, making David unique amongst some of his collogues in two ways: first, he desired to use his brain not just for stroking some egotistical feeling, but for doing good to the planet, and second, his devotion and regard for the community which had shaped his youth hadn't diminished, but rather grew stronger. For David, life was about honor.

Slipping on his heavy waterproof jacket and covering his dirty blonde hair with a warm cap, David noted it was about 3:30 p.m. and the little bit of sunlight was fading quickly. This was his second trip in a month to the Holstein and Jersey cow barns located just outside the southern city limits of Lebanon. But for Cutter's fields and barns, it no longer felt like country. Business, houses, and industry had all encroached closer and closer, creating clashes between inhabitants on what was considered acceptable or tolerable.

Standing up straight, which put him at five feet and eight inches, David took a deep breath, finding again, his senses inundated with negative perceptions: the bellowing from the cows held distress, the smell of death irritated the sensitive lining in his nose, and there was an unsettled feeling that David couldn't give a name to.

What looked to be a young veterinarian with a large toolbox was leaving the double door opening on the main barn. He was followed by a tractor with front end loader carrying two dead calves. Cutter walked angrily behind the tractor. David glanced at the grim faces of the veterinarian and Cutter. The men stood off to the side talking animatedly while the tractor continued on to the disposal dumpster which had been delivered to the farm in the last month.

David signaled the tractor driver and approached him. "I would like to look at these dead calves this afternoon. Could you leave them on the ground by the dumpster for the next hour?"

The driver nodded his head in the affirmative and proceeded on.

David kept a respectful distance away from Cutter and the veterinarian. He mulled over the details Cutter had given him three weeks ago. The calves born this winter were dying at the outrageous rate of seventy-five percent. Some died right after birth, others were stillborn, and some were premature and stillborn. The veterinarian had not been able to find any cause after blood work and post-mortem examinations had been completed.

David was appalled to hear about the farm's suffering. He knew the genetic stock of the herd was excellent, as new quality bulls were brought in each year. Cutter had given him the reports on feed, water, and blood samples. Although David didn't have a degree in the animal health field, it wasn't difficult for him to research the test results and understand them.

Last time David was at the dairy, he took a variety of samples from a large cross section of the cows, not just those pregnant, and submitted them to another laboratory who could analyze for additional parameters. None of those results showed any toxins or anything unusual, other than one interesting blip. The cows had very high levels of some adrenal gland hormones, specifically adrenaline and cortisol. Based on this limited data, but the only morsal of science he had, David theorized that a high level of on-going stress was causing the cows to abort or have difficult labors. Today he wanted to address this possibility with Cutter.

David noticed the conversation between the veterinarian and Cutter had stalled. The veterinarian shook his head, turned abruptly, and headed to his truck.

Cutter walked up to David and said, "That veterinarian is useless. He's a young kid who has never been on a farm. All he knows is what school taught him, which might not work in the real world." Putting his hand on David's shoulder he added, "Thanks for coming. If this problem continues for another six months, we won't be able to keep paying the loans on the new milking equipment. My grandparents trusted me with this farm. We have got to figure this out. So, what do you recommend for this afternoon?"

David replied, "I got back some interesting test results which might indicate that the cows are experiencing high levels of stress. Is anything different in the barns this year? It might be anything. Is it hotter or colder? Is there less room? Are they not going out in the fields as much?"

Cutter thought a few minutes. "I don't think there is more stress. We haven't changed anything other than the milking machines, which are quieter and better than the old ones. I have same number of cows in the same space. They have the same amount of time in the fields."

"Could you look at your milk production levels on certain cows and see if there might be a time frame when production went down? It might tell us something. I am going to take more samples this afternoon." Noticing the fatigue and stress in Cutter's face, David added, "You look a mess. Why not get home early tonight?"

The scowl on Cutter's face switched to one of sadness. He said, "My mother has been ill this month. I am headed to the hospital. Thanks for your help, David. I appreciate it."

Glancing at the barn, David squared his shoulders. He was tired. Tired of cow poop, tired of cows that didn't want to go in the squeeze chute, tired of dead calves which were in various states of rigor mortis, and tired of unhappy animals. Kicking up his resolve, he headed to the two dead calves on the ground. After that, he walked to the west end of the main barn to begin taking samples of the animals still alive.

Two and one-half hours later, the samples were carefully put into two buckets and loaded into David's pickup. He had a forty-minute drive to his lab, where he would put the samples in one of the large refrigerators specially used for samples. One of his students would box them up tomorrow and ship them out for overnight delivery.

Once he parked the truck in front of his office building, David quickly exited the truck and grabbed the full buckets. He turned, took three steps and slipped on newly formed black ice, which was impossible to see in the poorly lit parking lot.

"You have got to be kidding me!" David yelled as he tried to get back up. Broken glass and sample material littered the area around him. Finally regaining his balance, he headed toward his lab to find a late working and willing student to help clean up the mess.

Fifteen minutes later, with two students in tow, they headed out to the parking lot with brooms, dustpans, and garbage bags. While surveying the destroyed samples, David thought about giving it up. Maybe he should tell the Altree family to sell, get out, cut their losses. He had now tracked cow manure everywhere: from his truck to the lab and then to his office. But the students doing the cleanup convinced him that he was working on a good cause, which he already knew.

One student asked him, "Would you want us to give up on your research if we lost a few samples?"

With the tone of chastisement ringing in ears, David headed back out to the dairy, arriving close to 8:00 p.m. He walked into the barn, with new buckets and sample containers in hand, expecting to see the cows bedded down and chewing their cud. He stood stupefied near the barn entrance. All the cows were highly agitated. They paced, kicked out at anything, and rammed into the panels. Newly born calves trembled.

Considering how close the farm was to humans and human noise, David doubted that a cougar would be nearby. A pack of dogs roaming in the area might be possibility, but he couldn't imagine all the cows would become so agitated from roaming dogs.

David grabbed a flashlight from his pickup and began to walk around the outside of the main barn. When he turned the second corner, now on the backside of the barn, he abruptly stopped. He was assailed by an irritating high pitched grinding noise and a repugnant smoke, causing him to cough several times. Confused, David returned to the front of the barn to confirm the absence of the smoke and grinding noise. He realized the noise and smoke was also in the front, but only when he knew to look for it. Walking to the back again, he was amazed that the sound appeared to amplify off the back of the barn and the smoke stagnated in the field. On the opposite side of the field, David saw several doors of a huge industrial building were slid wide open, for light spilled out of them. The noise burst from the building, along with smoke and lots of particulate.

Thinking of the cows, David couldn't imagine trying to sleep with this irritating noise going on and the smoke made breathing uncomfortable. This, he knew, had to be the source of the cow's stress hormones, and the underlying cause of calf mortality.

Laughing to himself, David thought of how falling on black ice had led to a marvelous discovery. Perhaps his next paper would be on the importance of accidents and their contribution to science.

Wanting to give Cutter some hopeful news, David got in his pickup and headed past the barns to the Altree home, thinking that perhaps Cutter was home from the hospital. Once he got out of his pickup, still a hundred feet from the front door, he heard the television booming. No, that was an inaccurate description. The noise from the television almost blew him over, even with the wind and the icy rain. It was so loud; the entire family could have been sitting outside and would still be able to hear it without problems.

David slowly took the steps to the front door, holding the handrail to avoid any more falls. Ringing the doorbell twice, he waited. There was no answer. He rang it three more times. He didn't bother to knock because he figured no one could hear a knock over the television. David stood looking at the house; he was flabbergasted. The whole world was crazy with noise. He wondered who was failing to regulate all the noise.

Disappointed, David snugged his cap lower around his ears and headed for his truck.

-

The next day David spoke to Cutter about the pollution coming from the industrial building. Explaining that the noise and smoke correlated with the visible stress of the cows, he asked if someone in the family could check behind the barn every thirty minutes, starting after 4:00 p.m., to identify the onset of the noise. He suggested that the family keep a spiral bound notebook to record such things as: onset of the noise each day, variations in volume, description of the sound, condition of the cows, and information on the smoke.

Cutter said, "Well…my wife and I will be at the hospital with my mother. But I will see if the kids can do it. They always tell me how busy they are."

Thinking of the blaring television, David asked, "Who was in the house last night, about 8:00 p.m.? Do you have family visiting?"

"My two sons, daughter, and a daughter-in-law all live in the house right now."

David had heard about Cutter's children and their lack of ambition. "Cutter, your kids are adults and if they want to inherit the farm, then they need help with this problem. Why not have one of your sons go to the City of Lebanon and find out who owns that industrial building. Have him get a phone number for the owner. They are able bodied people, so they can step away from the television to make some observations at the barn."

Cutter finally spoke, "I'll see what I can do."

David checked in each day with Cutter for the next two and a half weeks. Everyday there were more excuses as to why the "kids" hadn't been able to check on the cows. David couldn't believe it. Not once had an adult-child gone to the barn. Cutter assured him that when he drove up to the house after long evenings at the hospital, the TV was off and everyone appeared to be cleaning or cooking or somehow, they were busy. Seeing that progress on the problem wasn't going anywhere, David asked one of his students to find out who owned the industrial building. He was curious; if the cows were impacted by the activity, wouldn't the neighbors be too?

After six more dead calves, David drove to the hospital one evening.

When David walked into the hospital room, Cutter's wife, Jennifer, was the first to see him. She said, "David, what a surprise. It is good to see you." Standing, she gave David a quick hug.

David spent some time with Cutter and Jennifer discussing the positives and negatives of the health care system as Cutter's mother laid silently beside them, her only movement was the shallow expansion and contraction of her chest. Finally, he broached the topic on his mind, "Cutter, when I went to the house several weeks ago, the television was blaring so loudly that I could hear it outside of the house. Your sons and daughter need to help with this problem because it isn't getting any better. You lost six more calves in seventeen days. Why don't we take my truck right now and I will show you what is going on at the barns and at your house. You wanted my help. Let me show you what is going on."

Cutter looked reluctant. He put his hand on his mother's head. He had limited time with her, as her strength waned a bit more each day.

"It will just take forty-five minutes and you can be right back." David smiled his most reassuring look.

A knowing glance went between Cutter and Jennifer. Jennifer spoke up. "Last time the kids didn't do what they supposed to do because they were watching television all the time, the television got busted with a baseball bat. We were without a television for three months. Cutter told the kids that another television would never be allowed in the house again if the kids couldn't be responsible."

David didn't understand the reluctance to hold the adult-children accountable again. He said, "Someday Cutter, you won't be around to take care of these adult-children, so they best learn about taking care of themselves now. How about we go take a look?"

To everyone's surprise, Cutter's mother took that moment to open her eyes and extended her hand to Cutter. Once he took it, she struggled to croak out a few words, "Go. I love our cows. Go help them." Her eyes, rarely open in the last month, pleaded as she looked from Cutter to Jennifer.

As they got to the David's pickup, Cutter asked, "Do you have any tools in the back of your pickup truck?"

Opening the canopy, David explained what he had with him. "Given all the ice we have had this month, I have several sandbags, two bags of rock salt, two shovels, and a pick-mattock."

Cutter reached in and took the pick-mattock, silently gaging its weight. Taking it to the cab, he settled in the seat, holding the tool with both hands. Cutter never said a word the entire drive to the farm and David didn't ask him any questions. No words were needed.

Chapter 14
Tele-devil-vision

(February - November 1997)

Jennifer Altree arrived back at the ranch house at 10:30 p.m. Her mother-in-law had actually perked up after Cutter had left with David, so she had stayed longer than normal. As she pulled up in front of the house, she noticed David's pick up, but all the cars belonging to the kids were gone.

Approaching the front door, she was relieved to see that it wasn't kicked in, but things were eerily quiet. Jennifer figured if there was a crisis, it had played out in the living room, where the large screen television took up its center throne. Walking into the living room, she saw David sitting on the couch, Cutter reclined back in his favorite chair with a pick-mattock at his feet, and the television was in pieces, strewn across the carpet in various stages of destruction.

No words were spoken. The silence reminded Jennifer of a mournful wake for some family member whose secrets were now exposed. When the doorbell chimed, Jennifer was surprised to find the Sheriff Bodenheimer. Sighing, she directed him to the kitchen table, calling Cutter and David to join them in the kitchen.

Giving a perfunctory nod in greeting, Sheriff Bodenheimer dove right into the accusations made against Cutter. He said, "Cutter, what is going on here? Those kids of yours say you threatened them with a pickaxe tonight. What am I supposed to do now?"

Jennifer put her hand to her mouth to muffle her distraught reaction. She knew Cutter would be beyond furious.

"You mean to tell me that my kids, who can't take the time to help me with all the calves dying, had time to see you and lie about what occurred tonight?" The muscles in Cutter's jaw pulsed.

Cutter turned to his wife and said, "You let them know they are to come here at 8:00 a.m., pack their stuff, and be out of house by noon tomorrow. They will never be allowed on the property again. I want the locksmith here before dark tomorrow."

Turning to Sheriff Bodenheimer he said, "No, I never threatened the kids. But I did threaten their best friend. Killed it, actually. Come see for yourself."

Sheriff Bodenheimer raised an eyebrow and followed Cutter to the living room.

David had stepped away to use the bathroom. When he returned, he found the three of them looking at the smashed television. Attempting to lighten the mood, he said, "Well, finally someone got rid of that lazy jerk, sleezy slob, foul mouthed idiot, violent moron, and poor role model. Now the television has reaped its reward for all of the excessive and ill-begotten humors it brought on the world. Off to the junkyard it goes."

The sheriff and Jennifer looked at David with concern, so he added, "Okay, Okay. It isn't all bad. Educational programs, the news, or something to uplift people - that is all fine. However, when entertainment become mind-numbing and more important than taking care of one's personal affairs, then it fails to serve humanity as it should. Cutter didn't ask his kids for much. He needed them to help collect information about the pollution coming from the industrial building across the field, as it appears to be causing high calf mortality. But noooo. They wanted to sit around watching the television and have Cutter do all the work."

Sheriff Bodenheimer asked David, "Did Cutter threaten those kids with the pickaxe?"

David replied, "Clarification. Pick-mattock. No. Did not happen. Saw the whole thing and he never once threatened those adult-children in any manner. The adult-children threatened Cutter when they saw what he was going to do. They said they would lock him out of the house if he dared touch the television. It is Cutter's television and his house."

The sheriff wrote down some notes, got David's address and phone number, then flipping the notebook closed, he looked at David and said, "Let's all have some coffee in the kitchen and talk about that noise and smoke."

Everyone headed back to the kitchen.

"How do you know about the noise and smoke?" David was shocked that the police knew about it.

"The City of Lebanon Police have been fielding calls from irate people. Since Cutter is just outside of the city limits, the calls are sent on to the sheriff's department. Things have become very interesting over the last two years."

David interrupted, "Wait. Don't say another word till I get my notebook, which is in my pickup. I'll be right back."

The sheriff put a quick damper on David's enthusiasm. "Don't bother. This will be surprisingly quick and ends, well, in a puff of smoke."

Cutter and David gave each other a look of concern.

The sheriff said, "Here is what I have heard. The problem began a year ago, about twenty miles away, in the neighboring town of Madison. As you might know, a huge employer in Madison is East-West Refined Metal Manufacturing (EwRM2). They started some secret process at one of the facilities in town and immediately the complaints started rolling in due to noise and a weird smelling smoke. At first, EwRM2, was working with the community and Oregon Department of Environmental Quality (DEQ). But then EwRM2 got a new president, and progress on the problem stalled and EwRM2 aggressively claimed that the problem wasn't them.

"After six or seven months, there was a writeup about the pollution problem in the Madison paper. Two days later, they printed a retraction of the article and the poor kid who wrote the article was fired. No more was ever printed about the noise or smoke. Even DEQ backed off, saying something nebulous about national security. Public perception of the "great employer" in Madison began to tank. Then, the company moved the process.

"Yep, it moved to the building on the other side of your field Cutter. We have been taking calls on it, but EwRM2 gave us the run-around. After a few months we were told to refer all calls concerning the issue on to the DEQ.

"David, if you are going to take on this issue, you be careful. There is power and money involved, and that power and money doesn't have much respect for the little guy. End of story."

David sat forward in his chair. Things just kept getting better and better. He had been struggling to get information and now it was handed to him over coffee.

David asked Cutter, "What do you want to do? Do you want to give up on the farm? I'll tell you what I want to do, and that is figure out who thinks they can push everyone around and get away with terrorizing communities."

Cutter snorted and then said, "Sheriff, if you are done here for the night, David and I will retire to my study. It is time to formulate a plan."

Sheriff Bodenheimer stood and said, "You both heed my warning. This isn't a game of patty cake. Good night."

-

Finding a veterinarian, Dr. Lisa Albright from southern Oregon, who would help David in researching the problem and assist in writing a scientific paper was cause for celebration for both Cutter and David. Lisa and David began their work two weeks after the television died. The farm became a hub of scientific activity. Noise levels were recorded. Air samples were collected and tested. Cow saliva, urine, feces, milk, and blood were tested. Three months later, David and Lisa were standing in front of the main barn when a huge semi-truck with hay pulled in.

Lisa looked at the truck with amazement and said, "Why didn't I think of this before! With all of Cutter's equipment, he can build a straw-bale wall and drastically reduce the noise in the barns. Straw-bale walls are outstanding for noise suppression. We can monitor the cow's improvement as the wall goes in. Better still, we can build the wall the same time the ceiling fans go in the barns."

When the wall and the fans were installed, life at the dairy farm improved tremendously.

David and Lisa published their work eight months after they started working on the problem. Their journal article did an outstanding job of corelating pollution with animal mortality. David felt satisfaction in helping Cutter, but he was anxious to get back to his microbiology research.

Everything was quiet for a few weeks after the article published, until the head of the OPI Agricultural Department (Ag) came to see David. The ruddy faced Ag head complained that although the paper was scientifically brilliant, it fell outside of the standard of OPI publishable material. A few days after that, everything started to fall apart in David's life. The Microbiology Department did a quasi-review of his work and determined it was in the best interest of OPI to remove David from the tenure-track permanently; OPI fired him.

To cement his firing, pictures of David and a graduate student were altered to show them in romantic embraces, and those pictures were sent to David's wife. Rumors of sex for grades abound. David's wife asked him to move out.

David was ruined. All that he loved was gone. Throughout 1998, his mental health suffered, as he became obsessed with seeking revenge again OPI and EwRM2. He dropped off the map. Although he was in the Lebanon area, near Jade Mountain, no one in town ever saw him. There was someone else who lived off the grid, and he helped David stay alive.

David knew he would get even; he just didn't know when.

Chapter 15
The Warmup

(July 1998)

Ed Keil, an eighteen-year veteran with the Securities Exchange Commission (SEC), working out of San Francisco, had been assigned to investigate possible insider trading and market misrepresentation at East-West Refined Metals Manufacturing (EwRM2). There wasn't much to go on other than a tip that had come in three months ago. After some digging and a thorough look at stock data, Ed was confident that further investigation was required and that would begin with interviewing some key people.

Arriving in Madison, Oregon, was easy for Ed, but not exposing his motives for the trip was a challenge. He knew how gossip surrounding a visit by the SEC would spread in a town such as Madison and that would make his job impossible. He needed to remain anonymous. However, the small town of Madison was very friendly, which meant, as a sign of friendship, the locals asked Ed questions, lots and lots of questions.

"How long is your stay? Why might you leave early?" asked the receptionist at the desk.

"What is the nature of your business?" asked the teller at the bank.

"Are you here to visit family?" asked a cashier.

"If nothing is wrong with the car, why do you want a different vehicle?" asked the rental agency person.

Ed found dodging all the questions took a tremendous amount the thought and planning.

Within a few days in Madison, luck struck. Ed came upon the perfect people to interview and that would mean his stay could become shorter than he had anticipated. Students from a local college worked part-time at the EwRM2 facilities. They were easy to find and easy to identify because they frequented the local sandwich shop for cheap food, either alone or in groups. They also were impressed by Ed because he was good looking without being stuffy. He took on a "cool" demeanor around the students. Getting them talking was easy. Getting them to stop talking about everything and focus on what Ed needed to know was the hard part.

Adeline S., a flirty blonde student-worker, became Ed's most plentiful informer. Yet, she presented a problem. Sifting through her incessant chatter to determine what was fact and what was fiction proved to be a serious challenge. Certainly, her student-worker position, much like a contractor, helped her to feel free from any loyalty to EwRM2, and Ed wasn't concerned about that. But her ability to either idolize people or talk trash about people showed a serious weakness in her character. Those types of personal weakness could negatively affect the SEC's ability to go from an informal to formal investigation in the EwRM2 case because the source was deemed too unreliable. Sources who were overly swayed by personal desires meant they misconstrued the truth.

Ed found other sources within EwRM2, but none talked as much as Adeline S.

Something else continued to trouble Ed. From some of his interviews and sources, one name kept coming up, Bernadette Engstrom. Bernadette didn't trade stocks. He checked records on her, and those records were very sparse. Adeline S. accused Bernadette of altering data, falsifying reports, and misrepresenting the truth in many documents. Ed wrote it all down, but he couldn't imagine that everything Bernadette did was a lie, or she would have been caught by now. He did some checking with the DEQ, and they assured him that Bernadette was an honest person. No DEQ audit ever found anything she did to be dishonest.

One day, when Adeline brought up Bernadette's name, again, Ed asked her, "Why do you keep bringing up Bernadette? What did this woman do to cause such animosity?"

Ed didn't expect an honest answer, so when he got a plausible explanation from Adeline, he was surprised.

"I got written up over a stupid safety violation because of her. She didn't have to press the issue, but she did."

Curious, Ed inquired further, "What was the safety violation."

"We were supposed to move this heavy carbon dioxide tank using some special equipment and I didn't have time to do it that way. I knew how to do it by myself. The tank fell over. It wasn't a big deal. We got it back up. But I got in trouble anyway."

Thinking the tank must have weighed thirty pounds or so, Ed asked, "How much did the tank weigh?"

Adeline said, "I think it is about three hundred pounds. But I knew how to move it. Bernadette is just a witch. Anyway, I have been complaining about her to human resources. I hope she gets fired someday. Would serve her right."

Ed wrote in his notebook, *Adeline is a witch, not Bernadette.*

There was another shocking event. When Ed had interviewed the president of the EwRM2, this highly respected man had implied Bernadette

Engstrom in the Environmental Department probably instigated this sham SEC investigation.

"She is a traitor for bringing you here for no good reason and taking my time away from more important company activities," the president spewed out.

Ed could not resist asking, "Why would a lower-level management person who works in the Environmental Department know anything about the company on such a level it would lead to the SEC asking a few questions of you?"

The company president turned several shades of red at Ed's question. Ed thought to himself, *this dude just threw more gas on the fire.* The interview was over shortly after that.

Other upper management sources also mentioned Bernadette Engstrom, in one way or another.

Ed came to a conclusion: people were willing to do whatever it took to hurt Bernadette. After all of the upper management interviews, Ed never got a concrete reason why Bernadette was being so professionally tortured. The only conclusion that made sense was alarming; Bernadette knew something. She knew something was seriously wrong and probably knew who was responsible. The EwRM2 criminals suspected Bernadette had knowledge of their activities, so they worked to destroy her; that was the only possible motive for the intense gossip. The information Bernadette had would certainly impact Ed's investigation. He had asked to interview Bernadette, but he was never granted permission. She never went to lunch or out to eat in the evening. He had gone to her house, but she never came to the door. Without a subpoena, and Ed couldn't ask for a subpoena because the investigation hadn't progressed to the formal stage, he was stuck, left to wonder what Bernadette knew.

After four weeks, Ed believed he had enough information to recommend a formal investigation. He told his wife he would fly back on Wednesday.

But a problem developed, and the bickering of intergovernmental agencies would do a huge disservice to Ed and his family.

-

Ed never made it back to San Francisco. When his wife called the Ed's office at the SEC Thursday morning; they were completely in the dark. They didn't know exactly when he was due back, and they didn't know if someone had requested him on another assignment in Oregon. By Friday his wife gave up with the SEC and called in a missing person's report. Her frustration and anger were mounting. She couldn't comprehend how the staff at the SEC knew nothing of Ed's whereabouts and possibly when he would return to the office.

The Regional Administrator (RA) for the SEC got engaged the next Monday because they needed the government car back that Ed had taken to and left at the San Francisco airport. With the RA's encouragement, the local Madison police finally went to the hotel. They found that Ed hadn't checked out of the hotel and someone, the hotel didn't have a record of that person, had paid cash to extend the reservation through the following Friday. His garment bag and suitcase were in the room, packed and ready to go. The rental car was in the hotel parking lot. But Ed, his notebook, and all his electronic equipment were missing.

The next call the SEC RA made was to the Federal Bureau of Investigation (FBI). The report given to the FBI was extremely vague. Because it was an active SEC investigation, they wouldn't release cell phone records or email messages. When the FBI became exasperated, the SEC just told them to do a "work around" and hung up the phone. The FBI stopped to visit Ed's wife in San Francisco, but for some reason she had become frightened and refused to even speak with them. Out of frustration, two FBI agents checked into Ed's former Madison hotel room and began stirring the pot with the hope that something would turn up.

124

Part IV

Chapter 16
Awards, Arrows, and Passing Gas

(Wednesday, December 9, 1998)

Bernadette half-zombie marched and half-sloth crawled out of her house and into her truck at 5:30 a.m., the time of morning when narcistic bosses compel worker bees to arrive at work even though the office is empty. She was accompanied by her bludgeoned brain containing a wealth of cannon fire going off inside of it. The headache pain was miserable and working though the roaring discomfort was akin to shoveling horse manure with a toothpick. She had resorted to taking a prescription drug to deal with the nausea, confusion, and neurologic suffering just fifteen minutes ago, giving her hope that she wouldn't throw up in full view of her coworkers today.

Multifaceted sources lead to Bernadette' physical pain and mental torture, but there was one main cause. That cause, which had begun as a wee itchy splinter between her shoulder blades six months ago, had grown to the size of a ten-inch metal wedge, normally used to fall a mature Douglas fir. East-West Refined Metals Manufacturing (EwRM2), where Bernadette worked as an Environmental Department manager at one of the company facilities in Madison, Oregon, had been under U.S. Environmental Protection Agency (EPA) assault and this assault bore no resemblance to normal enforcement standards. Several factors made the situation unbelievably perplexing for Bernadette: quasi-enforcement letters were delivered with the EPA expectation they would be treated as normal enforcement letters, surprise inspections involving nonscientific field tests were performed, and nonstandard and unpublished laboratory tests, of which only one laboratory in the entire US could do the test, were required.

Bernadette was distraught because the playing field used to determine what was considered a hazardous waste and then know how to manage it, had just been metaphorically bombed. She understood chemistry and the need to follow procedures to get correct results. EPA demanded that companies follow set procedures. Unfortunately, the EPA didn't want to follow their own rules this time around. After six months of playing Twister (normally a game kids play) with the EPA, Bernadette failed to acclimatize to the unprecedented and imaginative chemistry the EPA dabbled in, but she very well understood crazy, egotistical, power saturated government employees.

Today should have been a welcome reprieve from the EPA onslaught. She was tasked with setting up the EwRM2 President's Conference Room for the annual 9:00 a.m. Environmental Department Christmas Awards presentation with a light brunch served afterwards. Although she wouldn't have EPA stressors this morning, she found these types of events to exude their own uncomfortableness. Bernadette's normally full lips were set in a thin grim line as she picked up donuts from the store for this male chest-puffing event. Men were compensated, promoted, and exalted in these types of meetings while women where there to clap and gush gratitude for the opportunity to sweep the floor or mop up spilled coffee after the meeting.

Unfortunately, the feeling that Bernadette had everything ready for this Christmas award meeting and brunch was squelched with uncompromising finality by her boss, Tim Nelson, just yesterday.

Yesterday (Tuesday), just a few moments before Bernadette was to leave work, about 5:45 p.m., Tim called her and casually mentioned that the computer in the President's Conference Room didn't work, a fact he discovered during a meeting earlier in the day. Bernadette had hung up the phone and sat looking at her hands; they were shaking. Tim was setting her up for failure and he did that by not telling her about the computer problem until late in the day. Staring blankly at her desk, she thought about all the times men went out of their way to ensure success of their male coworkers and all the times she was gifted with a three-legged Arabian racehorse while everyone sat back to see if she could muster the guts to cross the finish line. If this time bomb of a fact had been mentioned to her earlier in the day, she could have worked with someone in instrument tech support (ITS) to get it fixed. But now they had gone home, and she would be forced to find an ITS person at home who would answer the phone and help her.

It was the unspoken expectation that everything had to be perfect for these types of alpha dog meetings. Even though the failure of the computer wasn't and wouldn't be her fault, it would somehow reflect negatively on her if she didn't have it fixed. To sum it up, if she did her job well, then the men believed anyone could have done that job, and if there was a problem associate with her work, then upper management believed that a man should have done the job. Bernadette was surprised she hadn't ground her teeth down past the enamel to the tender, nerve laden pulp, while attempting to survive in this organized system of jailers.

That Tuesday evening, she sat shaking her head with frustration while calling the ITS manager at home. He answered the phone. Miracle. Immediately in a snit, he began barking at Bernadette about how a work request should have been entered online, in a timely fashion, much earlier in the day. Waiting for patience to arrive and nudge out her stinging ego, she calmly explained the entire series of events. She then asked when someone could meet her in the conference room tomorrow, Wednesday morning, very early, before the awards meeting. He said he would have someone there before the meeting and hung up.

Once at work that cold and foggy Wednesday morning, she found the conference room door was locked. It took thirty-five minutes for security to meander about the facility, finally coming to the correct building. Bernadette thought she was going to lose her mind. She spent fifty minutes disconnecting and reconnecting computer cables; an inane attempt to get the system to work. It would boot up, show a lovely Microsoft Windows logo, and sit there. Nothing. A little after 7:00 a.m., Jeffery from ITS arrived and asked her to hold the doors open while he brought in the new computer. He had troubleshooted the network from home and decided the safest approach was to bring a spare computer.

At 8:30 a.m., Bernadette excused herself to begin setting up the conference room. The rectangular President's conference room had three doors; one at each end and a side door that led directly into the president's office. One end door was for entry off the main hallway. That is where most people entered for the meeting. The other end door lead into a preparation room where all the supplies for the conference room where kept. There were two doors into the supply room, one from the conference room and the other lead to the hallway. Finding the supply room completely locked, Bernadette grabbed Jeffery, who had a key to everything, to open the doors.

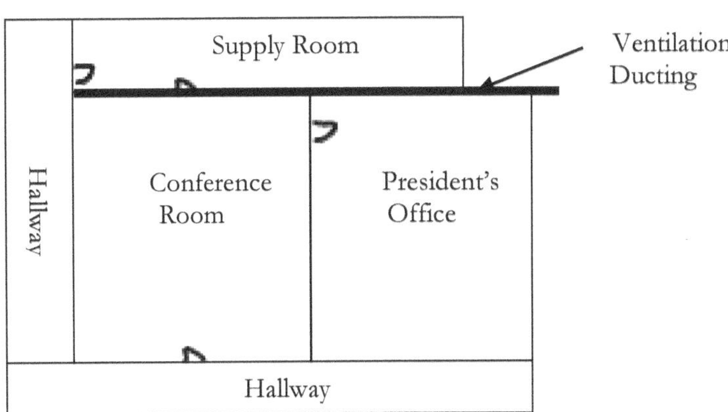

Once in the supply room, she found the coffee and started brewing a pot. As she assembled plates, napkins, and cups needed, she oddly heard the EwRM2 president's booming voice, "I don't care what kind of job she does. She won't be promoted under my reign. The men want someone who is more of a team player, someone who can understand their situation.

Personally, I don't think she is worth more than sludge at the wastewater treatment system she monitors. She is coyote ugly, if you know the expression. Hahaha. It is too bad that baby girl wasn't thrown out with the bathwater." Looking up to where the voice came from, Bernadette found herself glaring at the grating of a metal heating duct, as the laughter from a multitude of men trailed off. The voice had traveled through the metal duct work, probably coming from the Presidents room, as if on an intercom system. There were more muffled voices, but nothing she could understand. The EwRM2 president had not explicitly said that he was talking about Bernadette, but the description fit her completely. She oversaw the monitoring of the wastewater treatment system and she had been accused in the past of not being a team player. The men at the facility often made fun of her red hair and her looks. Friends told her the men said these things because they were insecure, but it didn't help the isolation she felt.

The relentless bitterness she felt toward the unfair working conditions at her job warped into supernova explosion status. She stood immobile, the formation of tingling goosebumps signaled the transformation of a woman who attempted to get along, be compliant, and sow seeds amicability, into a woman who detested a sexist system, held no tolerance for people who wanted to push her around, and took a more lenient view of what it meant to stand up for oneself. Quickly corralling her thoughts, she tucked away the coyote and baby comments; she could not cope with those words here at work. Roughly grabbing the supplies, she headed back into the conference room, smacking them down on a table. Well-worked muscles in her shoulders, thighs, and buttocks tightened, ready for a fight.

While finishing up, she fumed over the words team player; two words that locked Bernadette into a prison of frustratingly meaningless double speak. After observing and objectively listening to team players at EwRM2, she came to an unerring conclusion that team players underhandedly applied social pressure to promote deleterious behaviors from other team players. The sick team player system demanded a person abandon all unique talents given to them by creation and set aside one's moral compass of integrity and righteous duty.

At 9:00 a.m. Environmental Department Christmas Awards presentation started with Tim, the Environmental Director and Bernadette's boss, doing his best to give the peasantry credit for a good year. *Poor man*, Bernadette thought to herself, *submerging himself with the killer whales while still trying to suit up as a good-natured seal for the downtrodden worker.* Noticing the huge stack of new coffee cups had been reduced to less than ten, as the peasantry needed to keep their interest and energy level in line with management expectations, Bernadette slipped back into the supply room to find more. No additional cups were to be found anywhere, with one possible exception. There were two large cupboards up high, with interestingly, intricate locks on them.

She stood looking at silver locks, a unique design, remembering the first time Roger had shown her how to pick a lock at the tender age of eight.

"Be careful," Roger had said. "Not everyone will be thrilled with this talent."

They made a game of picking locks until there wasn't a lock on Roger's farm or anyone else's farm, she couldn't pick.

Bernadette couldn't think of a reason why cupboards in this supply room would have specific locks on them. The people-doors were locked if the room wasn't in use. *Forget it and move on,* she thought. Then, other words popped into her head. *Coyote ugly. Throw the baby out with the bathwater.* Bernadette's hurt feelings split open, and a yawning cavern of bitterness and vindictiveness began to discharge its poison. She attempted to stifle the flow, aware that hatred and revenge did not lead to healing but could consume her. In that moment of intense fatigue, head pain, and embarrassment, she gave up. "Boys, you should have played nice," she whispered to herself.

Rifling through a junk drawer, there always was a messy drawer housing a collection of odds and ends in any supply room, she found two paper clips; all she needed. She then closed both people-doors to the supply room, making sure they were locked. The cupboards were higher up and the locks were placed so high that she couldn't reach them without a larger step stool. Making the situation more difficult, these upper cabinets were directly over the counter, so it was impossible to stand on the counter and gain access to the upper cabinets. Having learned from her cats that doors of any type provide support and mobility, she decided to follow the feline approach. Opening the lower cupboard doors, she tested their ability to support her weight. One door couldn't support full weight, but if she stood on two open doors, she figured that the hinges wouldn't be damaged.

Knowing that a contingency plan was needed should she be interrupted, she eyed the corner cupboard. Corner cupboards were always a mess and this one was no exception. Kneeling before the assortment of worn-out tablecloths, damaged carafes, old Thanksgiving displays, tangled extension cords, and a stack of ugly charger plates, she pulled a multitude of items out on the floor. Leaving the corner cabinet door open, she went back to the serious business of trying to balance on the cabinet doors.

Sitting hunched over on the counter, she positioned her feet on the open cabinet doors, then used another upper cupboard door to pull herself up. She had to do a type of ballet plié because she was bumping the ceiling with her head. Her balance was precarious, but she found her practice of yoga postures had more benefits than one might imagine, keeping her muscles steady on the unsteadfastly doors. The locks were designed to hinder illicit opening, yet Bernadette was able to pick them in two minutes thirty-five seconds. Getting down, she opened the doors and surveyed her reward: a computer, five recording VCR units stacked one on top of another, a leather bag, and gobs of wires.

Standing back up on the cabinet doors, she tried to trace all the wires to and from the computer. One wire ran to an odd rectangular unit embedded in the sound insulating foam lining the interior of the cupboard. Realization swamped her. It was a camera and the president's office was being filmed and recorded on tape or perhaps just specific times were being recorded.

Out of place with the electronic equipment, an old fashion briefcase sat in a corner, not the hard type but a soft style, looking like a saddle bag. Pulling the bag out, she got down and opened it. Papers inside were old and yellowed. Finding a quart-sized Ziplock bag with odd looking screw-like objects in it, she looked at the fat sharpie writing on it: *Just as you asked for. Try not to use these everywhere.*

A larger test tube, the glass also a yellow tint from age, held several strands of metal wire. The label on it, mostly faded and illegible, had two things she could discern: the elemental notation of NiTi and a number X-512747. She guessed the wire was nitinol, a high-tech type of memory wire, for which EwRM2 manufactured both the precursor and final products. Most everyone at EwRM2 joked that nitinol was back-engineered, the original material was taken from an unidentified flying object (UFO) wreckage. Closing the bag, she was able to jump and shove the bag back in the cupboard, when she stilled.

The doorknob to the supply room imperceptibly jiggled. Not having time to lock the cupboards, Bernadette softly closed them, pushed the makeshift ladder doors closed, then stepped quickly to the corner cupboard and started digging through the mound of stuff while on her hands and knees. One of the Human Resources (HR) staffers, Sandie, who was sitting in for the HR manager currently on a business trip, entered with a key in hand.

"Why was the door locked?" Sandie asked, while glancing around the room, her focus coming to rest on the cabinets with locks. She began moving toward them.

This was going to hurt, Bernadette knew it. While half in and half out of the cupboard, she tersely replied, "Because I have stuff all over the floor while I search for the coffee cups. What a bunch of junk in here." With that said, Bernadette stood up with astounding speed, smacking the back of her head on the upper inside edge of the cabinet. As the tender scalp split open, blood smartly started to flow, with speckles of it flying over the other white cabinet doors nearby.

Bernadette has used too much force, but then she didn't know how much force would be needed to split her scalp. The headache pain spiked. She clutched her stomach and said, "I think I am going to be sick."

"Oh, oh, oh! You hurt yourself. There is blood all over! We will have to do a full safety investigation on this!" Sandie screeched liked worn out brakes on a logging truck.

Bernadette replied, "Could you get me a folding chair from the conference room, so I can sit in here for a minute? And put some fresh napkins on the counter so I can stop the blood from flowing. There are disinfecting wipes and gloves in that middle drawer. I'll clean up in a minute. Please be quick."

Sadie rushed around doing Bernadette bidding. As Sadie went to leave, Bernadette asked, "Would you please lock the door? I don't want blood tracked all over. Safety first." Once secured in the room, Bernadette, used the chair to reach the locks, clicking them back in place. Cleaning up the room was only a five-minute job, and although the wound on her head stopped flowing, she spent another ten minutes cleaning up her blood matted hair.

Entering the meeting fifteen minutes after it had started, Bernadette asked two other women in the department to make more coffee and refill the carafes. She explained what had occurred to her head and stated that they would need to take over, as she was sitting down for the remainder of the meeting.

Once seated on the side of the room, she glanced around while the Director of Maintenance droned on about how his department enjoyed working with the Environmental Department. Bernadette almost spewed her coffee after hearing another of several honeyed falsehoods about the deep mutual respect shared by the departments; a lie so huge she wondered if the planet would change rotation in revolt. While peaking at the other environmental staff from the corner of her eyes, looking for signs that others were trying not to laugh at such a farce, her gaze crossed that of Matt Reed, Vice President of Operations. As his eyes locked with hers, his face contorted with the ugliness of hatred, an actively steaming hostility projected towards her. Then the look melted from his face as he turned back towards the rest of the group. Searching her memory for something that she had done to cause such animosity in the last month, she came up with only bewilderment. Her confusion began a slow conversion into an agonizing sputtering acid pit in the middle of her gut.

Over the last two years, she had the increasing feeling that a negative sucking vortex was gaining strength somewhere in the underbelly of EwRM2. Today was just more of the same, causing her to feel a bit more weary and a lot more leery. It had started out as such a good job; great coworkers, a super boss, and challenges she could overcome. After one single announcement about a new company president, everything began a steady slide towards the cliff. The new company president ushered in an age of abuse, oppression, and persecution.

Once a confident woman who got the job done, Bernadette now felt like an amoeba under the microscope with every possible mistake just another fake reason to march her toward the inhumane resources department firing squad. She viewed the most innocent of emails from upper management morphing into lurking snares and policy changes were deadly trapdoors with no escape; any trust she had felt on the job sublimated away.

The only thing she knew for certain was that she had better watch her back, diligently, continuously, and stealthily.

Just as the meeting wound to a close, Bernadette's name was called by Tim. Gesturing to her, she was forced to join him at the podium, where she found herself presented with a surprise award. As she worked open the seal on the envelope, she glanced up to find the President of EwRM2, Devlin Holcomb, sharing a snarky smirk with Matt Reed. Bernadette's irritation upped even further. She had been here early, got things working, and now they treated her like the backwoods relation with rotten teeth. Bernadette still working the envelope, stared at Devlin, who narrowed a vicious stare at her before returning his attention to Sandie, who happened to be next to him.

Sandie was the most insecure HR specialist; treating humans with about as much compassion was the wrecking yard dealing with a broken-down Pinto car, after the gas tank exploded. Bernadette could see though Devlin's polish too, for he resembled an overly ripe apple, pretty and polite on the outside but rancid on the inside. He normally would never lower himself to speak directly with an unattractive lower-on-the-ladder woman like Sadie. If he turned his attention to Sandie, it was so he could snub someone else or because he was engaging in diversion and subversion.

Bernadette began to wonder if the card might have some anthrax in it or even another fun deadly bug. As she pulled the card out of the envelope and began to flip it open, Sandie patted Devlin's hand. Bernadette noticed the slight flinched of Devlin and again, he made eye contact with Matt, their faces beaming with conspiratorial malice.

Sandie was looking so smug, because HR always looks smug knowing everyone's weaknesses, everyone's surprises, and everyone's secrets. But that was about to change drastically for Sandie. In the space of a second, but a moment that she would relive forever, she let out a short, smelly, loud fart.

The room went completely silent. Devlin, the man of no weakness and certainly no bodily function, looked positively repulsed. Anyone who works in the corporate world knows that upper management never, ever, has any bodily malfunction.

Bernadette quickly began thinking of how she could save Sandie. Oh, Sandie didn't deserve saving in Bernadette's mind. She had written up Bernadette for loudly arguing with one of her employees, a student employee who spent too much time in the women's restroom gossiping. And when Bernadette's staff weren't working, it meant more work for her, which as already a huge workload. However, in Sandie's favor today, Bernadette wasn't feeling tolerant of the boys and hostility was making inroads into Bernadette consciousness.

Doing her best to have compassion for Sandie, who would be ostracized for this public mistake by the powerful white boys' club, her fate to be sunken in a lion den of frustration with no promotion in site, Bernadette shifted her focus to the VPs, directors, and her boss to assess their reaction. Yep, no one was going to try to diffuse this situation. It remained painfully quiet in the conference room. The boys didn't play nice, instead, they played together. Bernadette wondered why she ever played nice with them. These boys were going to fry her regardless of what she did. It was just a matter of time. Their unexplained hatred was palatable today.

She caught Devlin's eye, smiled, and gave it her best shot to save Sandie with the added benefit of throwing a crowbar into the boys' smoothly running timing belt. Speaking clearly into the microphone at the podium, Bernadette sweetly asked Devlin, "Devlin, there are so many reasons why being a vegetarian is a good thing. Did you eat one of those chili burgers at the Blue Ox Tavern yesterday?"

An anxiety broke out over the room. People suddenly found lint on their pant legs and those pesky dryer pills on their holiday cotton sweaters.

Devlin's eyes and mouth contorted with rage as he zoomed in on Bernadette. She stood her ground. With a slight tipping up of her nose, she looked at him as nothing more than an annoying fly at a summer picnic. Tim turned his back to Bernadette, eyeing the exit. Then, just in a moment, like a nice bleach job at the salon, Devlin's face returned to that of an attractive white man, with no sign of anger.

Devlin gave an insincere laugh and in a booming voice said. "I may have the digestive system of a cow, but at least I don't have the face of one. Bernadette. Why don't we focus on you and your wonderful achievements?"

She understood that punctuation. Their eyes met of unspoken challenges. She let her gaze bore into him. It wasn't until the catering company delivering the brunch accidentally dropped a clattering spoon that the forty-five second game of chicken slammed to a stop.

Bernadette nodded her head toward Devlin. Not to concede his win of put downs, but to acknowledge she was fully prepared to fight and fight she would. For you see, Bernadette had come to believe God enjoyed peace, but never promoted that one must be a doormat. Today, she didn't know how to be a completely evolved spiritual being, but she did know that she wasn't expected to be weakling on spiritual path.

She started to read the cursive writing on the award announcement, maintaining a pleasing countenance at all times.

"Congratulations on your outstanding performance this past year. As a show of our appreciation, East-West Refined Metals Manufacturing is providing you a with an all-expense paid trip to the World Environmental Waste Management Conference in British Columbia (BC)."

Bernadette smiled at everyone and in her most pleasing deep voice said, "Thank you so much for such a wonderful gift. BC sounds like a wonderful place to study the world of hazardous waste. Thank you again for having confidence in my abilities. It is a joy to work with all of you. Now let's serve up the food before it goes cold."

Everyone jumped up for the brunch. Bernadette spent most of her time looking busy in the supply room, away from management, while everyone was eating.

At one point, Tim entered the supply room. He looked very uncomfortable and more than a little disappointed. "Bernadette, there is more to your BC trip." He handed her a small piece of paper that would have fit inside the card and a larger manila envelope. "This is the information about the rest of the trip, but we didn't want others to know unless you wanted to tell them. The idea got circulating in upper management as a way to say thank you for all your hard work with EPA." Tim's crow's feet were creased with dissatisfaction, censure to the rudeness Bernadette displayed earlier. Most others would have muttered an apology under the boss's scrutiny, or a resignation, but Bernadette was not cowing down today.

Bernadette looked sternly at Tim under an arched right eyebrow, depicting her volume of displeasure. "Look, I got here before the crack of dawn to deal with a broken computer that could have been addressed yesterday. I picked up everyone's stinkin' donuts even though I had a massive headache, and not one person said thank you to me. Although it isn't your concern, Devlin and Matt gave me the evil eye today for I don't know what reason. I work hard, I do my job and more. But I refuse to be subjected to unwarranted hostility. Don't ask me to be spineless Tim, because I deserve more respect than that. I'm going back to my office."

Once back at her desk, she read the additional information about the trip to come.

In addition to the environmental conference, we have booked you a three-day and four-night complimentary ski trip in British Columbia. You will be staying in Vancouver for the conference and the Whistler Resort Cabins for the ski trip. You can enjoy downhill skiing at any skill level. The resort also offers snow shoeing, skijoring and much more. Your cabin comes with a fireplace and kitchenette. The enclosed packet provides you with all the details regarding the accommodations and vouchers for skiing.

Bernadette clutched her head in both hands, pulling on her massive hair, a method of massaging her scalp, harshly. This would be the trip from hell for two reasons.

First, she hated to fly and she would have to fly to Vancouver, BC, in winter! She could already envision the plane skidding off the runway as icicles hung from its wings.

Second, and worse, she couldn't ski to save her life. Many of her skiing memories just didn't match pictures in magazines. Her first ski experience, which set the tone for every trip thereafter, involved a pair of ski pants with an unimpressive zipper that decided to unravel at the top of the slope, and there just wasn't a way to get down the mountain hiding those pink panties. It was windy, snowy cold and tying her jacket around her waist wasn't an option given the temperature that day. She had been young, and sweet, and mortified. This was before a wardrobe malfunction was something to laugh off. The remainder of the day was spent in the lodge, confident that everyone was laughing at her.

It was her third ski trip that she learned the art of skiing on her back. It was an icy day and about halfway down the hill a ski tip hooked a huge ice block. She was catapulted up in the air, had flipped over her skis and landed on her back. Then to her dismay, she kept sliding at a dizzy pace down the mountain with her skis held over her head. Finally, she flew over a bank and landed on a trail made by a snow groomer. The air had been knocked out of her as she landed with a thud. She had slid so far on her back, it was then she realized how important it was to keep the skis on because she didn't want to have to walk back up the mountain to get them. She could honestly say that her skill at this inverted skiing position had improved with each ski trip.

If this ski trip was a company gift because they appreciated her work, she hated to think of the company gift Devlin would give her after he had time to think on her "fart" comment.

Later that afternoon, when the gossip regarding Bernadette's fight with Devlin had been told in every corner of the facility, James Bartledge, Director of Legal Counsel, slipped into Devlin's office. Closing the door behind him, he sat down, both of them knowing what the conversation would be about.

James looked at Devlin seriously and said, "Well, I don't think we will be laying off or firing Bernadette anytime soon. Not that we want to, but with that comment today..."

Devlin interrupted, "Why not? It is an *at will* state. We don't have to give any reason for her termination."

James continued, "I probably don't need to remind you of the enforcement action which is going on right now. Bernadette knows the rules of chemistry and can keep tabs on EPA. If we fire her, EPA will think it is because we are doing something seriously illegal. It will only increase the heat on the issue.

"And, after your comment today, the cow face comment, if you fire her then you can expect serious legal action. Bernadette will be laughing all the way to the bank while you are busy packing your stuff to leave town."

Devlin tried to back track. "I was up most of the night dealing with my sick mother-in-law. That woman is so bitter, and gets my wife so upset. I just wasn't myself today. I don't know when I have been so rude to an employee but then she wasn't particularly nice to me."

James, a very good lawyer, and good judge of people because of his practice prior to this corporate job, knew that Devlin was lying. He had been in the president's office when Devlin had called Bernadette coyote ugly. For some reason, Devlin held a great deal of animosity toward Bernadette. Unfortunately for Devlin, the arm of legal counsel had an incredibly long reach in the company. Devlin was trying to band-aid this miss step so he wouldn't have any bumps in the road to other corporate jobs further up the ladder.

"Well, I am sorry to hear about your mother-in-law. Whatever is causing the active dislike between you and Bernadette needs to remain unspoken. Bernadette is many things, but dumb she is not. For some reason, perhaps one you understand, she struck out at you, and it was a calculate decision she made. Not a random act. You keep your head low around her from here on out. Remember, she understands EPA weaknesses right now and we need that."

After James left the room, Devlin sat back with a smile on his face. He had been working to address the problem Bernadette presented; her understanding of the company created a risk. He sighed, relieved that a solution was close at hand.

When Bernadette got home, she ran in the bathroom, throwing up the toilet lid and seat, just before her stomach decided that regurgitation was the best solution for all the acidic contents churning there. The stress of the job wasn't going to eat a hole in her stomach, it was going to excavate her body cavity, if she wasn't careful.

Chapter 17
Gift Holiday with Bonus Stitches

(January 14-15, 1999)

Several weeks later, Bernadette found herself checking into Whistler Resort. She was surprised when the receptionist said, "The concierge will come by your cabin in thirty minutes with the extra items delivered for you yesterday?"

"I didn't send any extra items in advance," Bernadette explained.

"They are addressed to you, and I have no knowledge who sent them." The receptionist kept typing, making it clear he had no interest in the items or Bernadette's thoughts on the matter.

While Bernadette explored cabin 119, the concierge arrived with a medium sized moving box. Bernadette tipped him, then began opening the mystery box, hoping there would be a note inside. There was a note, *Happy Belated Birthday*. The box was filled with very high-end ski gear: jacket, pants, an odd-looking type of pack, gloves, several hats, turtlenecks, and long underwear. The items were very tastefully selected, fitting her very well. She knew that nobody at EwRM2 would never buy such items, and none of her friends could afford this, so that meant Carney knew of her trip and had selected these. It was standard for him to not sign a card or note.

Unfortunately, peering beyond the fancy accommodations and clothes, the trip still felt wrong. She had been convinced this trip was another opportunity for EwRM2 management to create a new Bernadette, easily tortured, voodoo doll; one sitting in a tin can 35,000 feet up in the air. She wondered what was wrong with her to think such negative thoughts. Here she was laying on an expensive bed, in a warm cabin with a spicy sent, and the outside was a marvelous winter wonderland; a deep sound absorbing snow had dumped on the mountain within the last week, hushing the harshness of man. The conference had been interesting: experts who understood hazardous waste regulations disclosed ways to untwist the convoluted, the newest treatment methods were explained, and all the trawling techniques regulatory agencies used on unwary industries who ventured in the waste arena were reviewed.

Regardless of her relaxing position, the muscles in her neck and shoulders were contracted, quiet like suspension bridge cables under the winds of adversity. The rigidity wound down the back of her ribs as if someone welded cool steel posts to her shoulder blades and hips. She wished a massage was all she needed, but usually a massage only served to cause back problems, so they weren't a consideration.

 Going through her purse to find her cell phone, she came across the card from work, which included vouchers for ski rental and the specific lift she could use. Again, she thought, *perhaps a day of reading instead of skiing would be better?* But then, if Carney bought her all these clothes, she felt compelled to use them.

Bernadette woke with worry and apprehension on her mind. Grabbing a cup of coffee, she set about changing her mental state with firm mental commitments: *Nope. No Way. I refuse to live my life in fear. Period. Action, best to take action.*

Grabbing the lift ticket, Bernadette compared the lift ticket numbers with the map on the wall, which showed all the lifts and runs on Whistler and Blackcomb. The lift ticket was for the east side of Blackcomb, which looked difficult to Bernadette because it wasn't labelled beginner. Blowing out a breath, Bernadette stood for some time, pondering. Could she even get down Ridge Runner or Crystal Road runs? It was a legitimate question. Picking up the phone, she called the ski resort and talked with them about the runs on Blackcomb. They assured her that there were moderate ski areas there. However, they mentioned that the east side isn't always open if the number of patrons were below a threshold, which it could be the situation on this Wednesday.

As Bernadette thought about the east side of the mountain, she decided to add a few things to the pack. The pack sent to her was unique, as it wasn't a backpack, but rather a front-pack. It would work well under her jacket, as she could get into it without taking off her coat. The pack could expand out, much like a full backpack, or collapse down with a zipper that went all around it, making it lay very flat on a person's chest and stomach. She added items that she wanted to have when out in the snow for a day: hankie, chapstick, a small bottle of vodka from the bar in the cabin (only extreme emergencies), an extra pair of gloves, extra hat, and her wallet. Being somewhat prepared, helped Bernadette to feel more relaxed. It was a natural outcome of spending too much time alone; being resourceful could get her out of a jam when no one else was there. She felt that too much of the American population behaved as if someone, or some government person, would always be there to save them. Bernadette didn't believe it. A time would come when resourcefulness would be the only method to achieve a life of basic needs met.

Bernadette got dressed and headed out the door, determined to have a beautiful day.

As Bernadette approached the ski lift, she noted one guy sitting in the hut at the lift and the chairs weren't running. Things were looking up. She was hoping that nothing was running so she would have a good excuse to go back to the hotel room without any guilt. She almost turned around without talking to the operator, but he looked at her, stood up, and waved her to the lift, but he didn't look very happy about it.

"Really slow morning, uh? Are you even running today? Where is everyone?" Bernadette tried to be polite and happy regardless of his puckered face. The guy said nothing, just held out his hand. Bernadette assume he wanted the lift ticket, so unzipping her coat, she grabbed it out of the front-pack. With her cold fingers, she handed it off.

Mumbling, the man fixed the ticket and attached it to her jacket zipper tab. He said, "Rich, little, society babes are all the same."

"Look, I don't need to ski this run. In fact, I would rather ski an easier run, and I am not a rich little society babe." Bernadette was thrown off by his nasty mood.

Slowly, the man looked up, closely noting the fancy ski pants, jacket, hat, and gloves. "Right. Here is your ticket. Here is the chair. Now get out of my face."

Again, Bernadette had the feeling it might be better to turn around a ski away. Everything felt wrong, but then getting on an airplane didn't feel good either. Ignoring the jerk and taking a deep breath, Bernadette moved toward the chair. Bernadette managed to get on the chair without a mishap, but then the lift wasn't running until after she sat down. She reflected that when a person is really terrible at something, you have to look for the positive wherever you can find it. The chair took off with a jerk, quickly speeding up, giving her that expansive feeling of partial flying. It was a cold ride up the mountain with foggy patches below and clouds above, the minor gusts of wind mildly rocking the chair left her feeling very alone.

When she saw the upper lift station, she started to scoot forward on the chair. There was no attendant at this lift station, which was more than odd, it was dangerous. Bernadette felt something was very wrong because the attendant at this end of the lift had to stop the chairs if someone ended up dangling from a chair instead of getting off of it. It was obvious to Bernadette that getting off the chair was a priority, even if it meant falling out of the thing. She thought for a minute about staying on it and riding it back down to the start. But what if the power was stopped and she was left to freeze stranded on a chair? With no one else on the lift she wasn't going to risk that option.

When her ski tips touched the snow, poles in one hand, she pushed off the chair with the other hand and stood long enough to get away from the chair. The next instant she was falling down, sliding on her side. The first fifty feet from the top of the chair exit had not been groomed; it was frozen, crusted with ice. Once Bernadette slid into some powder, she slowed and was able to push herself back up with her poles.

Bernadette reviewed the map of runs posted on a huge plywood board, color coordinated to show which runs were more difficult, noting which she could take, while getting snow out of her scarf and goggles. She skied along a ridge to the east for about fifty yards. Stopping to enjoy the fresh air and fortify her resolve, she noted that the air was undisturbed in this small pocket, somehow sheltered by a ridge behind her.

She felt the presence of others before she saw them skiing toward her. The three tall, fit men wearing tight ski pants and maneuvering the snow gracefully looked to belong in a magazine photo shoot with one notable exception, they all had on ski masks. She despised people who could look good in skintight pants and could ski well. The lead guy, who was actually the shortest one of the three, standing at probably five feet and ten inches, brought the group to a halt when they were only twenty-five feet away.

"You here all by yourself little lady?" he called out to her.

Bernadette's adrenal system began flooding her body with adrenaline even before one of the men pulled out a 9mm pistol and its magazine, neatly sliding the magazine into the gun with a smart sounding snap. Another took a rifle scabbard off his back and set the shoulder stock down, holding the narrow end with an eerie determination.

Bernadette frowned, squinted, at the unreality developing before her. A disorientation temporarily confused her ability to adequately respond. *Was there hunting allowed up here?* she wondered.

Then one of the guys answer for her. He said, "Too bad you came up here all by yourself today, huh?"

Bernadette looked down at the front of her jacket and the nice ski pants. She realized she had made a serious miscalculation. The clothes weren't from Carney. This was someone else's ploy to get her up on this mountain. That was the problem with having too many secrets. It was difficult to be sure who was doing what.

She had doubts about this trip and now she saw the truth, the trick and the treachery. If she ever got home, someone was going to pay. Bernadette looked heavenward, breathed in deeply, and asked God and her loving spiritual Guru for a miracle, for help, for guidance.

As fast as the prayer was thought, the wind began whipping around Bernadette's face. She was surprised by what should have been a bitter, biting sting along the neckline of her ski jacket, for the wind felt more like a whisper, a cooling relief to the emotions bubbling within her. Even the men, accustomed to the quickly changing weather on a ski slope, noted how the conditions went from calm to a rough, powerful wind in an instant, several of them making sure that the extra snaps on their jackets were fastened.

Comprehension flooded her and she knew this fact instantaneously. Anytime you are alone, and a bunch of guys ask if you are alone, it is time to muster all the bravado you cultivated in your life, and then add a mega amount to it. Fear was half of the enemy. If Bernadette was to become deathly afraid, then she couldn't think properly, she would fail to look like a serious obstacle, she would fail to fight and fight dirty if demanded. Although not a perfect alternative, probably not a highly spiritual alternative, Bernadette's current remedy was to get mad, once again. Really mad. Redhead mad. It would serve as a shield to keep the opposition guessing. Based on her years of experience alone, she felt that there is always a chance to throw negative intent off balance and therefore, fight you must.

Bernadette put her fury to the fore and did her best to take on a wrathful stance; holding her ski poles in one hand, she crossed her arms, put her skis shoulder width apart and settled into a good old "**A**" stance. **A** stance means *don't mess with me* in the world of body language.

Bernadette didn't say anything. She just watched the men, watched the snow blowing off the tree limbs. She thought about what was behind her and the image of the downhill runs on the board, where she might go that they wouldn't want to follow her. But that wouldn't happen, and she knew it. They were prepared and trained skiers and she was an uncoordinated woman in fancy ski clothes which amounted to very little at this moment.

In this game of life, she did have several, all pervading powerful shields: she was a daughter of Anu, she was a devotee of a loving spiritual master, and she had sincere relationship with God. She would still have to do the work, using her will and energy, but asking for outcomes that were for a higher good and that would conquer evil, was a true and just prayer. Pray she did.

"Want to play a game with us?" the tallest man called while closing the distance to Bernadette. "We have a great snow bunny game you might enjoy."

Bernadette detested the man as his words oozed sarcasm, but she would have disliked him under even casual circumstances. Most of his face was covered by his ski mask, but his eyes held all the information she needed. They were cold, not like the snow, but like a nefarious purpose. The corners of his mouth had deep creases caused by years of foul thoughts Looking at him, she nicknamed him Mr. Sociopath.

Bernadette still didn't say a word. She marveled at the resemblance between the wind and her heart; as the wind spooled more furiously around her, her heart pounded ever more strongly, like the beat of a thousand migrating geese.

Mr. Sociopath shrugged and continued, yelling louder as the wind whipped up more snow and ice. "Here's the deal, so listen closely."

Another guy came forward. Her attention was drawn to his trapper hat, which looked to be lined with real beaver fur. Bernadette called him Mr. Trapper. He clenched a seabag with draw-cord top, which obviously confined something alive, for the bag moved as if a fighter was punching to get out. Mr. Trapper chimed in, "We have a young bobcat in this bag. They are magnificent at running in the snow. You can help us chase it, and you will have to kill it. Then you get to go back to your warm little cabin." He came closer with the squirming bag, "It is just a baby, so it shouldn't be too hard to kill. Or the bobcat lives, returning back to its mountain home and we chase you for some fun. Now, I don't think we have to tell you what we will do when we catch you."

Bernadette's frustration soared and an inferno built inside her breast. She was roaring mad. She knew this was a ploy of someone at EwRM2. She thought about the times she had helped animals caught in some predicament at the facility: the goose in the oil sump, skunk in the spill pit, the hawk in the wastewater sump, the goslings next to the new construction, and the pigeons inhumanely left in a trap on top of a hot building. Staff had seen her sensitivity to an animal's suffering, and they ridiculed her at those times. She understood what this was about: someone wanted to exploit her gentle nature, punish her for caring, and make her suffer for loving those without a human voice. It was the only place she ever worked where being a degenerate immoral person was considered a good thing. Looking at Mr. Trapper, she mentally shredded him, for she would not lose, not now.

Bernadette's mind was scouting a plan. She knew, finding a way to release the bobcat and letting it get away wasn't a positive solution because bobcats are terrible at running in the snow. It wouldn't get far and they would just shoot it. She needed some time to formalize a plan and she needed some miracles. Her initial strategy was to engage them in arguments and delay action until she had a solid plan.

"Let's see this bobcat. I am not sure you boys know what a bobcat is. Maybe it is just a house cat." Bernadette kept drawing on her reserve of anger. If she got afraid, her voice would shake, and they would know, sense, her weakness. All would be lost then, her exposure of fear would embolden them,

She unzipped her jacket, never letting her eyes leave Mr. Sociopath. As she started to unzip the backpack, he sneered and with an annoyed voice barked, "If you are getting out a weapon little girl, don't even think about it."

She made a puff sound, loud enough to carry to all of them. "Oh right, I would have a weapon. Gee, did I bring it on the plane? Or maybe I just purchased a gun here in Canada so I can try to get it home, little boy." Disdain was dripping from her voice. "Look, I have cash. How about I buy the cat." As Bernadette talked, she started to put items from inside the front-pack and place them in her various zipper pockets on her jacket. She held up some of the cash, which fluttered madly on steady gusts. "I have about three hundred dollars on me. I can get more."

"Don't waste your breath." Mr. Trapper came closer to Bernadette, threw the sack on the snow, held it down the opening with a ski while he untied the cord. Once the cord was untied, he moved his ski, then jerked on a leash that was coming out the top opening. A confused and very young bobcat ejected from the bag, spinning and tumbling wildly as it attempted to outmaneuver the leash attached to a harness, a harness representing death. Bernadette was in awe, having never been so close to a bobcat. The fur was more grey than tan, covered mostly with black spots, except on its legs and down its back, there were black lines. Even when fearful, its face showed intelligence. Its brilliant hazel eyes and oversized ears zeroed in on Bernadette for a scant moment while behind it, the 9mm lined up with its innocence.

Mr. Trapper continued to elaborate on the game. "What we are going to do is put it on this very long bungie cord. Once you catch the cat, you get to mutilate it a little bit, then you let it go, and chase it again. You, my dear will kill it, giving it a painful death. Then we let you go. Or, if you don't want to hurt the bobcat, we just chase you." Holding up the bobcat by the harness, he pulled out a switch blade and swiftly cut the cat's right ear, which lead to hissing, screaming, twisting and turning.

Bernadette's gut was twisting like the cat. The game was a lie, and she knew it. They would not let her ski, walk, or run away from them. This animal would suffer all because someone was threatened by her, threatened by what she knew. Someone at work was sick. The stupid job! This game was designed to break her spirit, to show her that everyone will ultimately harm an animal to save themselves.

She let some of the money slip from her hands and it scattered in the wind. "Oh no." She acted like she was going to ski forward, an attempt to pick up the money. All the time she watched the cat on the leash.

Mr. Trapper signaled the other two men to help pick up the money. Putting the cat back in the seabag, he secured the cord and left it on the snow. The men began collecting the money fluttering haphazardly around. He warned Bernadette, "Don't try to get too far honey. It won't work."

"Ok, fine, You guys pick up the money. You're the good skiers anyways. Just don't steal any." Bernadette knew this group would not want American $20s fluttering about the mountain, as it would lead to more questions. It was precious time for her, as her plan was solidified. She needed to risk escape now, for her window of opportunity was limited. They would return to refocus on her.

Bernadette turned around, placed her pole tips in the snow and pushed herself back, in a casual stretch posture, toward the cat struggling in the seabag. Once at the seabag, she unzipped her front-pack so it expanded to it maximum width. Quickly, untying the cord, she pulled the cat out by the leash, grabbed it by the scruff of its neck, shoved its rear end into the bottom of the front pack, leaving just its head out and secured the zipper around the cat. She zipped up her jacket, which held the cat tight to her chest. For the briefest of seconds, their eyes met, Bernadette's angry and afraid, the bobcat's wild and afraid.

She worried that the cat would climb out of her makeshift pouch, but it only turned its head from side to side and kept its claws firmly anchored into the front-pack and the layers of clothing Bernadette had on, the snugness of the jacket most likely giving it a sense of security. Bernadette mentally pleaded that the bobcat did not bite her jaw or face.

Bernadette believed that most animals have a sense of who will hurt them and who will be kind to them. Unfortunately, the fear of humans can become overwhelming when there is a history of violence by humans toward a species; then the animals only know terror around people. She wasn't naive about the kitten's mistrust, but she hoped that it would respond to her positive thoughts.

The instant she pushed off to the east, Mr. Trapper looked up and sounded the alarm, only to have the words smothered by a ferocious gust, giving her a few more seconds to get ahead of them.

Mentally overwrought, Bernadette relied on her spiritual training and what she had read over the years to corral her run away emotions. *Trust. Trust in Anu, Master, God. Do your best and see success.* She brought the vibrations of the words into her being, causing fear to bring up the rear in the jostling emotional stew.

Recreating in her mind, the mountain layout as shown on the board by the lift, Bernadette scrambled to decide if she should immediately head down into the trees, the direction where she would eventually intersect three runs or continue further east on the ridge line which eventually would lead to a novice run. Further east from the novice run was an expanse of ungroomed snow, lots of trees, a small glacier, and areas of avalanche risk.

She glanced back. Mr. Trapper was right behind her, the other two weren't too far behind him. Looking down at the bobcat, she found his head tucked to the side, as if braced and ready. Bernadette would never be able to out ski these guys, solidifying the knowledge that a novice run was of no advantage. She was already slipping and sliding on the crusty ice just below a thin layer of snow. Pointing her skis down the hill, she chose to enter the denser stand of trees.

Navigating the stand of trees was challenging for Bernadette. Depressions in the snow at the base of the trees, weather stout tree trunks, and erratically developed tree boughs, all had to be avoided. The sharp turns she had to make were causing her to lose her invaluable lead. At five hundred feet into the fir stand, where the harsh winter wind lost some of its bluster, the snow bonnets on each fir bough were increasingly plump. At six hundred feet, Mr. Trapper had caught up with Bernadette and was coming along side of her. Bernadette dodged right as he grabbed for her coat. Slipping wildly on a patch of ice, she knew "it" was about to happen. She fought the feeling initially, then gave into the momentum. She wondered if perhaps she had spent all her embarrassing and awkward skiing moments preparing for this one hugely important moment. She threw herself into the fall, landing on her back, with the skis still on and up above her. She slid wildly towards a huge grand fir, its lower bent boughs settled close to the snow and ice, obscuring the view beyond. She heard Mr. Trapper laugh as he followed her on a huge ice patch, its solid, even surface protected from the meager winter sun by the tree stand. Bernadette's world spun. With every 360-degree revolution she had glimpses of Mr. Trapper doubled over with uncontrollable laughter. The panic in her was elevating and she felt deprived of air, which fueled more panic.

His laughter and resulting inattentiveness toward the downhill conditions would cost him the necessary time needed to ski off the ice and away from the huge bows. Bernadette heard him curse, as he dug the ski edges in to direct himself around the tree. While Bernadette careened, spinning and sliding, closer to the boughs, Mr. Trapper's ski edges failed to dig in causing him to slide sideways, directly following Bernadette. Bernadette hugged the skis and the cat to her, the snow finding its way into the neck of her jacket and under her hood. She saw the heavy bough, a few inches above the snow, looming just ahead and with a last-ditch effort, she threw out her left arm and used her hand and elbow to create friction with the ice. With the right amount of friction, she pulled herself around so her ski tips, now facing down the hill, could be guided over the bough first.

The first few inches of the tips went over the top of the heavy bough.

With a reverberating boom, her skis crashed into the fir bow just as Bernadette pushed hard off them. The bough, suddenly overcoming the heavy snow constraints which had kept it immobile, flung her in the air as it shed the weight of snow and ice, snapping back to its comfortable position. Bernadette half catapulted over the bough and half skied over it, the force sending her sailing through and past several more snow laden boughs, where she finally came slamming down on her side. The momentum carried her past a few more trees and down a bank to a maintenance trail. The last thing she heard from Mr. Trapper was the bough whiplashing back toward him, the crunch of cartilage and bone, a scream of pain, and a huge *wompf,* as snow and ice from higher up, felled the skier. The annoyance had been trounced.

In one smooth motion, she pulled her knees to her chest, planted her poles in the snow, pushed her torso up on top of the skis, and off she went. Following the trail west for several hundred yards, she found herself coming out of the trees onto a mogul ski run. Wanting to get down the mountain and closer to the other operating lifts, she would have to cross the highly exposed area. Sneaking a peak at the kitten, she found him with his head up, sniffing alertly.

Bernadette pushed off with her poles, skiing both down the hill and to the west. In minutes, she was going too fast for her ability. The moguls were serving as mini ski jumps. She was becoming increasingly conscious of the pain on her stomach, a result of the bobcat's claws sinking past her sweater and turtleneck while bouncing over moguls. She thought about ditching the cat and coming back for it after she spoke to the authorities, if there was an after. It sounded like a poor plan. If she tied it to a tree and she died, it might die from exposure before it was found. If she let it loose, she would never find it again and it would probably starve and die, or freeze and die. Truth was, if she ever got off the mountain, she was never coming back, that was for certain.

The second skier, Mr. Sociopath, had gotten not only ahead of her, but was above her. She was so intent on surviving the moguls that she didn't see him until he was next to her, blocking her path to the west. She didn't have time to figure out what to do; she had to turn abruptly. Her high center of gravity caused her to flip on her side and begin another slip-n-slide.

Mr. Sociopath was almost on top of her, attempting to stab her with his poles. Wildly flailing her skis in all directions, a defensive measure to keep the poles away from her, she accidentally caught the tip of her ski in his crotch. Once she found the vulnerable spot, Bernadette repeatedly jammed the ski up in the sensitive area, causing excessive pain on her ankle and knee because of the odd angle, but more importantly, causing the man to scream and fall back into the snow. They both slid a hundred more feet before Bernadette was able to use her poles and edges of her skis like mini snowplows, stopping her uncontrolled decent. Mr. Sociopath, rolled up in pain, bumped and bounced over the moguls. His skis, which had released from the boots, were independent toboggans wildly flying down the hill. Pushing back up on her skis, Bernadette aimed for the next group of trees.

The next stand of fir trees was much harder to transverse, for the support that ice had offered before was absent here. In its place was just fluffy, powdery snow. Lacking a skillful alternative, Bernadette was forced into an excruciating march, for her skis would sink down deeply into the snow, and she had to use her poles to push along, even grabbing onto branches to help pull her forward. An additional irritation, she had been struggling with the bobcat for the last five minutes; it continually tried to crawl out of the backpack while Bernadette kept trying to stuff it back in.

The bobcat let out an ear piecing scream, followed by Bernadette's scream, as gloved hands grabbed her jacket on the right shoulder and the small of her back. It was the last criminal. She hadn't heard him approach during all her exertion and panic and ungraceful thrashing about in the trees.

What happened next, was beyond Bernadette's imagination. The bobcat attacked the man's hand with the furry and ferociousness of a full-grown tiger. Launching partially out of the backpack, it used beautifully formed paws and claws to slice through the Gore-Tex fabric and insulation, biting down on the exposed flesh. There wasn't much Bernadette could do, for she had a hand holding her still and a bobcat's rump wiggling and squirming about on her chest. She heard crunching of ligaments and bone followed by a deep guttural curse, ending with a scream. The hands immediately released her. Skiing a few more feet, she stuffed the cat back in the pack. Profanity assaulted her ears. Looking back, she saw the criminal kneeling in the snow, bent at the waist, holding his hand in agony. Bright red blood was quickly coloring the area.

Bernadette glanced down at the kitten. It's cute head innocently peaked out. She snugged up the backpack zippers and zipped her jacket back up.

"Amazing. Aren't you the little helper today." Stroking its head, it shied away from Bernadette's hand and hissed. "Fine. Just fine. Don't get all pissy with me," she said.

"You..." the words of the criminal were lost to the wind and snow. Bernadette continued on her slow trek through the trees.

Almost two hours later, Bernadette had made it down the mountain. She was a wreck. Pain had made the decent an out-of-body experience. Circumventing the village, she headed back to her cabin through the woods, which took longer, but was necessary with a bobcat in her jacket.

Bernadette, cold, exhausted, and in shock, tied the kitten to the dining table leg, stripped and headed for the shower. As long as she kept the water to her back, the scratches on her chest and stomach weren't so dreadfully painful. Finally warm, she ate, drank some alcohol to deaden her pain, and waited for dusk to set in while flipping through the phone book, seeking to find a clinic which was privately owned and open during evening hours.

As darkness set in and with the bobcat in the pack again, she set out to find a security car or a police car. She needed it unlocked and unoccupied. She began by waiting in an alley near the local donut shop. It took another hour and 45 minutes to find the perfect police car, get the kitten in it, tie it to a seat belt, and slink away undetected into the darkness. She was careful to eliminate her tracks in the snow.

To accomplish her last errand for the night, Bernadette set out to Dr. Bensen's small office, open two days a week until 8:00 p.m. Bernadette was thankful that for some reason, this doctor saw a need in society and took it upon himself to stay late. She figured he was probably not frequented by the uppity resort class but here for the worker bees. Arriving just fifteen minutes before closing had advantages and disadvantages. There wasn't another patient in the office at that time, however the beautiful blonde nurse in the office obviously wanted to go home.

The minute Bernadette spoke, the blonde went from politely inquisitive to dumb blonde in a flash. She began to explain that she hadn't ever checked in an American patient before and suggested Bernadette go to the urgent care across town or perhaps a hospital.

Looking at the nurse's name tag, Bernadette took a deep breath. "Amber, I am sorry I am here so late. The dumb blonde thing was a nice try. However, you do know how to check me in, and I really need some help right now. I am barely holding it together."

Desperate and exasperated, Bernadette took off her coat, lifted her shirt exposing her stomach, "What do you think?"

Amber gulped; their eyes met with a look of instant camaraderie. Running to the side door, she escorted Bernadette into a room.

A guarded expression met Bernadette as she shook hands with Dr. Bensen, another good-looking blonde person. After Bernadette gingerly laid down on the table with a moan of pain, the doctor lifted the gown aside. Dr.

Bensen swallowed, glanced from Bernadette to Amber, and then returned to frowning a Bernadette's stomach.

Dr. Bensen said, "Ms. Engstrom, we can patch this up. Your chest isn't too bad, but your stomach will never look the same. May I enquire as to how this happened? We are required by law to report all injuries due to possible dangerous or diseased animals."

"Accident. Window accident." Bernadette turned her head, giving a pleading look to Amber. "Terrible window accident."

A woman of compassion, especially for any woman who suffered an injury that will result in permanent disfigurement, Amber came to the rescue, "Definitely looks like a French door accident to me."

"French doors are not windows, Amber, but then you already knew that." Dr. Bensen smiled at her.

Really trying to perceive who Bernadette was, Dr. Bensen replace the gown over her stomach, then looking at Bernadette in the eyes he evaluated. He didn't get any sense of malicious intent, and her willingness to meet his eyes told him that lying for some nefarious purpose wasn't a part of her. Her eyes held something deeper, kinder, maybe more ancient. "How did this come about?" he asked.

Understanding the question to mean, what series of events lead to this injury, Bernadette answered honestly. "I believe in truthfulness and goodness. I think that because I won't accept or tolerate things of an evil or unfair nature, I have become unpopular." Then she amended, "Unpopular with windows."

Firing off some rapid instructions, the doctor moved toward the door, where he gave his most trusted nurse an understood look. Bernadette stood up, snatched her purse, pulling out a wad of cash, and placed it in Dr. Bensen's hand. "Thank you for your help. It really has been a bad day."

He never looked at the cash, handing it back to Bernadette. He thought of the Hippocratic Oath he had taken years ago, its intent and essence so often manipulated and mutilated in the modern world. His modest practice allowed him to follow the oath according to its dictates and not the dictates of an insurance or drug company. "Ms. Engstrom, I will be back in five minutes and we will get this thoroughly cleaned. I will stitch up the scratches, ah, the cuts, that can't heal on their own. We will have you patched up. Your stomach will never look the same, even after it is healed and the swelling has all gone away. I am sorry to tell you that."

"No one sees my stomach but me, so it doesn't matter. Whatever you can do Dr. Bensen, will be much appreciated." Laying back down on the table, Bernadette smiled at them.

Dr. Bensen reflected how every five years or so, he would meet a patient who was so different he had to wonder about the origin of the species.

After leaving the room, the doctor stepped beside Amber, removing the page from the chart, then placing it in the shredder below the counter, he simply stated, "I just get so frustrated when we lose records on patients, don't you?"

Amber cocked her head to the side, looking at the Bernadette's patient screen she hit the delete key. "Now which key is the return button?" she asked, expecting no answer.

It was thirty-six stitches later and some strong antibiotics, plus pain medications, when Bernadette headed back to her room. She had been concerned about how she would get medication, but the antibiotics and the pain medications were samples Dr. Bensen had. Dr. Bensen corrected a terrible situation in her life, making it a manageable situation. She appreciated his willingness, to the fullest extent.

Laying in her cabin bed, drowsy from the pain meds, Bernadette thought about tomorrow. Would she see the authorities? She had looked at the problem from every angle. If the three men who tried to kill her were arrested, what good was that? She analyzed the issues once again.

- She knew secrets about EwRM2, but none of them were a crime, or could be related to a crime, yet. The hidden camera was a perfect example. The camera and NiTi wire indicated there were secrets, but it wouldn't get someone arrested. It would only make Bernadette look more irrational by her coworkers, delusional by the authorities, and put a bigger bullseye on her.

- The story of someone using a bobcat to torment her then kill her, sounded like Bernadette was taking too much medication or the wrong medication. People just shoot other people. They don't worry about "offending" or "emotionally tormenting" their victims unless torture is the goal. No one on the outside would understand why hurting a bobcat would be extreme torture for Bernadette. She never talked about being a daughter of Anu, ever. To talk about it to authorities would be a waste of breath.

- She wouldn't be able to explain why she thought the clothes were from someone else. So why did she wear them and go up on a mountain by herself? The police would be more suspicious of her.

- She wouldn't be part of a witness protection program, so to talk about this without understanding who was doing what, didn't make sense.

She had to wait, figure out the who and the why. She had to go back to work. Someone would be watching for a display of weakness and Bernadette was determined not to let that happen. Here, for the past year, she had naively thought that getting fired was the worst outcome possible at the job.

Now she had to contend with the fact that she might be killed because of the job. Just wonderful.

One week later, a person, of unknown association with a bandaged hand, walked into Dr. Bensen's office.

"We aren't open for another ten minutes." Amber smiled sweetly.

"Yah, I know. I came to inquire about a patient you may have had on January 15. An America woman."

Dr. Bensen, hearing this, came into the reception area. "All our records are confidential."

The man replied, "I am sure they are. I can sit outside your office for the next three weeks, scaring away all of your patients for the next three years. Or you could just help me out now and give a list of names and addresses for the people who were here January 15."

Nodding to Amber, Dr. Bensen gave her permission to print the information requested. Dr. Bensen wasn't going to fight this guy and he didn't have the information the stranger wanted.

Five minutes later, the man looked at the list. "Any sutures on this day?"

Amber turned and looked at both men. "I don't recall us having a Ms. Sue Churs here last week. Just look at the list. Isn't that what you wanted it for?"

Feigning irritation, Dr. Bensen put his hand on his forehead, rubbing up and down, imitating a man who is exposed to long suffering.

Shaking his head in irritation and wondering how a pretty nurse could be so stupid, the man put the paper down on the counter after a quick review and left the office. He bought the lie. Not because Amber was dumb, but because his limited view of the world. Her actions fit in with his narrow ideas.

Once he was in his car and leaving the parking lot, Amber turned to Dr. Bensen. "I hope Bernadette is safe. I wonder what happened to her?"

Dr. Bensen had trouble putting to words what he understood about Bernadette; it took several minutes before he could reply. "Any woman who could have such an injury and not be debilitated with the pain is... unique. And her eyes are so different, not in color or shape, but in depth. My guess is, Bernadette is a force that one would do well not to cross. Not because she is mean or evil, but because she is goodness."

Then Dr. Bensen retreated to his office to wait for the first patient of the day.

Chapter 18
The Beginning of a Scottish Mission in Oregon, USA

(January 16, 1999)

Quinn Moore gracefully took the porch steps to the rustic farmhouse four at a time, gaining the wide veranda in two jumps. He didn't know why he even tried to rush at this hour. He was late. He had made the poor choice of taking M74 to get through Glasgow. What a mistake. There was nothing to be done about it now, other than burn off the adrenaline coursing through his thickly muscled frame. So crossed by the impenetrable traffic, he would have kicked the door open, had it been locked. As the knob turned freely, he threw the door open with such force that is slammed against the wall securing the hinges and bounced back, hitting him on the arm.

Moving his thick brown hair out of his eyes and off his shoulders, he then grabbed the offending door, ready to throw it back against the wall, when a woman's voice said, "Don't do it. The door didn't do anything. You best get out to the barn. He has been there since the middle of the night. I am not sure if he is just getting the horses worked up or if they are calming him down." She appeared in the hallway, forced a smile at Quinn, who looked to be the immediate descendant of a marauding Norwegian Viking, then turned to head up the narrow stairs.

"Wait. Do you know what is wrong?" Quinn hoped to be more mentally prepared for the meeting, an attempt to make up for his lack of judgement with drivers of Scotland. Where did all the people, who were utterly incompetent at driving in the snow, come from? It wasn't like people from tropical islands sought out the winter of Scotland.

Quinn saw the jealousy in her eyes as she glanced back at him, the normally well concealed emotion was quickly extinguished. "How should I know? He doesn't confide in me."

He then knew with conviction what had led to the emergency summons. It was Carney's wife. Something was wrong with her. It had to be.

Carney's wife was a perplexing figure for many who associated with Carney. They never understood the source of Carney's devotion and love for his American wife who continued to spend the majority of her life living in the U.S. In fact, most of folks who had been part of the close-knit group when the wedding took place, failed to anticipate Carney's steadfast ability to honor his marriage vows year after year. His adherence to those promises chafed the women who either had relations with Carney prior to his marriage or had hoped to have extramarital affairs with him after the wedding, figuring their proximity to Carney would tip the scales in their favor. It was a false assumption on their part, only serving up a menu of dogged frustration for the hopeful women.

Quinn reflected on the oddity that a long-distance relationship, with not only emphasis on distance but lack of written or verbal communication for longs periods of time, was now the benchmark for any romantic relationship he wanted. Initially he had given the relationship a great amount of negative scrutiny. That very scrutiny convinced Quinn how solid and devoted relationships could be when both people had a sincere willingness to endure and love beyond themselves. Whatever tied Carney to his wife, it was something powerful, and something that many superficial people could not understand. Quinn wanted that extraordinary type of commitment in a relationship, and he was still waiting to find it.

Carney's marriage arrangement had come under speculation by others because he attracted women at an astonishing rate, for his looks were mysteriously striking. He was a man's man in height, build, and looks. Every woman hoped to be his. After the wedding, Carney would recognize women, but he now appeared board with their interest in him. His friends joked that the American wife must be a sorceress of some kind. Smiling at the joke, Carney nodded, simply stating that she was more of an enchantress.

Carney's respect for his wife was even more puzzling when people remembered what he said hours before the wedding; it was a relationship that would protect her, nothing more. That was a lie. Quinn knew early on the relationship was of great significance to Carney. It filled a large black-trust-hole he had with people who professed love to him.

After the ordained minister, Roger, privately spoke with Carney on the phone before the wedding, there were immediate changes in Carney; a strong but quiet reflectiveness and resolve emanated from him. Within the next few months, further changes occurred. Quinn noticed Carney becoming more watchful, less angry, less prone to frustration, and most of all, a better leader. So even when Carney couldn't touch his spouse every evening, even when the loneliness must have gnawed at his heart, he never wavered from honoring his wife.

Quinn turned and bound back down the steps, out toward the barn, which was just a few hundred yards to the west of the farmhouse. Instead of opening the gate, he leapt over it by putting both hands on the five-foot metal bar, then using his incredibly powerful biceps to flip over it. Spinning on the balls of his feet, he was ready to run into the barn, but Carney appeared in the door, solemn, tense, and ready for battle.

Punching the doorway, Carney let out a strangled, guttural curse. "She is in trouble and I can't get out of the stupid county right now."

Carney saw the surprise on Quinn's face and understood. He rarely gave into emotion that wouldn't improve a situation. As a good leader, he strove to set the tone of control. Punching a door was a stupid waste of good flesh.

"How did you hear from her?" Quinn's puzzled look was there for a good reason. No one ever knew Bernadette to contact Carney. If there was any contact, it was Carney reaching out to her.

"It's impossible Quinn. I thought that after our wedding and with time, my memory of her would fade. I would go on in life with the marriage there, but in the background, like having some type of nice whiskey on the shelf. But the opposite happened. Instead, she looms larger than ever. When I sleep, she is there. I know it will sound crazy, but I feel her and I can feel her heartbeat. And that is how I know if it is a good day, a bad one, if she is scared or happy. I know none of you understand it and I wouldn't believe it if it wasn't happening to me."

Carney looked at Quinn with eyes of pain, the white transforming into the stormy death grey of the angry ocean, the intense green iris filled with bitter worry. "Something terrible happened yesterday. When I closed my eyes and I waited for her feelings to wash over me, it came, and it was dread. Her heart was racing. Something is really wrong and I can't do a thing about it, personally." Holding up his hand to Quinn, "And no, it wasn't just a bad day at work. I know those too. There have been many. Someone tried to kill her yesterday. I still feel it. Someone made a very poor decision and they will pay for it."

Walking up to Quinn, his pace measured in an effort to control himself, he said, "You need to get Tierney to the U.S. now. He has the best American accent, he has connections there, and he is loyal. He needs to get there yesterday. I don't care what it takes. He needs to watch over her. If the situation is bad, he has my permission to physically remove her to a safe place."

Carney shouted, "You hear me, he needs to keep Bernadette alive. I will get there as soon as I can, when I can. If we have to, we will bring her back here."

Clinching his fists, Carney Gallagher lowered his head and walked back into the darkness of the barn. He thought about Bernadette's childhood, understanding the strength she had gained from her early years. She needed that strength now. He just hoped it was enough.

Chapter 19
With Chicken Justice for All

(January 18, 1999)

Greg Tucker finished his half-hour morning mediation. It was a gloriously clear winter day on Vashon Island. From his chair he could see the brilliant blue waters of the Puget Sound. The water was so still that ripples from splashing fish were quickly dampened into extinction. Greg thought the extreme stillness today must be a positive omen for an event that he had been anticipating for several months.

Flexing his arms above his head, he envisioned what the day would be like. He saw himself casually stopping by his boss' office, Dr. Brad Baily, Director for Solid and Hazardous Waste Enforcement at Region 10, U.S. Environmental Protection Agency (EPA) in Seattle, Washington. Greg often commented to his colleges that Region 10 was elite amongst all the EPA Regions. At this job, unlike his period of forced drudgery in the military as a yes-no-sir man, Greg's thoughts and infant ideas about hazardous waste turned into laws enforced by the EPA. He saw even his minor musings as tools to crumble huge corporations and his hundreds of thousands of dollars in fines turned shark like corporate attorneys into sweet little bowls of shaking, melting Jell-O. The icing on the EPA cake, there was no agency that investigated complaints about the EPA and no agency exerted any oversight on what EPA did. It was freedom extraordinaire.

He knew a midafternoon visit was best, when Brad would be more relaxed following his routine hour-long martini sipping lunch. Greg was still smarting from embarrassment he received during a staff meeting a month ago. Brad had derided him about the lack of decisive progress on the East-West Refined Metals Manufacturing (EwRM2) enforcement. This day, Greg didn't want to appear like a whipped dog, so he would have to wait for the right moment to bring up the progress he had made on the case. He was averse to appearing overly eager when discussing EwRM2, because he didn't want the boss to know how truly ill prepared he was. By keeping the conversation about EwRM2 as an apparent after thought, Brad would conclude that Greg had a textbook enforcement case.

Truth was, Greg should have looked at the laboratory data on the anhydrous calcium chloride weeks ago. He was up against a deadline now and would have to make a cursory glance at the data this morning be sufficient. The National Enforcement Center (NEC) in Denver did the testing. And given that such an important federal facility did the testing, what could possibly be wrong? There wasn't a person on the planet who could negate the tests, even if it was all dry lab. Greg chuckled at the idea of NEC doing dry lab work; an expression meaning the lab didn't do the testing and reported false results. Bottom line, no one could question the data, as NEC was above challenge. This complacency had led Greg to have absolutely no motivation to understand the data which was the basis for his enforcement.

Greg, regardless his grandiose feelings of being beyond reproach, still had a small nagging feeling that what should be a bread-and-butter enforcement with EwRM2, would meet some snag with Brad. Since Brad took over the position as director a year and half ago, things in the office had changed drastically and not for the better in Greg's view. EPA had operated in the past like the FBI; the criminal entity was told what they did wrong, and they were punished for it. With Brad at the helm, there had to be more "transparency" and "cooperation" during enforcement. That made getting an enforcement case though the process and fine money in hand, a longer and more arduous task. Brad had even lowered himself in a staff meeting by using the terms "customer relations" and "outreach". Greg had almost choked on his donut and coffee after hearing that. He didn't care about all this squishy stuff. Any reasonable enforcement officer could see that the best approach was to get in, get out, get the money, put people in jail, and move on.

Even after a long cool shower, Greg still felt hot and sweaty. Just the thought of a huge fine against EwRM2 and the possibility of a "kill" (sending a polluter to jail) made Greg's blood pressure skyrocket. The excitement made him feel more alive than he had in months, but it also made it hard for him to concentrate on the technical material, he was too jittery.

On his ferry trip across the Puget Sound to downtown Seattle, Greg was in such a heightened state that he noticed smells which usually were just background insignificance. The smell of fish in the Sound was so strong, it was like the fish market at Pikes Place. All the perfumes were extreme on the ferry; hair spray, aftershave, and shampoo were just the start of that problem. But what drove him outside on to the ferry deck was the smell of people with health problems. The pharmaceutical byproducts oozed out people's pores, making the boat lounge a cacophony of acrid illness. Getting off the boat was a relief to his tortured olfactory senses.

-

At 7:48 a.m., all the women on the sixth floor of the Region 10 EPA building made sure that they weren't at a copy machine, in the stairwell, in the breakroom, near a unisex restroom, or by any coffee machine. It was common knowledge that Greg Tucker would arrive any minute and the women never knew if the nice Greg would show up or one of his evil quadruplets. The woman had agreed there were four disgusting Gregs: a leering, ogle-eye guy; the hard-nosed, rude and insulting perfectionist; the passive-aggressive, knife-to-the-gut jerk; and the egotistical macho man of superior masculine traits. The women had thought of complaining to management, but Greg's sister, Natalie, who worked on the seventh floor, convinced them otherwise. She talked ad nauseam about what a nice brother Greg was, how he had protected her from an abusive father, and how he just needed to find the right girl. The women felt for Natalie, so they just did a "work around" with Greg.

-

Greg was relieved once he was in his plush office and closing the door. He could finally focus in on the EwRM2 analytical data electronically sent by the NEC. There were over two hundred pages to the data package, so he opted to send most of the package to the large department printer down the hall. The executive summary he printed in his office.

In a few minutes, Greg started reading the twenty-page executive summary. He felt extreme pride in knowing that he was one person on this planet who did something morally correct. He skimmed the data for what he could use, finding it on page three. The anhydrous calcium chloride heated up when exposed to water. When anhydrous calcium chloride reacted with water in a laboratory setting, it generated exothermic heat energy, given in units of joules. That was it. That was all he needed. It was unimportant to him that the very same material entered the US as a product, not a waste. He didn't care that the tests conducted were not standardized tests, that the NEC tests were not approved by any organization, or that the tests could probably never be repeated. Greg cared about one thing; no one could fight the EPA and NEC. EPA was righteous and everyone else was a loser.

Humming a tune as he walked to the department printer, he was glad he still had a good fifteen years at the EPA before he would even consider retiring. More time for him to right the scales that had historically been skewed toward criminals. The metals industry was about to burn in a litigation nightmare, and EwRM2 in particular, would suffer a stock toboggan run when this fat fine hit the media. An arrest during the case would be a fireworks display. The vague regulations were on his side again. There would be no way EwRM2 would take the case to court because it would be impossible to argue the slippery regulations, meaning any judge would defer to the EPA. They couldn't even argue the case to the media because it was so confusing that a thirty second sound bite would make the company look like a bunch of knavish hooligans.

As Greg neared the printer, he heard the grinding sound of a major paper jam. He slammed the top cover down after checking the feeder belt, moved on to checking the rollers accessed through a front door, and finally checked the paper supply carriage. Grabbing the paper tray out with as much force as possible, Greg tossed it across the room to hear it split into parts on a partition wall. He then struggled to rip the cover off the copier, finally succeeding and tossing it on top of the paper tray. Greg stood, silent, wondering if anyone heard. He had important work to do and didn't have time for all this poor, cheap, defective equipment. The government owed him a quality printer. Since this printer fell apart, the American people would buy him one. Greg headed off to see Tammy, the lead chemical engineer in charge of all EPA equipment, to let her know that the lousy copier was self-destructing.

When Greg got back to his desk, he felt it was time to take a mid-morning coffee break and maybe go pick up a good book downtown. He didn't see himself getting the laboratory data printed anytime soon and decided he probably didn't need to look at more of it anyway.

Tammy got the copier to use another default paper supply, since the main one was broken, and gingerly laid the cover over the top of the copier, like a lid to a coffin. As the report printed, she stood reviewing some of the information when she noticed a section on quality control. As she perused further into the summary, she found that the NEC noted how the samples collected didn't appear to be well mixed or homogenized, the calibration of the instrument was performed with standards that were at a minimum of a year past their shelf-life, and many of the results for standards used to check the operation of the instrument were extremely outside the recommended recovery limits. Gathering up the papers, Tammy headed back to her desk.

-

The meeting with Brad went as Greg had planned, with a promise to have the final enforcement papers ready for signing by tomorrow morning. When they discussed the information from the NEC, Greg had assured Brad that all was in order. Brad was prepared to recommend the case to the criminal division, who would assign two staffers to do the final criminal summary on location. Brad cautioned about any hasty arrests, suggesting it didn't appear to be a case of criminal intent and would require good investigative work to support such a drastic action.

Greg inwardly laughed at that comment of caution. He had already been talking with Calvin Rossberg, known as Ross in the office, about the case details. Ross had wanted to be the one to surveil the suspects and make the arrests. Ross said he had sources which were confident that an arrest was necessary and would be supported high-up in the government. Although Greg didn't know why Ross would want to go stay in Madison-Lebanon area, he didn't care. He just wanted his name associated with this case, the arrest, and the fine money handed over to EPA.

-

Late that evening, Tammy sat and looked further into the laboratory reports on EwRM2 anhydrous calcium chloride. The test results weren't worth anything and Tammy understood that enforcement was proceeding with EwRM2. There was no scientific justification for enforcement given the data EPA had from the NEC. She went over all the possible scenarios in her mind, from approaching Greg on the problem to talking directly with Brad. Tammy looked over at her five-year-old daughter sleeping on the couch. She needed this job. It was a dream job. And with that thought, she threw the papers in a box to put in Greg's office. If Greg never looked at the NEC lab data and summary reports, that was his issue. Her priority was her daughter, not EwRM2.

Chapter 20
Don't Walk Away

(January 16-18, 1999)

Bernadette went to the airport the day after getting stitched up. She wasn't about to spend three more nights at Whistler Resort, waiting to see if anyone stopped by to finish the job of killing her. She managed to get a first-class seat back to Portland, Oregon, before noon, on January 16. Thankfully, the flight and drive home were uneventful.

-

Monday, January 18, she went to work, sat at her desk, and waited. She wasn't sure what she was waiting for. People called her. Others stopped by her office with questions. No one asked her if the hazardous waste conference in B.C. was informative. No one asked why she so gingerly held her stomach when walking about. No one asked her why her face was contorted with pain.

Amazing, Bernadette thought, *this workplace is categorically sick.*

The job tried to masquerade as normal, yet nothing at the job would be normal again. Several times during the day she typed up a resignation letter for her boss yet couldn't send it. She had good reasons to stay.

- She didn't want to get shoved around and if she quit, then she was letting others force her into a state of joblessness. It would be their terms, not hers. Why were women always to leave the job so men could go on making money? Nope, she was not walking away like a kindergartener pushed off the swing set.
- She believed in what she was doing at EwRM2. She worked to help the environment and industry. She was good at doing it. She was born for this type of job.

She was staying for now She felt the best thing she could do was aggravate those who tried to kill her and the best aggravation was by not going away.

As she sat at her desk waiting, she thought about the words that rang down the ventilation ducting, *coyote ugly* and *throw the baby out with the bath water.* Her convictions surged. She refused to let the men treat her in the same manner as a snooker ball, something to shove around on cue. She would stay and win the game.

When Bernadette got home Monday evening, she collapsed on the couch in pain. The stitches in her stomach were screaming every time she moved. The band on her underwear rubbed more irritation into the injuries. Her stomach on the inside was felt like a hot pot of oil meeting some cool water; lots of splattering and sputtering inside.

Bernadette was determined to get through this. There had to be a way to fight back, to remain at the job which she had passion for, and ultimately get those people who were corrupt arrested. There had to be.

Chapter 21
Buying Rosie, A Real Farm Girl

(March - May 1999)

Bernadette dreamed of living on a farm and that dream amplified when neighbors were self-serving idiots.

She realized that most neighbors don't understand the rules which govern life on earth:

- What is a tolerable sound to the person making the sound, is an irritation to those who are impacted by the sound.
- Smells emanating from one's own domain, become olfactory corrosives within other's noses.
- What is a personally tolerable habit, quickly escalates into an uncontrollable annoyance for others.
- What was happily dumped on the ground as discarded waste, migrates as a hazard into someone else's area.

She also realized that most people weren't trained in the golden rule of consideration: *If you are polluting, keep it to yourself. And, anything can become a pollutant.* She believed that air pollution could be greatly reduced if cars were equipped with an emissions canister which would contain all emissions from the car. When a person got home from all the driving, they got to dump the emissions into their home and live with it. Air pollution problem would be solved.

When Carol, Bernadette's preferred real estate agent, a helpful and informative but not pushy professional, called about a small farm in Lebanon, Oregon, that recently came on the market, Bernadette cringed. How could the timing be worse? She was hanging onto the EwRM2 job today, but the fact that the job resembled the Titanic left her feeling insecure about tomorrow.

Then, on March 10, 1999, Bernadette got a call which tilted her axis and then righted it in a new place. Her mother had passed away. It was an odd situation. Bernadette had grieved for years for the mother she never had. Now, expecting Bernadette to grieve for a woman who had engaged in such emotional torture was highly irrational. The passing of Jan gave Bernadette a sense of relief and peace she had never known in life.

It was the inheritance and a new sense of freedom that helped Bernadette make the decision to purchase the house and barn on the smaller acreage. Svalbard, Bernadette's Irish Wolfhound, would thrive on a farm, further encouraging Bernadette to make the move.

The place was perfect when it closed. Of course, during the first night in her new house, the trepidation associated with this huge commitment began seeping in through all those old windows and drafty doors. Instead of running out to the hardware stores the next day, Bernadette found herself looking for the inexpensive draft horse of her dreams. She wanted to work the land with the horse.

After several weeks of searching for a draft horse, she was no longer confident that getting such an animal was going to be anything other than an expedient way to meet a doctor and probably an ambulance crew to go with it. How to choose? Would it be the two-thousand-pound gelding who made a fuss when the harness was put on? Or maybe Bernadette should have further considered the Clydesdale cross that had been so drugged-up, a person could only imagine its faults. The bandages on the owners' arms would indicate that the Clydesdale had a fondness for teething in all the wrong places. There was also a beautiful Paint-Shire cross who rode fine in the arena, but when outside she proceeded to go wild and lunge for the arena gate. Who would have guessed that a draft horse cross would fear the outdoors? Bernadette wondered if horses had become like people, no longer understanding the meaning of nature, the land, and the joy of the wind caressing your schnauzer (snout).

Standing, looking at the empty field, Bernadette wondered, why not go to the local auction? It couldn't possibly be filled with horses any worse behaved then the horses she had investigated from the advertisements in the local paper. All Bernadette knew about the auction was this: don't wave hello to anyone or you end up buying something at a price you didn't think was possible.

Bernadette didn't want to blend in with other farmers at the auction because she was going to need someone to take pity on her and give her some assistance. Wearing her western boots, shin-length western denim skirt with eyelet trim, and a white western blouse, she stood off to the side, hoping to be inspired with a solution to her predicament. As people were milling about, greeting one another with camaraderie that Bernadette always hungered for, she decided a trip to the restroom before the start of the auction would be a good strategy. Of course, there was a line outside of the women's restroom. As she stood waiting, a woman with a rotund derriere sidestepped, wedged, and shoved her way into the line in front of Bernadette. She pretended Bernadette wasn't there. Bernadette swallowed all the confrontational thoughts that came to mind, deciding that a discussion about the woman squeezing into pants a size too small and a few stiches away from a total rip out, just wasn't worth the karmic consequence of being rude to another person. Thinking of her spiritual training, she decided to use the restroom later.

She swung around, stepping out of the line, and met the stare of one blue eye and one brown eye. The Border Collie's eyes reflected the warring factions within any dog; calmness and loyalty to the owner, and desire for free abandon to search the hills and the valleys with the wind in between. The dog nuzzled up to Bernadette until it heard the shrill sound of a wolf whistle. Bernadette first noticed the boots then her eyes went up the man's form. He was very tall, probably six feet and five inches. Her eyes settle back on his beautiful silver belt buckle adorned with grizzlies fighting.

Stephen watched the redhead. Women who were caught eying his form fell into two emotional categories, he reminisced. One was embarrassment, which was accompanied by no eye contact and the other was overt sexual desire, which left Stephen feeling empty, a bit more like a ham bone then a person. The redhead woman moved her eyes further up to his face, smiling genuinely, and approached Stephen as if greeting a longtime friend.

The redhead said, "When were you in Alaska? Your belt buckle is something my father would have liked. The grizzles fighting inside the state outline is very stunning."

She kneeled down to pet Buffalo, rubbing him under the chin. Stephen understood that petting a dog on top of the head can be interpreted by a dog as a sign of dominance instead of camaraderie and knew the redhead must have understood that too. Stephen was impressed by her gentle gesture.

Stephen was pleased with this woman. She had been looking at his belt buckle, only that. Stephen laughed. *Leave it to a woman to complicate and confuse the situation*, he thought and laughed some more. Tipping his hat he said, "Stanford, Stephan Stanford. Last summer I was in Alaska visiting my cousin."

"Bernadette Engstrom. I have not been to an auction since I was a little girl. Would you be able to give me a ten-minute synopsis of the process, before I find myself the proud owner of a swayback, long in the tooth, mare? You look to be a very knowledgeable farmer."

Stephen was a knowledgeable farmer and he happened to be the owner of the auction yard, but he didn't tell Bernadette that bit of information.

The refreshing air of innocence in her request was pleasing and Stephen was happy to oblige. But there was another reason he wanted to assist her and that reason stood about five foot nine inches. Stephen had been assessing the interloper who was comically out of place because he wore blue suede tennis shoes. No one with common sense wore suede shoes, that couldn't get easily cleaned, to an auction. But this interloper had been watching Bernadette with a forced casualness, and that moved Stephan into action.

Offering Bernadette his arm, he said, "Let's begin with a preview of the animals we have for auction." Stephen pushed himself forward through the crowd with Bernadette following easily in his wake.

Bernadette was quiet, with the exception of questions for Stephen. She wanted to pet every animal that came to a pen fence and when Stephen mentioned some of the animals were designated for the slaughterhouse, much of the amusement in her eyes left, and didn't return. Most of the horses were showing the outcome of expensive hay prices, as dull coats and gaunt sides told the story of perhaps neglect or hard times.

Stephen was about halfway through the horse pens when Hal, his employee of 8 years, joined them for a few minutes.

Hall explained, "A lot of animals come through this auction each week. It might take you several trips or you just might want to wait until summer to attend some 4-H events. Kids have some nice family animals."

Bernadette looked at Stephen and said, "I found a horse I want to buy. Would you sit with me and help me during the bidding?"

Stephen leaned forward with an expectant look.

Understanding his meaning, Bernadette said, "No, I don't want to show you which one. You will just discourage me."

Stephen spoke with friends until the bidding started, then joined Bernadette on the worn bench. He said, "You got a horse trailer for this?"

"Oh, do I need one?" Then with one corner of her mouth turned up, and a dimple showing, she continued, "Oh my, they don't deliver?"

"Fine, just asking a good question for a greenhorn. As you wish."

Stephen knew when Bernadette's horse of choice was up for bid. She sat up straight and tugged on Stephen's sleeve when the animal appeared.

"She's got a beautiful mane and feather, don't you think Stephen? I am going to name her Rosie."

In the horse business, Stephen had heard a good many reasons for buying a horse; color, breeding, size, speed, but feather was a new one for this rural area. And feather was about all there was to look at. The Belgian Draft and Dutch Warmblood cross was horribly thin, and its dull coat showed the lack of nutrition.

After getting the animal loaded up in Bernadette's trailer, and Stephen watched her pull out onto Highway 20, Hal all but sprinted across the yard, dodging trailers which were backing up under inexperienced hands. The resulting vehicular dents to the walls and corners of the barns were too numerous to count. Repairs to the area were lucky to last into the next week.

"So, did you get her phone number?" Hal assessed Stephen with the look a mother gives a new bride.

"No." Stephen relaxed against the barn wall, picking a location where a vehicle mishap wouldn't stick him full of splinters.

"Alright, you get her address?" Hal was bobbing his head so fast, Stephen began to wonder if Hal shouldn't be the clown at the fall rodeo. Quirky bodily movements were a big hit for everyone.

"No." Stephen grabbed Hal's shoulder as he pushed both of them away from yet another trailer about to lose a taillight.

"So, you just spent the entire auction helping this good-looking redhead and didn't get any information about her?" As Hal got to the last words, his voice sounded like the whine when a belt slips on the old Ford pickup.

"Guess so."

"Stephen, you been out of action too long. Gee whiz, boy, look at you. You're like a bull afraid to leave the barn anymore. The gate is wide open. What in the hell is your problem?"

Stephen set his jaw, glaring at Hal under his eyebrow. "Hal, you know that forty-acre place at the end of Elmer Lane, where the Allen's lived? The one that butts up against my back eighty. Well, remember when I built my place and you laughed because sweet, eighty-year-old Mrs. Allen liked to prance around the tub without closing the blinds? Remember how funny that was for you? Here I was, newly divorced, and you practically peed your pants laughing at Mrs. Allen parading around in the buff. Well, Allen put the place on the market a year and a half ago and it finally sold. And you know who moved in? Yep, that tantalizing lady. The joke is on you, big guy."

Stephen spun around and headed to his office to review the auction receipts for the day. He hadn't felt this good in several years. He finally got to meet his shy neighbor and he had the confident feeling that he was about to see a lot more of her. It was about all he could do to keep from busting up laughing here in the yard. The mare Bernadette purchased had come in to the auction because it was a fence jumper. The owner had asked if there were any pens with 10-foot-high rails, claimed the horse would jump the fence to eat straw blown out of a truck on the road when it still had grain in the barn. Stephen usually abhorred fence problems with neighbors, which never left anyone feeling pleased. But this was about to be a very fun year, or at least he hoped it would be.

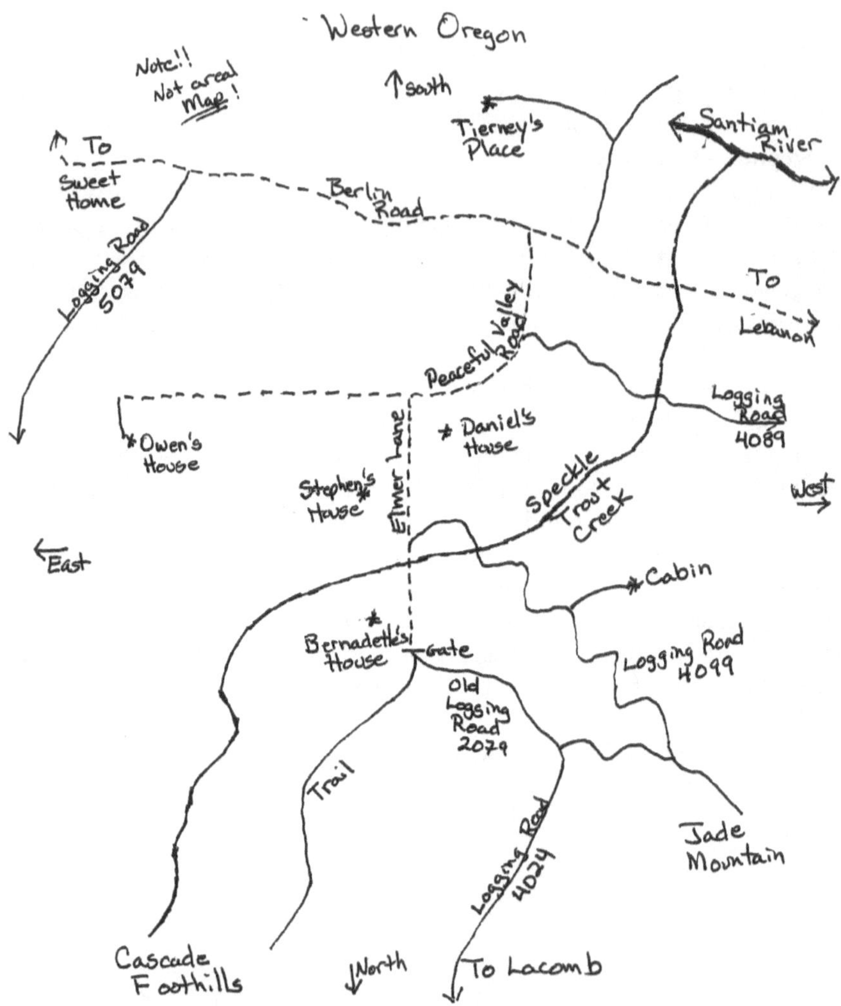
Western Oregon
Note!! Not a real Map!
↑ South
Tierney's Place
← Santiam River
↑ To Sweet Home
Berlin Road
Logging Road 5079
TO Lebanon
Peaceful Valley Road
Logging Road 4089
Owen's House
* Daniel's House
Stephen's House
Elmer Lane
Speckle Trout Creek
West →
← East
* Cabin
Bernadette's House
Gate
Logging Road 4099
Old Logging Road 2079
Trail
Logging Road 4029
Jade Mountain
Cascade Foothills
↓ North
To Lacomb

Chapter 22
Loving All of God's Babies

(Spring and Summer 1999)

Wiggly and Buster came into Bernadette's life when she needed them the most. She had been feeling monotonously selfish and perversely self-absorbed. This week, Bernadette slogged through thoughts of a human friend's recent abandonment. Nonproductive and ineffectual ruminations on poor human behavior culminated in an internal chorus of: *When will they help me like I helped them? When will they understand what I am going through and call to check up on me like I pick up the phone for them?* The inharmony plagued the internal serenity, leaving Bernadette's emotional state an exact replica of Rosie's corral; churned up earth with every blade of green grass stomped to death.

Just as the broken record of "feel-sorry-for-me" was reaching a crescendo, two babies of nature taught Bernadette how to deal with life's bruises: when presented with conditions not to your favorable interpretation, thoughtful action to the world is required. From that simple idea she then had to acknowledge that ruminating on toxic rubbish fails to incite conspiratorial spiritual help on this planet.

While the Oregon clouds had reduced their deluge this week in May, Bernadette decided to plant flower seeds in the pots sitting on a railing just outside the kitchen window. As she stood in contemplative thought looking at the seed package, Bernadette's heard a small distress call, not unlike a baby bird who toppled from its nest. Taking the time to push aside her dismal musings, she was surprised when realizing the same noise occurred the day before, only it was no more than a flicker in her consciousness, easily drowned out by the internal hurtful roar. Bernadette's awareness level raised up to scan for any creature newly introduced to or in the throes of agony. She visually probed the yard, her frown deepening.

After standing in the yard, alertly still for several minutes, Bernadette decided on a drink of water to sooth her emotionally heated system before embarking on a bush-by-bush search in the area. She headed toward the little concrete porch which served both the garage man-door and mudroom-laundry room door. As she bounded up the inclined gravel walkway, she heard the baby cry. Standing on the small concrete porch, surrounded by a cedar-stained railing, she happened to see a movement in one of the two plastic flower planters where the flower seeds were to go. Moving closer, she realized, there in the moss was a furry, open eyed, baby chipmunk. One of nature's perfect but immature creatures had just crawled out of a hole in the center of the flowerpot. This chipmunk's beautiful brown fur with perfectly aligned black stripes didn't conceal his weakness or distress. There he sat, crying, looking confused.

Rushing around the house, Bernadette grabbed gloves and a shoe box. Padding the box with some tissue, she returned to the flowerpot which had lost a mother and was now sprouting budding chipmunks. Not knowing how long the baby had been alone she decided that expediency was most crucial in this case. She was quick to securely but gently grab the baby, even while he was making a feeble attempt to bite the glove and wiggle away, depositing him in the box. Placing her finger in the entrance of the dirt home, she pulled up the roots of last year's flowers, removing soil without caving in the home. As she dug down in root bound mass there squirmed three more siblings, much weaker than the first baby. Setting up a bigger box with a heating pad and worn-out blanket, all the infants were place near the pad for warmth, but not on it, and a blanket was put over part of the box top to give the babies a feeling of security.

Although some internet information fell into the range of marginally incorrect to downright wrong, Bernadette had found the abundant amount of wildlife and farming knowledge to be immensely helpful. For periods of time, she would completely avoid the internet, its incapacitating drama and sucking emotional whirlpool. It was times like these, when the focus was on taking action to make the world a better place, that the internet worked harmoniously with nature, a resource to positively influence the land's survival. Running to the computer, Bernadette queried orphaned chipmunks, discovering they could be feed puppy formula and if the infant was dehydrated, a salt/sugar solution should be fed prior to puppy formula. Snagging a worn out and mended purse, Bernadette jumped into the truck and sped off to town to spend more money she didn't have on puppy formula and a few syringes.

\-

One sibling died each day. She just couldn't get the weaker ones hydrated nor would they take any of the puppy formula. They had waited too long to come out of the nest. They had waited for a mom that didn't return from her task of foraging. Although Bernadette grieved for the loss of such young life, she did her best to accept the terms of a world she didn't understand and instead focus on the things she could change. Life on a farm is in one of two states: something was in the process of being born or it was in the process of dying. That was life. The tipping point between process of dying, which occurs once we are born, and actively dying is almost infinitesimal at times. Bernadette learned to give gratitude to each day for all that was given.

The first baby that had come out of the flowerpot nest, now named Wiggly, wasn't going to succumb to any debilitating force without a fight. Even when he sat quietly, his eyes were alive with a zest for life. He was accepting of change. As long has he got food, no matter that it came now from a plastic cold syringe, he was enthusiastic about a meal. Warmth from a heating pad or from Bernadette was all the more cause to snuggle and grow.

Within a few days, Wiggly was scaling the walls of his cardboard box. After dragging an old cattle tank into the bedroom, she covered it best she could with hard-clothe, a very tightly woven mesh wire, to keep Wiggly from escaping and running wild in the entire house. She put new things into the tank to ensure he had mental stimulation, for Wiggly relished investigating and exercising. Bernadette gave him a variety of solid foods to try out; sunflower seeds, peanuts, and some special rodent food for helping him grow. Wiggly chewed and tasted all of it. But by far his favorite was the sunflower seeds.

Marveling at his fur, Bernadette figured he probably looked much like a rat if it weren't for his brown coat with the black racing strips. She was a bit intimidated by rats. The pointy nose and bare tail combination looked a bit off to her. But put the right fur on the guy and she was in love with him. Although she was busy and fatigued, she spent a half hour each night with him so he could socialize and perhaps, she could too.

Knowing that Wiggly would need to transition from confinement to the wilds with some type of supervision, Bernadette took time to read up on how orphans were introduced to the wild. Using plans from the internet and taking more time away from other things that needed to be done, she built him a special wooden house, outfitted with a unique entryway that would prevent predators from reaching inside it. Placing it in the cattle tank, Bernadette was pleased to see how he loved his wooden house, hauling sunflower seeds in and peeking out when called. Later, it could be moved when he was ready to be put in a cage outside.

By the time Wiggly had successfully escaped from the cattle tank and was retrieved from the closet, Bernadette had an outside pen built that was big enough to hold his house, a few small tree limbs, water plus food, and some running space. It was wire on all sides, so he could really feel and see the outdoors.

One day, while heading to Wiggly's cage for his morning feeding, Bernadette, in the middle of a step, as her right foot was in the air, extended her leg out in an exaggerated manner to avoid stepping on something that moved imperceptibly in the walkway. Stooping low, she could see it was hairless, and a baby, but wasn't sure what. Moving it with a stick, on to it back, it opened its mouth, and she knew immediately from the tiny sharp teeth and the hiss it was a baby bat, probably less than a week old. It really was a very ugly little thing, but then Bernadette figured mothers always loved the babies best.

With an internal moan, the orphan baby animal process started all over again, with Buster. She setup a heating pad on the side of a bird cage, covered it with foam then corduroy, so Buster's claws could cling to something and there were pockets for him to nestle in. She put up another such system without the heating pad, so if he was too warm, he could move to a different area. After ensuring the baby was hydrated, she started feeding him a watered-down solution of goat's milk, reducing the dilution with each feeding. Milking the goat Cinnamon was added to her list of chores each day, as she didn't want bacteria to get growing in the unpasteurized milk. After another visit to the pet store, she began introducing meal worms to his diet. This was not an appealing process, causing Bernadette to blanch at every feeding time. Buster had quickly caught on to the routine of being fed by a human. Because she didn't know much about bats, she decided that a call for Buster would be her trill, a sound she had been doing since young, but she never met anyone else who did it, or admitted to doing it. At each feeding, she would trill, then supply food. As he got older, she noticed how is ears would twitch when she trilled.

While Buster was growing hair, Bernadette kept Wiggly in his outdoor pen so he could see friend and foe with safety. When he appeared to be very aware of what was around him, Bernadette opened his door to the outside during the day, locking it at night when he showed up for sunflower seed dinner.

Finally, one night, Wiggly refused to come in his pen, instead sitting on a nearby tree, just out of Bernadette's reach, sashaying his tail in triumph. Although Bernadette didn't want to, she turned and walked away. He was free and if he was hungry, he could get the food and go in his safe box. It wasn't very long, maybe a day or two, and Wiggly was gone, not returning to his food or house. Bernadette worried a bit, but in truth was relieved because she was busy making a larger cage and bat house.

Luckily, Buster was flying in two weeks and one day. Added to her tasks, she had to make a bat house that would be moved outside, near the chimney where Bernadette suspected Buster's mother was located. Literature on bat rehibition suggested putting a flying juvenile bat back at the original roost location. Buster flew around the empty guest bedroom for 3 nights, coming back to her hand when she trilled.

When Buster was ready, Bernadette climbed a ladder to install the bat house near the original bat roost and then put Buster in the bat house. In the evening she trilled him, and he swooped by. During the day, climbing back up to the bat house, she looked inside, finding it empty. She almost sure he was back with his family, and they would teach him to feed. The next night, she trilled, and buster swooped her again, almost six times, before he was gone in the night. She checked on him each night for a week, until she was sure he was thriving. Finally, she took down the unused bat house, storing it in the barn, and fed the remailing meal worms to chickens.

About a week later Bernadette was walking on a path in the yard, when Wiggly bound though the fence, ran to her and climbed up he pant leg. As she reached for him, he turned to run back down her leg, glancing at her with one eye. Stilling her hand, she said, "Go on Wiggly and watch out for cats." He bounded back to the woods and he was gone, wild and sassy.

The sunflower shells, empty reminders of past friendships, strewn across the cage, finally molded, encouraging Bernadette to throw them out in the pasture. She threw his makeshift food and water dishes in the trash.

Bernadette's friendships with the wild animals remained in her heart, and she remained in theirs.

Chapter 23
Surveillance Begins

(June 1999)

A contractor coming out of Bernadette's place headed back up Elmer Lane. Anxious to leave before being noticed, the truck sped up to almost 70 mph (miles per hour) in no time, spewing fumes everywhere. In its haste, it didn't see the car coming towards it until very late, swerving to avoid a collision. The contractor's impatience turned to concern as he realized he narrowly avoided an accident with an unmarked official car, of what agency he didn't know. Having been in the military, the contractor did know it was a vehicle used by the enforcement arm of some government agency.

The car never went as far as Bernadette's driveway. Instead, it turned onto an old logging road going west, proceeding on to a Jade Mountain Forest Service cabin, a decrepit thing, currently situated on land managed by the Bureau of Land Management (BLM).

Peter Harris looked over at Calvin Rossberg, who went by the name Ross. Ross, an athletic brown-haired pretty boy, grimaced as he held tightly to the steering wheel, having narrowly missed the contractor's truck.

Peter, wanting to poke at Ross a bit, said, "Wasn't that the contractor you hired to put the camera on Bernadette's light pole? Where did you find that guy? I hope he does electrical work better than he drives." Peter settled further back in the seat, waiting for some playful sparing.

That didn't happen.

Ross felt superior about everything, and he wasn't going to let Peter think for a minute that he had made an error in judgement. Ross glanced over at Peter thinking, *who are you, but nothing. You came out of Alabama, some poor neighborhood in some poor town, born to poor parents.*

Ross aggressively said, "Look, I am the one who got you this assignment. This career-maker project is guaranteed to provide you with recognition, which as you know, can be used for climbing the ladder a lot faster than you have been in the past. Was good timing on your divorce; I figured that you wouldn't care about being out of town. All the extra money from over-time would look pretty good given all your bills from the divorce lawyer and the ex-shopaholic's credit card bills. I convinced everyone that you had all the right training and experience to make this a huge success, even if your Port of Tacoma project is a big mess. So, give me a break."

Peter was perplexed by Ross' comments for a few reasons. First, Ross' tone today was a big contrast to his jovial attitude the past few months. Peter held his tongue instead of snapping back. That self-control trait had served him well many times and he figured it would now.

The second source of confusion was more ominous. Peter thought back to the meeting Brad Baily had set up to discuss the EwRM2 project. Both he and Ross had been called to the meeting and the project had been explained to them. Peter was sure that Brad had been speaking to both of them as if they had no prior knowledge of the project. If Ross had known about the case, to the extent of having a major influence on who would be working the project, then why the appearance of a kickoff meeting for both of them? Did Brad know that Ross was familiar with the case? If not, who had Ross been convincing that a team consisting of Peter and Ross was a good one? Peter couldn't reconcile the introductory meeting with Ross' words.

His ex-wife was a sensitive topic for Peter. He did need the extra money on this job or he would have laid into Ross, as his remarks were overly personal and rude. Peter had an idea that his wife was cheating on him back at the start of 1998. He kept trying to do things, little things for her, in an attempt to win her back: dinner dates, theater, new clothes, doing the house cleaning, and some of the shopping. Most of the time his reward was a fake smile.

In the spring of 1998, Peter went to the photography shop his wife frequented as she was striving to become a professional photographer. He picked up two lens filters and film for the top-of-the-line Nikon he had purchased and given to her on New Year's Day. Just as an afterthought, he asked the store owner if his wife had any prints ready, and he would take those home too. Thinking that it would be a good conversation to talk about her work, show her he really cared about her mind, which he did, but she repeatedly said he didn't, he made the major mistake of looking at the prints. The photos started out innocent looking, a ferry on Puget Sound and seagulls. But then he came to photos of feet intwined on a lounge chair, legs intwined on the sand, hands on his wife's legs, and the romantic themes escalated, with Peter getting madder as each photo told more of the story. One picture was imprinted in his mind: a man's hand holding his wife's left hand, minus her wedding ring. That had ended his marriage. He had thrown the pictures at her and left.

Peter hadn't mentioned his divorce at work, yet Ross appeared to have a decent amount of knowledge about it. How would he have gotten that information and why would that personal information have been worth looking into? It looked as if Ross had been sizing up Peter's situation, finding it somehow useful. That troubled Peter.

Peter was glad when the car spun around in front of the decaying cabin, coming to a standstill facing back down the hill. He escaped the car with his thoughts. They were situated above Bernadette Engstrom's place, allowing them to amass information on her illegal activities at EwRM2. People always let down their guard at home, divulging information recklessly in the aura of safety found in one's house and Peter was confident that Bernadette would be no different.

There was power running to the one bedroom, one bathroom cabin. There were only five outlets and just four lights. The bathroom smelled of dry rot and it looked like the toilet might fall through the floor if a person sat on it. Peter walked around the outside, wondering about the abundance of footprints, both human and animal.

Ross came out of the cabin, a notebook in hand, and approached Peter. "Look, I will take charge of getting this cabin livable. I have a cousin who does all kinds of remodel jobs and things have been slow for him. Since we will be working this project in shifts, the person here will need to be able to make a meal and get some rest. We will need a functional kitchen and bathroom, plus lots of outlets for our equipment. You are scheduled to finish the Tacoma project in the next week. I will have my cousin get this mess fixed up and ready for our return. What do you say?"

Peter's scowl deepened as he glanced at the cabin and then down the hill.

He faced Ross and said, "Are we going to be here that long? If Bernadette is doing something illegal, won't we get the information in a few weeks, at most? You make it sound like we are setting up a lovely little home here. I can't imagine that we have all the funding to remodel a cabin. Isn't that why we have hotel rooms? Won't you have to get approval with Brad for all this?

"If we are going to be here any length of time, wouldn't it be better to find a place that is further away from the subject's home? It is going to be very obvious to the subject that a surveillance is in progress if we are so close, especially in this rural area."

Peter could see a sneer forming on Ross's face.

"Look, I am the lead on this project and will do all the reporting back to Brad. You worry about your stuff, like finishing up the disastrous Tacoma project and I'll worry about the cabin. We aren't just investigating Bernadette, but other EwRM2 staff too. This might take some time. Frankly, for this project it won't matter if we are close to the subject. She is just another stupid criminal. If you are going to complain about everything on this project, then maybe we should find a replacement for you."

Peter was shocked by the whiplash emotions and overtly threatening tone Ross displayed. And yet, he wasn't. As one of the few African American professionals working in Region 10, he had seen all kinds of behavior. Much of it, he had to forget about or go crazy. Today, he didn't even want to consider not being on this project because the overtime and out-of-town pay would be monumental. To turn his back on this windfall would be complete lunacy.

Peter said, "Look Ross, I am just asking questions to make sure we both succeed at this project. Don't you want someone to watch your back."

Ross smiled at Peter. "All right. Someone to watch my back. Let me write down dimension of the cabin, then we can go."

"Sounds good. Let me get my coffee cup and I can help," Peter replied.

Peter turned and walked back toward the car to retrieve his coffee cup and take a few deep breaths. As he approached the door, he glanced at the side mirror, almost stumbling at what he saw. Normally based on the mirror angle he wouldn't have been able to see Ross, but someone had adhered a two-inch blind-spot mirror to the mirror on the side of the car. Ross was pointing his gun at Peter's back! Peter went from mildly annoyed with Ross to completely consumed with anger. Staying steady, he took his time opening the car door so he could view Ross for as long as possible, sat down slowly in the passenger seat, picked up his coffee, and took a sip. He couldn't understand what just happened. Peter was so shocked, he wondered if he was dreaming. Why would Ross point a gun at his back? EPA staff on criminal investigations always carried, but common-sense dictates that you never point a gun at someone unless you are willing to shoot them.

Peter sat in the car, trying to keep a clamp on his boiling anger. Ross had turned and walked into the cabin. Who was this Ross guy? Having no understanding for what just occurred, all Peter could do was keep the information tucked away and hope it would help him navigate this project.

Getting out of the car with his coffee, he went back in the cabin to help take measurements.

Chapter 24
The Summer Solstice

(June 21, 1999)

The superficial town folks who engaged in small talk with Kal thought of him as some type of "want-to-be" artist. It was almost comical to hear their babble; he was described as a wastrel, someone barely able to maintain shelter and sustenance for himself and his wife. The few who took the time to befriend Kal knew that his real name was *Elk Standing in Snow* and that his artwork sold for obscene amounts of money to an international art dealer working out of Portland, Oregon.

Kal, a Calapooia Indian, lived on a two-hundred-and-thirty-acre parcel of land that he owned, free and clear. Both he and his wife, *Time of Blossom*, who went by the name Dora and was from the Warm Springs Indian Reservation in Oregon, bore a strong resemblance to their Native American heritage. But what truly set them apart had nothing to do with physical looks; it was a matter of essence. That was the quality of importance, for the essence drumming in Kal and Dora's veins was very different from the average person of today. Feeling no interest in the mountain of possessions that the average American had, they watched the constant rabbit-like scampering society with an odd detachment. The grounding land was a necessity for them, an escape from the heebie-jeebies present in a society hell bent on a hypnotic environmental desolation course.

Most of the other tribes in Oregon knew of Kal and the folklore that surrounded his family. His grandmother had been an extraordinary healer. As a young boy searching for a connection, she would tell him stories about the plants and the animals and the land, how those forces worked together to overcome sadness. She recounted how a mother raccoon had awakened in her a knowledge of things not seen with the ordinary light.

Much to Kal's liking, as a teenager he went to live a real life in the Cascades with his grandmother. Many town folks would have thought that their primitive way of living would lead to hardship and deepening ignorance. But modernization doesn't understand the calmness of the woods and meadows and it was within the pure wind that knowledge flowed fully into young Kal's system. Watching this gift seek out fulfillment within Kal, led to a renewed joy in his grandmother.

As his grandmother ripened from old to ageless, she encouraged Kal to sell his art. "You will need land of your own for times to come. The white money will help you to avoid the desolation in the city." Knowing Kal was objecting, she elaborated, "You don't have to be attached to the money to use it as a tool. The desire or hatred of money can lead to the same despair."

Most neighbors didn't even know that Kal and Dora lived on the land spanning between Jade Mountain and Snow Peak. A stark contrast to the fact that both Kal and Dora knew things of the land for miles around them. Often, they lived quietly by themselves, but currently their guest teepee was occupied by a broken white man whom they had calmly approached, over a year ago, at the edge of a sheer drop-off near the top of Snow Peak. On that wind swept peak, the man of strong convictions and discouraged spirit had contemplated suicide. Dora had walked up to him, took his hand, and he came to live at their place.

They left food for the man by the teepee each day, but didn't see much of him, which they understood. Healing great sadness took place in the fluttering leaves. The salve of peace would wither under the harsh daily scrutiny of *"how are you?"* and *"let's talk."*

When the new neighbor moved in at the base of Jade Mountain, situated in the rolling foothills of the Cascades, Kal and his wife were surprised that they had a positive awareness of the small farm. Obliviously, materialistic people made so much hectic noise and random bouncing energy, that anyone who was even remotely in tune with the land learned to recognize the senseless disruption and automatically filter it out. This new neighbor was different. A strange band of energy percolated there and they became more curious of the forces accumulating: thunder showers, snowstorms and bright spring days swirled around the little farm. It wasn't their business, they told themselves, nor had they been asked to help. Things changed when the summer equinox occurred.

-

Dora and Kal didn't need to chatter on with one another all day in order to communicate. The modern family of noise and uncontrollable talking was seen by them as a sure method for achieving discordant communication. On this particular summer solstice, a day of morning showers and afternoon cloud breaks, Kal rose early to find Dora already preparing a snack for them to take on their day-hike. The solstice had arrived with a calm peace but a shifting energy which both Kal and Dora understood.

After walking a flock of miles through forest and farm, and clambering over the many fences and gates, they found themselves along the lower section Speckle Trout Creek during the later afternoon. Most inhabitants around the clear stream didn't know that the waters originated from a huge spring and aquifer up on Snow Peak, on Kal's land. The truth was, most people didn't know much about the stream and didn't care, other than to see it as an inconvenience when building a road or when plowing a field right up to the edge of it.

Often, when walking in Speckle Trout Creek during the lower flows of summer, Kal would find artifacts from his ancestors and those before. Sometimes he enjoyed finding a tool of past, but often it brought him a sense of desolation; beautiful people gone, wiped out. Perhaps that was the way of this particular planet, but it didn't mean that everyone had to forget these people. Kal felt them and did his best to bring their memory into his art.

When given the opportunity, Kal liked to tease the government employees at the local Fish and Wildlife Department about all the speckle trout in Speckle Trout Creek.

They rolled their eyes and said, "Kal, that fish has been extinct for the last two hundred years, if it ever existed. If you ever do catch one, please bring it in so we can throw the book at you. Then we'll stop all logging, building, fishing, paving, or farming activities within miles."

Kal always laughed and walked away, knowing in his heart the fish in spirit were there. As a young boy he wondered how a people could possibly kill so many fish. Now as a mature man, he wondered how the fish has survived as long as they did under the ignorant ways of the white man. but figured the loss of the fish took more time than the destruction of his ancestors.

Walking in the water was not to be today. Both Kal and Dora were looking forward to greeting the whispering rapids. His grandmother had visions there, while sitting on the shearing bedrock that ran straight into the water, sheltered by a weather-beautified oak. He stood by the rapids holding hands with Dora and relaxed his mind to play with the shadows cast by the trees and sun dancing. They stood quietly for what would have looked to the casual observer as a long time, and there was a soothing peace.

After half an hour, Kal felt the presence of another coming up behind him. Releasing Dora's hand, he turned and came nose to nose with a beautiful horse in some type of ceremonial dress. *Was this a vision or real?* he wondered. The horse was magnificent, standing seventeen hands or taller. Beautiful red and black chicken feathers had been braided into the creamy white mane and tail. Black paint circled the left eye and ran the length of the white blaze on its nose. The horse stuck out its muzzle, as if expecting a treat for good behavior.

Kal's hand touched the soft muzzle. No vision here, instead a pair of wise eyes. "Dora, let's return the horse to its home."

Dora and Kal walked around the horse. This mare was a lady and waited until they were past her rump before spinning around and prancing after Kal and Dora. The three hadn't gotten very far when a woman's voice drifted on the moist air.

"Rosieeeee."

Rosie, looking perfectly happy to stay with her newfound friends, gave a loud whinny and refocused on Kal and Dora.

Kal addressed both Dora and Rosie, "I think we are about to become reacquainted with a friend of past."

They saw the riot of hair before they saw the woman. Hair on fire. No wonder they felt this neighbor. Every cell of her was vibrating with life, vitality, and passion. She was running like the fire was at her heals instead of on her head. Her jeans, cowgirl boots, and brown coat, were an interesting contrast to her partially braided hair adorned with colorful rooster tail feathers.

Dora and Kal immediately smiled at one another with a renewed spirit, for here was a woman pulsing with wildness in the deathless world of possessions.

Bernadette ran to within twenty feet of them, bent over at the waist with her hands on her thighs and tried to catch her breath. "Ah, Rosie, would you please stop jumping the fences."

With that Bernadette stood up, flinging her glorious mane to her back with a resounding thud.

Bernadette smiled and chewed her lip. "Rosie here hasn't been bothering you, has she? If she ate someone's favorite rose bush, I am going slip a gasket."

Dora spoke, hoping to put Bernadette at ease, "No, she came to see what we were doing at the whispering rapids. Your gaskets are secure around us."

Bernadette pondered the words *whispering rapids*. She looked closely at Dora and Kal, then focused on Rosie. As her gaze returned to Dora and Kal, her smile faded and a beep red blush spread on her fair skin, starting at her checks and spreading out with amazing speed.

With a dawning mortification, Bernadette realized these beautiful people were Native Americans. Here she was, with a horse dressed up in a bad imitation of a poor western movie, and feathers everywhere in her hair. She didn't know what she could do to not offend further.

Bernadette said, "Oh, I must look like an idiot. I ah…am just having a goofy dance for the summer solstice. I didn't mean to offend anyone with these feathers. Ah, I am really sorry. I bet this looks insulting and stupid."

Both Kal and Dora were pleased with Bernadette's sensitivity to their culture. Bernadette's obvious worry was actually a pleasure for Kal and Dora to witness, as most of society appeared to be on an oblivious outer space trip.

Kal said, "We will only be offended if you don't ask us to join you."

Bernadette immediately thought of the music she had recorded and would be playing as she danced around her little fire. Oh boy. Things were not looking up.

Struggling to explain, Bernadette said, "I would love to have company, but I am not sure you would like my playlist. Would you be able to sing?"

"I am Kal and this is my wife, Dora. We aren't offended by the song Indian Reservation."

"Bernadette Engstrom. I see there are no playlist secrets. I am glad that is settled. We will have a variety of music. The golden Hubbard squash is on the grill right now, so if we want it golden and not black, we have to get back soon."

Kal responded, "Let's all run. Lead the way."

Bernadette swiveled and took off with Dora and Kal right behind. Rosie stood for about half a minute, watching, her ears swiveling to detect what might have caused everyone to run. Finally, giving a snort and cresting her neck, she took off after them at a gallop.

Kal and Dora would always remember this night. Bernadette had a small cook fire set up in the dirt corral, with a picnic table nearby. They all ate their fill of herb seasoned Hubbard squash with a Greek yogurt dip and hot apple cider to drink.

It had become dusk and knowing that Bernadette was going to avoid the music if she could find a way out of it, Kal finally stood up and asked if they could start dancing.

They danced. They twirled and spun and hopped and every form of movement that Native Americans use to partake in a dance. Indian Reservation began, the drum beat, which wasn't loud, vibrated down to the whispering rapids and back up in the bedrock. Kal and Dora sang some songs and Bernadette followed their dance moves. After that, Bernadette played an instrumental Gaelic song by Cliar. The harp tones remind Bernadette of times past. She stepped quietly and gracefully around the fire until the tempo increased. Then it looked like Bernadette was dancing with an invisible lover. Dora and Kal held hand as the harps refrain took them up high cliffs and on wings of raptors. It was a dance of yearning and fulfillment, of the highs of love. As Kal and Dora watched tears start to fall down Bernadette's face, they bid their goodbye and melted away into the darkness, walking back home with both joyful and melancholy memories.

-

Peter watched the dancing that evening from the remodeled EPA cabin. As much as he didn't want to contemplate his life, the Native American dancing got him thinking about his ancestors and the customs he not only lost, but pushed away. He wondered if all the getting in his life was leading to a whole lot of losing. and the losing was more deleterious than he could understand.

-

Come the next morning, Dora had a few dark circles under her eyes and her voice held a worry tone. "Kal, perhaps you should go into town today. See if anyone is talking about Bernadette. You know, at that Blue Ox place. It would be good to know if she might need help in the future."

Kal nodded and took the car keys from Dora. He said, "I'll take David with me. Perhaps a trip into town would be of some benefit to him."

Chapter 25
Crash on Jade Mountain

(July 3, 1999)

Everyone rebels at some time in their life.

Rebellious. Bernadette couldn't corral her whims. She wasn't following her spiritual path. Specifically, she couldn't find the motivation to meditate or pray anytime: in the morning, at noon, or at night. She felt like a cork in Antarctica, stuck on one iceberg, then another. The icebreaker was nowhere to be seen. And, it was all of her own doing, this rebellion thing.

It was a windy, crisp morning and Bernadette was reflecting on her Antarctica. Birds weren't just singing; it was an opera complete with a tiny, fat, but very vocal, Plain Titmouse. To wake up early, hearing a melody which would inspire Mozart, grounds one in the sense of aliveness. The lure of the outdoors was too great.

With a quick brush of her hair and teeth, Bernadette was out the door. The sun filtered through the dust, stirred up in the barn by Rosie. The breath from Rosie's nostrils mixed with dust, looking like millions of sparkling lights dancing with the fresh energy of morning. Grabbing the halter, she would loop the lead rope around Rosie's neck for reins, Bernadette then pocketed treats needed for this morning's adventure. Today, Rosie, Svalbard, and Bernadette would re-explore the short trail up on Jade Mountain, where they hadn't been for a week. Using two hay bales to give Bernadette the needed height, she had just gotten her leg over Rosie's bare back when the horse started prancing. Once Bernadette was settled, Rosie immediately took off at a gallop.

Rosie and Svalbard knew this trail on Jade Mountain, but for them, every trip was a new exploration, as nights brought new scents to the world and days brought changes to the growth on the land. This particular day brought wonder to Bernadette. At their halfway mark, Bernadette's eyes noticed a brilliant white mushroom. Not just any mushroom. It was as big as a dinner plate and so white as to look almost silver. Sliding off Rosie's back, Bernadette got down on the ground to get a closer look at this fungus extraordinaire. Sleek, soft, fragile. Knowing nothing about mushrooms,

Bernadette figured it would also be very poisonous. She wondered who else looked at the mushroom and appreciated it.

Hearing a soft nicker, Bernadette glanced up at Rosie to find Svalbard nipping at her tail, the usual beginning of a game of chase. It was perfect timing. She couldn't get on Rosie right now, as there wasn't a handy stump near, so a game of chase down the mountain would be most exhilarating. Bernadette spun around and sprinted for the first corner, a giggling laughter followed her, echoing among the trees. With their ears pricked forward, both Rosie and Svalbard watched the human figure disappear. That laughter signaled the beginning of good frolicking fun with treats at the end. Rosie took a massive leap off her hind quarters, with Svalbard barking at her heals.

Bernadette was going to have to make good time down the steeper parts of the hill if she was to arrive at the meadow first, which would serve as an ideal spot to watch Rosie and Svalbard finish out their game of chase. Keeping her focus on the roots and rocks, she was picking up speed and into her third corner, a good distance ahead of the "kids", when she saw something on the trail in front of her.

"Oh no!" she yelled.

Accidents have an unreal feeling to them. This accident was no exception. She saw the person in the path. The African American man, she knew it was a man, had been distracted and now it was too late for him to hop out of the path. His surprised expression, once he saw her running pell-mell toward him, was comical. He held a cell phone in one hand against his ear and his other hand was stretched out in the universal signal of "stop".

Her tennis shoes skidded. She frantically tried to grab a nearby sapling but missed. All she could do was brace for impact as her feet connected with the man's shins. As Bernadette hit ground, she hoped for two things: an absence of rocks and a soft pudgy man. This particular man was solid and heavy. A knee hit her thigh, an arm came down above her chest, just by her neck. Then it was all a blur, the air was forced out of her lungs as the stout man came to rest on her.

Immediately, the man tried to push himself up and off Bernadette. She was aware of two more things: a gun holster was digging into her side and a knife holster was jamming her on the leg. As he tried to stand, one foot slipped on a tree root and his hand lost its support in the loose rock; he came crashing back down on Bernadette.

He looked down as Bernadette looked up, and he smiled, then began to chuckle.

Bernadette heard a rumble and a snort. Without thinking, she wrapped her arms around his waist and rolled several times, just as Rosie and Svalbard went cascading by. Bernadette frowned as she now heard an odd creaking, followed by whoosh, then a huge reverberating thud as a tree slammed into the ground. There was silence, followed by Svalbard barking and Rosie snorting and stomping.

Bernadette's love for her animal friends gave her strength to push the man off her. She was on her feet running down the path, where Svalbard and Rosie would be. A large Grand Fir now laid over the trail. Instead of trying to climb though the boughs, Bernadette ran around the tree, to find Svalbard with Rosie just a hundred feet beyond the downed tree. Both appeared fine but startled. The man came running, then walked, once he saw her.

"Are they alright?" he asked.

Bernadette said, "Startled, but fine. What the heck happened? Is the whole forest falling on us?"

"I am not sure. As long as you're all okay, I will go back up and see what is going on around here."

After few more minutes of calming Rosie, Bernadette tied her to a tree and headed back up the trail with Svalbard. She was curious what had happened, but more importantly she figured that the man didn't realize that his keys and other stuff fell out of his jacket when she rolled them across the ground.

She found him at the base of the tree examining something. He looked completely out of place on Jade Mountain, wearing clean cut slacks and a smart lightweight jacket. He wasn't a hunter or hiker, so she wondered why he was carrying a gun and knife. His close-cropped hair, freshly shaven jaw, and unworn hands reeked of a big city. Bernadette was bothered by the jacket, it looked familiar in some manner.

There was concern in his eyes. When she looked more closely, she saw the tree base had been cut.

"How is it we didn't hear someone cutting this tree? Where are they? There is no way a person could have been using a chain saw and I wouldn't have heard that."

"Well, the tree was cut most of the way and held upright by these chains. One chain had a clevis grab hook with an unsecured pin. And the pin was attached to a tripwire, which ran across the trial. When the horse ran into this tripwire, it pulled the pin out of that hook, which let the chain go free, which caused the tree to then finally fall."

Bernadette rubbed her eyes. She needed to figure out what was going on at work soon, before she was dead.

Bernadette looked at the man and said, "I am Bernadette, and you are?" Bernadette held out her hand.

The man hesitated just a fraction of a second before taking her hand. "Ronald. It is nice to meet you."

Bernadette noticed the hesitation and wondered what that meant.

"Ronald, do you live around here? I haven't seen you before. I am just down at the bottom of the hill."

He replied, "Oh, no, I was just out for a walk. I live off to the west there." And he motioned wildly with his hand. The man knelt back down, clearly wanting to end the conversation, and further examined the chains.

Bernadette walked back up the trial to find the spot where they had collided. Svalbard found the spot easily; his nose investigated the items which dropped from Ronald's jacket. There was a car key and a key card for Restful Night Hotel in town. Next to the keys lay a leather case. She knew what it was. It would hold a badge of some sort. Then she realized his jacket was the same style often worn by police and sheriff employees. Apprehension shook to her gut. How many problems could she have and how many would she survive? Glancing at Ronald, she opened the leather case up.

EPA Enforcement, Criminal Division, Region 10,
Seattle, Washington
Peter J. Harris.

Pocketing all of it, Bernadette continued to walk around looking at shoe prints above the trail. She had a choice to make. Give him back the stuff, or hold on to it, making his life more difficult. Honesty had always served her well, so she knew the actions she needed to take.

Ronald/Peter interrupted her thoughts. "Bernadette, I am not sure it is safe for you to walk around here. I am going to call the police and have them check the area."

Bernadette called Svalbard to her side, telling him to heal. She then walked over to Ronald/Peter and said, "Why do you say that, Peter? Who would want you or I to end up hurt or dead?"

Peter slowly stood, felt the pockets in his jacket by lightly patting them, then looked at Bernadette.

Bernadette took the badge, key and hotel card out of her pocket and waved them in the air. "I am going to tell you something, and I want you to listen. I could have made your life a real pain by hanging on to this stuff, but I don't believe in doing that. I am an honest person who hasn't done anything illegal. I don't know what the game is, but if you are going to be staying at the Jade Mountain cabin, maybe you could make sure nobody hurts me, or worse, kills me, okay? And by the way, there are all kinds of tracks above the trail. They might help you figure out something."

Bernadette walked up to him, looked him in the eye, and slapped the stuff in his hand. Then she and Svalbard walk off to get Rosie.

Blowing out a breath, Peter looked down at his important stuff. He had a few problems, that was for sure. The tripwire had not been purchased at the local hardware store, it was military. Peter had walked this trail the other day. Had someone anticipated he would be walking it today? Bernadette displayed honesty by giving him back his stuff, when he didn't even know it was missing. She is supposed to be a criminal. She then asked him to keep her safe. Why would she say such a thing? Was the tripwire meant for her? What was going on around this mountain?

185

Peter called the police and headed back down Jade Mountain to meet them.

Chapter 26
The States are Crazy

(May – July 1999)

Tierney Casey was able to set up camp south of Berlin Road. It was BLM timber and young enough that no one had plans to cut it for the next twenty-five years. There was a BLM locked gate, but for Tierney it was a simple task to pick the lock and have a key made. He worried a bit that someone would see him coming and going from the property and eventually report him. That problem was easily solved. He purchased a white Ford pickup that looked like all the Weyerhaeuser work trucks, stuck an orange light on the top, and had fir trees painted on the driver and passenger doors. No one gave his truck a passing glance.

Although he didn't want to, he needed to cut his long, light brown hair to match with the standard cuts around Lebanon. After a buzz cut and clean shave, his manly face blended in with all the other manly faces at Weyerhaeuser. No one ever gave him a second glance.

His living arrangements were a bit more challenging to set up. He got a decent sized travel trailer so he could be warm, shower, and cook. The trailer needed a good level spot and there had to be enough room to move it in a circle, as he needed to take it into town to dump the waste on occasion. He rented a dozer, improved the road, put in a driveway, cleared an area for the trailer, and had a good amount of rock brought in. Not wanting people to come up his driveway, should they be using the main logging road, Tierney came up with a cheap fix for that problem. Stealing a Weyerhaeuser sign from another location, he installed a gate and hung the Weyerhaeuser sign and a "No Trespassing" sign on the gate. No one ever asked him a question about what he was doing with the dozer, who authorized the dumping of rock, or what the gate as for. After that, he never wondered why crime was so high in the States. People here were oblivious to their surroundings.

Although, in defense of the people in Lebanon, everyone was busy watching and gossiping about Bernadette. He theorized that he could set up an antiaircraft missile site and no one would even notice.

From his comfortable couch he used his field glasses to see Bernadette's place. As he watched the antics of those around Bernadette, some days it was a toss-up if he should laugh, get mad, or just get drunk.

The two EPA clods on Jade Mountain who were watching Bernadette were completely inept in Tierney's mind. It was the most visible surveillance program he had ever seen. Tierney had meet both of them at the Blue Ox Tavern. He determined Ross to be a materialistic cheat. Peter, at first glance, was pathetically powerless, as he allowed himself to be pushed around by Ross. With a bit of study, Tierney realized Peter was very competent in many areas and underneath the city-refined facade there was a lethal man.

Bernadette's closest neighbor was watching her. Stephen superficially found the climate around his new neighbor a relief to boredom; a new energy surpassing all the potbellied men driving around looking at their cattle or fir trees. On a deeper level, Stephen was a shrewd farmer and respected Bernadette for working with her hands on the land. Tierney was confident that Stephen's sense of honor would cause him to defend Bernadette socially or physically if someone were to cross his firm "do not pass" mark.

The other neighbors hadn't interacted with Bernadette yet, so they weren't of any interest to Tierney.

There were the two FBI agents looking for leads into the disappearance of the SEC employee, Ed Keil. They visited Madison or Lebanon, or both, about once a month, for two days. It was an odd case that Tierney needed to watch closely.

The company where Bernadette worked was a hodgepodge of people, morals, and motivations. Some days, Tierney was surprised they could get any product out the door given the level of ineptitude, wasteful posturing, nonproductive bickering, and outright back-stabbing. His respect for her increased when he saw the obstacles she encountered every day. He was in the process of wading through the riffraff to determine a threat level for those working around Bernadette.

Tierney started networking to figure out who was the biggest gossip and had the most accurate information. His plan was to visit the Blue Ox Tavern on a frequent basis. Many people from Lebanon and Madison visited the tavern, famous for its hamburgers and beer. A good strategy for keeping Bernadette safe was to know the gossip in the area.

Chapter 27
The Ladder

(July 16-21, 1999)

Bernadette had enough time working at EwRM2 to understand the various ways one could climb the corporate ladder. One popular method was to align one's self with a point of view held dear by an upper management person. Given that Bernadette had fallen into disfavor with the President of EwRM2, Devlin Holcomb, (her comment suggesting he had passed gas while attending the Environmental Department Christmas Awards presentation would provoke even the most staid person) she was expecting any number of employees to align themselves with Devlin Holcomb's point of view, which could be summed up easily; Bernadette should be removed from the company.

The conspicuous alliance with Devlin's point of view and subsequently, the attempted dismissal of Bernadette from her job, happened in July.

The fire in the waste storage area at EwRM2 took off nicely. Normally, the hazardous waste paint material wouldn't have burned all that well. However, there was a major issue surrounding the waste paint management that had been circuitously navigated.

Someone was dumping excessive amounts of waste fuel and solvents in the waste paint drum. The Environmental staff had figured out the problem based on the last shipment of waste. The incineration facility had a highly charged phone call with Tim regarding the "miss labelled" waste paint drum. They told Tim that EwRM2 would be getting a bill for damages to the incinerator equipment resulting from an unexpectedly low flash point. The offending department, Maintenance, had then been retrained on waste disposal, new signs had been posted, and an additional two waste drums were provided for waste fuel (where was that coming from?) and for the copious amounts of waste solvents (why was there so much?).

After those steps, the Environmental Department figured that the problems would be solved. Wrong assumption.

It turned out, a union employee, Buddy Morris, was dumping paints, solvents, and fuels in an indiscriminate manner. He didn't care about following rules because his boss, the Maintenance Manager, scoffed environmental laws and refused to follow the environmental policies. He went so far as to slander Bernadette by saying since she wasn't married and didn't have a boyfriend, she must be sleeping with any number of undesirable men. Character assassination was a common method used discourage the workforce from following Bernadette's environmental programs.

Buddy was a jovial guy. He always had a smile on his face and was pleasant to everyone. He was also related to the Manager of Human Resources, Wilimina. He was the second cousin of Wilimina's half-sister's ex-husband's brother. Buddy had been disciplined eight times for serious production, safety, and environmental issues at EwRM2 in the last five years. Each time Buddy had been investigated for an infraction, he had repeatedly laughed it off, as he knew full well that the union contract was so full of loop holes a shot gun couldn't even hit it. It was common knowledge that no union person had lost a job due to disciplinary action in the last six and one-half years and counting. Buddy found management to be a nonthreatening type of irritation. His last disciplinary measure adjusted his lunch and break schedule to coincide with the department manager's. This was to ensure Buddy would always have supervision when on the job.

It was a Friday afternoon and the department manager had to leave due to a personal emergency. Buddy was being teased mercilessly by his union coworkers about not having his "mommy" supervisor nearby. In a fit of arrogance, he told everyone he would conduct his own fire test on some of his mixed paint waste because he was confident that the incineration facility had lied about damages to their equipment. Into the waste paint drum, he dumped fuel and solvents. Taking a wad of newspapers and matches from his locker, he got on the forklift, and took the drum down to the waste storage area for his test. His union buddies followed along.

Lighting the newspapers, Buddy found he didn't have a way to get the waste out of the small bung in the top of the drum. In a fit of insanity, he squeeze-lifted the drum with the forklift and tried to tip it over just a little, to dump some liquid on the fire. The drum tipped over, slipped out of the forks, and came crashing to the ground. The waste liquid flowed around the lit newspaper.

All the solvent and fuel on the ground went *poof* in a second. A ten-foot by ten-foot section of waste was on fire and spreading, as the drum lay on its side spilling it contents. The flowing liquid was heading toward twenty drums of waste oil.

Buddy grabbed a fire extinguisher stored in the waste area, but the flames were already too high and too hot to put out. A guard driving by called emergency services. By the time the first fire engine arrived, the one drum of waste oil had exploded into flames and six more were expanding with the heat. Hot flames from the exploding drum rained down on stacks of pallets some fifty feet away, setting them on fire. The pallets, stacked almost fifteen feet tall, fell over creating an inferno of nicely seasoned wood. The burning pallets landed next to a propane tank that had been removed from use, but still contained material. At that point the fire department moved everyone away. The tank exploded, creating a twenty-five-foot crater.

National Response Center was called, along with the EPA, and Oregon Department of Environmental Quality (DEQ), as required. Bernadette spent the weekend working with the agencies and contractors on the numerous problems.

Come Wednesday, Bernadette was called into Human Resources. Wilimina and Tim told Bernadette she was being written-up for not having a system in place to remove small amounts of waste material from bung topped drums.

Bernadette sat looking at them in disbelief. She said, "Let me get this straight. I am getting written-up because there wasn't a method or formal procedure in place to remove hazardous waste from a bung topped drum. Right?"

Wilimina tapped her pen on the line she wanted Bernadette to sign, stating that this was her first warning and following an investigation she may be dismissed from her position, or her employment terminated with EwRM2.

"Wilimina, what I hear you saying is that instead of reprimanding Buddy, who had failed to follow disposal policy and intentionally set a waste on fire, you are reprimanding me."

Wilimina replied, "This isn't a time to discuss Buddy and information regarding Buddy is confidential. This meeting is about your performance and how it led to the breaking of environmental laws."

Bernadette was fuming. She said, "Wilimina and Tim, let me help you understand a few things. If I had provided a tool and procedure so hazardous waste intended for disposal could be removed from the drum, with the intent it would be used for some other purpose, it would be against environmental laws. If Buddy removed the waste paint/fuel/solvents from the drum and put the hazardous waste in any old container and left it around some place, that would be against environmental laws. If he took the material and set it on fire, that is against environmental laws. So… you wanted me to write a procedure to break environmental laws?"

Bernadette knew that she was going to say something crude and wrong. She would regret it later, but she just couldn't stop herself. She would wonder about her self-control another day.

Bernadette continued, "If I tell you to get a backbone and think independently, will you reprimand yourself for not having a policy to address brown-nosing?"

With that, she got up and walked out of the meeting.

Tim sat looking at Wilimina. This was the dumbest meeting he had the displeasure of attending with Human Resources.

Tim said, "In the future, it would be wise to write-up Bernadette for failing to do her job in accordance with environmental laws. I will not attend another meeting suggesting she should break environmental laws, regardless of the people in the company who would take pleasure in her reprimand."

Tim stood up, pushed his chair back in, and walked out.

Once Bernadette was back in her office, she sent her boss a two-day vacation notice and left the facility.

The write-up was never mentioned again.

Devlin Holcomb was extremely disappointed that Bernadette wouldn't be fired over this mess. But he wasn't done yet. She would learn how to grovel with his tutelage, and he looked forward to further instruction.

Chapter 28
The Pucker

(July 22, 1999)

The morning began with a restless desire to explore the Cascade foothills. Bernadette had awoken with a burning desire for Carney and the fever it created pushed her outside into the cool balm, product of a dense overcast and a light misting rain. Surprised to find both Svalbard and Rosie had sore left feet, she ended up nixing a horse ride. Svalbard had split a pad and it took a good amount of time to clean it, then cover it with an antibiotic and some glue to keep it free of dirt for the rest of the day.

Not having the dog and horse with her would make it easier for her to slip off her property without the EPA geeks up at the cabin noticing. Having met both of them, she found Peter to be a pleasant guy, but Ross' arrogance gave anyone reason to shudder. Today, she hoped if she feigned "mending fences", Ross or Peter would become overly board with the monitor or binoculars and head to the refrigerator.

Her strategy worked.

-

After two hours at a brisk hiking pace, mixed with some running, Bernadette finally paused under an old fir tree. It had escaped the clutches of loggers, probably because of its location and its growth. It stood alone on an outcropping and had several Vs in the trunk. Bernadette leaned her head against the rough wood, hoping to soak up the tenacity of the tree. She needed the help. She felt worn thin, like a rag that has nothing left to give, except the sound of its last fibers rendering under a strain that was impossible to hold.

She never heard a sound, yet slowly turning toward her left with expectation, she found herself looking at a magnificent elk, just visible in a stand of scrub oaks. She wondered why it had appeared before her. The bull stomped his front hoof once, then again, and barked a warning. Not wanting to intrude, as animals rarely get a break from people, she turned and walked away, across the rocky ground with sparse grass and lush moss. Hearing the bull snort and retreat deeper into the brush, Bernadette glanced back, only to see Carney standing where she had been, under the old fir tree.

Carney wanted to run to her, but he realized it might startle her into thinking something was wrong. He walked towards her, controlled as possible, until he saw the tears being hastily wiped away with her hands. Then he bolted forward, running with the power of a linebacker, he was in front of her within a minute. His arms scooped around Bernadette, pulling her off the ground and into his embrace.

It was a phenomenal kiss.

Carney stepped back far enough to unzip his coat and hers, spreading them open, he pulled Bernadette to the softness of his shirt and the hardness of his belly. Feeling Bernadette's hands in his hair, Carney's hands snaked down to her derriere, drawing her tightly into his desire. Pulling her shirt out of her pants, his hand climbed up her back, loving the feel of her farm-girl muscles. His thumbs inched forward, stroking the underside of her breasts, softly teasing. As his hands slid down, with the intent of putting his thumbs down the front waistband of her pants, he encountered the first pucker and ridge, then another, and another. Carney had been told that his wife had been to a clinic after the attempt on her life. He had also been told she was fine and healthy.

Sensing a change in Carney, Bernadette backed up a step, smiling shyly. She said, "I am so happy to see you. What an excellent surprise. You look as gorgeous as ever."

The expression on Carney's face wasn't looking too happy now. Bernadette moved an eyebrow up in questions. She was so happy to see him, so overcome with their sensual kiss that she hadn't thought about the scars, until this moment.

Carney took a step back, slowly grasp the bottom front of her t-shirt in his hand and began to lift it. Immediately Bernadette was out of her sensual effervescence and putting both hands on his to stop him.

With a qualifier smile, Bernadette said, "I, ah, had a little accident Carney. I put Vitamin E on it every day and that helps reduce the…well, makes it so it isn't as noticeable. I didn't think it was worth trying to fix it with a bunch the plastic surgery. I guess I hadn't thought about how it might look to you."

Bernadette was no longer looking at Carney, but the ground. He could see and feel her embarrassment.

Releasing the shirt, Carney immediately dropped to his knees. "Look at me. I love you. You have been the best thing in my life since 1984. There isn't a day I don't think of you, hunger for you. I knew that someone tried to hurt you, but I couldn't get to you in a day or even a month. I am sorry that I have been such a poor husband. What your stomach looks like won't change how I feel about you, but it will change how I deal with others. I need to see what was done."

"No one did this to me Carney. It was an outcome of saving a little animal that was caught up in some twisted game. If I had to do it all over again, I would. I'll lift my shirt. You need to let me do it."

He remained on his knees and watched as Bernadette bunched the material up in her fists, taking a deep breath, she began to lift the shirt up, stopping just below her breasts. Carney kept his expression neutral for as long as he could, then his arms wound behind Bernadette's knees, bringing her to him, so his forehead could rest on her thighs. Bernadette let the t-shirt go and moved her hands down to massage his shoulders.

It took everything Carney had not to start sobbing. He knew that Bernadette was afraid that he would be repulsed by the scars and if he reacted strongly, she would think he was disgusted with her, that her wounds were grotesque. She wouldn't understand his emotion was caused by his own disappointment in himself; he had failed her. She wouldn't understand his intense anger to kill the people who tried to hurt her. She would withdraw back into herself if she felt scrutinized and it had taken years for him to peel away the layers that had once cloaked the beauty within her.

He stayed on his knees with his head resting on her thighs for a long time. Carney finally got up.

Bernadette stepped back, closing herself off from him. She expected to see his repulsion. Bernadette decided to tell him he didn't have to worry if he found her stomach horrendous. She wanted to tell him she could accept his revulsion. "Look, Carney, I know those scars..."

Carney put his thumb to her lips, silencing her. "Would you like to come live in Europe with me, again? I am very serious about it. While I am here, we can work on getting the animals new homes, your stuff boxed up, and the farm on the market. We still have to be discreet in Europe, but we would have a very good life and be very happy."

Bernadette knew that he was sincere, and she also knew that her living in Europe presented complications and an assortment of challenges for Carney.

She smiled and took his hands in hers. "No, I feel like my heart is here right now. My farm and the animals give me peace. Thank you for asking. I know it is complicated for you. It means a lot to me, that you would ask."

Carney just watched her for a few minutes, searching her eyes with his.

Finally, he said, "Leave your bedroom window open tonight. I will come to you. I need you Bernadette, in ways you can't imagine."

Sighing, Bernadette started to explain the EPA problem. "I have these EPA goons up the hill and ..."

Carney interrupted, "I know. Don't worry. They will suffer an odd power outage at the cabin this afternoon and probably won't be able to get it fixed for a good week. I need you tonight and nothing will change that or prevent it."

After giving her a kiss, he turned and ran back to the fir tree, turned back toward her, tipping his head at her, like he had done so many times before, as a sign of love and respect, then he was gone.

This wasn't what Carney had planned for the day, but he had to get away from Bernadette so she wouldn't see his anger, the intense rage boiling in him. He would find Tierney and they would commence a power interruption for the EPA cabin. Perhaps it would release some of his frustration to see their frustration. He ran through the woods until his lungs burned and his legs became wooden. Only then did he stop and think about what special things he might do for his wife this evening.

-

That afternoon the EPA cabin lost power. Peter called the power company, but because the cabin didn't have a formal address, only an account number, it would have to be fixed by one of their subcontractors who wasn't available until next week.

Peter said to the power company representative on the phone, "You must be kidding me. No one can work this Friday or Saturday?"

"No sir. Structures without a formal address can only be worked on by our subcontractor. It is stipulated in our union contract. And the subcontractor is out on a large job until middle of next week."

Peter disconnected the call and called Ross. "We are without power until next week. Let's go back to Seattle for a few days."

And so they did.

-

Later that night, Carney climbed through Bernadette's bedroom window, bring a backpack with him. Bernadette, sitting up reading in bed, looked stunning. Wearing a black tank top and black underwear, her sleek skin and toned muscles were well displayed.

Carney opened the pack and set up a little picnic for them: champagne, brie cheese, crackers, and grapes. They spoke in hushed tones with the lights off, all the while feeding one another the simple fare.

When Bernadette was a bit tipsy, Carney asked her, "Are you comfortable with me?"

She understood his question and said, "I think so."

After making love, Carney held Bernadette and cried. Then she started crying, until they both started laughing; what caused the laughter they didn't know.

After a few days together, they bother realized that Bernadette's injuries changed the depth of their relationship.

It was stronger.

Chapter 29
Poachers on Jade Mountain

(July 28-30, 1999)

Carney left the day EPA returned to their cabin, as their power had been restored. Up to this time, the EPA surveillance hadn't impacted Bernadette greatly. The threat of them being there hadn't been *real*. But today, it became very real and it had impacted her personal life. She was furious. She had hoped for more time with Carney, she needed more time with Carney. Their time together had come to an abrupt end and all because the EPA was on Jade Mountain watching her instead of at EwRM2 watching shipments of waste leave the facility or investigating upper management who sanctioned the movement of hazardous waste out of the facility.

After Carney left, Bernadette decided to take action. She wasn't just going to sit and wait for EPA to do something. She wasn't going to wait to get arrested, if that was their intent. She wanted EPA to rethink their strategy and she was going to help them along. She needed her privacy.

Bernadette could not believe her good fortune. The weather was cloudy this Thursday and it was raining. This summer had been one of the wettest on record for Western Orogen. Her constant EPA companion, the one on shift today, was most likely in his cabin and probably not coming out unless to get in the car. Sneaking around the farm, she jumped a fence and hiked up Jade Mountain, coming near to the EPA cabin. As she got closer to the cabin, she found trash everywhere. Peter and Ross were slobs. They had been collecting trash in thirty-gallon plastic trash bags and throwing it outside in a pile. Of course, the wild animals had gotten into it. She spent under an hour photographing tire tracks, boot prints, and trash, which included bones, rotten vegetables, wrappers, paper, plastic, aerosol cans, and even batteries. After sneaking back down the mountain, she headed into town to get the prints made at the one-hour photo shop.

Sam Cooper had worked for the City of Lebanon for fourteen years and had never been so stumped by a section of road as the long ally that ran from South Main to Conifer. The alley was gravel and there were no plans to pave it. Once your paved one alley everyone would expect their alley to be paved too, which was a financial impossibility for the city. Therefore, the war with this section of headache-inducing road had to be fought with three-quarter inch minus gravel and a road grader. Regardless of the volume of gravel poured into that alley in July, August, and September, the soft, slimy clay ate it up; the gravel sunk in and just kept sinking all winter long. Beginning each February, Sam began driving all over town looking for the missing gravel, expecting it to reappear somewhere. He never found it and only got ridiculed by his coworkers for his efforts.

Once a Buick got stuck in the clay in the third week of December and couldn't get removed for over two weeks due to the Christmas holiday; the local tow guy, Marty, who had the tow contract with the city, went on vacation and didn't care about backups. By the time January hit, the car had sunk to just below the taillights and headlights. Marty got stuck trying to get the Buick out and it took the local crane company to remove both vehicles. The crane company decided not to charge for this debacle because the press went wild showing photos of the vehicles being removed, which lead to a huge influx of business for the crane company.

Universities in Oregon sent in engineering students to study the gooey mass. Sam figured it had resulted in more theses than any other section of road.

The locals took to keeping a gate up to prevent anyone from driving on it, and the city was fine with that, but no locks. Fire ordinance and easement access made sure the gate was for looks only. Of course, everyone, fire department, police, cable…, they all knew not to drive there. Everyone knew that the alley was only good for getting stuck. That is, everyone local.

This year was particularly troublesome for Sam. Usually, by July, he could work on the section of alley, adding more gravel and grading it. Not this year. The continuous summer rain kept the alley closed.

-

Once home from getting her photographs developed, Bernadette exaggerated the motions of loading the camping gear into her truck bed, making it impossible for EPA not to question what she was doing. She knew, if they started questioning the activity, they would most likely follow her. She took her time bringing one item after another out to the truck, let the truck warm up before she left, and she drove slowly down the lane.

She pulled up three blocks from the gate which kept unsuspecting drivers off the alley of "perpetually vanishing gravel." She took her time to put on her backpack, hat, and really stretched into her black leather gloves. It was all to create a sense of leisure, knowing that Ross would get bored quickly and start using his cell phone. Just as expected Ross looked down, failing to question Bernadette's motives. Knowing she had about a minute before Ross would look up, Bernadette opened the tailgate, pulled the mountain bike from the pick-up bed, did a quick little jog, and swung onto her bike.

She had traveled a block when she heard Ross gun the car, squealing the tires while coming away from the curb. As she edged around the gate, Ross was only one-half block behind her. She was counting on his total disregard for other's property and the next few seconds would measure the man. Sure enough, he plowed through the gate, smashing it open and mildly denting his bumper.

Bernadette knew to stay on the center ridge of the alley, as she heard it was the most stable section of the road. That position supported her for about three quarters of the way down the alley. Then the clay stuck to the tires like dog poop to a shoe, encasing the tires and causing the pedal motion to become excruciatingly difficult. A few more feet and the clay jammed in between the wheel and the fender. She was slipping and wobbling along. With only ten feet to reach asphalt, the front tire sunk in the muck, pitching Bernadette down toward the ground. She hit the clay with her shoulder, fell on her side, and the bike came down on top of her.

Getting up, she immediately glanced back to see how Ross was fairing, initially more embarrassed about falling than concerned about being run over by him. Ross was taking the entire thing pretty hard. His face was bright red. He had only gotten about ten car lengths before the entire car spun sideways. With the front of the car directed toward a neighbor's fence, he was initially hesitant to gun the engine, so he gently gave it some gentle gas and turned the wheel. Nothing happened. He put the car in reverse and applied more gas. He could hear tires spinning but he didn't move backward. Instead, the car was beginning to tip wildly to the passenger side. Ross jammed the car in neutral, threw open the door, pushed himself out only to find himself sliding, like on an ice-skating rink. He ended up on his hands and knees.

"What the hell is going on?" was the last thing Bernadette heard Ross scream before she crawled to solid ground and ran off with her bike.

Back at the truck, she thew the bike in the back, ran to the passenger door, opened it, and stripped. The truck would be filthy if she got in with clay covered clothes and the clay would never come off the upholstery. She had brought along a change of clothes figuring it was highly probable she would fall. She slipped on jeans, a flannel shirt, and cowboy boots for phase two of her plan. As she sped away from the area, Ross watched his car sink deeper and deeper into the muck.

-

The Lebanon Fish and Wildlife branch office didn't see much business in July. Nothing big was in season right now and usually complaints or tips were made discretely to Bob Schmidt when he stopped by the Blue Ox Tavern for lunch. When he heard the bell at the front desk at about 3:00 p.m., he figured that someone from out of town must have gotten lost.

Sighing from the boredom of it all, Bob rounded the doorway to get behind the desk, and was surprised to see what looked like a good ol' fashioned cowgirl.

Smiling, Bernadette started in, "Good afternoon. Is this the right place to be to report poachers?"

Bernadette thought Bob grew about a foot as he stood up straight and squinted his eyes.

"That is a pretty serious charge there little lady. Maybe first we ought to talk about why you think there are poachers."

"Is Jade Mountain in your jurisdiction? If not, I don't want to take up your time."

This was the most excitement Bob had in the last year, possibly five years, and he didn't even know what the excitement was yet. "Sure is. No bother at all. This is what we are paid to do. Enforce the regulations."

Bernadette said, "Good, I would like to show you some photographs I took this week." Taking out the pictures, Bernadette began to tell her tale about all the suspicious traffic on the mountain near her property.

Chapter 30
More Surveillance

(August 3, 1999)

Dr. Brad Baily looked out of his seventh story window at the Region 10 EPA headquarters, his face mottled with angry red splotches. He went over in his mind what had happened this morning.

The Regional Administrator's assistant had called him just before 11:00 a.m. and told him to come to the Administrator's office, now. She sounded stressed. When he questioned, she was curt and hung up the phone. The Regional Administrator was the highest office in the EPA Region 10 and normally a meeting would be made days, if not weeks, in advance.

Administrator Mitchell Robinson was not looking anymore pleased than the assistant had sounded. As Brad sat in the chair looking across the beautiful executive mahogany desk at Administrator Robinson, he noticed that the Administrator's calm was belied by the pencil constantly twirling in his left hand.

Was Robinson going to sack him, he wondered? Impossible. No one ever got sacked at EPA and Brad couldn't even remember the last time someone was demoted.

"Brad, tell me about the East-West Refined Metals Manufacturing case you are working on."

Brad relaxed while he talked about the case and how it could lead to an important arrest plus a nice fine that would help with the budget.

Finally, Robinson held up his hand, signaling Brad to cease speaking. "One of your employees, Calvin "Ross"" Rossberg, was arrested early this morning, before 9 a.m., on Jade Mountain for poaching. Calvin, as you probably know, is the nephew of Robby Rossberg, who is currently the Senator for Colorado. He is a very well-connected man. I got the issue cleared up, but not before Calvin had suffered the humiliation of being arrested and taken to the county jail. When will you be able to conclude this case?"

Brad was highly in tune with the seriousness of this embarrassment. "We don't have enough evidence for an arrest. The agency would look incompetent if we took action at this stage."

"Brad, I want your staff to bug all the buildings on that farm, including the corral, the chicken coop, the pump house, and the cat box, if necessary. I will sign for the increase in expenditure this morning. I want this case concluded in EPA's favor, with a good amount of positive publicity and soon.

"And one other thing. You can tell Calvin Rossberg that he has been given a promotion, *several* levels, to a GS-15, effective immediately. Human Resources will be sending you the paperwork to sign in just a few minutes."

Robinson picked up his phone, effectively dismissing Brad.

-

Now, as Brad stood in his office looking out at nothing, a big fat zero called life, he reflected on his humble beginning with EPA. He had worked hard in college and struggled to get his master's and PhD. He started out as an intern with the EPA and worked longer hours than anyone so that he might get his dream job with the EPA. The biggest mistake of his career, by far, had been hiring Calvin Rossberg. He thought it would have been a boon to EPA to have ties with the senate and especially a positive for his department. But now, this idiot who got himself arrested, would be paid more than Brad by at least twenty grand a year. Rossberg was just given a huge raise for what? Nothing. Brad was seething.

Brad wanted to be mad with Miss Bernadette, as he called her, but he found himself rooting for her. She was clever and she had guts. He knew from the file she had a tough life, worked hard, and was never even close to being pampered like the relatives of the Robby Rossberg family. Brad had never once in his career felt compassion for someone being investigated for an EPA crime. How was he going to mentally reconcile these conflicting emotions?

EPA would now spend more money on the case, a case that Brad hadn't found particularly noteworthy. It had been the constant talk by a few people around him that encouraged him to conclude the case was substantial. All this surveillance extremism would put considerably more pressure on them to make an arrest. The stakes in this case had just gotten much, much, higher. Brad was hoping that Miss Bernadette would have some excellent tricks up her sleeve, because she was going to need them.

Madge from Human Resources had already left Brad's office with the signed paperwork for Calvin Rossberg's promotion. She hadn't said anything. Just tapped her finger on the two lines to sign, looked Brad in the eye, and walked out with a scowl to match a mad hornet.

Morale all over the building was going to tank today. And it did. Brad left in the early afternoon and didn't take any vacation or personal leave for it. He just didn't care today. And maybe tomorrow he would start coming in at 8:00 a.m., instead of his usual 6:30 a.m. Why the hell was he trying so hard?

Chapter 31
Getting the Goods

(August 1999)

After Ross was arrested and released on August 3, he went back to Seattle for a week. Peter was thankful. He didn't see Ross the day of the arrest, but he could only imagine his rage. During the week following the arrest, Peter got just a few terse emails from Ross. The first email described the increase funding for the case and how those funds were to be spent. A list of items for purchase was shown as an attachment, noting that Ross was responsible for securing the orders and delivery. Three words caught Peter's eye, *mounted posse supplies.*

Peter sent back an email, asking if there were some typographical errors. The reply showed the extent of Ross' anger and the extent of his obsession to have Bernadette arrested.

Ross wrote: *The EPA has limited ability to adequately surveil the suspect because the suspect has modes of transportation which are off-road. To ensure an adequate program, I will be procuring all the materials necessary for an EPA Mounted Posse Program. I have several years equine riding experience and I am working to secure the purchase of a quality horse. A contractor should arrive in two days to install a temporary corral and horse shelter.*

After Peter reread the email, he had one thought, *I am glad this is all on Ross' purchasing account because explaining this to the Regional Administrator will be impossible!* Then he amended that thought. If you are the nephew of a Senator, perhaps it doesn't matter what you spend.

The new cameras for installation at Bernadette's place arrived by special currier on August 6. When Bernadette and the neighbor, Stephen, were at work on Monday, August 9, Peter helped the installation contractor placed the new cameras at the following locations: in the living room, main hallway, equipment and food storage room, barn interior, and barn exterior overlooking the corral.

The new EPA temporary horse corral and lean-to were completed on August 9.

Ross returned the next day, August 10. Peter found an unpleasant note from Ross when he arrived at the cabin in the evening. It reiterated that the expenditure increase allowed for ten, not just five, new cameras and a new computer to handle all the data. The five additional cameras were in the cabinet next to the desk. He was to install the other low light, infrared, wide angle cameras at the following locations: looking out over the chicken coop, view of horse lean-to, inside the garage, kitchen corner, and view of driveway.

The messy missive also stated that Ross wanted to take over the night shift, figuring that he would have the best chance of nailing Bernadette's coffin shut by watching her nefarious activities in the dark. The result of Ross' nagging: Peter worked a night shift, installed five more cameras in the morning and covered a long day shift. Peter's patience was waning. He couldn't help but wonder if they would be communicating by notes for the rest of the project. He had tried to call Ross early on, but he had been told to "shut up".

On August 11, Peter called a buddy in the office, Dan "the tech man" Flanagan, who assisted with any technical questions regarding equipment. Two of the cameras weren't operating consistently and Peter needed help troubleshooting them. During the call, Dan gave Peter the office chatter: Ross had been given a raise the size of the Holy Roman Empire following his arrest; the mood of EPA's entire nine floors was dour; and staff were now secretly rooting that Bernadette could pull off another fast one. Peter found this information most amusing: the woman's restroom on the third floor had a whiteboard installed for making suggestions as to how Bernadette could get Ross arrested again and the whiteboard showed the current Ross (0) – Bernadette (10) score. It had been suggested to Dan that the equipment purchased for the project should have the lowest ratings for quality and reliability.

After getting all the office yarn, Peter wasn't sure he wanted to talk with Ross again.

When Ross did start talking the night of August 11, the baby-faced pretty-boy was gone, to be replaced with the visage of curdled milk. Peter regretted that he hadn't appreciated the silence, because Ross was going on a poorly thought-out rampage.

Ross said, "While I was in Seattle, I made some key phone calls to the IRS (Internal Revenue Service). This entire town is going to squirm in the next few months. I am going to show them a thing or two about respect."

Peter blew out an exasperated breath and said, "Ross, it was an innocent mistake. Fish and Wildlife and the Sheriff thought they were doing the right thing. Let's not anger the entire town."

Ross looked down his nose at Peter and said, "Shut-up. You're a yokel and you come from a litter of hicks. I make the tough calls here."

Peter stood up so fast his chair flew over. He walked up to Ross and said, "You ever talk to me like that again, I will make sure you sing two octaves higher for the rest of your miserable life."

Peter walked out and slammed the door shut. He headed to the Blue Ox Tavern. It sounded like damage control would be needed in the foreseeable future.

-

Ross did make phone calls to the IRS and Lebanon suffered through terrible bouts of IRS audits. The town of Lebanon detested Ross more and more as time went on.

-

The next morning, Peter was surprised to see Ross' car still at the cabin. He thought Ross would high-tail it out of the cabin early, to avoid further confrontation.

Once Peter entered the surveillance room, Peter said, "Well, wait until you hear what Bernadette said last evening." Ross was facing the monitor and didn't even turn around to look at Peter, however his venom sounding voice told the entire mood.

"Let's hear it," was all Peter said.

Ross punched at the keys. The picture on the monitor didn't show anyone, but a person could make out Bernadette's voice. In a whisper, she said, "Rosie, this is our secret. Be very, very quiet. You are my favorite girl. We can't let anyone know about this secret. What a good girl you are. Such a good secret keeper."

Ross stopped the recording. "What do you think?"

"This is encouraging." Peter sat down and looked at Ross, "I am a little curious. What exactly does EPA think Bernadette is doing at home? Is she stealing hazardous waste and taking it home to put in the barn? I haven't been able to get a good sense as to exactly what we are looking for here. Wouldn't the problem or issue most likely be at her work?"

Ross rolled his eyes and said, "She isn't married, and she doesn't have any family. People like that just do unscrupulous things. Bernadette's kind of mentality doesn't have anything to live for, so they do things to get back at the normal people. EwRM2 has been involved in the illegal disposal and shipping of hazardous waste, the anhydrous calcium chloride. Bernadette is obviously involved in it and promoting it because she gets a raise if she saves the company money. This isn't rocket science."

Peter felt his teeth clinch and his jaw muscles flexed several times, in a very noticeable way. He was beginning to think that this was like some very bad comedy movie. "First of all, married people and people with children and people with large extended families do illegal things too. Second, EwRM2 ships five dump trucks and pups of that particular waste each day. If she was bringing it to her house, don't you think we would notice it? And third, how was the company to determine the waste was hazardous if there isn't a standard test for it? NEC Denver had to dream up a test to use. EPA doesn't allow companies to dream up tests, so why should NEC be able to dream up a test without going through rule making. Finally, why would EwRM2 think it is hazardous waste when the same anhydrous calcium chloride is shipped into the U.S. as a product, from the same process done in a foreign country, and may I add, not labelled as a hazardous waste."

Ross was groping for a weakness in Peter. "Are you in love with Bernadette or something? If this case is going to be a conflict of interest for you, maybe you need to go back to Seattle."

The smug look on Ross' face was almost too much for Peter. He knew this ploy and found it childish. Time was on Peter's side, so he decided to continue watching and not react too harshly.

"So, I can't ask any questions about the case? You want me to follow along when there doesn't appear to be any leader? Why don't you go get some rest? You look like you've been up all-night big guy."

Ross swaggered out of the cabin. Peter reminisced that there was one thing wrong with people who thought they had the upper hand. They didn't access the situation to see if they were right.

-

Peter spent the rest of the day, on and off, looking and listening to the footage of Bernadette admitting to a secret. Something was nagging at him. It took him until 5:00 p.m., as the shadows started to crisscross the mountain, to figure out what was bugging him. Sitting back in his chair, he watched the shadows move as the darkness crept in. With a synaptic jolt, he bolted upright.

Replaying the footage, Peter found that the shadows changed quickly before and after the section Ross had pinpointed. There was missing footage. Ross was good with computers, but Peter was better. He was able to retrieve the deleted section within ten minutes.

He listened to entire section. Bernadette said, "We don't have to tell them about this Rosie."

Then in the background there was a loud "Baaaahhhh".

"Rosie, this is our secret. Be very, very quiet. You are my favorite girl. We can't let anyone know about this secret. What a good girl you are. Such a good secret keeper."

Then another louder "Baaahhhhh".

"Oh no Rosie, they found us out. Our secret alfalfa treat has been exposed. Eat fast big girl."

Peter wanted to throttle Ross. He didn't know what he could do to put Ross back on a mentally stable course. Ross was deeply embarrassed and finding a way out of that would be impossible for someone so arrogant.

-

When Ross pulled up, Peter still hadn't thought of a good way to confront Ross about the altered tape. Problem was solved easily.

Ross took one looked at Peter that evening and said, "You figured it out. I knew you would for your girlfriend."

"You know Ross, it may not be good to alter evidence."

Ross smirked, "What would you know. I am a GS-15 now. I got a raise because I have been handling myself so well on this case. I am taking a few more days off to see my wife and celebrate the raise. Car is packed."

Peter found Ross to be so annoying, that he figured another break from the guy would be a relief. He was also glad that he already knew about the raise, so he could express pleasant surprise.

Giving Ross a pat on the back and then a shove toward the door, Peter said, "You just enjoy yourself and commence with spending the raise. I'll be here when you get back."

Ross turned at the porch, looking Peter up and down. Immediately, Peter knew he might look just a tad too happy at Ross' departure.

Peter stuffed his hands in his pocks and put on a squint, "Now, you will be back for your nightshift soon, right? I can't do back-to-backs forever."

Ross relaxed and shrugged. "Should be just three or four nights, but will let you know if the lady wants me around longer. Should be back no later than August 17 or 18. And when I get back, I think I want the day shift again."

Peter mustered up a frown as Ross jogged to his car.

Chapter 32
Meeting of the Minds

(Saturday, August 7, 1999)

Rosie was gone. Bernadette blew out an exasperated breath. She had scanned every minuscule pasture concavity, scrubby stand of inconspicuous trees, slight swale borne of creek erosion, spiderweb filled barn corner, and dilapidated shed. A creeping irritability slithered out of her mind to set up camp in the currently tightening shoulder muscles, much like a ratchet wheel with a failing tension release knob. The early morning sun marched higher in the sky all the while Bernadette was tediously searching, instead of accomplishing some labor on the ever-growing task list of summer. Doing her best to tamp back down the impatience, a particularly unhelpful personality flaw, she endeavored to replace it with something much more useful, a sense of positive expectancy. She was beginning to see how much of her life, as of late, was lost to a cesspit filled with wrong emotions. Nudging in some Pollyanna mental habits was supposed to make life much better, or so the great spiritual leaders implied. Bernadette pushed her mind to contemplate that perhaps a Cascade foothills walk-about this beautiful warm day held the key to solving her confounding problems.

Since it was before noon and the wilderness excursion's duration was unknown, Bernadette threw supplies that might be needed into one of her larger backpacks; extra sweatshirt, water, food, first aid kit and gear for Rosie. The navigation equipment was efficiently supplied by Svalbard's keen Irish Wolfhound auditory and olfactory senses. Knowing he could find his way all over Jade Mountain and Snow Peak and far beyond, Bernadette didn't pack for an overnight outing. If she didn't find Rosie before four that afternoon, she would give Svalbard the "go home" command. Her trusted guard, companion, helper, and therapist would deposit both of them back at the farm with or without trails to follow.

Slamming the back door closed, Bernadette sprinted toward the three stairs bridging the house porch to the lush dwelling of the outdoors. Instead of slowing as she neared the steps, she sped up, following Svalbard with an impressive leap from the porch to the gravel walkway. What might be a strenuous hike for some today, would be easy for Bernadette, as her dog was a top-notch athletic trainer.

Svalbard could be very good finding stray animals, but sometimes he appeared to be in cahoots with the escapee. Today, animal camaraderie was in full swing on the farm. The more frequently Bernadette said "go find Rosie" the more Svalbard stopped and looked at her with a tilt of the head and innocent eye. Bernadette needed a work around and she already had a plan for circumventing Svalbard's relishing attitude of accomplice.

A few stars had aligned in Bernadette's favor and with this in mind, she was confident that today she would be able to find Rosie's exit point from the pasture. Rosie was extremely muscular this time of year, weighing in at eighteen hundred pounds and as this Oregon summer would have it, the clouds had blessed the plants with rain recently. Hoof prints in the pasture would not be unusual, but wherever she jumped the fence, her hoof prints on the other side of the fence, the size of a salad plate, would be very noticeable. Bernadette was always amazed at how a whopping draft horse cross could sneak around quiet as a gliding hawk, startling everyone from Bernadette to the chickens. Luckily, they would be trying to follow hoof prints, not hear the movements of the colossal horse who had the stealth of a panther. Today, tracking Rosie's feet could practically be done in the dark, as long as everywhere she went was soft ground.

Rosie had gone missing three times since coming to live with Bernadette, this was the fourth. But it wasn't concern for Rosie that caused Bernadette to jog along the pasture fencing searching for stray hoof prints, rather her desire to positively accomplish the mission before the other animals had to be put to bed this evening. Rosie was never off eating someone's favorite garden vegetable or in a dangerous predicament. It was the deep understanding that only an animal could possess which prompted Rosie's foray into the serene foothills where she was always found with a distressed human in need of a horse therapy session. Just two weeks ago, the County Sheriff called Bernadette while she was at work, requesting she hitch up her horse trailer and come retrieve Rosie at McDowell Creek Park, for the gentle but stubborn mammoth horse was refusing to leave the side of a depressed person, a person who had just come down from the ledge above the falls. In some way, Rosie was able to comfort human nerves, frayed ragged from a noisy, insensitive society that didn't know how to soothe or care with silence.

Bernadette picked up Rosie's exit point at the northeast corner of the property. The fence showed no signs of horsehair, but as Bernadette jogged along beside it, she noticed the trampled Oregon grape. Leaning over the fence, she could see the how Rosie had sunk in the ground a good two inches during the landing. From there Rosie followed Speckle Trout Creek, walking up into the hills where the creek cascaded over huge slabs of red lava rock. Moss and fissures in the rock purified the water to such an extent that the air was suffused with freshness and energy. Then the creek was left behind.

Higher up to the northeast, the land hadn't been disturbed since a late wave of settlers in the early nineteen-hundreds; those who were inclined to avoid the new ruckus from the sprouting cities. With a desire for self-sufficiency and a love of the land's bounty, they had planted a diversity of fruit trees to ensure a supply of storage hardy apples, pears, and quince. Some trees had long ago tilted in the wind, finding themselves hugging more of the ground than the sky. Elk and deer had sensitively nibbled the trees. Suckers and seedlings had spread out in areas where the evergreens were stunted or didn't do well. The thriving diversity lured such an array of creatures to the area that Bernadette felt an intruder in this richness. Heeding the resilient peace of nature's health spa, Svalbard was given the request to heel so as to minimize disturbance. They walked on quietly.

When the hoof marks were lost to a particularly rocky patch of volcanic rock, Svalbard kept at the trail. Bernadette was aware that they were now on Kal's land. She had not gone to visit them since their surprise visit and was a bit concerned that Rosie's keen intuitive senses had sniffed out a problem with Kal or his wife, Dora.

They had been walking for over two and three-quarter hours when Bernadette heard Rosie's nicker, well before seeing her. Bernadette whistled Svalbard to her side and approached, softly humming. She didn't want to startle anyone. She found Rosie showering fancy upon an elderly, unkept man standing within the shelter of a noble oak certainly approaching two hundred years of majestic joy. As she stepped within sight, both looked at her, but with distinctly different messages: Rosie, always welcoming and thinking of treats; the man, hurt and distrustful. Approaching with comfortable steps, Bernadette came to realize that this man wasn't as old as she originally thought. He was in fact, quiet young. The retrospection creases at his mouth, eyes and forehead combined with a pallid complexion added almost twenty years. However, it was the feeble energy, as if the last drop of vital blood in his system was about to extinguish, that gave him a good thirty years past prime.

Bernadette smiled, hoping to set the man at ease. "I see you and Rosie have become friends. I am a friend to be, Bernadette Engstrom." Extending her hand, the man looked at the extension as if it could only represent betrayal and made no move toward it.

Instead of dropping her hand, she reached to Rosie, stroking her nose.

"I came to collect up Rosie unless you want to spend more time with her. Or I can bring her back here another day." Bernadette watched the man, seeing intelligence in his eyes along with immense hurt. She was impressed with Rosie. This man needed love, needed some comfort that only a horse's essence could convey. With the intuitive knowing that this man had spent time in deep study, Bernadette speculated that his hurt stemmed from other's acceptance of a falsehood instead of looking at facts, for this type of betrayal all too often drove analytically minded men and woman to the emotional precipice. This was a conjecture of relevance, for she also found the acceptance of opinion as fact a very scary disappointment and since it wasn't hard to find instances of it in the news every day, she was challenged to find forgiveness of the personal hurts.

Bernadette waited. She understood broken things and wild feelings. Not everyone could attain the idyllic mood of a Norman Rockwell romance painting on even a sporadic basis. Svalbard approach the man, sitting at his feet and looking up. Abruptly, the man turned and began to stumble off at a surprisingly quick gait given his unsteadiness. Rosie and Svalbard were having none of it. Rosie actually trotted after him and nuzzled his neck while Svalbard ran to the front, blocking his movement. A laugh erupted, in a hollow and cynical way.

"I don't think Rosie and Svalbard are letting you go that easily." Bernadette called after him.

He then turned and looked at her, really looked. "Women are a pain in the neck." Focusing on the ground, as if embarrassed for his rude comment, he studied his boots, shoving a worn toe into the dirt. He looked at Bernadette again. With clarity, his eyes shined through his long, unkept hair as he continued, "I became insane, with long intervals of horrible sanity."

Edgar Allen Poe. Bernadette felt a pleasure at meeting this man. He quoted Poe. Here too, in the beauty of wilderness, was the constant battle of light and darkness.

She worried that the quote she was about to give him by Walt Whitman would look superficial when contrasted with Poe. "Keep your face always toward the sunshine and shadows will fall behind you." Bernadette upped her smile. "Glad I am not the normal woman." She had to dig deep in her memory. Because she had pegged him to be intelligent, one way to identify with him would be to pique his mind. Biology vocabulary tests came to the rescue. "I am sort of something else, really. I have a lot of male qualities and some good female qualities, but basically I am a classic example of homomorphy (resemblance in external character but widely different in fundamental structure) when you compare me to other people."

"I think you are an example of homophyly (resemblance arising from common ancestry)." Pushing his hair back from his face, he started to laugh again. This time a deep belly laugh, a laugh shared with those you trust. He shuffled more than walked to Bernadette and held out his hand. "David Bernstein. Your horse is beautiful. Do you worry about her wondering around the country?"

Bernadette took his emaciated hand but didn't shake too hard. She wondered if he was starving himself to death up here in the wilderness.

"Well, she usually has a goal in mind and doesn't wander off to the city. I don't necessarily like it, but she has a keen mind of her own. We appear to share life instead of one owning the other. Come visit us. We would like it." Bernadette worked the halter on, then attached the lead to Rosie. "Would you like to come with us now?"

Shaking his head negatively was David's only reply.

Bernadette led Rosie to a rock. Efficiently heaving herself up on Rosie's back using her powerful quadriceps and biceps, she was fully seated in a matter of seconds. They all turned expectantly and looked at David. A sense of warmth spread out over his skin and a tingle rose up his back. At that potent juncture, David became convinced that miracles of soul healing happen in the woods and the city is where it all gets torn asunder. Then the three headed back down the mountain.

David stood for a long time in the shady spot, watching where they had vanished from his sight. Marveling at Bernadette's magnificent horse mounting ability, he looked down at his arms where muscles shriveled from more than the disease of disuse, but also from a type of energy atrophy. After meeting Rosie, Svalbard and Bernadette, he realized that his mental fragility had improved but his overall vitality was deadlocked in the painfully ruined past. His soul felt pure and free up in the mountains but the whole of him had not improved. He knew, with a calm and nonjudgmental clarity, the problem's source was in his lack of initiative. Kal and Dora had been taking care of him, but he hadn't been doing anything. This entire time he hadn't put even a smidgen of effort into his own healing. He wanted someone to fix it from without, but the truth was, complete healing lied within the twisted mess of confused emotions aggravating his mind. The lack of self-effort had left him still feeling lost and he often wondered, *if the wind blew just the right way, wouldn't he scatter into pieces all over God's universe?*

Looking out over the grandeur the Cascade Range, a view suffused with invigoration, David knew he had been and would continue to choose life over death. From this moment forward he would ratify his current internal covenant, a hodgepodge mess of damaging thoughts, and put renewed zeal into creating a new life for himself. With a smile, he thought about not only turning toward the sunshine, but rekindling a light within.

-

Bernadette wanted nothing more than to bound in the house and look on the laptop for a David Bernstein the minute she got home. With a disgruntle sigh, she accepted the current responsibility; animals needed to be fed and settled before nightfall. Readjusting her mental stance, she was able to chirpily embrace the extra task of brushing Rosie and picking out her hooves, checking for any problems incurred during her mountain excursion. As she worked, Bernadette's mind contemplated how real farming demanded a backbone of steel and the fortitude of the mountains. She had often speculated that factory farming got its initial start when someone wanted to make their human life a land of lethargy. Or perhaps they wanted to consistently indulge in tomfoolery entertainment instead of caring for an animal, regardless of what happened to any animal. No matter how many layers of explanations were put on the factory farm farce, it still reeked of spirit short-sightedness. She found that taking care of animals was about discipline, excessive amounts of discipline needed when tired, or sick, or sick and tired. Bernadette figured anything less than complete commitment and honor was playing the odds that mother nature wouldn't or didn't eventually seek indemnification.

While relieving the tangles from Rosie mane, Bernadette kept mentally revisiting her short interaction with David, dissecting each word and nuance that might provide clues to explain his worrisome mental and physical state. Initially she had speculated on the possibility that David was some type of criminal hiding out in the mountains. Regardless of how odd his presence was there, she just couldn't believe that he had malicious intent, even if he was evading the law. The reasoning was simple. Rosie and Svalbard wanted to be with him. If he was dangerous, Rosie would have sensed it, exhibiting a nervousness, and Svalbard would have been a watchful spectator, ever on the alert that David might get too close to Bernadette. She completely dismissed the idea that David had escaped from some mental institution. His Poe quote was more of a reminder how life is fraught with horrible moments causing one to wish for insanity as a method of relief. When he said women were a pain in the neck, Bernadette understood that women were a source of frustration, but the betrayal was far deeper.

Finally, getting into the house just before dark, Bernadette settled on the couch with tea and the laptop. It was easy to find that David had been a professor in the microbiology department at Oregon Polytechnic Institute (OPI); however, the online library for professor publications held a big zero for him. Because no university would ever keep a professor who had never published a thing, Bernadette was confident papers had been deleted from the online database.

-

The following Wednesday, Bernadette was able to make it to the OPI library after work, only to admitted defeat after three hours of futile searching. Apologizing again to the librarian, with the lovely name of Myrtle, for pestering her a minimum of ten times in the last few hours, Bernadette joked that the woman more than earned her pay today. As Bernadette slid her old, out of fashion, leather fringed purse over her shoulder, Myrtle cleared her throat.

Myrtle, who secretively watched Bernadette for the last few hours, decided to help this country polished woman, because for once someone found a librarian's work to be of consequence. Being the head librarian for the last four years, Myrtle had seen a steady stream of pompous professors and conceited students, for many at OPI considered Myrtle inferiorly educated. She detested the constant parade of snobs. Conspiratorially glancing under her stern eyebrows, Myrtle confided to Bernadette that some university publications for which the research was considered of "questionable" quality by bombastic staff, were entombed in the infrequently visited upper-level room of the library. Guiding Bernadette to the location, Myrtle divulged that a small percentage of the papers were just on the wrong side of the university funding equation, so regardless of the quality of the research they were expected to remain "secluded".

Bernadette stood looking at the jumbled mess of papers, held in over sixty magazine organizers. Turing to Myrtle in astonishment, she said, "How can there be so many papers which contain facts offensive to university supporters? Does anyone complete their research?"

"Oh, many of these papers here are students' master theses. Not up to par with the graduate level work, or so the graduate students tell me. They ended up here." Myrtle gave Bernadette's shoulder a knowing pat and walked off.

Instead of starting from the top left, where she would have to stand on a stool to pull the boxes down, Bernadette sat on the floor to ease her tired feet and started pulling boxes from the right side of the bottom shelf. Luckily, in the sixth box there was gold. The publication was by Dr. David Bernstein and Dr. Lisa Albright.

Bernadette copied the paper and headed home.

That night, when Bernadette should have been sleeping, she was working herself up into the lather. Bernadette should have known about the facility that was originally in Madison, then moved into Lebanon to spew out noise and dust. The Environmental Managers met once a week to go over problems at all of the Madison facilities; the issue should have been discussed then. When EwRM2 had been approached by the community about the problem, the engineer working on the issue should have notified the Environmental Director, at a minimum, to understand if something had to be reported to the Oregon Department of Environmental Quality (DEQ). Picking up an operation and moving it wasn't a solution to the pollution issue, but from what she could infer, DEQ and EPA had done nothing about it either.

Bernadette got up for some Tums.

Returning to the couch, Bernadette put the bottle of Tums on the coffee table, as she started searching online. She went to the Lebanon Herald newspaper archive webpage to see if there was something about David or the EwRM2 facility. She found notice that a pending divorce was on hold because David had gone missing. Tomorrow she would call the person who wrote the divorce notice on David, someone who happened to be from Bernadette's graduating high school class, and try to find out more.

The next morning, Bernadette had the full story on David from Sammie. Sammie, once learning that Bernadette had seen David Bernstein, gave Bernadette the details on how the Lebanon Herald had received pictures, anonymously of course, of David in an embrace with an undergraduate student. David lost his professorship for failure to follow protocol when publishing a paper and what OPI called *quid pro quo*, favors for grades. His marriage was in shambles because of the picture. But Sammie said she was suspicious of the picture. She tracked down the student, now working in Iceland on a grant to study lichens. The student had no idea why someone created that picture and said she never had any relationship with David. She hadn't even seen David outside of the classroom. Sammie dropped the whole thing because she felt someone had an axe to grind with David.

By the time Bernadette had gotten home from work and finished chores for the day, her agitation level was inextinguishable. Someone in the company was circumventing the Environmental Department and destroying the livability of a neighborhood in Lebanon. The issue was not *if* she would do anything, she wondered what exactly she would do.

David was a broken man, not because he lacked morals, but because someone in EwRM2 had put David on a dingy, pushed it out to sea, and dusted their hands off, thinking problem solved. Someone at that company was out of control, and she felt an odd pleasure knowing she wasn't the first victim. She thought of David's haunted eyes, his bent over posture, all he had lost because he cared for the truth and found joy in seeking it. That was her last thought before the synaptic earthquake happened.

She headed out the door, avoiding the outside EPA surveillance cameras. Once Bernadette got to the EPA cabin, she was glad to see Peter's car there.

She knocked on the door and said, "Peter, can you open the door?"

Peter came to the door, looking astonished. "Bernadette, I can't be cavorting with you. I will lose my job."

"We aren't cavorting. You're going to lose your job if we don't figure out what is going on around here. Look at this research paper. I didn't even know there was a EwRM2 facility in Lebanon. We need to go into town and look at this facility."

Using the light behind him, Peter started reading the David Bernstein paper. After perusing a few pages, he looked up at Bernadette. "Maybe EPA doesn't know about this."

"Yes, they do and so does DEQ. They both shoved it under the rug."

Peter watched Bernadette closely. "Is this a trick?"

"No. You aren't like Ross. But you are not getting all the information about this case or this company."

Peter didn't like the situation. If he was thought to have duplicity in his loyalties, he might never get another job. Then an image came to mind and more importantly, the feeling that went with the image. The memory of Ross pointing a gun at his back on the first day they got to the cabin left him wondering if loyalty was just effervescent idea in his mind; a good deal of fizz leaving behind a lackluster substance.

He said, "I'll get my coat."

Peter and Bernadette said very little as they watched the EwRM2 facility in Lebanon spew out smoke and noise. And hour later he dropped her off on Elmer Lane.

As she got out of his vehicle, he said, "No talking about this, right?"

"Right. Have a good night. Oh, and don't forget to delete the surveillance footage from tonight."

Peter wondered if Bernadette realized the number of cameras they had recording her moves. He said, "Already on my to-do list."

That was Thursday night.

As darkness settled in Friday night, August 13, Bernadette got on her coat for her next excursion. She would probably get fired for this stunt tonight. Who cared? They had already tried to kill her so if she got fired and killed or if she got killed and posthumous fired, what was the difference? If they thought to whip her and David until they crawled around like subservient imbeciles, then they didn't understand infuriation. She got in her truck and drove to town.

When she got to Mrs. Bernstein's door and rang the bell, Bernadette wondered how to approach this issue. All she could think of was honesty.

A well-dressed woman, perfectly manicured, like the house trimmings and yard, answered the door.

"Mrs. Bernstein, I am Bernadette Engstrom, and I was hoping to talk with you about your husband."

A frown creased Mrs. Bernstein's perfect forehead that had either been the lucky recipient of some very expensive creams or some surgery or both. "Why don't you people leave me alone." She started to shut the door.

Bernadette pleaded. "Wait, I wanted to talk with you about how your husband is innocent of wrong behavior. I know what is going on. Please let me talk with you. I have taken a great risk just by coming to see you."

Mrs. Bernstein looked torn, and a tiredness was creeping into her eyes. She wanted her old life back. Her sister was always telling her, *ad nauseam*, "How can you ever get past this mess if you never do anything to fix the problem?"

Seeing Mrs. Bernstein's slight wavering, Bernadette forged ahead. "I cannot talk with you about it outside. You need to trust me to come in your home. I won't even take off my coat. I won't stay long."

Again, Bernadette's eyes worked in her favor. The depth and the caring were there. Mrs. Bernstein opened the door so Bernadette could pass inside. In the entryway there were two chairs and Bernadette, after taking off her shoes, walked to one, and sat. Bernadette looked with compassion at a woman who was fighting the illusion of betrayal and had no concept of the battle.

Bernadette began, "I work for East-West Refined Metals Manufacturing. For the last few years there have been some unusual problems there. Someone has secrets at EwRM2 and I am not sure how all the secrets fit together. I don't know the extent of the problem, but I do know EwRM2 will do just about anything to cover up an issue, even hurting others. I saw your husband the other day, up in the Cascade foothills, near Jade Mountain. I didn't realize what had happened to him until I did some research. Your husband may have discovered a problem that some person in EwRM2 doesn't want anyone to know about. I believe they photoshopped those pictures of David and the student so you would think David had an affair. I am confident that the same EwRM2 person made sure he got fired from OPI."

Mrs. Bernstein looked doubtful and interrupted Bernadette. "I don't know what conspiracy theory you are dreaming about, but I can't imagine anyone doing such a thing to David. I think you should just go."

Bernadette stood and instead of taking a step to leave, she shrugged off her coat. "Someone in the company tried to kill me. Let me show you the effect of that mishap."

Lifting up her T-shirt, she showed her stomach to Mrs. Bernstein, knowing well that time had eased Bernadette's pain but not the ugly scars and grotesque puckering that wove across her stomach.

Mrs. Bernstein gasp in horror, her eyes showing dismay. "Oh my God, what happened?"

Bernadette slowly lowered her shirt and spoke deeply from her gut. "The same thing probably happened to your husband, but he is suffering emotional and professional employment scars. I want you to think about this. Really dig deep to your core. Mrs. Bernstein, look beyond the manicured lawn, the white walls and white carpet I see in the living room. For goodness' sake, stand up for something important, your husband. My guess is, someone of influence destroyed your husband's career and personal life so he would go away and not pursue an environmental problem. Get a backbone and look at the evidence. Take that stupid picture and ask yourself if it looks real. The woman in the picture, who conveniently is in Iceland right now, says the picture is fake. Don't just sit here and let your marriage and husband rot because he had the guts to ask a question, not realizing what it meant to someone."

Putting back on her coat, Bernadette slipped on her boots and let herself out.

Mrs. Bernstein went to the kitchen sink and filled up the tea kettle. She made peppermint tea, put more water on to boil and made more tea. Several hours ticked by and she was still in the kitchen making tea. She wasn't thinking, and yet she was deep in thought.

All she had ever wanted was a perfect marriage and a beautiful house, like her sister, like she had growing up. Now this. Why couldn't David have left well enough alone. But like Bernadette had said, he hadn't known it was a huge issue until it was too late.

When Mrs. Bernstein went to bed, all she could see was Bernadette's stomach. Whatever had happened to Bernadette, it was serious and still the woman was willing to talk with her. She just didn't know if she had the strength to do anything and that was her last thought before falling asleep.

-

Dreams about our lives have a way of falling apart with the axe of reality. Mrs. Bernstein was ready to let the entire conversation with Bernadette go forgotten until a week later. It was Friday, August 20, 1999, when the police showed up at her door with a search warrant. She stood there astounded.

"A search warrant for what?"

"We have a legitimate claim that there is manufacturing of methamphetamine on site."

-

After all the "investigating" was done, Mrs. Bernstein stood looking at her torn apart house, the white carpet covered with dirt, and the neighbors rubbernecking as they drove by the Bernstein house. If this was a warning for her, some threat that she should stay away from David and Bernadette, someone had just made a huge mistake. She cleaned and vacuumed the white imported carpet every other day. She had bragged about the loft of the carpet, the whiteness of the carpet, even the sexy feel of the carpet, to everyone who would listen and everyone who didn't want to listen. She was boiling mad because no "lift my carpet stain" chemical was going to fix this mess. That carpet had come from the Middle East and was the only one of its type in Oregon, or so the sales lady had told her after the special order was placed. There didn't exist a product at any store that could possibly clean this mess. It looked like one hundred dogs had lived and pooped on the white carpet for a month.

Digging though the study desk, she found the envelope holding the picture of David in an embrace with a young topless woman. She walked back into the kitchen. Grabbing a bottle of Irish whiskey, she poured a shot. Looking at the bottle and the shot, she chose to take the bottle and the envelope back to the desk. This was also new. She never, ever drank straight from a liquor bottle, as it was incredibly uncouth. She sat drinking from the bottle and looking at the picture. Good golly, the shadows and lighting on David were completely different from the woman.

Gaining resolve hours later, tomorrow, which had become today, she would go to Jade Mountain and find David. She realized, all this time she had been hoping that life would somehow become normal and beautiful again. She would wake up and her marriage would look perfect, and the house would be the envy of her sister, and the neighbors would all respect and adore her again. When someone had killed that dream, they didn't realize they were cracking a fake nesting doll, of which the inside consisted of a real feeling tigress, not just an infinitesimally small doll. By God, someone had ruined her snow-white carpet and now they would pay.

Chapter 33
Peeling Away the Layers

(August 1999)

Mrs. Bernstein was not at her best this Saturday. Drinking directly from a liquor bottle was not only uncouth but led to a highly unsettled stomach. After stopping at the local sporting goods store to purchase hiking boots, and they insisted she needed heavy socks instead of her nylons, she stood inside the store door, packages in hand, wondering where on Jade Mountain she was to go. Normally, she would not have tried such a foolish adventure, but every time she thought of her white carpet, which would now best assist a psychologist in conducting some sort of huge inkblot test, an energy rose up within her that was most impetuous and vengeful.

Turning back to the salesman, she smiled sweetly, inquiring about maps of Jade Mountain. She was painfully informed that the mountain was not necessarily tall, but the area was large. The salesman, quite smitten with such a refined woman in his store, inquired as to her exact destination.

Mrs. Bernstein was not about to explain the situation to a stranger. She inquired as to any campgrounds on the mountain and was informed there were none.

Lodges? The salesman said there were none.

Bed and Breakfast? Same answer, none.

The only thing she had was Bernadette's name. Because there appeared to be no other way to find David she asked, "I think that a woman by the name of Bernadette Engstrom might be able to help me. Tall, red curly hair. Lives near the mountain. Do you know of her?"

The salesman brightened at the prospect of finally having an answer. Pulling out a map, he highlighted directions to Bernadette's place. Everyone knew Bernadette in this small town because she was such an entertaining source of gossip.

-

Bernadette was in the garden, August 21, when Mrs. Bernstein pulled up in her immaculate Cadillac.

She mumbled to herself, "Fat is in the fire now." So much for secret meeting with Mrs. Bernstein. Work would know about this by Monday. If

Ross was at the cabin, he would be rubbing his hands in conspiratorial glee. And whoever felt threatened by David and Bernadette would probably have a momentary seizure just before getting every gun out of the gun cabinet.

Stripping off her gloves and shoving them in her back jeans pocket, she approached the woman who looked completely out of place anywhere near animals and manure. As Bernadette got closer, she noticed that Mrs. Bernstein looked like she had indulged in a major alcoholic bender.

"Good to see you, Mrs. Bernstein. Can I help you with something today?" Bernadette smiled and sized up the bags on the hood of the car which came from the local sporting goods store."

"Bernadette, I can explain later, but I need to find David. I have no idea where to look. I was informed that Jade Mountain doesn't have a lodge, no bed-and-breakfast, nor even a campground where I might start looking."

"I will get our ride. Best get your gear on." Bernadette walked off to the barn.

Mrs. Bernstein, sitting in the front seat of the car with her legs hanging out, had just finished lacing up her boots and was wondering what sort of vehicle they would take. She had on her newly dry-cleaned tweed jacket and it would be a shame to have to clean it again so soon. Hearing a strange sound, she glanced up and jumped out of the car.

"Oh my gosh! It is a horse." The horse part came out in a high-pitched squeak. Rosie put her ears back and snorted.

Bernadette rubbed Rosie's neck. "Easy."

"You wanted to see David. Throw that purse back in the car, lock the door, put the keys in your expensive jean's pocket, and get on up. We are already through half the day and I need to be back before dark."

Mrs. Bernstein stood and gaped at Rosie.

Bernadette dropped the reins on the ground and walked over to Mrs. Bernstein. Easing the purse off Mrs. Bernstein's shoulder, she threw it in the car, moved Mrs. Bernstein away from the car door like a small child, locked and shut it, and put the keys in Mrs. Bernstein's pocket.

"Come stand on the picnic table bench, put your left foot in this stirrup, hold on to the horn, and pull yourself up till you can throw your other leg over."

"I can't do it." Mrs. Bernstein looked like she would faint.

"Ok, come over here to the picnic table and stand on the top of the table."

Mrs. Bernstein carefully got on the picnic table.

Bernadette led Rosie over to where Mrs. Bernstein stood. "Now get on."

Mrs. Bernstein looked a shade more pasty.

"If you don't get in that saddle, I will personally go find David and tell him he needs to find a wife who can at least fight her way out of a paper bag. Now get in the saddle."

The insult worked and Mrs. Bernstein threw her torso over the saddle, which meant she spent a great deal of time trying to get her leg over and sit up. All the while Rosie's ears laid back, showing her displeasure with this flailing about of arms and legs.

Once seated, Mrs. Bernstein said, "I don't know how to steer her."

"I know." Bernadette jumped on Rosie's back, behind the saddle, flipped one rein over Mrs. Bernstein and clicked Rosie forward.

"I am steering. Just relax. If you are all tense Rosie will think that something is wrong."

It was quite a journey with Mrs. Bernstein's "Oh"s and "Oh my!"s and "Ah"s. Bernadette got her talking after about ten minutes just so the horse wouldn't bolt from all the exclamations. Once the tale of the search warrant and white carpet destruction began, the acid level in Bernadette's stomach started to rise.

Bernadette tried to steer Rosie to the old oak, where she had first met David. But when the horse spun a circle in defiance, Bernadette gave up, giving the horse her head. They climbed through an area covered with black, rather than red, volcanic rock, causing the fir trees to be stunted in growth and sparser. Bernadette had been focused on the rock, trying to determine if it was sharp enough to cut Rosie's frog, when she heard Mrs. Bernstein's shaky voice whisper, "David, oh my God, it is David." Glancing up, there stood David, looking at them with an expression as bleak as the black rock around him. Yet, he looked different today, more rugged, a bit more color in his face.

After sliding off Rosie, Bernadette then held the reins while Mrs. Bernstein dismounted for herself. Bernadette intuitively felt that Mrs. Bernstein needed to show David the depth of her willingness to reconcile with him, which would include overcoming her fears during an ungraceful and awkward dismount from a draft horse.

Once Mrs. Bernstein had touched the ground, Bernadette began walking Rosie back the way they came. She never asked the Bernsteins how they would get back or if they needed a ride. If David lived up here, he could take care of Mrs. Bernstein from this point forward. Bernadette knew that any further loitering would be most intrusive into a special moment for this reunited couple.

Bernadette found herself anxious to get home. The carpet story was not a nice magic carpet story, giving Bernadette a new feeling of exposure. Once off the volcanic rock and back in the saddle, Rosie galloped home.

That evening, when Peter arrived at the EPA cabin to relieve Ross from his shift, he found Ross to be agitated and irrational. Ross had a foul mouth tirade about Bernadette for almost ten minutes.

Peter finally asked, "Something happen today?"

Ross just glared at Peter, then walked out the door.

Peter sat down at the work desk, knowing that something important had happened. His foot bumped and knocked over an over-flowing trash can. Curious why there was so much trash today, Peter began flattening out the various crumpled sticky notes, printer paper, and food wrappers. The reward came two minutes later. A sticky note had an Oregon license plate number and the name Bernstein written below.

Peter sat back in the chair and stared at the ceiling. Ross knew Bernstein. Why was that?

Sunday, down the road came the Bernsteins, Kal, and Dora, all on horseback. Bernadette continued working in the garden, only acknowledging their presence by calling Svalbard to her side. No words were said as the Bernsteins dismounted, then drove off in the
Cadillac, now wearing spots of chicken poop.

The car had finally become a proper chick-mobile.

Chapter 34
Rockin' Rooster

(September 3-4, 1999)

Ross, having gone back to the dayshift, had been watching Bernadette this afternoon. He detested her. He was bored. He was ruined if he just kept sitting, idling away the time.

Bernadette, however, was bone tired this afternoon. She had worked at EwRM2 all day, then came home to work in the garden. Her shoulders felt like someone had stabbed her in the back and then stitched it up, leaving a hot poker inside. Why hard work couldn't loosen up these muscles was a mystery to her.

The chickens had been watching Bernadette work in the yard with increasing interest. In winter, the chickens were allowed in the yard to eat up bugs. But, for most of late spring, summer, and fall, the yard was off limits because Bernadette didn't want them messing in the garden. The chickens did get to roam the entire orchard area, which had plenty of room and provided them with abundant forage. Yet, the swiss chard Bernadette was picking had their attention.

Listening to the increased clucking from the hens, Bernadette selected a few of the older swiss chard leaves and went in the chicken pen to hand feed the enthusiastic hens. All was fine until WHAM, something slammed into the back of Bernadette's legs.

Spinning around, Bernadette saw the rooster standing in full fight mode. Make no mistake, a rooster with his neck, wings, and feathers stuck out, ready to fling his beak and spurs on a wary victim, is nothing to laugh about. A rooster spur can leave a scar or take out an eye.

She didn't have much time to think and the rooster effectively blocked her access to the pen gate. He came at her again, and she did the only thing she could, connect her boot with his chest, sending him tumbling back several times. She watched him closely, hoping his ignoble tumbling would lead to termination of the fight. For the rooster, it appeared this was just the beginning of his retaliation; a result of a long-standing frustration with the human who swept away the attention of his hens. He came at Bernadette a second and third time, his beady eyes fixed on the Bernadette target, only a fool would mistake his anger.

Bernadette misjudged her fourth kick and connected with only air. The rooster came in closer, having developed a strategy for avoiding Bernadette's kicks. Fearfully, she took another wild kick as he jumped toward her. He easily flew up in the air and avoided her boot.

Both Bernadette and the rooster stared at one another, breathing hard. The rooster has not lost his murderous beady eye squint, and Bernadette was scared she would forever be trapped in this pen. She noticed a good size branch on the ground, a gift from an overhanging pear tree. With several quick kicks, Bernadette caused the rooster to lose ground, giving her a chance to get to the stick. Swinging wildly, she hit him in the chest several times. It did nothing. Frowning fiercely, she took aim and hit him on the lower neck He actually backed up. She jabbed at him some more with the stick, forcing him away. She backed up to the gate, unlatched it, and got out, never taking her eyes off the winged terrorist.

Ross was on the phone to the American Animal Society (AAS) before Bernadette had gotten out of the pen. Frustrated with the slow service, Ross was rude to the woman who answered on the fifth or sixth transfer. Curtly, he said, "Can I speak with someone who runs this organization?"

"You're speaking to her. Mr. Rossberg, let me tell you, your uncle, Senator Rossberg, has fought every legislative initiative we attempt to introduce. Your uncle has called me every name in the book. I have no interest in your petty problems in Oregon. Good day."

"Wait, Wait. I would guess that my uncle probably confused you with another environmental group, one that slandered him during his campaign. In fact, it probably wasn't even his misunderstanding, but an erroneous decision of an employee. If I were, you know, just theoretically, to make a contribution at this time, would that make up for his staff's misjudgment?"

The phone was silent for almost thirty seconds.

"Only a substantial contribution would encourage the AAS to forgive your uncle's staffing problems."

"Consider it done. Let us discuss an amount and how I might get a few of your employees out to a farm in Lebanon, Oregon." After another twenty minutes on the phone, Ross hung up and smiled. Bernadette was toast this time.

-

The next day, about noon, Bernadette was hoeing around her squash when two cars pulled into the driveway. Two women got out of one car and a man got out of the other. They began unloading things from their car.

Irritated, Bernadette walked up and said, "May I help you?"

The man spoke. "Hello. I am Sean with the American Animal Society." He stepped forward and held out his hand, which Bernadette shook.

A brunette woman stepped forward and said, "I am Sarah and this is Cara." She pointed to the other woman. "We also are with the American Animal Society."

Bernadette stood watching with folded arms as they unloaded a tripod and an expensive video camera. They all looked like they were on safari, wearing tan shorts and tan shirts.

Sarah finished working with the video camera. She turned to Bernadette and said, "We have reports of you abusing farm animals, especially your chickens. We would like to take a look around."

"What? I appreciate what your organization does for the rights of animals. I wouldn't hurt my animals and I work all the time to take care of them. I don't understand why you are here."

This time Cara replied, "We aren't really interested in your excuses. We received a credible tip that you are abusing your chickens. We would like to video tape the conditions of your animals, starting with your chickens."

Bernadette rubbed her eyes. It was all making sense now. This was another plot by Ross.

"And if I say no, you can't video tape the animals or look at them?"

Sean puffed out his chest and said, "Then we will seek a court order to remove the animals from your farm after the Sheriff is notified."

Given that Bernadette had nothing to hide, she decided the best approach was to go along with this absurdity. "I see. Choices and more choices. Okay, please turn on your huge video camera and get ready. Which one of you is the most fit?"

Sean stated, "We are all fit enough to walk around the farm. Please, let's start with the chickens."

Bernadette picked up her hoe and headed to the chicken pen with the three AAS employees trotting behind her.

When they got to the pen gate, Bernadette said, "Here they are. Did you want to feed them?"

Cara said, "I would like to go in the pen and check their health."

Bernadette sighed and said, "Here, you will need this hoe." She handed the hoe to Cara, then turned to unlock the pen gate.

Sarah, Cara, and Sean couldn't believe what Bernadette just did. Cara signaled to Sean to make sure he was recording everything right now.

Cara asked, "Why do I need a hoe in the pen? Do you normally use it on your chickens?"

"No, I don't ever use it. But you might get afraid in the pen and want it. Let me get you some swiss chard to feed to the chickens."

Bernadette picked some swiss chard just twenty feet away, handed it to Cara, and opened the gate for her to enter.

Cara entered the pen and bent over feeding the hens. She kneeled down to look closely at them. Bernadette saw the moment the rooster thought his territory was threatened. His eyes went beady.

Bernadette yelled, "Cara, you better stand up and hold on to the hoe."

Cara stood up and gave Bernadette a disgusted look, as if Bernadette was an evil witch with a wart on her nose. The rooster took that moment to charge. "

Cara stumbled back as the rooster's talons raked her calves. Screaming, she waved the hoe wildly. As the rooster came at her again, she put all her weight into the swinging the hoe. Accidentally hitting the rooster at the base of his head, she succeeded in knocking him out, or so Bernadette hoped, as he fell over and appeared dead.

Both Cara and Sarah screamed as the rooster laid lifelessly on the ground. Bernadette opened the chicken pen gate and said, "Get Out!"

Cara was wildly dancing around, holding her hands over her mouth as she repeatedly screamed. Blood was flowing down her legs.

Bernadette yelled at the top of her lungs, "Shut up. Stop screaming. Get out of the pen. Now do you see why I had to kick the rooster and hit him with a stick? It is terrifying to have him attack you; not to mention dangerous. At least I never killed him. Get in your cars and leave. I will send you a bill for the rooster."

Cara came running out of the pen and Bernadette went in the pen to pick up her limp rooster. Cara and Sarah sprinted for their car.

Sean was standing with the video camera at his side.

"Did you get the abuse on tape?" Bernadette asked.

"Maybe he attacked Cara because you beat him," Sean accused.

"Nope. I never did anything to him. He just got jealous yesterday because the girls were around me and not him. Some roosters just get mean. I don't know why that is. Some are very nice. If you want more footage you will need to take the dead rooster with you."

Sean trotted to his car. Sarah and Cara had already left Bernadette's place. That was the last she ever saw of them.

The rooster was back on his feet strutting around after about an hour.

Ross was fuming.

-

When Peter arrived for work that evening, he could tell something had set Ross off, yet again. Ross didn't fuss around with any niceties; he went for Peter's jugular. "Been able to pay off the divorce attorney yet?" he sneered.

Peter mused to himself, *yup, Ross is like a cornered racoon, looks all cute till it rips your hand off.*

Wanting to find a new topic of discussion, Peter zeroed in on Ross' sweatshirt, just because it was hard not to notice it. "Nice Alaska sweatshirt Ross." And it was. It was a deep forest green with a huge grizzle's head and open jaws in black. Below the jaws, red drip lettering said *Alaska.* "When were you in Alaska?" Peter was hopeful this would move things away from the topic of divorce attorney fees.

"What?" Ross' forehead bunched up in puzzlement and it took him a few seconds to figure out what Peter was talking about. "Oh, I wasn't. My Uncles goes up here every year for a few weeks. He always sends me something. This is better than the mug I got last year." Ross' voice had taken on a distracted tone.

That was when Peter started to feel the hairs on the back of neck tingle. "Your uncle, the Senator Rossberg?"

Ross nodded yes.

Peter wanted more information but needed to keep the conversation casual. He also needed to keep Ross from wanting to leave, as his shift was up. "You want a beer? I picked up some local dark beer on the way here."

Ross, feeling tense from the rooster fiasco welcomed some relief. "That would be great. Just half a glass, I have to drive to the hotel."

Peter got two bottles out of his vehicle, opened them, poured half a glass for Ross and handed it to him.

Keeping Ross engaged, Peter asked. "I used to do a lot of fly fishing. Always wanted to go to Alaska to fish. Your uncle does a lot of fishing up there?"

"Nope. My uncle says fishing is for people who are too sissy to fire a gun. He has some old friends up there. He went up there right after high school. Worked that summer in the oil business before he was to attend University of Alaska." Ross had been quickly sipping the beer and looked more relaxed.

"Good thing I don't fish much anymore," Peter said. Both Ross and Peter laughed.

Taking swig of the beer Peter gently pressed, "So why isn't Senator Rossberg the senator of Alaska instead of Senator of Colorado?"

Ross snorted, showing that he doubted what he was about to say. "There are some family rumors, probably a bunch of rot, that he fell in love with an older woman and she broke his heart. Left Alaska before school started. Went to Colorado State and has been in Colorado ever since. Anyway, I better get going. I don't get paid to work a double shift. Thanks for the beer."

-

Once Ross had pulled away, Peter whistled, long and low. He marveled at this delectable information; he had stumbled on to something important, he felt it. He knew Bernadette was born in Alaska, that her parents had lived there for several years prior to having children. Peter knew he was going to have to be very careful, for as soon as the hound scented the racoon, the racoon knew it was hunted. Problem was, the racoon was his enforcement partner.

Five minutes after Ross had left, Peter got on his phone to call his old college roommate, Jimmy, who now worked intelligence for the Navy.

Jimmy answered his phone, "What a pleasant surprise. You and I haven't spoken in what, over five years." Jimmy's tone was upbeat, as usual.

"That isn't true. I call you every Christmas. Or do you forget about that?"

Peter and Jimmy spoke for five minutes about family and friends.

Switching subjects, Peter said, "I need your help. Remember that day in the dorm room when you were in a bad way, compromising your engagement, and I got you out of that mess. You said that if I ever needed something, you were the man to come to?" Peter was hoping the offer still stood.

Jimmy never missed a beat. He clearly heard the desperation in Peter's voice. "You don't have to remind me. Let's forget about that. I will help day or night, even though my wife knows all about that dumb event. What do you need?"

"I need you to investigate a senator. But I need you to do it in a way that no one will know you are looking into it. You up for that?"

Jimmy was surprised. "Don't tell me you have a senator breaking environmental laws. Let me guess, like most politicians, this senator is releasing excess air emissions. Too much hot air."

That was what Peter needed, some levity. Both of them laughed.

Peter gave Jimmy all the information he had about Senator Rossberg and Jan Engstrom. However, he didn't tell him about Bernadette, Ross, or EwRM2, letting him know it was better if he didn't have details of the enforcement case.

Jimmy said, "Let me work on it. I'll get back to you when I have something."

The next Monday morning, in the third floor EPA women's restroom, the whiteboard had been changed. Bernadette had been awarded ten more points due to a vicious rooster. Her total was twenty. On Ross's side it said zero points, due to inept rooster. There was no doubt in anyone's mind who was the emasculated rooster.

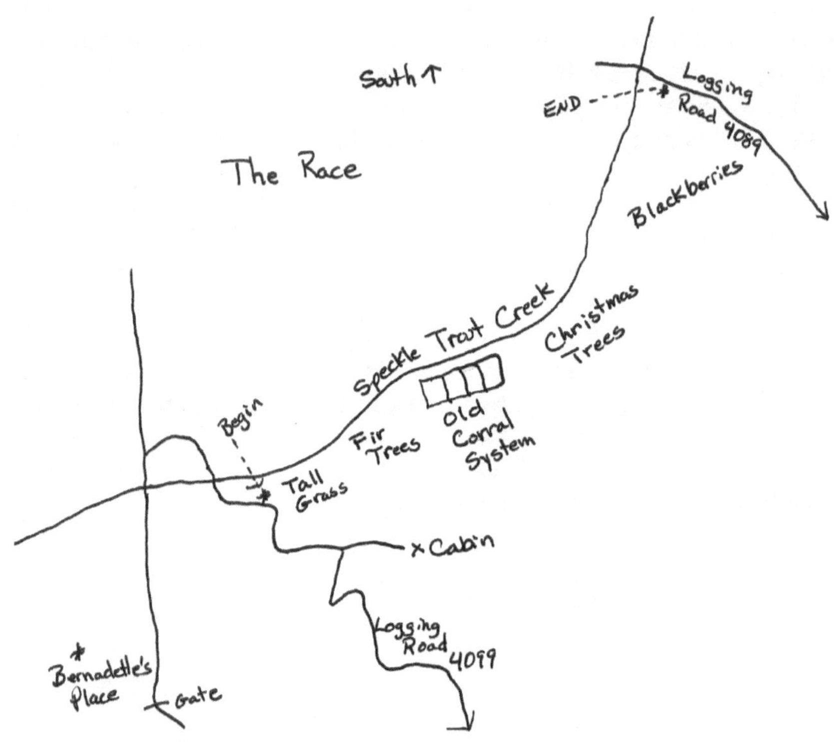

South ↑
The Race
END
Logging Road 4089
Blackberries
Speckle Trout Creek
Christmas Trees
Begin
Fir Trees
Old Corral System
Tall Grass
× Cabin
Logging Road 4099
Bernadette's Place
Gate

Chapter 35
When Did Money Eclipse Honesty?

(September 10-12, 1999)

Another Friday. Bernadette made it through another torturous work week. At 7:30 p.m. she was picking up an expensive meat-free pizza, excited at the prospect of a good book, and a satisfying meal to reset her emotional state. Returning to her truck, Bernadette did a misstep; there was a yellow sheet of paper under the driver's side windshield wiper. How could she get a ticket for parking? She was at the grocery store! There wasn't a meter or parking limit for half of a mile. Putting the pizza on the passenger seat, she hesitantly walked to the driver's side, yanking out the slip of paper.

Meet Me at the Noisy Volcanic Rock Sunday

Relieved that it wasn't a ticket, Bernadette slipped the sheet in her pocket, making a mental note to burn it in the wood stove when she got home. There was no question in her mind, David Bernstein wanted to talk about EwRM2, Lebanon location. She would need to go alone, as EPA was not invited to this meeting. If they were interested in the smoke and noise issue, they should have addressed it several years ago. Most of the evening Bernadette spent deliberating how she could lose EPA while riding Rosie on Sunday. That might be a challenge, as Stephen recently informed her that EPA had acquired horse, of very good quality.

On the positive side, she had new knowledge in her arsenal. Two weeks ago, the goats had gotten out and ventured down Speckle Trout Creek. She had found them, with the help of Svalbard and Rosie, munching on luscious blackberry leaves and succulent blackberries. The fattest and sweetest blackberries always grew right along the creek. After getting the goats home, Bernadette went back to the area with buckets; the berries were in perfect condition for freezing. In her quest to get to the best blackberries, she walked in an area of slow-moving water along the bank. Walking became more difficult, for her shoes were sinking into yucky sticky silt. However, with blackberries on her mind, she didn't head the tickling warning; instead, moving on as the muck and the water deepened into a wide lazily flowing pool. When her right shoe became stuck in the mud, Bernadette realized how soupy things had become. As she tried to pull one foot out, the other became stuck. After ten minutes, Bernadette had to abandon the bucket on the bank and leave her shoes in the bottom of the creek. She then swam to the center of the creek, where the water must have been over eight feet deep, used the sidestroke to swim downstream and finally walked out on a sandbar.

Now in bare feet, she had to get back to Rosie and ride home to retrieve old tennis shoes. She then returned to the same spot, a third time today, for the buckets of blackberries. It turned out to be a very long day, with Svalbard, Rosie, and Bernadette exhausted and cranky when the sun finally set.

In hindsight, the day had been a gift. She had advantageous insight into that section of the creek and now knew how to navigate it to avoid problems, whereas the EPA would not. It would be an excellent place to ditch a horse and rider in a chase or race.

To understand her chances of success, she needed to visit the new horse up the mountain. That would be tomorrow.

Saturday, Bernadette rode up to the cabin to meet the new addition. On Rosie's back, Bernadette sized up the warmblood. It was a beautiful horse, all black except a white blaze and three white socks. It pranced around the corral, a long black mane and tail flowing on the winds of money. This picture immediately put Bernadette at ease, because in all likelihood, the horse was bred and purchased for looks and groomed fields. There might be some redeeming qualities about the horse and it's sixteen hands suggested it was a good height for jumping, but Bernadette's gut told her the horse was not country flesh.

Spinning Rosie around, Bernadette headed back down the hill at a trot when she heard Ross' elitists sourpuss tone.

"This is a private operation and you are trespassing."

Turning Rosie back around, Bernadette faced Ross, who stood on the cabin porch in full English riding gear. Raising an eyebrow, Bernadette wasn't sure if she was hallucinating this seen of Ross in stylish tan pants tucked into just-below-the-knee black leather boots. A white shirt and black blazer completed the look. *Good grief, was he attempting to enter the Olympics?* she wondered. She was repulsed by his baby-man face; a face that women all too often swoon over.

"Hello Ross. Good to see you looking so fit today. I was just admiring your new mode of transportation. Very nice." Bernadette sat comfortably in her jeans, old boots and flannel shirt, waiting for Ross to make his move.

"Like I said, you are trespassing." Ross walked off the porch, coming toward the horse. As he stood by the corral, the horse never approached him, eyeing him nervously.

"Since this is BLM land, how could I be trespassing? Just to go along with your assertion, how about you saddle up and we go for a ride off of *your land?*" Bernadette was even shocked this came out of her mouth. This man made her life a living hell; she had to watch every word.

Tilting his head, Ross tried, in vain, to give Bernadette a scare with his condescending regard.

She was just tired of this problem, so more of EPA power plays wasn't working today.

Ross said, "I don't think Gustavus wants to associate with riffraff like Rosie. Gustavus is prime warmblood flesh, experienced in steeplechase races with years of professional training. And by the way, this is the last time I will ask you to leave."

"This is the last time I will say, this is BLM land, Ross." Swinging Rosie around, they headed back down the road. Bernadette thought about Gustavus. It was possible he could excel at running in a steeplechase, but chances are there would be training issues if he was ridden here, as this was "rough" country and not a course. There isn't a perfect horse; there was always a weakness. That was all Bernadette needed to understand, what was the horse's weakness. It was possible, in a race Rosie would know the other horse's weakness and be able to take advantage of it. She was a smart girl.

Hearing Ross open the gate into the corral, she slowed to hear how the horse reacted to him. There was a neigh, glopping, yelling, skidding, and a horse running on gravel. Since Rosie was turning her head to look back, Bernadette swung her around to see Gustavus heading for them at a full gallop. Gustavus stretched out his neck with his ears back and teeth showing. He was attacking them! Bernadette was stunned but Rosie was not. She immediately swung around and prepared to kick the other horse. Bernadette felt Rosie's powerful back and side muscles thicken and her flanks tuck in. She waited for the kick. Rosie's kick was huge and powerful. Gustavus skidded sideways to avoid a full kick in the face and chest. Rosie swiveled and moved her hooves in direct line with Gustavus, ready to give another punch if needed.

Bernadette just waited. She let Rosie have her head because to do otherwise might mean that both of them would get hurt by the demented Gustavus. Ross, holding a lead, came running up, attempting to approach Gustavus' head. Instead, the black horse reared, striking out with its front hooves. Rosie moved quickly to protect Ross, spinning, opening her mouth wide and lunging at Gustavus' neck. She forced Gustavus to come down on all hooves to avoid Rosie's side attack. Bernadette could tell that Rosie meant to put this gelding in his place. As Gustavus came down on all fours, a bit off balance, Rosie lunged again, placing a well-deserved bite on the horse's upper neck. Rosie held her ground, mouth wide, head going up and down, demanding submission from Gustavus.

Gustavus turned, trotted a few steps away, and pawed at the ground before standing still. Ross cautiously approached him, snapping the lead to the halter, then backing up to put a good five feet between him and the horse.

Ross, unwilling to moderate his speech said, "Well, I guess we can tell that Gustavus doesn't like the criminals or the animals consorting with the criminals."

"Ross, you idiot. Rosie just saved you from ending up with a horse's hoof in your mouth and that is all the thanks you can give?" Then Bernadette realized what Ross had said. Giving a good belly laugh, she gave back with equal gusto. "Yes, I suppose that is true. Since he just attacked you, that puts you in the lot with the criminals."

Bernadette was surprised. When she accused Ross of being a criminal, he looked like a guilty young man as a puffy redness took over his face. She began to wonder what secrets he was hiding.

Wheeling Rosie around, Bernadette clicked and they flew for home, all the while Bernadette wondering how much the taxpayer spent on Gustavus.

That evening, Bernadette pondered if she could orchestrate losing Gustavus in a race. If he had experience in steeplechases, he would be familiar with jumping fences and running on straightaways, meaning that obstacles to be jumped and speed alone wouldn't give Rosie the advantage. She would have to outmaneuver the horse with her knowledge of the environment. That was where the blackberry picking day on Speckle Trout Creek became important, her knowledge of the area and its sunken treasures were her best weapon.

Sunday awoke to be a beautiful sunny day. The wind out of the north was Alaska fresh and strong. Because the day might be full of surprises and the weather could change, Bernadette packed a change of clothes, extra boots, food, items needed for Rosie, and water, all in zip lock bags or water proof containers. Everything was stashed in saddle bags. Saddling up Rosie was a challenge today. First, she shied away from the saddle. Then, sticking her nose up in the air, she avoided the bridle. The freshness of the wind apparently brought rambunctiousness into everyone's spirit. Bernadette often rode without a saddle or bridle; today, she would want and need them. The saddle was a very old Barnsby, used for jumping. Bernadette adjusted the stirrups as high as they would go to ensure that nothing snagged on them while jumping. She was glad she was in shape from working on the farm. Riding at a leisurely pace was easy, but to ride a running and jumping horse meant she had to be in shape and mentally prepared. She also decided not to take Svalbard with her; she would need to focus on Rosie should she race against Ross and Gustavus.

Bernadette started out going toward town on Elmer Lane. Before Stephen's house she turned west to follow Speckle Trout Creek, just as she did the day the goats had gone on their juicy blackberry quest. Most of the fences in and around the creek were half on the ground and presented a tripping hazard for people or animals. She was glad this land hadn't gone the way of other places in Oregon. So many forgotten farms of ethical allegiances withered under the drunken fountain of feed lots and their offspring, factory farms. The fertile land went idle if it did sprout into a mall. Rich retirees from other states came in, purchasing farms with no intent of farming. As the materially covetous retirees sang their tale of "the stock market will work for me because I deserve to have a blissful golden age," the land grew to know future lumber, chemical lawns of vast expanse, and nary a seed to feed a bird. Even the stately old fruit trees of heritage birth were bulldozed over to ensure the heady occupants could have a sweeping vista scene from every room.

It was still wild here, but for how long she wondered?

Crossing the old logging road 4099, Bernadette got off Rosie and pretended something was in a hoof, or all of them. She wanted to stall, be sure they were being followed by Ross. When this entire surveillance debacle got started, EPA followed her all the time. As the weeks passed, the perpetual hounding decreased until now it was about a fifty percent chance that EPA would shadow her. She wondered if that meant they had put tracking devices in all her shoes or if they had some criteria to determine if she should be followed. Or maybe some days they were just tired and didn't want to bother. Since this was the first opportunity to follow on horseback, she was counting on Ross wanting to show his stuff. Cleaning out the hooves, she kept an eye out for movement.

Bernadette winced as she heard Gustavus whinny, high and shrill. Pausing, she worried that this race would end in an injury. Then she dismissed the worry; what horse EPA chose to ride was their problem, not hers.

She looked up as Gustavus came trotting down gravel logging road. Ross was dressed for a *Horse and Rider* magazine shoot. Too bad the rest of the picture was so distressing, with Gustavus pulling at reigns and constantly chewing the bit.

They came to a halt about twenty feet away from Rosie and Bernadette.

Based on a hunch, Bernadette asked, "Did someone in your family own or train Gustavus? He is a beautiful animal. Normally it would be hard to find an animal like that."

"My mother-in-law raised and trained this horse from a colt. Was one of the top show horses in Washington. Several highly selective equestrian farms were interested in buying him, but she felt selling him to the EPA for such a noble cause was the true sign of a prominent horse woman supporting our country."

Bernadette bent and grabbed the back left feather so Rosie would lift the last foot to be cleaned. Listening to Ross and his twaddle was so sickening, she didn't want him to see the grimace on her face. Unfortunately, Rosie was always more sensitive about lifting this foot and gave her leg a few shakes, jerking Bernadette around, before relaxing and allowing Bernadette to lift it up.

Ross tipped his head back giving a hoot, then laughing. "Bernadette, that horse is just a piece of crap. Poor breeding, poor manners, and hell, its confirmation looks like it didn't know if it was growing up to be a horse or an ass." Slapping his thigh several time, Ross laughed some more at his own joke.

Bernadette carefully put the tip of the hoof down, letting Rosie settle it as she wished. As Bernadette stood up, she found Rosie stood with her ears flattened back against her poll. Rubbing her neck, Bernadette cooed to her. "Easy. We'll show him. Just trust me. Take it easy."

Bernadette led Rosie to stand in a ditch, so she could reach a stirrup and get on. Bringing Rosie out of the ditch and to the road, she walked up to Ross and Gustavus. "Well, why don't we find out today who owns the better horse. If you can keep up with Rosie, then I will concede that Gustavus is the better horse. If you can't, then you will need to admit that Rosie here is the finest horse."

"I have a better idea. We race to the intersection of Speckle Trout Creek and logging road 4089. If I win, then you must come with me to the Region 10 EPA office in Seattle and make a full confession as to what you and East-West Refined Metals Manufacturing are doing."

Without thinking, and the was the weighty word here, thinking, Bernadette spewed out, "I can't make a confession because I haven't done anything wrong. As you wish. We will race and if I lose then I go to Seattle with you. Just fine!"

The look of conquering haughtiness that Ross gave Bernadette told her that she had made a mistake, serious mistake.

Bernadette was ruffled. She didn't immediately see that her comment was a commitment that Ross could enforce. Couldn't she later, if she lost, just say she wasn't going anywhere with him? She would break her word, but that was a rare occurrence. After what happened to her skiing and what happened to the Bernsteins, she would never get in a car with Ross or go to Seattle alone and take on EPA. She wondered if he was recording their conversation. Would this conversation sound like a confession of sorts? Would she be forced to go to Seattle? That didn't sound likely.

Somehow, she had agreed to something, and Ross considered it a coup de maître. What had she done, she wondered? What had she allowed her ego to do?

Bernadette shook her head and mentally put an end to her confusion.

Regardless of what had just happened, she had to be confident of Rosie at this moment. There was no room for an insecure horsewoman in this race. Doubt was a sure way to make a horse act up. She knew the area and she had a strategy.

Bernadette decided she and Rosie would hang back for a bit, until she felt this moment of withered confidence get pummeled with Rosie's hoof beat.

"As you wish." Bernadette swung her arm wide, in a mocking bow.

Bernadette hadn't seen a riding crop until Ross was suddenly bringing one down on Gustavus' rump. The horse jumped, and luckily Rosie did too, as she was narrowly escaped being rammed in the shoulder by Gustavus. Bernadette nudged Rosie's flank and they were off the road in a few bounds running through tall dry grass of summer. It took a good quarter mile for Bernadette to coordinate her muscles with the powerful surges of Rosie. The conversation had made her tense, so she bobbed and bounced along until she started to focus on her weight position in the stirrups, the feel of the reins woven between her fingers, and her center of gravity rocking with Rosie's. Instead of reacting, Bernadette began extending her perceptivity out into the surrounding grasses, further into the brush and deep into the trees, so as to accumulate all the information needed to take the best path.

Ross was a good seventy-five feet ahead of them, and had brought the crop down on Gustavus' rump several more times. Knowing that they would have to slow once they got to the tall fir trees, Bernadette leaned up higher on Rosie's withers, and pressed her heals into Rosie's sides. Rosie immediately responded with a burst of speed. Bernadette felt the incredible muscles working this amazingly strong horse that she loved. She had never ridden Rosie so fast and her gut instinct was to slow down. But that wasn't possible given this quagmire agreement with Ross, where she didn't understand the implications of Ross winning.

Rosie gained on Gustavus quickly. Once Bernadette's eyes were looking back at Ross, his irrationality intensified, causing Ross to use the crop five more times. Bernadette could have sworn she saw Gustavus slow every time Ross pelted the flexing muscles. Gustavus was accustomed to running on shorter grass. This field had tall and thick grass, old brown blades were woven with green new growth, making it a tangled mess. Both horses were forced to lift their front hooves higher to avoid tripping. This wasn't just a run down the field, it was running with a great deal of bounce.

Adjusting her focus to the large stand of firs looming ahead, Bernadette knew the trees were about a half mile deep. They were not planted in rows, so there was no straight way through them. There were also lots of dead logs, some on the ground, some that hung at odd angles from stumps which were two to five feet tall. The trees grew right up to the bank of the creek. Bernadette was not opting for running in the creek at this location. Gravel quickly gave way to sheets of overlapping bedrock which was slick with slime. A horse couldn't run on it, she knew, as a person could barely walk on it. Her only hope was a trail used by elk and deer further to the west. It was better than the maze of trees, but only marginally.

With two hundred feet before the tangle of trees, Ross began steering Gustavus toward the creek and Bernadette took it as a cue to head to the west.

Bernadette worried that she was riding Rosie too hard. Yet every time she asked for speed, Rosie gave it instantly and willingly. In Bernadette's haste, they almost missed the beginning of the elk/deer trail, hidden in scrub oak and Oregon grape. Bernadette was going to ease Rosie through the brush, but Rosie had other ideas, taking a huge lunge, then two more, and they were on the trail. Bernadette knew that horses who could smoothly change their leading leg, a show ring must, but she never imagined it to be of value in the forest. Rosie changed leading legs as she cornered around huge trees, allowing her to maintain speed, almost like banking into a turn with a car. A few times Bernadette had to pull her leg up, on top of the saddle, as they got too close to a tree, which was ultimately Bernadette's steering problem.

By the time they left the forest and headed toward the old corral system, both Bernadette and Rosie were covered in sweat. Bernadette had a good view of the flattened old barns and aged wood fences. There was no Gustavus or Ross anywhere in sight, causing Bernadette to think they had already come out of the creek and were far ahead of her. Sometimes in life, it is just too late for regrets, and this was one of those moments. She had put Rosie first by avoiding the bedrock in the creek and she wouldn't have changed that decision even knowing the outcome in advance.

As Rosie and Bernadette neared the old corral system from cattle days long gone, Bernadette herd Ross yelling or perhaps screaming. She kept going, picking up speed to jump the first corral fence, which was only standing at four feet or so. In its heyday, it had been much taller, but the elk and deer had broken most of the tall, half rotten boards. They had just cleared the third corral system, with one left, when Gustavus and Ross came up the bank and into the fourth corral area, only thirty feet ahead of them. They were both completely wet, but still running. Rosie and Gustavus were neck and neck as they cleared the final fence. The next field was again tall dry grass.

Rosie was easily over taking Gustavus, so Bernadette glanced back to see what Ross was up to, only to see Gustavus' right foreleg bleeding. Reining in Rosie, Bernadette yelled at Ross, "Gus is bleeding. Let's stop Ross and see how bad it is."

Ross screamed back several obscenities. Shaking her head, Bernadette focused on what was to come.

The next obstacle was a field of small Christmas trees, many of which were three to four feet tall. They were in rows, but the rows ran perpendicular to the direction Ross and Bernadette were going. There were so many, it would be hard to jump them and going around each tree in their path would be like speeding through a corn maze. Bernadette opted for running around the small trees. Ross tried to jump them, but Gustavus quickly balked, refusing to jump as he couldn't get up speed. It was slow going, for all of them.

With Bernadette in the lead, ahead she saw where the Christmas trees became consumed by the largest blackberry mound ever, probably twenty feet tall in areas. It must have covered several acres. She started heading toward the creek. Slowing Rosie down, they reached the creek bank, which dropped about three feet; Rosie easily slid down it. Bernadette took her to the middle of the creek, where the water was the fastest, and encouraged her to go forward, down the creek. She side stepped several times, arching her neck in an elegant but rebellious look. Bernadette would not let her walk near the bank as that was the location of the sticky muck.

Reaching down, Bernadette caressed her neck. "Rosie, it is fine. Let's go girl. Come on. In you go." With a bit more prancing, Rosie began walking in until she was forced to swim down the stream. Bernadette heard Gustavus' whiney, and a commotion but didn't dare look back. She had never ridden a horse in water, and although the distance wasn't long, she wanted to be sensitive. Several times Rosie headed for the bank and Bernadette kept her at center. It was less than three or four minutes and Rosie found footing again. When they were finally out on the sand bar, Bernadette spurred Rosie toward the bank, where they would soon find logging road 4089. Glancing back, she saw Ross, his face red with rage, standing in the creek by himself; there was no Gustavus around.

As Ross watched Bernadette ride off, his thoughts turned ugly with ideas for metering out revenge. In his mind, he could no longer tolerate this continuous humiliation. She was nothing and yet, she had become greater.

-

It was a long winding way to get from logging road 4089 to the lava rock. At the first opportunity, Bernadette stopped and gave Rosie some grain, a huge thanks for her efforts. Bernadette changed into her dry clothes. The stirrups were lowered, and the bridle came off. A halter was fine for the remainder of their trip, as it would be calm ride.

David wasn't waiting for them at the lava rock. The old oak where she had first met David wasn't far off, so they went there. David stood with his back to the tree, smiling as they approached. There is nothing like seeing a person who went through the depths of despair and came out the other side. He had conquered the darkness. In his struggle he gained an emotional and spiritual muscle which shown with immense energy. David looked brand new.

"Bernadette, how nice to see you. Anyone follow you?"

"It is wonderful to see you, David. EPA Ross followed on his new horse, but with Rosie's excellent skills we managed to lose him. So how are things and are you still working on the noise problem?"

David smiled and began petting Rosie, "Good. The answer to the second question is more complex. Have you ever been to the Lebanon EwRM2 facility?"

"No, I didn't even know it existed until I read the paper you wrote. No one ever talked about it in a meeting. No engineer ever mentioned it. Very strange." Bernadette looked confused as she spoke about the secretive facility.

"After I went to live with Kal and Dora, from what I have heard, the noise problem there reduced overall, but continued just twice a week. The last few weeks I have been watching the building at night. Near the end of the night shift, about 3:00 a.m., a guy who doesn't do much but watch the process, he comes by in a white pickup and gets anywhere from one to three buckets of something. On the days that specific guy isn't there, then an employee will drive around the back, stop, run in to the building, come back out with a bucket or two, and leave. To me, it looks like they are stealing. Just the other morning a fancy black Audi drove up at the end of the shift and this white hair guy in a suit goes in for a few minutes, comes out with two buckets and leaves the facility. Any idea on what is going on?"

Bernadette said, "There could be a few people who drive the black Audi. EwRM2 has a lot of employees. But the person I know who drives a real fancy Audi and wears a suit, is the president of the company, Devlin Holcomb.

"The topic of stealing from the company is a sore one with me. We had a contractor doing some work on a large project a few years ago. The union employees approached me multiple times about theft of company tools and materials by contractors. I finally approached the project manager on the issue. You would have thought I was complaining about something as trivial as one-ply instead of two-ply toilet paper. I was basically told to shut up and get lost. From what I have seen, it is rare that the company actually cares about theft of materials or process secrets."

Bernadette got out of the saddle and stood next to David. She couldn't believe his transformation.

David said, "I followed the expensive car. It went to this very secluded and ritzy place just outside of Brownsville. It is funny though, the house is just a few hundred yards from property owned by a buddy of Cutter's, his name is Hobson. Hobson owns land all around the house and on both sides of their driveway."

Bernadette searched her mind and then asked, "Who is Cutter?" She was unfamiliar with the nickname.

"He is the farmer with the dairy near Lebanon EwRM2, Cutlas Altree. His calves were dying, and I associated the calf mortality with the noise and dust coming from that process."

Bernadette was already hatching a plan. "This Hobson guy, what does he do with the land around the fancy house?"

"I guess the land isn't that great. He has a good stand of fir trees there and runs cattle on it for part of the year." David was more interested in the EwRM2 facility, so he tried to tamp down his impatience with Bernadette's line of questions. He had hoped his observations of staff stealing company materials would provide an inroad into the noise and dust problem.

"Can you get a tractor or equipment up there?" Bernadette asked.

"I am sure you can. It is fall, so don't have to worry about getting stuck in mud."

"Well, looks like Ms. Karma is going to Brownsville, to the Holcomb house. Fall is harvest time and that might go on all night and day, right? If a belt isn't tight on some harvest equipment and it screeches like a banshee, that can't really be the farmer's fault, can it? There are probably lots of other things Hobson could do to make their quiet estate a living horrorville. When they complain, you just ask why they are concerned when they do the same to people in Lebanon. Let them know that if they want to poop all over others so they can take home a huge salary, then they should expect to be pooped on.

"There are other things you could do. Set up a chicken operation where you are raising chicks and need to run a super loud generator at night to keep the little chicks warm. Or put an equipment overhaul operation up there. Test drill for oil outside their window. Endless opportunities up there. Noise, the gift that keeps on giving."

David hesitantly walked up to Bernadette and gave her a hug. "Thank you for being so creative." Standing back, he said, "This could be the only way to fight them. Nothing else has worked. I will talk with Cutter and Hobson and see what they want to do. From what I can tell, farmers always have some old equipment just right for such a sacrificial operation."

-

As it turned out, Hobson had thinned fir trees in that area over a year ago and it was a perfect time to mill them. Several hundred yards behind Devlin Holcomb's house, he set up a rough milling operation to cut some nice 2 x 6 x 10-foot boards that could be used for fencing. The equipment was old, rusty, and resulting cacophony was enough to make a person beg for hearing loss. They started up the equipment after 5:00 p.m. Once it became dark, they started several generators to shine high powered lights on the operation. One light was accidentally pointed at the house.

When a sharply dressed woman with an equally sharp tongue stormed out of her house to speak with the men operating the mill, she didn't get far. People in the logging and milling business are a tough breed and if a man is willing to take on the deadliest profession, he probably isn't concerned with some hen cackling in the hen house. When you deal with trees that split up the middle, dead treetops waiting to fall down, cables that lose their hold, logs a split second away from uncontrollable rolling, and equipment that knows no difference between tree and man, then dealing with a woman yelling about noise is as simple as dressing her down and walking away.

Two and one-half weeks later, Cutter noticed that the doors on the EwRM2 Lebanon building didn't open at 8:00 p.m., as was usual. The doors never opened again. The building was cleared out and sold.

Chapter 36
Hot Summer Night

(September 13, 1999)

Peter stopped by the Blue Ox Tavern before his night shift officially began. *Who was he kidding?* he reflected. Ross left town this afternoon, like a confused bird on some crazy migration pattern. He had announced his imminent departure, which meant Peter was on all-the-time shift.

Just when his sandwich was brought to his table, Peter was jarred out of his critical musings to focus on a brand-new twist. Tierney, who frequented the bar, usually reclusive in a back booth, appeared to be completely inebriated and picking a fight with another customer, Frank. Everyone knew everyone's name at the Blue Ox Tavern and everyone knew a lot of gossip, most of it false. Rumor mill said that Tierney was some type of operative with a secret agency and Frank worked at the mill during the day while cheating on his wife all night. During Frank's latest expounding on his debauchery with a girl in high school, Tierney had turned on him, slamming down his drink and shattering the glass, spilling the fine soda water mixed with something across the table.

As the argument regarding underaged girls moved across the tavern, Frank pushed Tierney in the chest, causing Tierney to fall on to Peter's table. Quickly, Tierney grabbed a chair and sat down across from Peter, with his legs arrogantly splayed and arms crossing his chest.

"Oh, look at the tough boy Frank who pushed me. What you going to do now?" Tierney was heavily slurring his words.

Other men in the bar grabbed Frank by the suspenders and pulled him several tables away from Tierney. Tierney kept up his drunken monolog for another half minute, then while attempting to stand, slid a piece of paper under Peter's plate. Tierney stumbled back to his regular booth in the back.

Peter slipped the paper in his coat and asked for a container to take his sandwich with him. Getting in his car, he turned on the dome light to read the lightly scribbled note: *Hit order on Bernadette for tonight. Meet at barn at 20:00* (8 p.m.).

Tingles went up Peter's back and the hair on his arms stood up. Peter was not in the mood to face this decision this afternoon. He wanted his life to follow a path based on easy and clearly defined decisions. Helping someone whose life was threatened was on an entirely different level from helping someone under investigation for a crime. But what was the crime? That question kept coming back to him.

Why ask him? Peter knew the answer to that question. Although he had left the military after years of service, with the firm decision that all the killing was behind him, those who understood lethality, saw the potential for it in him. Peter mentally ticked through the options. If he turned his back on this information and Bernadette died, would that be acceptable? If he called the police, and they showed up, causing the hit to be delayed to another day, would that be better? If he went to help Bernadette live another day, what would his career look like after that and more importantly, what would the man in the mirror look like? If he was killed tonight, what would his family be told about who he was and what he was doing?

Peter didn't doubt the note was true. The whole ridiculous operation reeked of someone slithering around on their underbelly trying to gain something, probably money or power. Anymore it all seemed to come down to money.

After driving to the cabin, Peter sat staring at nothing. He finally came to the conclusion to dust his hands of the whole thing. Bernadette wasn't his concern, and he didn't engage in hand-to-hand combat for the EPA. Grabbing a beer to go with his sandwich and punching in a movie, he was fully intending to zone out, until his phone rang at 7:15 p.m.

It was his sister, Margery, and Peter thought the call would be good tidings for him. His sister's tales of his three nephews and two nieces would distract him into a happy oblivion. Instead, he was given the news that his niece, Milly, who was coming home late from a swim meet, stopped by a store to pick up a gallon of milk and ended up getting her purse stolen. While fumbling with the car keys and the milk, a man approached her from behind, knocked her to the ground, took her purse, and ran off. In the parking lot with her were four biker dudes, the father of one of her teammates, two beefy men in a pickup truck, and a store employee picking up some garbage. None of the witnesses said or did anything. They just watched."

Peter was inwardly groaning. He knew what was coming.

Margery asked, "When will you be back home? We need one good man amongst the rot of them. Your nieces and nephews rely on your compass to make it through the cesspit of the poorly behaving public. Their father can't be the only good man."

Glancing at his watch, it was 7:45 p.m. "Margery, dear, I appreciate your faith in me. I should be home soon, I hope. Got to be somewhere in fifteen minutes. Love you."

After clicking off the phone, Peter glanced at the expensive beer, open, fizzing away. Was that his life too, just fizzing away with the beer and movie? Goodbye beer, hello Bernadette bodyguard, once lowly EPA guy.

Although Ross had made most of the extravagant purchases under this operation, the few purchases that Peter had encouraged included a gun safe and night operations gear. Walking over to the gun safe, he dialed in the combination with a bit of apprehension. He had gone sloppy. Should have been checking on equipment and guns in here daily. Luckily, as the door swung open, he found all in order. He wasn't sure what he needed, so he dressed for a night operation, like his old military times. Overdressed rather than underdressed was best when one didn't know their opponent.

It was 8:05 p.m. when Peter arrived at the barn. With the night vision goggles he easily saw Tierney, looking relieved.

Tierney said, "Was beginning to think you weren't coming to our party. I don't know how many to expect and from what direction. Tierney handed him a two-way radio."

Peter had been thinking about this down the mountain. "My guess is two. One to do the hit and one to secure the area. What about Svalbard?"

"Already fixed that problem. Shot him with pureed hamburger from a water soaker gun. Bernadette has him inside because she trying to figure out what is wrong with him. She will probably give him a bath. If he isn't barking or getting shot, it will keep her in the house."

Peter took the barn loft door, which gave a good view of the field and back of house, while Tierney took the front of the house.

Peter saw the men easily, two, with two huge German shepherds. Calling quietly on the radio he said, "Approaching. Two and two dogs. Going to secure all barn doors." Peter was please that all the doors could be locked from the inside, not just the outside.

Back up in the loft Peter secured a rope to a six by six, ready to rappel down when he needed to.

They waited.

The hit men reached the barn and house.

One man tried to gain entry to the barn. The goats were starting to yell, but the doors held. He then approached Rosie's corral and lean-to.

Peter knew (because of the camera directed at the corral), that Bernadette never locked the horse in the corral for fear of trapping the horse with an attacking cougar or dog. When the two German shepherds were set free, they went after Rosie. She immediately kicked one, knocking it senseless, and the other chased her out of the corral. The man growled in frustration. Peter had dropped to the ground and came at him from behind. The man was a decent street fighter, attempting to flip Peter over his back. He didn't manage that and he was quickly incapacitated.

The other man approached the front yard from the road. Tierney was confident he was waiting for Svalbard to make an appearance. He ran toward the side of the house. Tierney jumped off the porch railing, landing on top of him. Being that Tierney was an excellent fighter, the struggle was over before it began.

Tierney and Peter loaded the unconscious and bound men into Tierney's truck bed. The German shepherds had long vanished.

Tierney asked, "What do you think these men were going to do?"

Peter was surprised by the question. "Why ask me? You said it was a hit job." But the minute the words were said, he knew why the words were inaccurate and why Tierney asked. "Inexperience. Wrong equipment. The German shepherds."

"Aye." Tierney elaborated. "These were not professional hit men. I think we are seeing the Battle of Medway. Ensure your opponent is worn down so they are unprepared and unsuspecting of the event to come. Plague, fire, in this case animal trauma, can distract and make a person sloppy. It can also be easier to break their spirit, get them to talk, or make the wrong choices. It is time for me to do more checking around town. All the stars suggest we have a big event coming up."

Peter asked, "What are you going to do with these boys? Will you tell Bernadette about this?"

"I am going to take them way up into the Cascades and let them wake up there. I think that will encourage them not to come back, if they ever make it back. And no, I won't tell her. She already had one attempt on her life, has the scars to look at every day. Thanks. Thanks for helping Peter."

Peter didn't reply, he just walked away. He wanted to be alone with his thoughts.

-

When Peter was back at the cabin drinking his flat beer, he began going over this mess. First, the hit didn't come from EPA. EPA was lots of things, but they never killed people who might be breaking environmental laws, or kill an offender's animals, did they? To think EPA had any part of this evening went against history. But Peter had to admit, history was filled with people who were villains.

Having no answers to who was doing the tormenting, Peter moved on to the troubling questions of why. People were tormented and killed for several possibilities and Peter ticked though those.

First, people were attacked because they are on the "other side". War, spying, gang activity, mafia relations, and even unhappy, cheated on, spouses can lead to death. Peter was certain Bernadette was not involved in any of these. She just didn't have the make up for any of those activities. This fact had confused him from the beginning, because to be investigated by EPA meant you probably weren't doing the right thing. He had a gut instinct about people who were shady and Bernadette just didn't fit that description.

Second, people were killed because they bought and sold materials in dangerous markets. Drugs, guns, explosives, gems and the list went on. Again, he didn't see evidence to call Bernadette a dealer of anything. People didn't show up at her house at all hours of the night. Fairly confident, he marked that off the list.

Third, people were besieged and killed because they know something, and someone doesn't trust them to have the secret. Or, someone thinks they know a secret, but they really don't. This had a high probability of being Bernadette's problem. She was smart, quiet, took initiative, investigated things, and didn't like dishonesty. Did she know something? If she hadn't told people about the problem, there was a reason she wasn't talking about it. Or maybe she had spoken about it and now it led to this crazy circus filled with a bunch of clowns. Peter was willing to bet a year's salary that this was the source of Bernadette's problems.

But how to remedy the situation would require more thought and time. It was unlikely that Bernadette would come to the conclusion that she should confide in him. If he had understood the complexity of the problem in the beginning, he would have approached things differently.

Chapter 37
A Change of Plans

(September 14, 1999)

Bernadette got into work almost a half hour late this September 14th morning, a Tuesday. She had spent the better part of the night giving Svalbard a bath and blow-out because he had gotten into something dead, horribly decomposed based on the mushy texture. Initially, she thought the dog had a major injury, but after inspecting him and washing him, there was nary a scratch. Then she had to clean the bathroom and some of the floors in the house of blood, mud, and dog hair. She had no idea how dogs managed to find the most vile substance and then get such delight in rolling in it. She wasn't tired just from the late-night dog washing event, but also the stress of thinking something terrible had happened to Svalbard, that was until she couldn't find a scratch on him.

Tuesday was normally the day when Bernadette performed the weekly hazardous waste inspections, required by government regulations. She began in the facility's process areas furthest north and worked her way south. At about 11:45 a.m. Bernadette reached the area she called the "back forty". A creek, wetlands, and fields lay beyond the hazardous waste storage area, some of it EwRM2 land, some of it not.

A pair of eyes watched Bernadette enter the area and they admired her. She walked with confidence. Even when wearing an orange hardhat, steel-toed boots, and a safety vest, she blended beauty and strength, or perhaps her unconventional beauty came from her strength.

As Bernadette began checking the labels on the drums, a voice said, "Good morning, Bernadette.

"Ha!" Bernadette jumped as she sucked in a breath. She thought she was alone at the waste storage area. Turning, she said, "Carney, what are you doing here? You scared me."

Carney looked at Bernadette with green eyes holding concern. He stayed behind a stack of pallets, just his head and chest showing a smidgen; he could easily vanish should someone else come by the storage area. Bernadette set down her clipboard and walked closer to him, looking concerned.

She said, "You wouldn't be here unless something was really wrong. What is it?"

"Bernadette, I need you to come with me. Now. I have a motorcycle hidden down by the wetlands, so we can leave quickly through the fields."

Although she wanted to give him a welcoming kiss, she kept her distance, ensuring she could easily return to the inspection should they be interrupted. "I should finish up a few things and I have an important meeting this afternoon. Can I meet you someplace later, say 4:00 this afternoon?" Bernadette tried to be conscientious about her job, yet she felt the intense tug of wanting to spend time with her husband.

Carney shook his head, looking sad. "No, we need to go now."

Bernadette sighed. Having a husband who couldn't exist in front of family, friends, or coworkers was such challenge. "Okay. Let me go to my office and get my purse. I will ask someone to finish this inspection and decline the meeting notice for this afternoon. I'll be right back."

"I took care of your purse. I hacked into your work email account about an hour ago and asked one of your coworkers to bring your purse down here and put it in the operator shed. "You" explained that you were getting a migraine and the medication was in your purse."

Bernadette tilted her head to the right, raised her right eyebrow, and stared at Carney. She thought, *well, at least he is efficient.* Shaking her head, she walked over to the little shed which served as an operator station. Sure enough, there on the desk was her purse. She slung the purse over her shoulder.

Returning to Carney, she hesitated to leave, not wanting to be responsible for an incomplete inspection form. She said, "Let me just take this inspection form to a coworker and I will come right back. It won't take more than fifteen minutes. These inspections have to be done every seven days or we get fined. It is called a paper crisis if it doesn't get done." Bernadette smiled, hoping Carney would understand the joke, a sharp contrast to the crises they experienced together.

Instead, Carney clinched his jaw. He was going to have to explain this dire situation to her here. "Bernadette, if you go to your office, I will never get to see you again.

"EPA, your boss, the company president and HR are waiting for you in a conference room right now, in the administration building. When you go to your office, your boss is going to escort you to the conference room. EwRM2 worked a deal with EPA. They are going to say you committed illegal activities in the management of hazardous waste. For that admission, EPA will reduce monetary penalties against the company. You are to be arrested and immediately taken to Seattle. There you will be put in jail and there you will die by suicide.

"I can't protect you in jail Bernadette. I can only protect you outside of a jail. You must come with me now."

Bernadette stood several seconds shaking her head in confusion. "What? What are you talking about? I haven't done anything illegal. Are you saying there is a warrant out for my arrest?"

"No, the EPA has no evidence that you have done anything wrong. Your boss and the company president will each give a statement that you have committed certain illegal actions which will allow EPA to arrest you."

A frown and squint took over her expression. "Why are you talking about suicide? I don't feel suicidal!" Bernadette was becoming visibly upset and her voice was starting to increase in volume

Carney held out his arms and Bernadette walked into them. He said, "Someone doesn't want you alive. Killing you by hanging, when you're in jail, would be easy. Officials would say that you were distraught over being arrested; you were a loner who had nothing to live for. It is an excuse used all the time to kill people in jail."

"I like my job. I feel like I can contribute here. I feel like this is important for the environment. How can I just walk away?" Bernadette asked. Tears were beginning to swim in her eyes.

"If you are dead, you aren't any help to the environment. And I love you. This job isn't worth dying for, I know that. Come with me. We are going to take a vacation in the mountains for several weeks; destress from this company."

Bernadette continued to push back, "Maybe you're mistaken. How do you know my boss is waiting for me at this facility?"

"Call his landline. See if he is in his office. You can leave him a message that you are taking two weeks' vacation and giving two weeks' notice, on the same day, today."

Bernadette called and she was connected to voicemail after several rings. After resigning from her job, she hung up the phone and said, "I need to put this phone in the shed. It is company property." She jogged to the shed, set the phone down, then took her hardhat and vest off, setting them by the phone. She stood in thought for a few seconds before running back to Carney.

"Let's go before I think too much about this," she said.

Carney drove them to Kal and Dora's place. Tierney was already there. He handed two large backpacks containing Bernadette's clothes to Carney.

Bernadette stood quietly sobbing while Kal got two horses ready.

Tierney walked up to Bernadette and said, "I will be staying at your farm. I have got it covered. Don't worry about anything."

She just nodded her head.

Carney got up on one horse, then extended his hand to Bernadette for her to get up behind him. Their supplies were on a second horse.

Kal watched them ride off. Early this morning, he had helped Carney and Tierney prepare a temporary tepee and corral at a beautiful location just an hour ride away. They would have to come back in a week for additional supplies. He was confident the quiet would help Bernadette heal from this betrayal. Nature would sooth the hurts that only mankind could inflict.

-

The whiteboard in woman's restroom, on the third floor of the EPA Region 10, was illuminated with words – profanity. Greg and Ross, trying to manipulate the arrest of Bernadette, were called every name imaginable. Finally, someone offended by the talk erased most of it. Bernadette was added fifty points (+50) for integrity and ingenuity. Ross, and Greg's name was added this time, were given a negative number of fifty (-50).

Chapter 38
The "You're Not Welcome" Committee

(September 15, 1999)

With Ross out of town, Peter left the cabin at 7:00 p.m. and headed to the Blue Ox Tavern for dinner. Sitting down at his favorite table near the bar, he waited for his order to be taken.

After twenty minutes of being ignored by the waitstaff, Peter got up and approached the bartender. "Hey Jeff, could I get a cheeseburger and soda?" He was completely ignored. "Jeff, what is up man?"

Tierney approached Peter and Jeff. "Jeff, Peter doesn't know what happened yesterday. He wasn't in on it."

Jeff looked shocked, "He is EPA. How could he not know?"

"Because Ross kept it a secret. Ross and Greg Tucker were at the meeting. Give Peter some food. I will fill him in on the details."

Peter stood looking from Jeff to Tierney and back again. "What details?"

Tierney spoke kindly to Peter, "Come sit at my table and I will give you all the EPA news from yesterday." Tierney winked at him, "Everything you wanted to know but were afraid to ask about subversive EPA enforcement actions."

As Tierney told Peter about the deal EPA and corporate EwRM2 had made, Peter began losing his appetite. When he learned how Bernadette had quit her job in the middle of the day to avoid being arrested because Devlin Holcomb and Ross had a plan to get rid of her, he didn't want his cheeseburger anymore.

Peter said, "Now I understand why you drove her truck home yesterday and stayed at her house last night. You have animal duty while Bernadette recovers from this absurdity EPA is calling an enforcement."

Tierney stood up and said, "That reminds me, I need to get back to the farm and feed the dog. Peter, you watch your back. Until this mess gets cleared up, Ross would happily ship you out with the hazardous waste if it was beneficial to him."

Peter left for the cabin, his cheeseburger in a box. Take-out food was becoming the norm.

Peter walked in the cabin, put his food in the refrigerator, and then went to sit at the work desk. Tonight, as he walked up to the new, fancy, ergonomically correct chair Ross had purchased, a question pulled at him, *who was approving the purchase of all this stuff?*

The list of items purchased was outrageous when seen in totality: cabin remodel, cameras, monitors, corral, horse, gun safe, hotel rooms, food, and salaries with overtime. Sitting down, he tried to access the EPA purchasing system only to find the search function and historical records system were blocked for him. He called the after-hours IT (Information Technology) person. IT troubleshooted Peter's account while they were on the phone and concluded it was an issue of authority. IT would have to contact the project lead to get Peter more access. Peter told them not to bother and hung up. The lead was Ross. How convenient.

Peter was feeling more than frustrated. He had tried to look at the history of use on the computer, only to find that it was erased for today and every day it had been erased. Why would Ross want to do that?

It was time to call Jimmy. Peter was relieved when Jimmy answered his phone.

Peter said, "Sorry it is so late, but I know you are a night owl. Jimmy, you better have something for me. I am counting on you."

Jimmy chuckled. "Well, you and a bunch of other people are counting on me.

"I have some interesting news. First, your hunch that Senator Rossberg and Jan worked together was incorrect. But I have something better for you. Jan's first marriage was to an Anthony Watson who was killed in a 1956 automobile accident outside of Anchorage. Anthony Watson was a distant cousin of Senator Rossberg. Jan and Anthony didn't have any children and Jan suffered greatly when Anthony died; she had a severe mental breakdown. She met her second husband a few years later. I doubt that Bernadette was even told her mother had been previously married because the topic would be too disturbing to Jan.

"The Rossberg family didn't stay in touch with Jan, not until 1997. Senator Rossberg was in Portland, Oregon, for some republican event and Jan met with him for lunch. It was just luck that I found that out. A reporter happened to snap a picture of them leaving a Portland restaurant. Rossberg was in Portland and Seattle in the spring of 1998 for more republican fundraising, but I don't know if they met again at that time. Since Jan passed away in the spring of 1999, we know they didn't meet after that."

Peter asked, "Did Senator Rossberg have an affair with Jan when he was in Alaska?" Peter was cringing at that thought. Sounded too much like a bad show on T.V.

"I am still digging into his summer job and why he left in a hurry. My gut says no. He is an ambitious man, and my guess is, if he were to have an affair, it would be with someone who had status. I'll let you know when I hear more. Happy now?"

"Sure am. Thank you and good night."

Peter was floored to find out that Senator Rossberg knew Jan Engstrom. Peter couldn't shake the reoccurring notion that Ross was being motivated by someone else. This entire situation was not how EPA ran an enforcement. Senator Rossberg was the logical person to pressure Ross, causing him to behave in abnormal ways. But why? Had Jan done something to encourage the attacks on Bernadette? What mother would do that?

Peter had been in special forces for the Army and based on just a fraction of his experience there, he knew this situation couldn't end well. There was an iceberg here and Peter wondered when it would ram his boat and the big ol' EPA cruise ship.

He decided he would pass this information on to Tierney tomorrow.

A few weeks later, Jimmy called Peter with more information on Senator Rossberg. The summary was enlightening: the Rossbergs liked to manipulate and sabotage company equipment or products to make money in the stock market. That modus operandi had gotten Senator Rossberg fired from his job in Alaska.

254

Part V

Chapter 39
Loving Ways

(September 14-28, 1999)

The tepee nestled in a small valley between two foothills. Big leaf maple and white oak trees filtered out the sun in summer and in fall the abundant leaves gave back to the earth. A plentiful artesian spring a quarter mile away brought the animals to the area. Sheltered from the wind, it was a peaceful place.

Carney circumspectly watched Bernadette, for she barely spoke twenty words the last two days. They rode the horses or sat under the trees in silence. Carney gave her time. He understood betrayal. Bernadette had been there for him when he was in the thick of betrayal. She had saved his life. In his opinion, betrayal was one of the hardest wounds to heal but the most liberating when that journey was accomplished.

Bernadette felt she had undergone a mental and emotional triathlon these last two days; many, many thoughts and emotions crossed her mind. She kept circling back to a few key points.

- She grieved the loss of her job, which had held meaning and importance to her. The hard work and repeated attempts to instill ideas of good environmental stewardship now dissolved into nothing, like a worthless deflated balloon ready for the landfill.

- The enthrallment with EPA ideals failed to resurrect itself in any manner or form. EPA had become just another organization prone to the same human failings as any other organization.

- She wouldn't miss the tight gut and headaches resulting from working in a place that found women to be servile distractions. All her efforts to fight those attitudes had only targeted her for slaughter with upper management.

- Compassion for others increased as she began to realize why a person stayed in an abusive relationship - familiarity. The bullying and disrespect she had endured at EwRM2 felt normal after its continual daily onslaught. Going forward, she was walking into the unknown job world, and she hoped, a more professional one.

-   Her hurt spurred the creation of a new path; she was ready to strive and hope for better. It was time to move on.

She had been sitting with her back against the huge trunk of a stately oak. Carney rested on a blanket, cushioned by the lush grass, in the sun. Quietly, Bernadette stood, walked over to Carney and laid down beside him. Rolling over on his side, he ran his hand through her hair and caressed her face. "Are you feeling better?"

"I think so. Thank you for bringing me here. It is beautiful."

"Are you ready to talk about work? My guess is, people think you know something, even if you don't know that you hold critical information. The only way we can fix this is to figure out what scares them. What is threatening them."

"I haven't seen anything or heard anything illegal. But we can walk through a few things that were odd or unusual or one might say bad for the company. I think you will find all of it rather boring."

Carney kissed the tip of her nose. "I think together we can solve this, so please begin."

Bernadette started in. "I was checking things at the wastewater treatment system one day about two years ago and found that a switch for a pump was malfunctioning. I needed it fixed quickly because it was only a matter of time before we would get into an overflow problem at a wastewater sump. I couldn't reach anyone on the radio, which was so typical. I figured someone was hiding or lazy or both. I am not being judgmental here. Just to give you an example, one time I went in the instrument shop and found the guys playing chess. They looked at me straight-faced and said they were too busy to help with a problem. Some of the employees were excellent, but others you needed to hunt down with a bloodhound.

"Anyways, I called on the radio and no one answered, so I walked to the south instrument shop, hoping to find someone working, or someone taking a break, or someone in the storage unit attached to that instrument shop. No one was in the front area and I headed into the back room where they had a lot of supplies and tools. No one was there either. I heard the front door open and started to call out, but stopped when I heard people yelling at each other. Men were screaming and saying things like, "you did it" or "you caused it" and then it turned into "if you ever tell anyone I'll kill you" or "you're already dead". It sounded like they started punching at one another. I did what any reasonable woman would do, I opened up a large closet for storing gear and hid in it. Luckily, I remembered to turn off my radio. I was so scared; the men sounded completely out of control.

"Excessive amounts of profanity went with all the anger I heard. Turns out, they were yelling about the new natural gas lines that had been installed, a multimillion-dollar project replacing and upgrading thousands of feet of natural gas pipe. This had been a huge project that had taken three years to complete and involved shutting down process areas when some of the work was being done. They completely redid the natural gas delivery system. From what I heard that day in the closet, all the below ground connections, fittings connecting pipes to pipes, or pipes to flex hoses, or pipes to a process, were the wrong specification. The fittings were purchased from a cheaper source in a foreign country and people in the instrument shop who specified the buy had not realized that this other county's standards were different from the ones in the U.S. The lower grade fittings, suited for above ground use, not below ground, were now installed all over the facility. These connections ran the risk of early failure, as the metal would corrode more quickly at the connections. The men disagreed on several key points: were the fittings really a serious issue, should they tell the corporate office; and who would redo and pay for the project the second time around.

"Someone said that maintenance should think about all the people who could be killed if the system had catastrophic failure and it resulted in an explosion. The shop went silent.

"Then I heard the door again and the manager's voice spoke in low tones. I know his voice well. He said this wasn't a safe place for such a serious argument. Everyone left. I don't know where they continued that discussion.

"I came out of the closet about two or three minutes after everyone left. The problem was, as I was leaving the shop, I ran into one of the instrument technicians. He looked surprised and asked where I came from as they couldn't reach me on my radio. He pasted on this fake smile, reached over to me, and turned on my radio. I blustered my way through his questions and told him I had been everywhere looking for someone to fix a switch at wastewater treatment. I tried to act urgent about the situation, hoping to deflect his suspicion. We walked to the switch, and he began troubleshooting it. I don't think he believed that I had just arrived at the shop; he kept glancing at me with mistrust.

"I later left an anonymous note on my boss' desk briefly mentioning the possibility of a natural gas line problem. Nothing was ever mentioned or done about the issue in the two years since that day. I don't know if it was determined not to be a problem or if everyone wanted to look the other way. The problem could even be bigger. I knew that they had redone some of the natural gas systems at sister companies too. Maybe the lower grade fittings were installed in multiple facilities in multiple states; maybe the problem doesn't exist at all. I don't know and I didn't feel comfortable asking about it after I heard the many threats flung around the instrument shop that day."

Carney said, "Interesting. The problem could impact company profitability. Maybe they would try to avoid costs though insurance fraud in some manner, or possibly they just forget the problem and hope they are long gone when the pipes leak. Complicated. Go on."

Bernadette continued, "That wasn't the only thing suspicious at the shop that day. When I got in the closet, I was up against a wall and felt something move. You know how much I like to discover hidden compartments, and well, there was a hidden compartment. I was only able to glance in it briefly, when I opened the large door to the closet and let light in. There were bags of different metal objects. Some looked like snaps, some were like a heavy-duty screw, but I didn't know what they were. They were labelled by numbers alone, no words or chemical notation. I know that some alloys are manufactured at EwRM2, so having different metals at the facility is normal. But it is odd they would be hidden in such a manner. If they are used in the process, I would think the departments using them would have them locked up, especially if the materials are expensive or can lead to a quality failure if the wrong amount is used.

"I never told anyone about those bags of metals. However, I once asked a production manager how they stored materials used in alloys. The had a locked cabinet in the area for various metals. The production operation looked very standard and nothing like what I found in the instrument shop that day."

Carney reached over and squeezed Bernadette's hand. He said, "Bernadette, storing metals for alloys in a secret cabinet makes me think you found a problem. Do you think they have hidden cameras in that shop?"

Bernadette thought for several moments. "I don't think so, but it is possible. Maybe the fact that I was leaving the shop, just moments after the arguing men left, was enough to make others think I knew something I shouldn't."

"Is that it? Do you know anything about the anhydrous calcium chloride that EPA doesn't know?" Carney asked.

"I don't understand all the machinations going on with the calcium chloride enforcement. EPA has behaved in odd ways. I don't know if they are confused, or have a hidden agenda, or are just using it as an excuse to pursue me.

"One other unusual thing happened at EwRM2. It was the day of the annual Christmas awards. I heard the booming voice of the company president through some ductwork, I think he was insulting me. Then, when trying to find coffee cups, I picked some locked cabinets in the supply room that is off the conference room and president's office. There was a camera imbedded in the wall and it appeared they are taping activities in the president's office. Plus, I found an old sample of NiTi wire, nitinol, a high-tech type of memory wire. The rumor is that nitinol was back-engineered, the original material was taken from an unidentified flying object (UFO) wreckage. I don't know why the nitinol sample was locked in those cabinets with a camera, recording device, and a plastic bag containing the very same screw-shaped metal objects I saw in the instrument shop. I almost got caught by HR getting into those cabinets but managed a way out of that situation."

Carney smiled. "I bet you did get out of that situation. You are the most incredibly inventive person. Which probably scares the hell out of everyone at that company.

"I can see why you couldn't do anything with this information. Sure, it might look odd to those who understand the company, but nothing stands out as illegal. If you told someone about the hidden camera, EwRM2 could easily say they have signs up regarding areas are under video surveillance within the company. They could remove the camera and then there is no proof it was there. Period. Having materials around for making alloys is nothing unusual. On the surface it appears normal."

-

That evening, Carney put his everything into loving Bernadette. He seduced her, teased her, and kept her on edge for a long time. He did every trick he knew to love her up and take her to the sexual stratosphere.

As they laid quietly in the aftermath of love, Carney felt a satisfaction with himself. He hoped to give Bernadette a reprieve from the thoughts of hurt and betrayal and he felt he had succeeded.

Pulling Bernadette on top of him, he massaged her temples and asked, "What are you thinking?"

"I was thinking of Wiggly. No matter what life brought to him, he fought for his life and he was happy. I respected that about him and learned from that."

Carney tried to hold back a groan. "I just spent hours loving you, wanting you to know how much I care about you, wanting you to forget about the sick EwRM2 company, and you are thinking about a chipmunk?" Carney began laughing and honestly, he laughed so hard he could hardly breath. When he lay exhausted from laughing, he said to Bernadette, who was pink with embarrassment and worry that she had hurt Carney, "You are the best Bernadette. Let's hear about the chipmunk in a minute. First, I want to tell you something important.

"Both Roger and I are convinced that God displays his love for you like a billboard sign. If I didn't see God's hand is in your life, protecting you, loving you, giving you strength, I would never, ever believe it. You make me a better man Bernadette, because I get to see the most beautiful relationship on display; through your love of nature, you are always a best friend of your creator. You care in ways that most people can't imagine because you look outside of yourself and immediate family. Without you in my life, I never would have developed into the better person I am today.

"Thank you for your loving ways. Now tell me about the chipmunk."

Instead, Bernadette began loving up Carney.

Chapter 40
Who is Culpable?

(September 21, 1999)

Bernadette wanted to check on her farm after being gone a week. They returned early, before dawn. Carney and Tierney left to buy supplies and Bernadette started the clothes washer. After checking on the animals, she noticed that everyone was getting fed more than enough. Rosie girth had expanded and the goats were eating through alfalfa like candy.

She decided to ride Rosie around the farm to check on fencing and perhaps help Rosie burn a few calories she was amply consuming. A misting rain fell while the sun rays warred with the clouds filling sky above the Cascade Range. This morning was chilly, but the glow on Bernadette's face reflected the warmth of her lover's caresses during the last week.

Dressed in her riding gear and long waterproof riding cape, Bernadette saddled up Rosie. The sweet calls of the chickadees were interrupted by a high-pitched squeal (the timing belt was going) upon startup of Stephen's old pickup. Bernadette knew that it would be about five minutes before he left. Smiling, she realized she knew quite a few of Stephen's habits and none of them were annoying. A perfect neighbor.

The Stephen's truck rumblings had vanished up the road when the first bleats of his sheep started. Svalbard was on his feet, bounding out the back of the barn and toward the sound with his hackles up, clearly agitated. The bleating quickly grew into panic. Bernadette ran back in the house, grabbing her loaded rifle. She didn't have time to attach a scabbard to the saddle; the over-the-back scabbard, less convenient if one needed to shoot from the horse, would have to suffice today.

Bernadette had a hunch as to cause of the commotion. Two months ago, the local paper had a front-page article about a pack of dogs, eight of them, who had gone wild. They were attacking livestock in the Lebanon area. Stephen had lost a lamb and ewe last week to them. Bernadette locked the goats up in the barn each night, something Tierney had been doing the past week, so she hadn't lost any livestock, yet. She guessed that this morning the rogue dogs had returned for another meal.

Because the goats were still in the barn, and Svalbard would be outnumbered by the dogs, she locked him in a stall with her favorite doe, Mocha Poka. Leading Rosie out of the barn, she locked everything up behind her, quickly lowered the stirrups to ensure she could easily mount and dismount under any condition, and mounted Rosie.

Rosie had jumped the first fence separating the properties, crossed Stephen's lower paddock, and was galloping full throttle to the south when they came upon the panicked flock. It was the bleating of a lamb in a stand of juvenile oaks which had captured the wild dogs' attention. The dogs, more skittish in the increasing light of day, were unorganized, some slinking along a fence, others standing alert, and a few creeping toward their soon to be killed lamb. Bernadette dashed Rosie into the middle of the pack, skidding up to the lamb. Off the saddle in an instant, she had the lamb in her arm and was back up on Rosie in moments.

She watched the dogs as they turned their aggressive sights to the horse and rider. This was the wrong place to fix the problem. Rosie would get surrounded, Bernadette could get thrown, and once on the ground, she would be the dogs' next victim.

Bernadette quickly decided on a precarious strategy; she bleated like a sick distressed lamb. She moved Rosie into a trot, going south, away from the panicked flock. Bernadette continued to give a sheep's distress call and the dog's senses were quickened. They began to follow. Holding Rosie back from her top speed, they galloped three-quarters of a mile at a clip compatible with a dogs' speed. The dogs, their senses captivated with the chase, were silent and close behind. Bernadette brought Rosie bounding up steep bank, breaking into a wide spot in Berlin Road. Crossing the road, she dismounted, put the frightened lamb in a saddle bag, tied Rosie to a sapling, and took the rifle from her scabbard. Sprinting to the middle of the road, she knelt and focused the rifle to the north, toward the embankment where the dogs would rise in their last pursuit. She waited.

A semi-truck crested the rolling hill to the east, and a 4Runner rounded the curve to the west. Both stopped, seeing Bernadette on her knee with the rifle pointed to the north. A German shepherd reached the top of the embankment, never slowing as it came at her, its ears back and teeth bared. Bernadette fired. Three more dogs arrived on the road, slightly leery from rifle fire, but too excited to stop their instincts. It was nerve racking for Bernadette, she had to work the bolt to eject the casing, which meant the third dog was almost three feet away when she aimed the rifle and fired. Bernadette understood the impact of what she was doing and hated it.

Peter was in the 4Runner. He wanted to jump out and help, but he couldn't justify using his firearm while on shift. EPA enforced strict rules regarding when firearms could and could not be used and dogs running in a pack did not meet one of their acceptable categories. He looked at the frustrated face of the semi-truck driver, understanding the feeling. A dog had entered the road further to the west. Crouching, it worked its way toward Rosie. Bernadette turned, aimed, and killed it. Peter blew out a breath. She was an incredible shot given the stress and tightness of the battle.

Then a minivan pulled up behind Peter, and he saw the horrified look of a woman with her two impressionable kids. A Camaro SS was behind her. This wasn't a good situation. Five dead dogs were on the highway and Bernadette hadn't moved, telling Peter that there was more to come. Warily, another German shepherd began to moved up the embankment. Bernadette couldn't see it yet, but Peter and the ditz of a woman behind him could. To his horror, Peter watched as the woman jumped out of the minivan, leaving the door open, and ran between Bernadette and the dog coming up the bank. The woman began screaming at Bernadette, raging that she shouldn't hurt the little dogs. The dog crouched at the top of the embankment, the look of menace in its eyes. The women spun and knelt with her hand out to the menacing dog.

Bernadette was mortified. City folks just didn't understand that wild dogs are predators, and they aren't in any manner like your good old pet at home. Bernadette started walking forward. She didn't have a good shot at the dog, and if the woman moved at the wrong time, Bernadette would probably shoot her by accident. As she moved forward, so did the dog. At that moment, Peter and the semi-truck driver got out. The movement incited the dog; it lunged for the woman's arm. She screamed as the dog tore into her. Bernadette moved away from the woman; she needed a good shot without distractions as more dogs would be coming up the bank.

The truck driver beat the German shepherd several times with a stick as it tore the woman's flesh. With lightning speed, it adjusted its grip to bite her in a new location. Peter was close and took the easy, clear shot. He hoped this fell into life and death situation by EPA or he was going to lose his job over an idiot woman.

Two more dogs appeared on the road. Bernadette killed them with the same emotionless façade she had killed the others. Her grip on the gun and focus on the dogs never wavered. She worried she would be out of rounds before this was over; that was her only concern right now.

When the police arrived, Bernadette returned to Rosie and the lamb. Traffic was backed up. Bernadette led the horse and carried the lamb a short distance away from the road. She bent over and threw-up. Peter watched her puking and thought, *my God, if I only had such guts and conscience.* The women with the bloodied arm screamed obscenities as the ambulance staff tried to help her. The cops were about ready to handcuff her.

Bernadette could feel her pulse in her temple. A bad sign and a sure foreshadowing of the migraine to come. The gossip from this escapade was going to kill her. Then Camaro driver approached her. "Ah, miss, can I help at all?"

"Well sure. Why not? Can you hold back the tide of gossip that is already brewing. Can you change human behavior? Could you save me from the phone calls I will get once this reaches the papers? The accusations will fly and I will be persecuted even more."

His eyes danced with light and love, causing Bernadette to pause and relax, just a fraction. "Many are misunderstood. You and I know that God does not respond based on a social popularity contest. How God views you and how society views you are probably worlds apart."

The man returned to his car, did a U-turn, and was gone.

All the fight was gone from her, as she realized that she was focusing in the wrong direction. She should focus on what God thought of her, not people. Ignorant dog owners caused the dogs to become a danger. Bernadette had been forced to address the problem. In sorrow for the ignorance which lead to death, Bernadette dropped her gaze and stood, waiting for the police to dismiss her.

That evening, after she and Carney returned to the tepee, Bernadette got in her sleeping bag expecting to be woken up early with a roaring headache. When 6:30 a.m. arrived, the headache never appeared. As Bernadette wondered why, she came to realize that she had charted a course with the wild dog pack; she took action. Thinking about the threats on her life and EPA hounding her, she mostly reacted. She wasn't charting her own course. With a sense of resolve, she decided it was time to remedy that problem.

Chapter 41
Subbing - The Joy of Daniel

(September - October 1999)

On September 28, Bernadette returned to her farm, leaving behind the tepee filled with passion and comfort. She was uncompromisingly warned by Tierney; nothing had changed here. EPA was still at their cabin, EwRM2 was still doing whatever, and whoever found Bernadette a threat, still found her a threat.

Yet, Bernadette didn't find that a reason to let time waste away with a gloomy attitude. She thought about what profession she could do and took the steps to do that job.

She was excited to get accepted as a substitute aide with Lebanon School District. It was a relief to have some income, but also nice to have a job where she might make a difference, perhaps people would appreciate her efforts. She began to navigate the job at a number of elementary schools, but she didn't find her stride until she was at the high school. Many substitutes didn't want to deal with the older kids, but Bernadette found more purpose when working with them; they would soon turn eighteen and legally be adults, facing all the adult decisions. The kids still needed supervision and she was happy to give it to them. Many times, when giving direction, she was met with a sledgehammer attitude. It didn't stop her enthusiasm for instructing others in the art of self-discipline, whether the pupil was a kid or teacher.

A number of problems didn't begin in the 700 hall of the high school, but they found a secure footing there. The hall was only a few hundred yards from the main school building, but in reality, it was detached, alone and sullen, just as the kids who hung out there. They were kids who were last at many things. It was in the 700 hall they tried to be something because it gave them some feeling of existence. The school system that they didn't respect, and parents who couldn't parent, led them down wondering paths of disrespect which turned into dead ends, except, there wasn't a dead end to the feeling of hopelessness. They looked to the adults for guidance on how to be a grownup and what they got was a bunch of gibberish talk; something about three tries and endless open-ended options that would quickly evaporate once the real world of drugs or violence embraced them with open arms.

There were times that Daniel, who call the 700 hall home, wished someone would do something of strength. Just once, he would then know, with finality, that it really wasn't okay to use profanity, or talk back, or fail a class. But all everybody did was talk, little baby talk, about this and that, choices and time out. He tuned it all out with the efficiency of a switch. And that didn't matter because tomorrow would be just a bunch more talk about not listening to the talk from the day before. The endless mind-numbing emasculated lectures put all of those boring physic equations to shame.

Daniel's dad said it was the school system that was causing him to fail. Even Daniel laughed at that comment. Daniel knew when the problem started. It was third grade and he had been forced to sit next to crazy Damian. The kid was so violent that Daniel was always afraid at school. He never was able to listen because Damian was always trying to punch him. Because of "no child left behind" laws, even violent kids were required to be in the classroom. All the rest of the kids suffered because a crazy kid disrupted the classroom, turning it into a constant recess. Damian sucked all the learning energy out of the classroom.

Daniel got behind and never caught up; not in fourth grade or fifth and so it went. Daniel hated crazy Damian. He complained to the teacher about Damian threatening him on the playground and punching him. All he was told to do was focus on his schoolwork and learn to play with everyone. Everyone said that Damian's father was so huge, and a big mouth to boot, that nobody wanted to talk to him about his son's behavior. The school system let it go and waited for Damian to move on to the next school.

Daniel wasn't able to answer many of the questions asked him in class, so the kids always picked on him and called him stupid. Finally, in junior high, wanting a solution to all the name calling, he went out for wrestling. Wrestling helped Daniel's confidence because he became the best wrester at the school. But what he really wanted was to be strong. He never wanted to be picked on again and the weight room was the path to being respected.

He didn't do his homework, ever. His dad talked about taking away this game or that video if his grades didn't go up. Daniel knew nothing was ever going to be taken away because then his dad would have to help him with homework and that would take his dad away from all his girlfriends. Teachers didn't try to teach anymore because the classes were so disruptive and parents didn't want to parent, so Daniel just felt frustrated and mad most of the time.

That was why he was egging on a fight in the 700 hall. He didn't like either of the kids involved, but what he really wanted to see was someone who believed in something enough to stand up for it. Which was more than any adult did these days. Joey's girlfriend, Abby, had been called a name by Cory. Daniel felt compelled to embellish on the names she was called by Cory, just to add fuel to the fire. The cat calls were reaching a fevered pitch when Joey slid off his backpack and pushed Cory.

Bernadette, working as a substitute hall monitor this day, had just rounded the first corner in the 700 hall when she suddenly stopped to see what the group of kids were doing. Once she saw the shoving, she ran down the hall and placed herself between the Joey and Cory. She was facing Cory, as being the larger kid, she figured he was the instigator in all of this.

Bernadette put her hands up and the age-old sign of stop. "Easy, everybody just take it easy."

Joey, who was behind her, grabbed Bernadette's favorite, from the thrift shop, Ralph Lauren blouse, by the collar and started yanking her backwards. Joey said, "Get out of here lady. Cory and I have something to settle."

Bernadette had been working on temper management for years. As long as the adrenaline hadn't kicked in, the problem was manageable, most of the time. But Bernadette was off center, being pulled back, and as the blouse collar got tighter against her throat, Bernadette was getting madder.

"Let - Go - Of - My - Shirt," she snapped, as she struggled to pull the blouse forward so it wasn't choking her.

Joey snarled, "What you gonna do? You can't do anything, can you?"

That was it. Some little time bomb exploded in Bernadette's system. She could see students looking at her with the question of, *well, are you a weakling like every other adult, or can you do something?* Finally, the shirt was so tight at her neck, it no longer felt like the button was on the outside of her skin.

Bernadette didn't want to remove her grasp on the collar, for it was protecting one side of her throat, but if she was going to get out of this, she had to. Moving both hands to chest level, she put her fingers in the spaces between the buttons, tightened her grip and yanked. Buttons flew off, hitting the kids nearby and it was completely silent by the time the buttons came to rest on the cool linoleum floor. All anyone heard was Bernadette's rapid breathing. Usually, Bernadette wore a camisole under blouses in case the dress shirt gapped near the buttons. But today, as there were more clothes in the laundry basket and few in the drawer, she had put on a tank top that barely reached the top of her pants; it was too short to tuck in. She figured it was better than her bra showing if her blouse gapped.

As she pulled her arms free of the blouse sleeves, she was glad that she had worn the tank top, for she could feel confident in her current state of undress. Spinning around, she glared at the kid who uncomfortably stood with Bernadette's shirt in his hand. Grabbing his hand with shirt, she put her palm over his fist, and without even a strain on her part, she took Joey to his knees as his wrist threatened to break.

"Ow, Ow, OW. Stop."

Bernadette did let go, and she stood looking at Joey like she could pull him apart and scatter the parts around the school.

As Joey assessed Bernadette, he figured humor was the only way out.

"Want your shirt - ah - to put back on?" He tried smiling and holding her shirt up to her.

"No, it doesn't have any butt - ons."

Joey didn't have any more to say, as he knelt staring at Bernadette's upper body and shoulders, just like all the other kids.

They were massive; they were muscled.

No one would have guessed what lurked beneath the delicate exterior of Bernadette's blouse. Bernadette's shoulders were big, bone wise. She was always ripping shoulder pads out of everything she bought so she could wear stuff comfortably. But the farm had added sleek muscle to the bones: deltoid, pectoralis major, triceps, and brachioradialis. Even the muscles in her neck stood out right now. As she took a deep, calming breath and her chest rose up and she looked more massive.

In the silence, Bernadette assessed Joey.

"That was a very stupid thing to do young man. Get on your feet. We are going to the office." And for emphasis Bernadette grabbed the shirt out of his hand.

"What about Cory? He started this."

"I don't really care. You tried to strangle me. You can explain it to the office."

Joey was so surprised by the amount of muscle looking at him, he got up, turned, and started walking. The crowd parted like the Red Sea as Bernadette followed him out of the hall and toward the main building.

Daniel's eyes were huge as he watched Bernadette walk down the hall. He could actually see the muscles in her back move in ripples as she marched after Joey. She was badder than the football coach. Hell, she looked badder then those guys in the wrestling federation. Wow, if he had muscles like that, he would never get teased again. In fact, he could take state, get a scholarship, and go to college. He was sure of it.

Daniel nudged his friend, Andy, standing next to him. Daniel asked, "Think she gives lessons in body building?"

"Why don't you ask her, stupid. She is your neighbor."

"What? How do you know that?" asked Daniel.

Andy rolled his eyes. "Don't you ever look out your window? I see her some mornings pulling out of Elmer Lane when we are on the way to school, idiot."

Daniel didn't tell his friend that he didn't look out the windows, for a variety of reasons. His dad had boarded up the front window after it broke and couldn't afford to fix it. Daniel knew the real reason it wasn't fixed. All the money his dad made at the mill went to the bar and the women at the bar. His dad took him and his sister to school at 5:45, while he was on his way to work. They huddled under doorways waiting for school to open and breakfast to be served. Some mornings Daniel wondered how long he and his sister would have a home or if they would find themselves seeking permeant shelter in building entrance ways.

If the muscled woman lived just down the lane, he could walk there. He was confident, she was filled with solutions, unlike his dad, who was filled with problems.

-

Daniel tried his best not to go spy on Bernadette, but after two days, he just couldn't hold back the curiosity. After school on Friday, he headed down the lane. He found the perfect covert location by climbing a fence and hiding behind a huge old fir. His view of the barn, field, and house was excellent. Bernadette was everywhere: in the barn with animals, in the garden working, and in the field dealing with a fence issue. After a time, Daniel sat down, resting his elbows on his knees, allowing for the easy support of the binoculars he had snitched from his dad. He was just getting comfortable when there was a noisy crunch behind him.

"Something I can help you with son?"

Looking back, Daniel saw some worn, but clean, cowboy boots. Getting up, he dusted off his rear end with both hands. Noticing the very expensive leather jacket on the tall, rugged man, Daniel sighed. "I was waiting for a chance to talk with Bernadette. I live up the lane."

"Looks like you want to watch her. Name is Stephen. Don't blame you one bit. I have been entertained by Bernadette since she moved in. I am surprised I am not charged for this comedy show. It is a laugh a minute around here." Odd, but Stephen wasn't laughing as he said this.

Daniel relaxed immediately, knowing he wasn't the only one wanting to watch this woman. "She has amazing shoulder build, and really good back muscles. Do you think that she would help me get bulked up like that?"

"Shoulders... hum...This younger generation is different. I can't say as a young man I was all that concerned about a woman's shoulders." Stephen frowned at the young man. Times were changing he had heard, but this was an unexpected change.

"You don't understand. Bernadette has incredible upper body form. I am on the wresting team, so I need to look like her. I would get into any school I wanted if I had her form."

Stephen frowned at Daniel, cocking his head to one side. "How do you know she has incredible upper body form?"

Daniel never saw the confusion in Stephen's face. "She ripped her shirt off at the high school the other day when she was substituting. Do you know her very well?"

Shaking his head, Stephen said, "It sounds like we both need to go talk with her son. Let's go."

With that, Daniel and Stephen climbed over another fence and went off in search of Bernadette.

Chapter 42
Striking a Deal

(October 1999)

Daniel and Stephen intercepted Bernadette as she was finishing a chicken coop cleaning project. Smiling at Stephen, she held Rockin' Rooster in a tender, but secure, embrace. Bernadette said, "Stephen, how are you?" Then, looking quizzically at Daniel, she said, "Don't I know you from the high school?"

"Yes, I was there when you took Joey to the office."

Stephen cut off Daniel. "Daniel here told me that you took off your shirt at school."

Daniel interrupted Stephen in return. He said, "Yah, as I was going to say. I saw your upper body build and wondered if you would help me strengthen for wrestling."

Bernadette immediately handed the rooster to Stephen and put her arm around Daniel's shoulders, steering him toward the barn. "You bet. Let's talk about projects here that really work the upper body."

While the rooster pecked at his shirt buttons, Stephen watched an animated Bernadette begin a sincere conversation with the young man, never giving Stephen even a backward glance.

Stephen raised his voice, "Uhm, Bernadette! Did you want to comment on something?"

Turning, Bernadette looked confused. "Oh, once you put the rooster down, you better run, fast. And to clarify, I didn't take my shirt off at school, I ripped it off."

Daniel and Bernadette entered the barn talking about strengthening.

After outrunning the rooster, Stephen walked back to his place, muttering as he went, "I never get any respect around here and nobody tells me anything."

Daniel and Bernadette came to a deal on upper body training even though Bernadette assured him it would be nothing short of full body training; he could help with chores, thereby getting his workout, but he had to stay and do some homework. After several hours of working amicably together, Daniel confided in Bernadette that he had a very unhappy sister, Macie, who stayed in her room almost all the time, unless going to school. Bernadette immediately thought about how she could help Macie too.

Normally, this kind of arrangement, Bernadette working with youth on her farm, wasn't possible since Bernadette lived alone and would worry about being falsely accused of some action related to the children. This entire concern evaporated because, thanks to the EPA, there were cameras all over the farm recording all the areas where she and Daniel, or any child, would be. She would have study time in the living room, with EPA watching and recording. Finally, a good use of taxpayer dollars.

Daniel's father, Ben, was to stop by Bernadette's place to give his blessing on the chores-workout-study arrangement. After four days, with Daniel pestering Bernadette every day to let him begin, she could see that leaving it up to Ben to stop by and grant his permission was not an action-oriented option. When Bernadette announced that she would seek out Ben for permission, Daniel commented that if Bernadette was to gain his father's attention and a positive response, she must dress-up a bit more.

"What does "dressing-up a bit more" look like? No muck boots?" Bernadette teased.

With a grimace, Daniel explained, "He will be more likely to listen and give approval if you look pretty."

Bernadette's look of exasperation gave way to a smile. "Anything for upper body strengthening."

—

It was a Saturday night, perfect for a black skirt, black high heels, black nylons, and a shiny purple top. Daniel told her what Ben looked like and she figured she could easily find him at the Blue Ox Tavern just by the purported number of women hanging from his sleeve. It was almost 9:30 p.m. when she finally walked into the Blue Ox, uncomfortable and self-conscious about her dressed-up appearance. Picking the first open table, she sunk down in a comfy chair, hoping that she could quickly find Ben and succeed in her mission.

After a few minutes, Bernadette focused on a man sitting at the bar; she deduced he was Ben. But the women had long forgotten his once handsome face, which now sported saggy jowls from the oft consumed beer and the once sparkling eyes of excitement were now narrow slits in a puffy red face struggling to keep toxins at bay. Daniel must remember and idolize the man he once was. Getting up and shrugging back on her coat, to keep most everything covered to the knee, Bernadette approached the chair beside Ben.

"Ben? I am your neighbor, Bernadette Engstrom. May I have a few words with you about Daniel?"

Slamming down his drink, Ben said. "What has that boy done now? I'll tan his hide."

Resting a hand on his forearm, Bernadette sought to calm Ben. "Nothing. Daniel hasn't done anything wrong. I am a substitute at the high school and Daniel was telling me how he wanted to improve his upper body strength. I think he might benefit from all the chores at my place. And if Macie can come along, I would like that too. After chores, I could give them dinner and tutor them in their studies. I was hoping to help them with school since I hear you are very busy at work."

Ben's face hardened. Already knowing this approach wasn't succeeding and an immanent "no" was on the horizon, Bernadette switched tactics quickly.

"I am sorry to trouble you with this. I am a single woman trying to farm, and if Daniel could help me a little, I would much appreciate it. I have trouble doing some things on my own."

Tierney, who was in his usual spot at the bar, had just taken a drink. Hearing Bernadette's comment, he first choked, then spit the drink across the table. He couldn't believe she said that she was unable get things done on her own. That was the biggest lie he ever heard from her.

Bernadette gave Tierney the evil eye, then turned back to Ben and smiled.

Bernadette asked, "What if we give it a two-week trial. Doesn't work? No problem."

Ben was relieved. Two weeks of not having to deal with the kids would be like a Hawaiian vacation. No harm would be done and he wouldn't look like a bad parent. "Ok, two weeks."

Bernadette outlined a schedule with Ben and got him to sign an approval slip to pick the kids up from school and have them at her house. Monday would be the first afternoon they would visit Bernadette's place and Ben was to pick up the kids at 9:00 p.m. that Monday night.

On Saturday, Bernadette had a moment of inspiration. She stopped by the used clothing store and picked up work clothes, sweats for lounging, and pajamas that she hoped would fit Daniel and Macie. She also got sundries and food for lunches. By being "casually" prepared she could avoid embarrassment for the kids if Ben failed to pick them up Monday night.

On Monday, everyone had a blast doing chores. Bernadette now had twenty goats and they made a mess in the barn, frequently and routinely. While Daniel cleaned the goat stalls, Macie and Bernadette brushed Rosie and gave Svalbard a bath. Then she taught them how to feed everyone and put them to bed.

By 6:00 p.m., she had everyone march in the house, get a shower, and when they were clean, she had dinner on the table. It was hamburgers and homemade French fries. After dinner, Bernadette made them milkshakes and they started on homework.

Bernadette wasn't surprised when they tried to stall on the homework.

"What are you going to do while we do homework?" Macie whined.

"I am going to sit right here and read a book, so when you need help, I am ready."

Both kids looked at Bernadette with confusion.

"Go on, get working," Bernadette added for emphasis.

Immediately she could see that Daniel needed help and was embarrassed to ask. She started asking him questions, then took out paper and began to teach him. She didn't look at the time until it was 10 p.m. Jumping up, Bernadette looked at her phone. No calls.

"Should we call your dad and see if he is coming to get you?" Bernadette asked the kids.

"Dad probably had to go back to work. That happens a lot." Macie explained, her head down doing her homework.

Bernadette got them set up for bed in the living room. She explained to the kids she had some old but clean pajamas they could use. After Daniel and Macie had brushed their teeth and were lying down, Bernadette sat in the living room listening to the kid's rhythmic breathing. Bowing her head, she silently cried. *What had happened to all the mothers and fathers,* she wondered?

Peter, watching this odd turn in event, wasn't unaffected either. He made a mental note to spend time talking with Ben at the Blue Ox.

As the days went by, Bernadette often found herself surrounded by these beautiful children. Grades were advancing up to A's and B's. Daniel was pleased with his new muscles and Macie was coming out of her shell. Bernadette taught her to sew her own dresses.

Everyday Bernadette wondered when this joy would stop. She didn't want to think about it. It felt like family and the joy was so great she feared she would shatter from its purity. Would Ben wake up one day and realize that he was missing out on true happiness?

-

The gossip suffered by Bernadette throughout the town began to change. Instead of salacious ideas, there was more compassion surrounding her; everyone watched in wondered as two children blossomed under her attention.

Chapter 43
Whiplash

(October 4, 1999)

Peter was relaxing at the cabin, reading a good book, when he heard a vehicle. His tension level went up. This would be a confrontation of no winners.

Ross walked in and Peter pretended surprise. "Hey, good to see you back. How are things going?"

"Not as well as I would hope. This case keeps dragging on." Ross plopped down in a chair across from Peter.

Peter set the trap and bait for Ross. Peter nonchalantly asked, "I was curious, did you and your wife go to that Seahawks game September 14? What a wild game." Peter had a big smile on his face and since Ross was so self-absorbed, it didn't register that the smile was a sham.

Ross said, "No, we went up to the in-law's cabin for a few days. Real nice spot on the Puget Sound."

Going for Ross' jugular, Peter asked, "How is that possible Ross, since you were in Madison at EwRM2 waiting for Bernadette to show up at her office? All of Lebanon knows about your foul methods and slimy deeds that day. You are not a well-liked man in Lebanon."

Ross exploded, jumping out of his chair. "What do I care? This is just some ignorant town filled with ignorant people. I am trying to enforce environmental laws here, which is more than what you do!"

Peter remained calm, "Really? Working a deal to arrest Bernadette while upper management is "off limits" and the monetary fine for EwRM2 is reduced once Bernadette is arrested - that is enforcing environmental laws? Or how about the use of test methods on the anhydrous calcium chloride which aren't approved or used on foreign material brought into the country - that is environmental policy? I heard from sources at the regional office about the quality control data associate with the calcium chloride; it is a complete fiasco. All of that is enforcing environmental laws?"

Ross yelled, "I am going to get some lunch and when I come back, we won't talk about this anymore. You are just like the rest of this town. Idiots." Ross walked out, slamming the door.

Peter said to the empty room, "Thanks for the compliment, Ross. I hope I am like this town."

Ross didn't return until much later in the afternoon.

Peter didn't hesitate to make a verbal attack, "Well, how was that four-hour lunch?"

"Shut up. When I came out of the restaurant my car had been vandalized. Had to file a police report. I am heading back to Seattle. I'll be back in a week."

This time when the door shut, Peter said to no one but himself, "Good riddance."

That evening at the Blue Ox Tavern, Peter ordered his cheeseburger. When Tierney waved to him, he joined Tierney at the dark corner spot.

Tierney said, "Did you hear what happened to Ross this afternoon?"

"Yah, he was upset about the vandalism to his car."

Laughing, Tierney continued, "That wasn't all he was upset about. He called the police to the parking lot to report his vandalized car. When they arrived, it happened to be the K-9 unit. Well, the dog smelled drugs in Ross' car! You should have seen Ross sweating that situation. The police told him if he ever harassed anyone in this town again, he would be arrested for possession of illegal drugs."

Although Tierney was laughing, Peter was not. He knew, the next move made on Bernadette might be the last. Ross was not finished with this situation, just very, very furious.

Ross did return on October 11, but he kept a very low profile around town. And his attitude changed; it was worse. Peter did his best to be cordial, but Ross, with a permanent pout on his face, said very little.

Chapter 44
The Plane

(October 1999)

Bernadette never really understood why people worshipped the developments of the industrial revolution. She theorized the infatuation stemmed from a lust people have for easy and sensual mobility: cars, planes, trains, boats, and any manner of transportation. Bernadette was dismayed over the hidden costs associated with all these transportation items: the loss of productive land, the noise pollution, air pollution, land claimed for roads and airports through eminent domain, and all the life that died when innocently attempting to navigate around a transportation system. Bernadette was convinced that motorized mobility allowed a person to do terrible things in someone else's backyard and then go back to where they came from, expecting a wonderful environment free from all the transportation pollution.

She believed the freeway was a perfect example. Normally, no one wants to live right next to a freeway, but everyone wants to drive on it; not caring how the noise or air pollution might impact someone. Or people drive a super loud motorcycle past a quiet neighborhood, but park it in their garage with the motor off, thus not impacting their environment with noise. Why not keep it running in the garage so the owner can enjoy what he/she just gave to everyone else during his journey? The same question applies to semi-trucks when using brakes. She wished truck drivers would engine brake at their home, constantly, when their children were trying to sleep.

Bernadette believed that one mode of transportation above all others lead to the dastardly spread of an earth destroying gangrene: the airplane – *it went everywhere.*

It all started in October, when a neighbor, the Olsen family, decided to oblige their friend who was a pilot and owner of a Piper; the Olsens allowed him to use an abandoned section of road on their land as a runway. The insanely high-pitched motor in the shiny, narcissistically engineered plane was landing and taking off from the abandoned road, for no other reason than *fun.* And, just for additional giggles, the pilot routinely buzzed Bernadette's house and barn. This irritation was followed by a steep climb, accompanied with massive engine whining, and disappearance over Jade Mountain.

She had gone to visit the neighbors, Owen and Olivia Olsen, only to find out they didn't think the plane was a big deal. The pilot, Ralph Waldock, did "free" work for them. In return, they were letting him use the abandoned road for his personal enjoyment. Bernadette politely told them that they needed a permit to operate an airstrip. The neighbors had smiled, been so friendly, and said they would take care of it.

They did that; the problem got worse.

Instead of happening once or twice a week, it began to happen daily, always in the afternoon.

A day after the conversation with the Olsens, Bernadette was out working with Rosie and found a ten-foot section of the woven-wire fence on the east side of her property had been vandalized, completely removed. The plane took off that afternoon, not only once, but thank you very much, five times.

Bernadette called the sheriff regarding the fence vandalism and visited county land use and planning in Madison. She also contacted the FAA (Federal Aviation Agency), but they were useless and appeared to want to promote plane activity, of any kind, not actually regulate it. The sheriff was supportive, but quick to note that usually this type of retaliatory vandalism was a single incident. How reassuring. Land use planning sent Bernadette a complaint form, which she diligently filled out every day and sent back to them once a week. She followed up with phone calls to the county. They assured her they were doing everything they could, which wasn't helping the problem.

The noise was driving her batty.

After three weeks of this, she walked up to the cabin to ask Peter what he thought of the plane.

Peter just shrugged. "Sure, it isn't legal. But I don't need to worry about it; I don't live here."

Bernadette replied, "Yep, that was exactly what I was thinking. Nobody cares unless it is in their backyard. Well, I will continue to work with the county on the issue."

Peter had a sharp rebuttal, "Bernadette, I thought you didn't like government. Weren't you saying that all we do is meddle and create wages for ourselves?"

Bernadette didn't give an inch. She said, "Well, government is not my hero, yet. Weren't you saying that government is composed of people, ordinary people who make mistakes while doing their job; ordinary people who have to consider their own lives, sometimes above consideration for the position they hold?"

Peter nodded his head and said, "Let's call it a draw for today."

-

Sunday, October 24, it was blessedly still and quiet. Bernadette was adjusting the harness on Rosie, getting ready for some fall plowing, when she thought she heard something, something in distress. With all the banging of the leather and chains on the traces, she wasn't sure if she had heard a bird or an animal. She stopped and waited. Rosie snorted and pawed the ground, ready to get going.

Rubbing Rosie's neck, she said, "Quiet, wait a minute."

As a minute ticked by, all she could hear was Rosie chewing. Nothing sounded unusual. She was about to hook up the single tree (a piece of wood used when pulling an item behind a horse), kneeling close to Rosie's hind legs with the chains, when she heard it. There was a man's scream, and then a faint "Oh God, somebody help me!"

Bernadette had excellent hearing; it was the reason she was so strung up by the plane noise. She knew it wasn't Peter, Stephen, or Ben because the noise came from the east. That meant the call for help probably came from the Olsen place."

Quickly securing the chains back up on the harness hooks, releasing the clasp to Rosie's halter and tossing the reigns over Rosie's head in one swift motion, Bernadette held onto the surcingle while she stepped up on the leather trace, which runs the length of the horse, and threw her other leg over Rosie's back. She had ridden Rosie a few times this way, with the harness on. Holding on to the hames she gave the kiss sound and nudged Rosie's flank with the heel of her work boots. It was going to be a chafing ride, with stiff leather straps rubbing Bernadette in all the wrong places. Rosie, loving to run, was across the field in minutes and clearing the fence like it never was there. They were on Olsen's land in record time.

As the panic and fear eased from Owen Olsen's gut, his temper started to kick into high gear. He had specifically told his son, Dave, not to fix the combine platform auger until he got back. Now he was on his cell phone with a Lebanon EMT (Emergency Medical Technician), Ricky, who had not been at the scene of the accident but had heard the call go out.

Ricky said, "I heard your neighbor did a nice job saving your son's leg. Got the reel tines pulled off his leg by using a pully and applied pressure to the bleeding. Smart thinking that ..."

Not waiting for Ricky to finish, Owen said "Ricky, I got to go. We are almost at the hospital. Thanks for the call buddy."

Owen let the phone slam shut and glanced at his wife, who was driving over the speed limit with amazing skill. Turning his head to look out at nothing through the dust laden window, Owen said, "Hon, maybe you should let me out before we get to the hospital. It sounds like our son will survive his injuries, but I might kill him."

Olivia understood her husband's frustration. With deep worry in her voice, she said, "He just wanted to empress you by finishing the job before you got back. All he ever wanted was your approval. Go easy on him."

"How can I go easy on him when he never thinks about anything. If he would listen, then I would give him lots of approval."

-

Olivia put her arm around Owen's waist as they entered their son's hospital room. She figured with her hand on Owen's side, she could pinch him when he started to lecture Dave. The lecturing never fixed anything between them.

Owen and Olivia were surprised to see Ralph Waldock standing near the head of the bed, casually talking with Dave. In that moment, Owen made an assumption, an erroneous assumption.

Owen stepped forward clasping Ralph's hand, "I want to thank you for saving my son's leg. I have always been impressed with your mechanical abilities, especially with that plane, but now I am impressed with your life and limb saving skills." Placing his hand on Ralph's shoulder, he directed him toward the door, "I bet the next month might be good weather for you to do some more test flights from our place. That Bernadette and the county can go to hell." Then whispering to Ralph, "I need a few words with Dave alone. Do you mind?"

"Oh no, just waiting for you and Oliva to show up. I'll see you soon." Waving at Dave, Ralph smiled and walked down the hallway, whistling as he went.

"Ah... Dad. Ralph..."

Owen cut him off. "Son, it is a good thing that I let Ralph use our field, even with all the whining from the neighbor. Thank God he was there to help you. You need to start developing and using common sense, like I do. I don't know why you can't pay more attention."

Olivia was pinching her husband's side like a lobster caught. Owen looked away from his son and blew out a breath. Leaning over to Olivia he kissed her cheek, "I'll go wait in the truck."

As his father's footsteps echoed down the hall, Dave looked up from his bed to meet his mother's eyes.

Dave said, "Can I get two words in? Come on, it was only three years ago that Dad crushed six ribs. What a hypocrite."

Sitting on the edge of the bed, Olivia took her son's hands. "I am glad you are ok. I think it is time that we help you move to a place of your own and help you look for another job. I don't think I can take much more of the bickering between you two."

Grabbing his hands away from his mother, he said "You don't take the time to understand me and you guys never listen to anyone. I am not going to say anymore. You're right. I need to leave. You guys figure out this mess on your own."

-

Rosie was limping a bit the next day. The running and jumping with all the harness on had thrown her balance off. Bernadette sighed thinking that plowing would have to wait a few more days. All day she waited for the

Owens to show up and thank her. They must think saving Dave's leg was worth something, didn't they? She was going to savor that moment, a bad attitude she knew. They had treated her like dog poop and now they were going to grovel in it.

But Owens didn't show up that day. She figured they might be busy or still at the hospital. But no one stopped by the second day.

It was the third day that put Bernadette into orbit. The plane landed, took off, landed, took off, landed... After six landings and takings off, Bernadette lost count.

Bernadette put her head in her hands and kneeled down. She we going to burst a blood vessel. She was going to have to sell the farm. She just couldn't take the high-pitched noises.

Then something Bernadette had read the night before entered her mind: *for every battle on the physical plane, there is a corresponding spiritual battle within.*

With a conviction to do spiritual battle, Bernadette went into the house, put in ear plugs, and sat in prayer. Really, it was the only thing that made sense. Karma would have to sort this out.

Chapter 45
Can't Get Enough of Them Sunflowers

(November 10, 1999)

Wiggly, now one of the biggest males in the area, excelled at wild, rowdy chipmunk life in the meadows, fields, and forest. There was one thing Wiggly would never forget about his time in captivity: the smell and scrumptiousness of sunflowers. They had been his favorite. Everyone in the area, including Bernadette, who tried to grow sunflowers during the summer by direct seeding had a devil of a time doing it. Before the seed could collect up the strength to form the tiny white root designed for bursting open the shell, the seed was snuffed out with tiny claws and sharp teeth. Oddly, even with Wiggly's thorough quest to commit sunflower seed eradication in the area, he kept smelling sunflowers, to the west, up on Jade Mountain.

Forging through forest, up and up the hill, Wiggly explored the world with action, purpose, and direction. The direction was sunflowers, and they were finally found strewn about on a picnic table, forgotten in the straw of a horse shelter, discarded in a vehicle, and left unattended inside a cabin. He showed his friends the stash of food. The supply was so great, they took great pleasure in burying many of the seeds for a later winter or spring day.

All was fine until the rats, large and intimidating Norway rats, moved in. After a scuffle under the cabin, Wiggly and his buddies were forced to keep a distance from the cabin and temporary horse shelter. Finally, outnumbered and pursued by the bare-tailed species, the chipmunk clan moved back down the mountain.

The rats set up a serious camp. After gnawing a hole through the floor of the cabin, the rats worked on enlarging cracks and crevices into the kitchen and its cupboards. Once inside, they skirted along walls in search of food, residing behind the refrigerator or desk should their exploration be interrupted. With such excellent food sources found in trash cans rarely emptied, they began tearing apart materials that could be used for nest making, the beginnings for new families.

It was just this sort of rat activity that led to Ross' discovery of the rat infestation and his consequential berserk behavior on a Wednesday. When he had left for the store, around 10 a.m., all the electronics at the cabin had been working fine. He had left some of his favorite chili cheese flavored sunflowers on the desk in an open package. The grocery store run took longer than expected as he decided he wanted goat cheese and the best goat cheese was in Corvallis, twenty-eight miles away. After getting to Corvallis, he realized how hungry he was; he settled in for a long lunch at the Indian restaurant.

Ross returned to the cabin at 2 p.m. Sitting back down at the computer, with coffee in hand, Ross reached out to grab a sunflower, only to find a mostly empty bag. His irritation rose as the monitor failed to come to life once he jiggled the mouse and the screen saver wasn't even working.

Glancing down at the tower near his feet, he realized the power light wasn't on. Pushing the power button, he waited for the familiar sound as the computer started up, but there was nothing. Putting down his coffee, Ross rose with exaggerated patience and headed toward the circuit breaker. Not knowing if he should be relieved or dismayed, he found none of the breakers to be tripped.

The work desk, an ornate, heavy, functional piece of furniture, was appropriate if you were an attorney. For an EPA surveillance job in a luxury cabin, it was beyond the needs of Peter or Ross. Locking file draws were found on both sides of the mahogany-colored expansive writing and typing area. Real wood enclosed the back of the desk and a shelving unit was situated above the writing area.

Grabbing the back right side of the desk, Ross had to put his weight into pulling it away from the wall to gain access to the wires and surge protectors stashed in the five inches of space below the filing drawers. Once it was about eight inches away from the wall, Ross walked around the front of the desk to the left side, maneuvering that side away from the wall. The flooring had a bit of a ridge in just the wrong place, causing Ross to grunt and groan during his five minutes of straining. Walking back to the front of his desk, he grabbed his coffee and a flashlight from the top drawer. He figured if he studied the wires long enough, without doing any actual work, his shift would be over, and Peter would fix the problem. With flashlight on and coffee mug near his mouth, Ross walked to the wall, shining the light on the lower back of the desk.

In a split second, something shrieked, hurtling itself at Ross' lower pant leg. The mug of coffee flew in the air, crashing against the wall, with a resulting irregular fountain of hot coffee spewing around the room. Ross' back peddled so fast he slipped, landing on his bum only a few feet from the desk. The momma rat, startled by the coffee mug and liquid hitting the floor near to her babies, retreated to the nest of blind and almost naked bodies.

Ross couldn't get his legs to move fast enough. Twisting over on his side, he was able to push up, regaining his footing. At a crouch, he was already sprinting for the door. Not remembering how he actually got outside, he found himself on the porch, with all the physical symptoms of having run a four-minute mile.

Problem was, now that he was on the outside, he had no keys, no wallet, no phone, and not even a gun. Sinking into the porch chair, Ross glanced at his hands which were shaking in fear and rage.

This stinking enforcement case! As Ross sat, he couldn't stop thinking about how this case had been a disaster from the beginning. He absolutely hated the countryside with its bugs and vermin - all those things that should be exterminated. He loathed his partner; a liberal brainwashed idiot parading around as a respectable boxer-short kind of guy. Ross found Peter's southern heritage to be an effeminate trait, like the idiot was wearing woman's panties. Ross was forced to be away from his wife and family. His wife, beautiful and successful, was the center of attention just walking out the front door of the house. If she was tricked into having an illicit affair, she couldn't be blamed, as her husband (this stupid husband now sitting on the porch) had been ignoring her with a stupid job that didn't give the Rossberg family further status in the neighborhood. He wasn't even respected at work anymore! It was a despicable situation.

Getting up, he peered in the front window. His phone wasn't in sight, which meant it was probably in the kitchen. Running around to the back door, which lead into the kitchen, he found the door locked. To get to the kitchen from the front door, he would have to go through the rat-infested cabin. He wasn't doing that. Sprinting to the horse barn, he grabbed the flat shovel, still shining new as he never used it. This would be his ticket into the locked back door.

When Ross was done, he was sweating heavily. The shovel was no longer recognizable as anything other than a crumpled piece of metal. The back door, now open, was mostly splinters of wood around a mangled doorknob and dead bolt. Both of Ross' hands were bleeding.

Speaking on the phone with every exterminator in the area, Ross agreed to pay them double time to show up late in the day. Four exterminator vehicles, six men with white Tyvek suits, two dozen live traps, two cattle prods, two tranquilizer guns, and forty pounds of rat poison greeted Ross as the forces of death parked at the cabin.

-

When Peter arrived that afternoon, Ross' face was so grim, Peter knew better than to say anything.

Ross said, "Watch out for the rat traps and bait. I'll be back in the morning." Ross' car door slammed shut and Peter jumped out of the way before the tires ran over his toes.

-

It was a Friday, November 12, in the afternoon, and Bernadette was walking back to the house when she noticed Svalbard in some tall grass by the fence, crouching and barking, then bouncing and circling, then more barking. Running to the scene, Bernadette was confident something was trying to fight off the dog, and not wanting the dog to get hurt with an ensuing veterinarian bill, she yelled, "Svalbard, NO! Stop. Down."

Finding a writhing rat, Bernadette immediately grabbed the Svalbard's collar and hauled him off to his dog kennel, used just for these times. Returning with a plastic tote, she slid the rat in with a stick and lightly put on the lid. There was blood coming out of its nose and an odd foam in its mouth. She didn't believe it had bitten Svalbard as it was so weak.

Something nagged at her. Finding dead rodents on a farm usually wasn't a big deal. But this rodent's illness looked serious and mysterious. Running back in the house she made four phone calls before she found what she needed. Putting the plastic tote on the passenger seat, she climbed in the truck and gunned the truck for town.

-

"I appreciate you seeing me on short notice. I know it is a Friday, but I am concerned that there might be rabies going around and if it is, I need to see about vaccinations for all the farm animals. Here is the rat I told you about."

The veterinarian took the lid off the tote. She poked and prodded at the rat, using tools to keep her hands away. She raised its eyelids and shone a light on them. The rat, taking only sallow breaths, died in five minutes.

"Bernadette, the only way we can know if this is rabies is to do a necropsy on the brain. I am going to give you my opinion on this, which is negatively influenced by the small amount of time I had with the animal. I don't think this is rabies. I think it is rat poison, probably what we call second-generation anticoagulants. Do you put out rat poison?"

Standing in shock, Bernadette said, "No, never. I have too many animals and wild animals around. If I need to remove a mouse or rat, I always use the snap traps. Those darn things always snap shut and scare me to death. But no, I wouldn't use that bait."

"Somebody did. Ask your neighbors. Suggest that they consider another means of controlling a problem. Or they need to be sure they are using the bait in a safe manner."

The veterinarian handed the tote back to Bernadette. She knew everyone was wanting to get home.

"Thank you. What do I owe you?"

The vet smiled kindly. "Nothing Bernadette. I have heard about your... challenges. Keep up the good fight and good luck."

Friends in an odd way, thought Bernadette. Does everyone gossip? Bernadette felt exhausted. Gossip, even if it helped her, wore at her heart.

Once in the truck Bernadette called Stephen. "Hey, are you using rat poison?

Stephen replied, "Well hello Bernadette. No. Should I be?"

"No." The phone went dead. Stephen looked at the phone and laughed. Somehow, he just knew the EPA guys up in the cabin were in trouble. He had seen a convoy of pest control trucks go up there a few days ago. As Stephen thought about the EPA in trouble for the improper use of a rodenticide, he almost fell out of his chair laughing.

Bernadette drove home to get her camera. Sneaking out of her house, she stealthily jumped a fence onto Stephen's property, crossed his property, and ran up the logging road to the cabin. The cabin was lit up and Ross was there, but she couldn't see him through a window. Bernadette explored the horse area and yard, taking almost fifty pictures of rat bait strewn here and there. Some of the bait was mixed with bird seed and placed in aluminum pie tins. The pie tins were placed under trees, near the base of the cabin, or around the horse hay.

Bernadette was seething.

In the horse shelter she found sunflowers mixed with rat bait; it was laid out on a board. She doubled over at the waist, stifling back a scream of rage as she thought about Wiggly. What if he ate this shit all over the place and suffered an agonizing death?

Finishing her pictures, she stomped towards the front of the cabin just as the door swung open.

"Bernadette, surprise, surprise." Ross used his best Gomer Pyle imitation. "I thought we had discussed how you cannot trespass on our property."

"Yes, and I know we discussed how this is not EPA property and I am certain it is not your property personally. This is BLM land or perhaps BS land. Look, you can either be nice today, or we can do this the hard way and you can figure out your problem another way. Completely up to you."

Bernadette heard cars approaching, but Ross must not have.

He pulled out his 9mm and leveled it at Bernadette's head. That action only incited her.

Bernadette screamed at him, "You piece of crap! You have broken every FIFRA (Federal Insecticide, Fungicide and Rodenticide Act) law up here. You're poisoning all kinds of animals and you, who should be enforcing FIFRA rules, are flagrantly breaking them. Then you stand there with a gun. You are an embarrassment to the EPA!"

Two vehicles skidded to a stop. Peter and Tierney jumped out simultaneously.

Peter ran toward Ross yelling, "Put the gun down, Ross. Put that gun away!"

Tierney ran to Bernadette, put his arms around her shoulders and began pulling her to his truck. She was dragging her feet.

Peter was not in a good mood today. Expenses had been through the roof this week with Ross' requirements for a complete "securing" of the crawl space so no other rodent could get under the cabin. He had also insisted on a complete sanitization of the cabin, top to bottom, by a professional firm out of Portland. Finally, all brush one hundred feet from the cabin had to be removed and additional gravel areas put in. The cabin looked like an electrical substation; the area was completely denuded. Now Ross was pointing a gun at someone. Peter's temper was about to launch.

Taking a deep breath, he approached Ross' side. "Ross, let's lower the gun. Just put it away and we will go in the cabin and figure this out. Just…just lower the gun."

Ross moved, but only to keep the gun trained on Bernadette's head.

Peter reached Ross and put his hand lightly on Ross's arm, then began applying pressure to push his arm down. "Lower your arm, Ross. Come on, let's go in and talk about this."

Suddenly swinging his arm, Ross pulled the trigger, blowing the bark off a nearby tree. He screamed, "Bernadette you get the hell out of here or the next shot will be your head!"

Bernadette got in Tierney's truck. As they drove down the logging road she said, "I am finished with this attack on my life. I won't tolerate anymore. By the new year, this…this mess, will be over."

Tierney remained quiet. He didn't doubt that Bernadette would end this fight and Carney made it clear that she should be allowed to fight. Once at her place, Bernadette said, "Thank you Tierney. You're a good man."

-

The Lebanon newspaper came out three times a week: Monday, Wednesday, and Friday. The following Monday, on the third page of the newspaper, was an article warning all families in the vicinity of Jade Mountain to keep all pets locked up indefinitely. Included with the article were pictures of the EPA cabin grounds and horse shelter strewn with so much unsecured rat bait it was surprising that it hadn't been delivered by dropping it from an airtanker.

On Tuesday, Ross and Peter had been immediately summoned back to the regional office for a meeting with the EPA Compliance Unit. A HAZMAT (hazardous materials) clean-up crew, which charged by the mile, hour, and exorbitant disposal fees, had been sent out to Jade Mountain.

-

The EPA women's restroom scoreboard was buzzing with activity. Bernadette's status as a savior of "all that was good" had been elevated to new levels. The EPA women were wondering if Bernadette might come to Seattle and run for a political office. Perhaps she could work for the UN (United Nations). Even the Red Cross might be a good fit.

That night, the women at the EPA went home with a swagger on their hips and smile on their lips.

Chapter 46
The Auto Store

(Friday, November 19, 1999)

Bernadette pulled up by the high school and waited for Daniel and Macie. They were to spend this afternoon working in the barn and then it was time to catch up on homework in the evening. She smiled and waved when she saw the kids running toward the truck.

As they got in, Daniel said, "Bern, I need to swing by the auto parts store. Dad's car is low on oil and he says he is too busy to pick it up."

Bernadette was familiar with stories of how busy Ben was, so this extra errand wasn't surprising. "Okay, do we need to drop it off at your house on the way home?"

"No, I will just add it to the car tomorrow, after you take us home."

At the auto parts store, they were standing in line to pay the cashier for the oil when Bernadette noticed the purchase made by the man in front of them. She had heard him asking for tire studs, and a bag was brought to him. The salesperson said, "These are the best tungsten carbide tire studs we have. They won't wear out easily."

As the clear bag filled with small screw like objects sat on the counter, Bernadette sucked in a breath, and the blood drained from her face. They were the same objects she saw in the instrument shop hidden compartment and in the locked cabinet by the president's office.

Good grief! Someone had been sabotaging the products at EwRM2. Tungsten carbide created inclusions in the titanium metal, making it unsuitable for certain applications because an inclusion made the metal more likely to fail under heat and stress. She knew this because the company went to great lengths to keep tungsten tipped ball point pens out of the facility.

She swallowed and immediately decided to keep quiet with this new information. This had to be the reason why someone tried to kill her. It had to be.

The following night, Saturday, she stopped by the Blue Ox to see Tierney. Sitting down at his table, but never taking her coat off, she said, "Tierney, I would like to talk with you and Carney when it can be arranged. It isn't a crisis, but I think I now know what everyone thought I knew, if that makes sense."

She didn't wait for him to question her, immediately getting up and walking out.

Chapter 47
What is Thanksgiving All About?

(November 1999)

It was four days before Thanksgiving and Bernadette needed to get all her supplies stocked so she didn't have to go into town again until December. People drove like crazed rabbits around the time of Thanksgiving and it was just better not to get in the truck and risk life and limb while people, with glazed over eyes, frantically sought out turkey and stuffing.

Bernadette was a bit depressed. She had no family or friends with her this Thanksgiving; everyone was busy with their own families. What she really wanted was to have Daniel and Macie with her. She wondered if she could convince Ben to let them come to her house for part of Thanksgiving Day.

As fate would have it, Ben was pulling out of his driveway when Bernadette was driving by. She stopped in the road, rolled down the window, flagging him to stop.

"Bernadette, I am sorry, but I am in a hurry. Thanks for all your help with the kids."

"You're welcome. Real quick, I don't have any plans for Thanksgiving and it looks to be lonely for me. Do you think I could be selfish and ask for the kids to come by during part of the day? Or maybe they could come by in the evening and spend the night?"

Ben's face cunningly went blank. "We are headed to my girlfriend's house that day. I really like to spend the day with them, but I don't want you to be lonely. What time would you want to pick them up?"

"Would 3:00 p.m. be too early? Is it alright if they spend the night? It is really up to you. I don't want to take away from that family time. I am sorry if I am just being too selfish Ben."

Inwardly Bernadette cringed. She knew that there wasn't much "family" time in that house. The girlfriend was rumored to dislike the kids. But Bernadette knew she had to protect Ben's pride, or this Thanksgiving idea wouldn't fly. He would be defensive, or worried about some government agency stepping in, if Bernadette spent too much time parenting the kids.

"Well, I don't know. It doesn't give me much time with them. But you have been real good at helping Daniel with homework. Yah, I guess it will be okay."

"Ben, thanks so much."

Bernadette made out list of things to get done over the next few days: getting movies to watch, cleaning, meal preparation, and baking. Given her excitement, the energy flowed in copiously.

At noon on Thanksgiving Day, Bernadette got a call from Daniel. His dad had gone to the store in the morning and never returned. Bernadette asked, "Do you want me to call the police to see if something happened to him?"

"No, Dad said he might stop by his girlfriend's house on the way back. This happens all the time. Can we come over now?"

Bernadette didn't hesitate. "I am on my way to get you. And be sure to have a change of clothes because you're spending the night at my place."

After the kids were loaded, she headed down the road, then up the old logging road to the EPA cabin.

"Where are you going Bernadette?" asked Macie.

"To pick up Peter. He is alone. I want him he to join us. Are you okay with that?"

Daniel asked, "Are you going to trick him?"

"No, I reserve tricking for Ross. I am going to offer Peter a twelve-hour armistice."

The kids were quiet after that. At the cabin, Bernadette jumped out of her truck and rushed to the door. The kids watched as Peter and Bernadette argued for a solid five minutes. Finally, Bernadette and Peter turned and looked at the kids. Tentatively, Daniel waved to Peter, then Macie joined in. Peter vanished back in the cabin and Bernadette gave the kids a thumbs up.

Peter brought his 4Runner to Bernadette's house. He wasn't at all keen on this idea, but it had been hard to say no when two kids were watching. Once he walked in the house, he was impressed with the good smells. The meal turned out delicious and Bernadette, a staunch vegetarian, even cooked plenty of meat dishes for everyone. Then it was board games and movie time.

Peter watched the festivities unfold with a new awareness of Bernadette, which he kept attempting to snuff out. He didn't want to recognize the depth of her compassion for others. His job demanded a certain amount of detachment; he held on to it desperately this evening.

After the kids went to sleep in the guest room, Bernadette and Peter stayed up talking and reading. A slow and easy pace.

Peter finally looked at Bernadette and asked her, "Bernadette, how do I go back to this job knowing what a kind person you are? Something has been wrong with this whole thing from the beginning. It looks like an enforcement case, yet it doesn't."

Bernadette said, "I have been hoping you might be willing to explore all angles of this enforcement. I am going to give you a bit more to think about.

People tried to kill me in Canada; it was just the beginning of this entire misadventure. I will show you the result of that attempt."

Standing she pulled up her sweater so Peter could see her stomach.

When Peter saw Bernadette's stomach, he immediately went into military mode. He had seen gruesome injuries during his duty and the last thing a person needed when injured was for someone to freak out.

Peter's eyes moved from Bernadette's stomach up to her eyes. "Can you tell me all of the story?"

"Sure." Bernadette told him the story starting with the Christmas awards program and ending with getting back on a plane to the U.S.

After Bernadette finished her story, they both sat in silence.

Peter finally said, "I should go back to the cabin and get some rest. And more importantly, I need to think when I am not so tired. Thank you for a great meal and lots of fun."

It was the day after Thanksgiving that Ben landed in jail for a second DUI (Driving Under the Influence).

On Saturday, the mom came from Eastern Oregon, packed up Daniel and Macie, and they left. Bernadette spent the entire Sunday crying. Peter finally shut off the equipment and went to visit her.

Peter walked up to Bernadette in the barn and said, "I could have told you things would end up this way. These families and their kids come and go. It is better not to get involved."

Bernadette continued to repair several two by fours that Rosie had knocked down, all the while wiping away her tears.

Peter, thinking she agreed with his line of thinking, continued warming on the topic. "These quasi-parents don't even realize how much energy a person might invest in their kids. They deposit the kids someplace and withdrawal them to another place, with all the emotion of a banking transaction. The bleeding-heart types tell us to donate our time and energy to this kid or that kid; to what end or purpose? Then bam, the kids are moved, and some caring adult is left all broken up over something that was completely predictable."

"I'll give you bam!" Bernadette swung one of the two by fours with moderate speed till it connected with Peter's derriere.

"Ow, what are you doing?" Peter jumped out of the way to avoid getting smacked again.

"Off. Off my property now." The two by four was being poked at Peter like a long sword. "It is people like you who promote the breakdown of our society. People like you who are too fragile to love and maybe lose that connection because of a move or death. You sit around in your clinical chairs analyzing but not participating. Well, I participate, and I want to help. The kids will be back someday. Now take your attitude and scat."

After Peter left, Bernadette felt better. She wouldn't forget Daniel and Macie and she would love them from afar. That was all that mattered.

Chapter 48
Where Detachment Takes Us

(November 29, 1999)

When this Monday afternoon came, the plane was still practicing take offs and landings at the Olsen's place. Even Peter marveled at the audacity of it. He left the cabin at 1:30 p.m. and headed to the Blue Ox. The noise from the Piper was driving him crazy. That plane had done more landing and taking off in the last few weeks than all the planes at Seattle International Airport, or it sounded that way. Bernadette, who had been spitting mad about the plane, was oddly quiet.

As Peter's eyes adjusted to the darkness of the Blue Ox, he was surprised to see Owen Olsen there. Peter took his standard table near the bar. Owen had his head in his hands. Apparently, he couldn't stand the plane noise either.

Someone sitting next to Owen motioned to Peter, "We got us a Reg-u-la-tor in here now. Maybe he can get Ralph to stop flying that plane."

Owen looked up blurry eyed. "Since he saved my boy's leg, no one is going to do a thing. Don't do a thing or I'll have to break someone's neck."

Peter took a drink of his soda and then said in a quiet voice, "Ok, who is going to tell Owen. Someone is going to have to tell him."

Owen said, "Tell me what?"

Suddenly everyone found the bottom of their glass very interesting. The place was quiet. Peter figured as much. Owen didn't know who really saved his son's leg because the bunch of guys were gutless.

Peter drained his glass. He had been hoping to enjoy the root beer, but it looked like getting out of here would be better. "Owen, you need to go get the copy of the accident report. But considering that we might not have time for that before we all lose our hearing, let me give it to your straight. Bernadette heard your son's cry for help. She rode her horse over to your place, risking her neck riding the horse will all the harness garb on, then she threaded a cable through a pulley, secured one end of the cable to the combine part sitting on your son's leg, and used the horse to pull the weight off his leg. Rosie, the horse, stood there, while Bernadette pulled Dave out from under the darn thing.

"Ralph was in the hospital seeing his father. He went to Dave's room when he heard what had happened. Ralph never saved your son's leg. He has been laughing at you this entire time."

Peter turned and walked out, after slapping a five-dollar bill on the table for his drink.

It was later said that Owen's expletive, once understanding the real story from Peter, could be heard over into the next county.

—

When Ralph saw Owen's truck approaching on the old asphalt road, he knew the truth had been found out. Life was a game for Ralph and tricking Owen was just more of the game. It wasn't his fault if Owen had jumped to conclusions at the hospital, he told himself. He spun the plane around, wanting to take off immediately and avoid a confrontation the Owen. He didn't have the usual distance for take-off, but Ralph wasn't worried. Skimming the top of Bernadette's house would be funny and would give him the time needed to gain altitude.

When the house shook from the plane flying so close, Bernadette didn't do anything. She leaned her head against the kitchen wall, breathed and breathed some more. She wasn't prepared for the next sounds: a high-pitched engine whine, tree limbs snapping, metal bending, a huge thud and big whoosh. Running out of the house, she looked at Jade Mountain. Flames were shooting up amongst the trees, close to the EPA cabin. Bernadette dove for the phone.

Peter had been on the phone arguing with his ex-wife. Stepping outside, he gulped in the cool air and clinched his fists. He didn't understand how a divorce could turn good people into ugly people. Seeing the horse, he ran back in the cabin for an apple, then headed to the corral for some horse therapy. As he walked toward the corral he stopped, looking up to identify the plane making the awful whining noise. There wasn't anything. Then he looked over Bernadette and Stephen's places, only to see a plane headed straight for him.

He sprinted down the gravel logging road.

The plane hit the cabin as if it were a target. The tail flipped up and the entire plane flipped over, then it burst into flames. It was immediately an inferno.

Bernadette met Peter on the logging road, as she was heading up the road in her pickup to help.

"Thank goodness you are okay. Get in and we will check on the horse."

They looked at each other with the understanding that Ralph wouldn't have made it.

The wind pushed the flames up and over Jade Mountain, away from Bernadette's house, but a total of two homes were lost before the fire could be put out. Animals and pets were gone because of selfish, weak people. Gustavus broke a leg trying to escape his corral. It was tragic. Bernadette called her veterinarian, who arrived within an hour. The horse had to be put down.

Once it was known that Bernadette had complained to the county about the plane, a number of lawyers called her, wanting information for their clients who lost their homes and animals.

Peter stopped by the Bernadette's house the next morning and told her that they were leaving permanently.

"You're kidding, right? A plane crashes into the EPA cabin so you decide that you don't want to play the EwRM2 enforcement game anymore? I don't believe it. You spent too much money on this to walk away."

"Bernadette, I know it sounds weird. But that is what I have been told. Someday maybe this entire thing will make sense." Peter stood looking lost.

Bernadette eyed Peter for several moments. "No, it doesn't sound weird. It makes perfect sense. Someone is just going to try another tactic. You keep thinking this enforcement is about pollution. It isn't. The case will make sense to you when you see it as a front for something else. Have a save drive." Bernadette shut the door.

As Peter walked to his vehicle, he knew Bernadette was right.

Before Peter left town, he had someone else to visit, Tierney. Peter walked in the Blue Ox Tavern, went to the bar for a soda, then headed to Tierney's table.

"May I sit for a few minutes?"

Tierney eyed Peter and then shrugged.

"Look, I am leaving town now, since my assignment here has been, well, let's just say, closed. I am more concerned about Bernadette then when we started."

Tierney just raised his eyebrows and nodded his head.

"The agency spent hundreds of thousands of dollars on this investigation. EPA can't just walk away. People would look too stupid. Eventually, someone would be called on the carpet and the mudslinging would begin. There is only one solution I know of at this juncture. Bernadette is arrested for nothing or dies."

Tierney looked board.

"Look, I know it sounds crazy. But power and money make people crazy."

Tierney sat up and frowned at Peter. "Why are you telling me about this. Don't you think you should be warning her?"

"I didn't want to upset her more. She understands much of this. She will need someone to protect her."

Tierney sat back and laughed. "You must be blind. When you drive home, I want you to think about all the things Bernadette has done to take care of herself. Sure, we helped with those two idiots, but my guess is, she could have handled it fine. Bernadette is more deadly and cleaver than you or I. Think about that while on the freeway. And, think about how you harassed an innocent woman for months on end and she still had you over for Thanksgiving."

"That was my job. I was just doing my job." Peter knew it sounded lame the minute he said it.

Peter saw Tierney move. There was a flash and then Peter felt something sticking him in the side. "Maybe it is my job to terrorize you. We all have a responsibly to evaluate our ethics - all the time - and determine if what we are doing is causing undue harm and pain to someone. Governments do lots of illegal things. Just because you are government doesn't make what you do right."

The gun quickly vanished back inside Tierney's coat. "We have got it here. Have a safe drive."

Chapter 49
The Camel's Back

(December 1, 1999)

Carney and Tierney appeared in Bernadette's house the evening of December 1. She walked out of her bedroom and they were sitting in the living room watching T.V.

"It is a good thing I don't get spooked easily. Can't you guys use the doorbell?"

Carney got up and gave Bernadette a deep kiss. Then he asked, "Is your doorbell ringing yet?" He smiled and sat back down.

"She grabbed some drinks, turned off the T.V., and sat down with them. "I would like to tell you guys about tire studs and tungsten inclusions."

When she finished the story, Carney said, "Very interesting. Now we would like to tell you about Ross, whose name is Calvin Rossberg and he is the nephew of a Senator Robby Rossberg. And, just as a side note, we need to give credit to Peter; he got much of this information from an old college buddy.

"When Robby was just out of high school, he went up to Alaska. He knew your parents. We were initially concerned that he had an affair with your mother, but are rather certain he didn't.

"The story about Robby Rossberg goes like this. Robby had an apprentice position in the maintenance department at the Swanson River oil pumping station in Alaska. Staff in the maintenance department started noticing an increase in breakdowns at the facility. They had approached several suppliers about change in quality, had meetings with staff, added an additional shift to deal with the problems, and still things were causing major delays. It was starting to impact profits because they couldn't get the oil off the facility. Then Robby was caught sabotaging equipment. At first no one could figure out why he would do that. They concluded that he and his family were trying to influence oil supplies which would allow them to manipulate the market. Robby's career in Alaska was abruptly ended.

"In 1998, an SEC employee named Ed Keil was in Madison investigating people trading EwRM2 stock. There is a rumor he tried to interview you, Bernadette, but his request was denied. When it came time for him to leave town and go back to his office, he vanished and no one has found any evidence of him. The FBI shows up every so often and snoops around, but they haven't found Ed, nor do they know where to look for his body.

"We suspect that the Rossbergs are attempting to manipulating the metals market like they tried to manipulate the oil market. Based on what you just told us about the tungsten carbide, I would guess they try to time stock transactions with success or failure of the product, making a bundle of money. To do all of that, they need people in the company to also participate. That is probably why people feared you Bernadette, and what you knew. They assumed you would not be easily manipulated."

Bernadette watched Tierney and Carney fidget. She asked, "Is that it?"

Carney came and sat next to Bernadette. Putting his arms around her shoulders, he said, "Your mother met with Senator Rossberg in 1997, at a restaurant in Portland. Your mother's first husband was related to Senator Rossberg. Did you tell your mother anything confidential about EwRM2 which she could have passed on to him?"

In shock, Bernadette stared at nothing. "I didn't know about her first husband. I also don't know if I told her anything confidential. I would have to think about it. She might have just told him the best way to torture me, since she was so good at it."

Lifting Carney's hand from her shoulder, Bernadette got up, walked out of house, and went toward the barn. Her face was red and her hands were shaking with rage. How her mother could betray her to such a level was beyond Bernadette's imagination. The hurt was immense. It was time to channel the rage.

Chapter 50
Watch Your Backside

(December 1-7, 1999)

Peter's return to Seattle left him feeling off center. A sense incompleteness nagged at his mind.

He didn't have an office or even a computer to use at U.S. EPA Region 10 office, so for five days he worked from home. Finally, on a Tuesday, he went into work to find himself relegated to the intern area, a maze of cubicles in a dank and dark forgotten part of the building. Ross wasn't anywhere to be found, but that didn't mean he wasn't the instigator to Peter's latest irritation.

At noon, a wonderful woman, Janna, who always had the hots for Peter, and now, since Peter was divorced, could act on it, stopped by. She frowned at the way Peter's legs were crammed under a desk better suited for a kindergartener. Welcoming him back, Janna blushed, asking Peter if he was up for some tea or coffee. Peter suggested Starbucks, but Janna wanted something quieter. Peter obliged, seeking out a less popular and more eclectic coffee shop.

At the table, after fifteen minutes of polite talk, the conversation became stilted and waned into uncomfortable territory. Peter, already feeling strange, decided to get to the point. "Janna, is something wrong? I am a big boy. Whatever you have to say, I can handle it."

Running her hands though her straight black hair, she took a deep breath and pushed off into a probable political nightmare. "When I get back to the office today, I will be setting up a meeting to review the expenditures for the EwRM2 enforcement case, with the chief of finance and Brad Baily, and, uh, you."

Janna, looking at Peter expectantly, waited to see how this information would affect him.

"Ross will be there, right? He did almost all the purchasing for the case. I don't know how he is going to pull off this meeting, but he definitely needs to be there." Peter leaned back, for once thinking that being at an EPA meeting might be more on the entertaining side.

Janna frequented the woman's restroom on the third floor just to stay informed on white board commentary, so she knew the talk about Ross. She was suspicious about the project purchases and found it more than unusual that Peter had made over ninety-five percent of the purchases yet was not the project lead, Ross was. Getting in her bag, she took out a two-inch stack of papers. "All these purchases for the EwRM2 project show that you requested the items, and you alone approved all the items. According to the purchasing system, Ross purchased very little on the project." Janna slid the stack of papers toward Peter.

Peter didn't move to take the papers at first. His eyes met Janna's. She watched his brown eyes go from a general interest to furious anger in a matter of seconds.

Janna said, "Look, I just thought you would want to know before the meeting." Then whispering, "Did you really buy a horse for jumping fences and chasing Bernadette?"

After five minutes, Peter was still leafing through the papers. Janna asked, "Are you going to be okay? Do you want to talk?"

"Yah, I am fine. Just thinking. Can you schedule the meeting for week after next?"

"I can schedule it for later, if you block out your calendar."

"Reaching for his wallet, Peter took out a twenty and put it on the table. He handed the papers to Janna, who put them back in her bag. Peter held out his hand to Janna and pulled her into the hallway leading to the restrooms, out of sight from patrons. Peter leaned back against the wall, spreading his legs, he pulled Janna into his embrace, and kissed her like it was the last kiss he would ever have. After being beaten down on the job by Ross, he felt alive as his fingers ran though Janna's hair and down her back. When he finally came up for air, she was smiling.

"Wow, I think that was the best, most intense kiss I have ever had. Will we get to do that again?"

"Count on it. Ross bought most of the stuff, including the horse. I need to go clear up this mess. Wait for me. May I take the stack of purchase orders with me?"

Janna, keeping one arm around his waist, used the other to fish the stack of papers out of her bag. Then Peter lifted Janna away from him, winked at her, he turned and was gone.

As Peter walked to his car, he attempted to give understanding to the unknowns:

- Someone had to have given Peter's purchasing password to Ross. Or, someone hacked the EPA system to get the password. Peter suspected it was someone within the EPA who had helped Ross and there would be no back door to determine who did it.
- Peter's purchasing power had mysteriously increased to such a status that he didn't need approval from anyone on any purchase, regardless of monetary value. Usually, this situation

only applied to division directors. Who had manipulated the system in such a manner was a big question. Peter suspected that the person who made the change would never be known.

- The purchasing system was altered in his account so that sole suppliers specifically listed were accepted without going out for three bids. The purchase orders had to have been printed and mailed to the supplier's address. Who did that?

On his drive back home, Peter kept seeing a vision; Bernadette asking him to believe she was innocent of any wrongdoing. Now, only several days after the close of the case, he faced the same fate; he was innocent, but no one would believe him. He had thought he was immune to the conniving craziness Ross had created. Nope. He was now shoved in the league of Bernadette, and frankly he couldn't be happier. Before this moment, he didn't want to help Bernadette for fear that he would lose his job; now he was jumping into help Bernadette for fear he would lose his life. Finally, he felt on the right side of the equation.

His travel bag, empty but still by the bed, was quickly refilled with the items he would need for another stay in Lebanon.

Chapter 51
Hope for the Best, Plan for the Worst

(December 4, 1999)

Bernadette put on a blue silk suit and high heels for her upcoming visit with the two FBI agents. Tierney and Carney were surprised when she asked for information on where and when she could meet them. When they pressed to understand what she hoped to achieve with the FBI, she didn't respond directly, telling them she wasn't sure if she would be getting information or giving it.

She had come to a private decision, and she didn't want anyone dissuading her; she was going to draw the instigator of this mess to her. She felt ready to fight, fight to gain her life back, fight for normalcy, fight for what was right in life. Bernadette abhorred gossip, but now she was going to use gossip to let the threat know she had information and intended to use it.

At 6:30 p.m., once in Lebanon Travel Lodge parking lot, she strategically parked her truck near the thoroughfare, hoping that those driving by would notice her truck and begin gossiping about it. Entering the lobby carrying both her purse and a briefcase, the receptionist looked up to great the new customer and found the redheaded woman to be completely overdressed for this motel. Bernadette asked for Jim Bray and Scott Sanders in Room 116, then sat near a window in the lobby waiting for them.

Tierney had mentioned to Bernadette that the two FBI agents were young preppy kids trying to look mature. When Jim and Scott walked in the lobby, she was transported back in time to what it felt like when having that first professional job: to be young and unjaded, eager to change the world for the better. Bernadette introduced herself to the neatly dressed, dark haired, and clean-shaven men. She inquired if they might discuss Ed Keil. Both men looked surprised, then pleased, and took a seat across from Bernadette.

"I have been told that Ed Keil was investigating EwRM2. I am sorry to hear he disappeared. Have you had any luck understanding what happened to him?" Bernadette knew they would not give her information, but she wanted to pique their interest immediately.

Jim took the lead, "Since this is an active investigation we can't comment on the progress in the case. Would you have information for us?"

"I might. I didn't know anything about Ed until after I was no longer employed by EwRM2. I have heard that Ed tried to interview me while I was working there, but his request was denied by someone very high up in the company. However, I do know something that could be of interest to you. The company president, Devlin Holcomb, was secretly recording transactions in his office. I accidentally found a camera in locked cabinet and the camera was embedded in a wall adjacent to Holcomb's office. The uses for that secret camera might be important to your investigation." Bernadette was fudging with the information, as she didn't know how the camera was used, just had theories.

Jim and Scott looked at each other. Scott said, "Perhaps we should find a private meeting room to discuss this."

Bernadette quickly responded. "I don't have any other information you can use right now. I was thinking the existence of the camera might be useful in your investigation."

Pausing, Bernadette added, "You know, there might be something else of interest to you. EPA has been involved in a strange case with EwRM2. You might want to see if there is a connection between Calvin Rossberg or Senator Rossberg, and Devlin Holcomb. Ed may have found an unsavory connection between those men."

Smiling kindly at Jim and Scott she added, "And please be careful. I have found Calvin and Devlin to be rather conniving at times. I think the reason for that behavior lies in ulterior motives. If you need to reach me, here is my information." Bernadette handed them a slip of paper with her name, address, and phone number. She turned and walked out of the lobby.

-

Jim and Scott got to work and found not only a long-time friendship between Senator Rossberg and Devlin Holcomb, but also a familial connection between the Rossberg and Holcomb families. The more they researched the families, the more the investigation progressed.

Chapter 52
Twister

(December 7, 1999)

Bernadette had just sat down for a nice cup of tea when she jumped off the couch as the front door swung open and Peter marched into her home.

"Ah, you nearly gave me a heart attack. Good grief, don't you knock? Why are breaking into my home? You went back to Seattle, Peter. What is wrong now?" Jumping over the back of the couch, Bernadette put distance between herself and Peter. "If you have come to arrest me, forget it. You will have to kill me."

Eyeing him suspiciously, she wondered why the dog hadn't barked and she, with excellent hearing, never heard him in the yard or walking on the porch. How creepy. Really analyzing him, she noticed he looked terrible.

"What happened to you. Did you drink excessively? You look like hell."

Peter said, "Look at this." He tossed his jacket on a chair, unzipped a bag, and handed Bernadette the stack of papers Janna had given him.

Bernadette could see they were EPA purchase orders. Glancing though them, she whistled. "It cost you $6,474 to put a camera on my telephone pole. And holy cow, you spent $3,565 dollars to clean the cabin of rat poop. I would have done it for $1,000."

Squinting at Peter, she asked, "Why are you showing me this stuff?"

"Look at who made and approved the purchase orders."

Bernadette set the papers on the back of the couch and started leafing through them. She paused when looking at the purchase of the horse. "Looks like you made all of them. Which doesn't make sense. Ross told me he bought the horse. But here it says you did."

"I probably only made five percent of the purchases. Ross hacked into my account and made it look like I did all the purchasing."

With a dawning realization, Bernadette stared at Peter. "Oh my, you are toast."

"Not yet. I know one thing about Senator Rossberg. He likes manipulating companies through the use of sabotage. Which means his nephew probably likes it too. You, Miss Bernadette, are going to tell me what you know about that topic."

"Why should I trust you with that information? You might think I am a weakling, but it would take a lot of work on your part to force me to talk."

"Bernadette, it is almost midnight. I don't have time for this. I need to know what you know. Then I can work to resolve this mess. If you would have told me what you knew before, it would have saved us from losing the good part of a year."

"No, that is a lie. I would just be dead. You wouldn't have cared. You care now, because you are about to land in jail due to no fault of your own. But no, a year ago you were preoccupied and didn't listen to me. People often suffer from this common but unnamed affliction: *I won't listen until it affects me, then I hope I can fix the problem and it isn't too late.*"

"I care now. I wasn't myself the last year. I was thinking about a marriage that was never a marriage because I wasn't the one who was the husband. Money was the husband, and I was just a tool to get the money. Let's start your story and I promise you, I am myself now."

Really looking at Peter, Bernadette evaluated her options. It was better to have someone in the stew pot with her, because then they would really be on her side. After standing in silence for a good five minutes, Bernadette told him the stories about the instrument shop, the hidden camera, and how the odd material at both locations was tungsten in the form of tire studs.

At the end she said, "I am one hundred percent confident that the rumor mill led to my problems. Someone at work thought I knew a secret about EwRM2, a secret of most importance. I didn't even know that what I heard or saw was of importance until people tried to kill me. I think it is time I use a rumor to trap those people who are trying to destroy my life."

Stepping to the recliner, Peter let himself fall in the chair.

"Please sit, make yourself comfortable," Peter told Bernadette.

Leaning his head back, Peter closed his eyes and contemplated what Bernadette had suggested as a solution to this confounding mess. For the past year he thought continually about what was gone; he had ruminated on his failed marriage. His ruminations had been exacerbated by the rumor mill. The vicious rumors his wife said about him made him stew on the divorce, feeling ever more a failure. What was it that made a rumor like a festering boil, impossible to ignore? Did anything positive come out of rumors?

With that thought, Peter began to smile. If rumors drove everyone to go bonkers, what would be a good rumor to bring Ross and the Senator to town for a roasting.

Peter said, "Rumors."

Not knowing where this was going, Bernadette piped up anyway, "Yup, time to make those rumors work for us."

Looking at Bernadette thought barely open eyes, he agreed, "You need to spread a rumor to make the Rossbergs think they must take action here and now." Speaking from a deeper place, Peter's eyes closed as he said,

"Bernadette, you know, you are the perfect person to take on this crime. Like Winston Churchill during WWII, he performed his roll so well for that particular span of time. You are what is needed right now. You are clever in spades. You don't back down. You understand nature and are close to it. And your confidence in spirit is phenomenal. Most people would have run away by now, moved, hit the trail. But not you. Maybe you are here to inspire the rest of us to get off our rear ends and do something."

Bernadette said, "You should be happy to know that I have already been working on rumors. I went to see the FBI guys who are in town investigating Ed Keil's disappearance."

Peter grinned at the ceiling. "See. Perfect person for this." Getting up he said, "I am going to get my bag and crash in your guest bedroom tonight. See you in the morning."

Peter slept well that night. He had a woman on his mind, Janna, and another woman had his back, Bernadette. Couldn't get much better than that.

Chapter 53
Gathering Forces

(December 8, 1999)

Bernadette woke-up tired. She had tossed and turned much of the night thinking about how she might fight Senator Rossberg, Ross, Devlin and all the goonies they might bring along to destroy her. She needed some help. That morning, leaving before 7:00 a.m., she headed to the Bernstein's home. When she arrived, David and his wife, Cynthia, greeted her warmly, inviting her in even though they were still in their bathrobes.

David looked kindly at the woman who had helped him and Cynthia when so much had been lost. "I hope you are here to ask for our help. We need some action to help us get out of bed at a decent time." He pinched his wife's side and she yelped.

Giving him a seductive smile, Cynthia added, "Right. We do need to get up earlier."

Bernadette, feeling impatient, got right to the topic on her mind, "I feel badly asking, but I could use your help. I am actively working to bring this mess with EwRM2 to a conclusion. Obviously, there are lots of unknows and serious risks. But if any of us ever want a normal life again, then we must obtain a resolution. I wondered if you could do a few things for me?"

David rubbed his hands together in happy anticipation. "Anything to take down EwRM2! Just tell us what you need."

"First, I need about six live, wild, juvenile rats. I thought perhaps Cutter would have them around the dairy and you might be able to live trap some for me. If you get me a dozen, I will determine which will be a good fit for my plan."

Cynthia looked mortified. "Could you maybe buy some in a pet store?"

Shaking her head, Bernadette said, "Nope. I need wild, mean rats, but young ones. Second, I anticipate that several individuals will use logging roads to get close to my place and attack me. I need USGS (U.S. Geological Survey) maps of all the logging roads which come within five miles of my place and where landings are located. I also need to know the most likely spot on all of those logging roads where people will be forced to transition from vehicle to foot as they try to ambush me.

I need the rats this week and the other information next week. Are you up for that?"

Cynthis looked at the face of her husband. He was beaming with happiness. She understood. David wanted to be part of the solution so he could feel satisfaction with metering back the pain that was dished out to him.

"Consider it done," David said.

Bernadette smiled. "Excellent. I have a live trap in the truck. Let me get it."

After Bernadette left, David looked at his wife and said, "I will call Cutter to let him know we will be by the farm in a few hours. We better get the maps today so we can go explore those logging roads in the coming week. We should bundle up and take some food along when we go exploring."

As they got ready to leave the house, David kept thinking about *purpose*. He felt alive with purpose.

Chapter 54
Shoring Up the Net

(December 8-15, 1999)

For over a week, Bernadette methodically spread rumors to former coworkers, high school friends, casual acquaintances, or anyone who would listen to drivel, which included most of the town. Enthralled with Bernadette's new compulsion, people began seeking her out once her vehicle crossed into the city limits.

Her standard bewitching comments promised to stoke up the agitation. "I am doing great since leaving that EwRM2 job. I just felt it wasn't a good fit there because of a few shady characters who like to pressure people into corruption. Certainly not the type of pressure I needed. I do know a good deal of the inner workings at EwRM2 and there were some questionable practices." And, on it went. After three or four days, Bernadette was becoming quite good at her vague statements filled with veiled accusations.

On day five of spreading prattle, an EwRm2 accountant approached her in the feed store. With his arms crossed over his chest, he got right to the point. "Bernadette, I don't know you very well, but I would like to give you a bit of advice that I would give any friend. I would suggest not talking so much about EwRM2. I am hearing rumors that upper management is more than prepared to take legal action against you for your role in the improper disposal of hazardous waste. Cost them a lot of money in legal fees while they worked through matter with the EPA."

Bernadette tittered at the submissive fool, and put on her brightest smile, "Oh, it happened again, to you. Didn't anyone tell you that I have all the emails from my boss giving me very detailed instructions on how I was to manage the hazardous waste? Because I like you as a *friend*, I would be happy to make you a copy of those emails. Just let me know how I can help."

Her comments sent the accountant back to his desk and calculator, abandoning his hopes of getting a quick promotion by eliminating some of the boss's irritation.

By the end of the week, Lebanon was getting high off all the gossip in the air. Bernadette decided it was probably enough gossip and she didn't want the town to become addicted to her manipulative moonlighting position as rumormonger.

Tierney, in Colorado keeping an eye on the Senator, sent back reports that the man's nightly toddy had ramped up in volume and strength to all night Turkey Trot benders, a sure indication of impending imprudent behavior. Senator Rossberg vaulting ambition for power would incite him to extinguish the constantly resuscitating threat Bernadette represented.

David and Cynthia delivered the rats on Saturday, December 11. Peter had predicted his imminent eviction from the guest bedroom and found other lodgings the prior day. The rats went in the guest bedroom. Using very tall bird cages, modified to keep a rat in, Bernadette commenced with their training, spending hours with them, developing bonds of trust and understanding. A sign was placed on the door informing anyone in the house that the room was off limits to all, but her.

The following week, the Bernsteins came by again, spending several hours with Bernadette. They went over maps of logging roads, vista points, turn around areas, landings, and locations where roads became impassable. Cynthia and David's checks were flushed with color and they both looked refreshed.

Curious, Bernadette asked them about their renewed energy. "Both of you look so invigorated. What has happened?"

David reached over and took Cynthia's hand. "I think we found that exploring the old logging roads, hiking the more inaccessible, highly rutted roads, and riding horses on the mountainous roads, has helped our relationship. We are thinking of writing a travel guide on what to see on old logging roads."

"That is a beautiful story. Cynthia, you should write about your blooming romance."

When they left Bernadette's house, they cheerfully climbed in their newly acquired beat-up Jeep and sped off to new adventures.

-

Since December 1, Carney had been less discrete; hanging around the house during the day and sleeping with Bernadette at night. She wasn't sure of why things had changed. When she asked, he said only a few sentences, "I have been extracting myself from duties in Europe. I want to spend quality time with you."

Although Christmas was approaching, and no one expected uninvited company from December 20 through January 1, Carney was often out checking the farm and beyond for intruders during the early evening. During the night, after he took a shower, he would join her in bed, keeping both of them awake for hours. They often talked in the darkness, about something or nothing in particular. On the night of December 21, as they lay in bed waiting for sleep to take them, Bernadette asked, "Would you be able to help me make a fake tactical vest?"

Carney turned on his back, pulling Bernadette on top of him. She rarely asked for help, and to his dismay, he had no idea what she needed right now. But given this rare opportunity, he would never show any doubt in being able to accomplish this task, even if it was impossible. "I would be happy to, if you would just explain to me what a fake tactical vest is."

"I have an old black fishing vest with all the zippered pockets and clips on it. I want to make it look like a tactical vest with a switch blade, handcuffs, duct tape and ... well other things you use when capturing someone or fighting. But I don't want any of the stuff to work. The switch blade won't open, and the handcuff ratchets are filed, making them open with a little bit of pressure, we could put baby oil on the duct tape and wind it back up, maybe a 9mm pistol that won't fire."

Carney looked up at his beautiful wife to see she was completely serious about this project. She had sat up and was astride him wearing a lovely old fashioned flannel nightgown. Yet, for her to want tactical equipment that didn't function was completely contradictory to the sweet purity she projected in her nightgown. Carney's mouth started to turn at the corners. Taking a deep breath, he tried to think of something serious to keep from laughing. Then he looked back at Bernadette and burst out laughing. "Why," more laughter, "would you," his head thrown back on the pillow laughing, "want survival equipment that doesn't work?" He reached up and caressed both her cheeks with his hands. She didn't appear concerned that he was highly amused.

"I'll tell you, but you must promise that you won't tell anyone, not Tierney, Peter, no one. And I want you promise to help even if you find the reason stupid."

Carney stopped chuckling and smiling; he became very serious. "Bern, you are the smartest woman I know. I have learned that you are far more clever than 99.99% of the population. I might not understand what you are able to intuit, but I would never, ever, find anything you do to be stupid. I promise."

Taking a deep breath, she explained her reasoning to Carney, "Well, criminals are often overconfident. They like to think they are smarter than everyone. I can't overpower and out fight the senator and some goons with guns unless I am able to exploit their overconfidence. In the event that I have to directly deal with them, I want them to think that my equipment is functioning and that if they use my own equipment on me, I will be helpless." Then she smiled. "What do you think? Can we make it not work?"

Shaking his head with a grin on his face, "I am so glad you are my wife and not my enemy, you gorgeous woman. We will make the vest tomorrow." Carney pulled her head down so he could show her just how glad he was.

-

Peter decided to leave Lebanon and return to Seattle for Christmas and the New Year. On his way out the door he said, "Call me if we get a fish on the line."

The fish was on the line December 29 and Tierney called Peter that day to suggest he return to camp. Senator Rossberg left his home for a New Year's "hunting" trip, as it was described to his family and staff. The only problem with the hunting trip was the species he was hunting: *Homo sapiens.*

Tierney followed Senator Rossberg for several days; going into Wyoming and Montana then heading toward Washington. Finding all the sightseeing a waste of time, Tierney abandoned the winding path of the Senator and decided not to trail him; he returned to Bernadette's place.

When Tierney arrived at the farm and everyone had settled into the living room, he told Carney, "Senator Rossberg is circumferencing."

Bernadette, grabbed the dictionary but didn't open it. "That is not a word. Try another."

"Doesn't matter, it applies here. He is going to spiral in closer and closer, however, he wants to ensure the path looks devoid of a human target. Make no mistake, he is working his way here to be sure this job gets finished, finally."

Looking at Peter, Bernadette asked him, "Where is Ross? Shouldn't he be scheming along with his uncle right now?"

"I never saw him in Seattle. I heard that he had taken extended leave. He is around. I will put more effort into finding him tomorrow."

Inclined to believe the situation was reaching a point of force overcoming friction, Bernadette felt it was time to go over the logging road information. They all needed to strategize their approach. She said, "Why don't we order in pizza and go over our defense plan on the logging roads this afternoon?"

Everyone was in favor of that.

Bernadette said, "Since Polly Doodle Pizza closed three months ago, no one will deliver this far out of town unless you order a minimum of five large pizzas." Warming to the idea of excess pizza, Bernadette glanced at Carney and made a proposal. "You guys could get three meat pizzas, I'll get two vegetarian, and freeze what we have left over. That would be a great solution for days when I'm too busy to cook, or too tired."

An hour and half later, Tierney and Peter were arguing about logging roads while Bernadette and Carney were getting plates dished up. As she loaded a slice on the spatula for herself, it slipped, landing with a *plop* in the floor, splattering sauce all over.

Glancing at Bernadette, Carney smiled and winked at her. "Glad to know you are human," he said.

"If you will take the pizza out to the living room, I'll clean this up and be there in a moment," Bernadette said.

Although she usually didn't feed human food to the dog, she scooped the slice from the floor into a dog dish and put it outside for Svalbard. Returning to the kitchen, she was down on her knees wiping up tomato sauce when the dog began barking. Because Bernadette was on a heightened alert due her sense that Rossbergs could strike anytime, she responded quickly whenever Svalbard barked, setting aside anything she was doing to see what the problem was. She got back up, leaving the rag on the floor, and headed to the front door.

Carney watched as Bernadette walked to the door. Glancing at the guys, he observed them as they picked at the pizza, taking off the mushrooms, which Peter has specifically said they didn't want on the meat pizza.

Opening the door, Bernadette found Svalbard barking at his dish, with the pizza still in it. Doing a double take, she grabbed the dish, turned and yelled, just as Carney shouted, "Don't eat the pizza!"

Peter, having just taken a bite, spit the slightly chewed piece out on the plate. Tierney tossed his slice on the plate, which was sitting on the coffee table, and looked up shocked.

Standing by the door, dog dish in hand, Bernadette's face turned bright red. She was furious. "If that Ross kills the dog with poison, I won't just kill him, I will fillet him till he dies. That man is a piece of garbage!"

Carney stood and walked quickly into the kitchen. He opened up all the boxes of pizza and tried to find something in common amongst the boxes that looked odd. He again zeroed in on the mushrooms. Peter and Tierney joined him.

Bernadette marched to the mudroom and then returned to the kitchen, her face flushed with frustration. She slammed newspapers on the counter with tightly corded muscles in her powerful forearms. "Put three to four pieces on a several sheets of newspaper, roll it up, and I will feed all of it into the wood stove tonight. Those bastards almost killed the dog!" With tears in her eyes, she walked to her bedroom and closed the door.

Carney turned to Peter and Tierney. "We have gone to flab. We continue to treat this issue as a woman's problem. Because she paid attention to the dog, she just saved our saggy butts." Peter started to talk, but Carney held up his hands and continued with what he had to say. "You haven't been living with the fact that someone wants to kill you, so this event might be excusable, if you were both just ordinary guys. But you are not. You both have training that is supposed to make you aware, cunning, decisive, and lethal. The boars were on the verge of becoming bacon right now, so we best get a quick tune-up, eh."

Then, Carney released the tension from his face, taking on his most angelic expression, he gave voice to the humor that Bernadette worried more about the dog then the four people in the house, "Besides, we have to avenge these idiots. They almost killed the dog. I can see why that would upset Bernadette, because the dog is the only one paying attention right now." Putting his head back, he gave a ghostly howl that would do a wolf proud.

Going in the bedroom, he spoke to Bernadette for ten minutes, before they both headed back out to the living room to join in the map conversation.

Carney, Tierney, and Peter were convinced that an attack on Bernadette would come at night from the east, off logging road 5079. Logging road 5079 provided easy access from Berlin Road, wasn't traveled but by hunters in fall, and provided cover while approaching Bernadette's farm. Bernadette didn't agree completely with them, but she didn't tell them that. She believed that Senator Rossberg would attack from the north using the logging road 4024 originating in Lacomb, a small town with just a gas station and grocery store. Based on Senator Rossberg's history of sabotage, she surmised that the Senator thrilled in the element of surprise and the pain inflicted on others because of the unforeseen. The 4024 logging road held the element of surprise because of the distance the senator and his brood would have to travel on rough road to get to Bernadette's place.

A mean smile crossed Bernadette's face as she thought of the pleasure in meeting Senator Rossberg for the first time. She was ready.

Chapter 55
Time to Make Soufflé or Get Out of the Kitchen

(January 6, 2000)

The cold numbed Bernadette's finger and toes as she cleaned the goat stalls this windy winter day. After she finished cleaning, she checked on all the stock tanks, filling them as needed and removing the ice, since it wasn't thawing much during the day. While waiting for the stock tank in the south field to fill, Bernadette noticed the deer, seven of them. It was about noon, the wrong time of day for them to be moving in such an open area. They weren't forging, looking here or there for a tasty green morsel which had survived the cold, they were on the move. Something or someone was pushing them out of their winter area. That was when she knew, Rossberg and friends were coming tonight.

Finishing up the tanks, she returned to the barn. Rosie and goats were fed and watered, then locked up for the night.

Getting back in the house, Bernadette grabbed some lunch with Carney, Peter, and Tierney.

When they stopped talking about their favorite ice hockey team, Bernadette said, "Rossberg and his friends are coming tonight."

Tierney asked the obvious question, "How do you know?"

"The deer. They are getting out of the area. Several other things get deer to move out of their home area: hunting season and cougar. Those aren't the reasons today. We will have a New Moon tonight, no extra light, which is what they want." Bernadette cleaned up her dishes and went in the guest bedroom.

Bernadette had her clothing all laid out. All of it was black: long underwear, ski pants, thick socks, gloves, an insulated flannel shirt with special pockets she made to hold her rats, a heavy raincoat, and her fake tactical vest.

Four of the rats would come with her tonight. David and Cynthia had brought her twelve, but four were too wild and afraid to train, so they went back to Cutter's place. She worked daily to train the eight. First, they were taught that Bernadette provided good food and tender belly rubs. Once she could hold them, they were taught to attack. She would toss them at a stuffed dummy clothed in a combination of Peter, Tierney, and Carney's plundered clothing. They learned where to enter the clothing, either at the collar, top of the pants, or bottom of the pant leg. Once inside the clothing, they were taught how to scratch and rip apart inner clothing to get at food inside the dummies.

She tested her training by having Carney momentarily enter the guest bedroom. The rats went wild in their cages when they smelled him, which was exactly the behavior Bernadette wanted. In contrast, her smell soothed them, her hand-fed scrumptious treats filled them, and behind the ear rubs pleased them.

A black cap was the final touch to hide her hair and a black backpack held a few extra items. Bernadette silently escaped through the bedroom window. The minute her booted feet touched the ground outside of the house, she knew she was transforming into something better. Her desire to bring a conclusion to this confounding problem couldn't be shuffled off to another time or place.

Svalbard was left with the goats in the barn. She had other plans for the night, and she needed to focus on the enemy, not worry about her beloved dog. Her pace was quick as she sprinted north, down Elmer Lane, past the logging gate, and onto logging road 4024.

-

Peter, doubting Bernadette's method of surveillance, made a few calls around town. It was quickly confirmed, Senator Rossberg had been seen in Madison yesterday. Carney, Peter, and Tierney all changed into black and layered their clothing. It was going to be a long cold afternoon and night.

After fifteen minutes of discussion about the maps, Carney reiterated, "Peter, you and I will go east, and attempt to intercept them as they travel down the logging road. Tierney will stay around the house and yard, but not in them, the last line of defense here."

Peter said, "And Tierney will watch over Bernadette, right? Is she in the house or barn?"

Carney shook his head, "She is already gone. She left through the guest bedroom window."

Looking surprised, Peter asked, "If you knew she was going to slip out, why didn't you stop her? You let her go?"

Carney remembered. Roger had given him words of wisdom regarding Bernadette and how to be in a relationship with her. Many years ago, he told Carney: *You and I cannot fully understand this woman. She is the goodness and force of nature. She is a spirit seeking to progress in understanding. Respect and love her, but do not hem her in. She seeks growth over comfort. She seeks experience over shelter.*

"Peter, I vacillate between wanting to protect her and wanting her to experience life as she wishes. Stand back and look at who was actually taking care of Bernadette. I had to face the reality that more often than I wished, I did very little for her, other than be a source of heartache. Just as you and I don't want to be hemmed in by a woman, she doesn't need us to limit her experience. So let's get going, see if we can't rally on her behalf."

—

Off to the east, at 10:15 p.m., three men attacked Peter and Carney. Within five minutes of the first shot, which was very wide, Carney's battle instincts told him that the oppositions purpose was solely to engage, not to conquer. Carney worked on a plan to finish this foray, but it would take some doing as the three men were smart. He needed to be careful and not let this understanding of battle motive, and his growing concern for Bernadette, get him injured.

—

At 11:17 p.m., Bernadette had been sitting for hours, with her back against a tree, fifty feet from a vehicle-impassable section of logging road 4024. She heard people in the woods and waited for them to find her. Hearing a man's yell at least a football field away, she moved her hand, lowering the zipper on her jacket.

"Get up, slowly." The male voice came from behind her, perhaps two hundred feet off. Standing, she turned toward a man wearing night vision goggles. She slowly moved her hands, making a big production of trying to remove the pistol from its secure holster on the front of the vest.

The deep voice boomed, "Put your hands up now! Get your hands away from the gun!"

She complied, doing her best to appear flustered and unsure. A large hand reached toward her, releasing a snap holding the pistol secure in the vest pocket.

Grinning, his white teeth showing in the darkness, he said, "You have to remove the strap holding the gun. Here, I'll take it for you. Look at all this equipment, and not a brain cell to use it. Tsk, Tsk." Holstering his own gun, he checked the magazine of her gun was loaded, then kept her gun in his hand.

Bernadette looked at the silent Doberman Pinscher, extremely large but skinny, who stood by the man's side. The dog had already been kicked twice by its handler for some imagined infraction. Making eye contact with the dog, she found no malice. She hoped the dog wouldn't complicate her rat plans.

She needed the men to underestimate her completely. Doing what she felt would meet those ends, she started to cry and blubber. "Please, don't hurt me. I haven't done anything wrong. Please."

Another man, also in night vision goggles, approached from behind. Bernadette turned to evaluate this additional threat through her fake tears. Neither man was the senator, which was expected. The senator was probably sitting on his rear end somewhere, waiting for the underlings to do his work. Reaching out, the goon pulled the handcuffs from a pocket on the vest and put the key in his jeans pocket. Putting a hand on her shoulder, he spun her around, then secured her hands in the metal cuffs behind her back.

Once they had the handcuffs on her, they marched up logging road 4024, going in the direction of Lacomb. She felt her pulse quickening and fear seeping into all parts of her brain. She had to maintain control of her mind. Trying to corral her thoughts, she began to mentally chant, *God, Christ, Guru,* her favorite blood pressure reducer.

Bernadette knew where they were going. The turn out and landing area for the old logging operation; one that David and Cynthia had pointed out to her on the maps. It was a large gravel area built upon loads and loads of rock brought in by dump trucks to create an artificially level, brush free area. Of course, that is where they would park their cars. It also would make an escape into the brush more difficult, as a person would have to outrun a bullet if they were to flee while in the barren area.

There were two black SUVs (sport utility vehicle) parked in the turn out area. Both SUVs were off, but one had its headlights on, infiltrating the peaceful night with more human machinations. As they approached, Bernadette could see the senator, hands clinched in fits, by one of the SUVs. After loading the cowering dog into one of the SUVs, the men gathered at the hood of their car which was illumined by the other SUV's headlights. After removing the night vision goggles, one man grabbed Bernadette's jacket, forcing her to within a foot of the senator. "She wasn't too hard to find," the man said.

The senator's face contorted with distain and viciousness. "You vulgar brat. Wasting my time and affecting my money." He slapped Bernadette with all his force. Afterwards, working his elbow back and forth, he prepared to continue his assault. "Your nothing but a tramp. These men will be happy to kill you. I can't wait to hear from them, later, how their adventure goes. You are a stupid woman."

Bernadette saw another blow coming. Although she could have deflected the force to her face, it would destroy her fake tactical vest plan. Taking the slaps created three good outcomes for her: her fear decreased, her fury increased, and the rats, sensing the violence, became aggressive.

After the second blow, she sensed the immediate change in the men's disposition. They had been bored with this task until now, until they learned that they could do as they want. The violence aroused them. The one man laughed and put the dog in the SUV to devote his full attention to Bernadette.

The senator, noticing the increasing viciousness in the men, abandoned his desire to beat her and abruptly turned, marching toward the SUV with the headlights on. He was followed by an assistant of some type. She suspected they would drive off and let the two other men feed their violent passions.

Bernadette pleaded, for she wanted to keep the senator here, "Wait! I have money. I can pay you. The right inner pocket of my jacket has one-hundred-dollar bills. If you just unzip that pocket, you will find the money." It didn't have hundred-dollar bills, it had ones, but she was hoping she could bluff for as long as possible. She started to work her right hand out of the handcuff, as a minimum amount of pressure caused the filed ratchet mechanism to give.

The senator's sinister laugh cut the chill air.

The goon, with Bernadette's gun pointed it at her, said, "I'll be happy to unzip everything."

Backing up, she moved toward the rear of the SUV which was parked furthest south. She was on one side of the SUV and not between the SUVs. Cunningly, her movements took her toward the shadows, where the headlights didn't penetrate. The idiot with her gun, getting impatient with her movements, quickly walked toward her.

This was the time. The darkness presented opportunity. Wrenching her right hand free, she said, "Here, let me help get the money." Her left hand opened the zipper to her jacket while her right hand slipped into a pocket of her flannel shirt, closing carefully over one of her favorite rats. The man stood astonished, watching her hands move freely. She tossed the rat at the man's neck, where it found its footing and slithered inside, as it had been trained to do.

The man stepped back quickly, batting at the animal running around inside the front his jacket. Bernadette leaped forward, grabbed his gun from the holster, and jumped back out of his way. He fell backwards as the rat attacked his upper torso. The screaming and cursing began as fear took over the man and training took over the rat. The other henchman came running around the side of the SUV.

Putting her hands behind her back, Bernadette said, "Something attacked him! Help him!"

The man kneeled to attend his friend and Bernadette quickly approached him, sliding a rat down the back of his coat. He jumped up and yelled, trying to unzipper his coat. The senator and his assistant ran back to find the two men fighting some unknown assailant. Bernadette jumped around screaming, attempting match the actions of the two men with vicious rats in their clothing. As the senator's assistant tried to help the one man unzipper his coat, Bernadette stepped close and threw a rat on his shoe, which promptly ran up his leg.

The assistant turned on her, "What did you do?" He grabbed his gun, but with a rat biting his inner thigh, he wildly missed Bernadette.

Bernadette ran around the SUV and grabbed a pair of night goggles, just as the Senator turned with his pistol trained on her. She threw the final rat at him and dove for the ground as he fired at her. Crouching, she ran for the rock embankment and the trees beyond.

The resounding boom of a second discharge was followed by the scream of another man. Still another shot went off, and she heard the shattering of glass. She heard the senator yelling and another three rapid successive shots. There were more screams and the dog barking. Another shot took out a tire with a resulting hissing sound, somewhat hard to hear amongst the commotion.

Reaching a bank about 15 feet down and very steep, Bernadette threw the goggles around her neck, then went feet first over the bank, using her feet and hands to slow her decent. She laid at the base of the embankment for a moment, listening, breathing heavily. There was more yelling and cursing. A voice above the others screamed, "Get this thing off of me." Two more shots were fired and the senator was heard cursing this time. Putting on the night goggles, Bernadette ran into the woods. The voices became more muffled. She ran to the west, away from the turn out area and the continuing gun fire.

Carney, Tierney, and Peter arrived on the scene thirty or more minutes later. They found two shot up SUVs, three men writhing in agony on the ground, and a dog cowering in one SUV. There was no sign of the senator.

They tied up the three men, threw them in the drivable SUV with the dog, and Peter drove them off to the local hospital.

Tierney and Carney began tracking the senator. He was bleeding. They finally found the senator a quarter of a mile away, hiding in a huge logging road culvert. His face and neck were covered with scratches, and he had shot himself, not seriously, in his left arm. They brought him back to the SUV.

Carney and Bernadette had long used animal calls to communicate in the appropriate situation. The all-clear call was two wolf howls. Carney called to Bernadette, knowing she was unlikely to reappear uninvited.

Forty minutes after the wolf call, Bernadette came walking down the logging road. Carney greeted her with a kiss. Then both he and Tierney headed back to the house, telling her to take as much time as she needed. She approached the SUV, setting her attention on the Senator.

The dome light cast a bright glow in the vehicle. The senator was naked, except for boxer shorts, and tied to the SUV passenger car seat, with the door wide open.

She started to laugh. "Oh, you look positively like a trussed-up walrus, with no insult intended to the walrus. Aren't you just the worst specimen of pasty white human."

The senator growled, "When I get out of this mess…"

Bernadette cut him off. "No, no more threats. You ever try to hurt me again I will solve this disagreement permanently. Your career is finished as of today."

His head flopped around and his words slurred, "I'll pay you. One million and you just go away, shut up."

Turning around she headed down logging road to return to the ranch. "I'll be sending in the sheriff for you, you stupid maggot. Hope you freeze your ass off."

Some of the pulsating pain gave way to the Senator's anger. He thought, *this little fool, this nothing of a woman, couldn't just walk away. He wasn't going to jail.* Kicking the glove compartment with his feet, his facade of egoistic human grandeur crumbled into stench pot of spiritual malnutrition. He yelled, "You are just like your mother, you idiot carcass."

Bernadette stopped. Why did every political disagreement end up with a comparison to Nazism and every insult thrown at her always end up with some comparison to her mother? Shaking her head, she turned around walking back to the Senator. She evaluated his hard eyes which spoke much more truthfully than his mouth. He said, "Untie me. I won't hurt you. I have to pee."

Bernadette momentarily examined her feelings. There was exhaustion on the surface, but deeper, there were darker emotions, their evasiveness to her self-scrutiny meant they had been taking up residence in her mind for some time. She hated these people, and she knew it was wrong. She tried to drum up compassion and understanding, but it was futile at this moment.

Then the senator urinated on the seat. She watched as his jaw clinched, the muscles working back and forth, as the urine slid back on the cushion, creating a small pool under his bottom. She watched as he tried to spit on her. This scene of redemption for Bernadette was turning into numbness. He was a pathetic figure.

"I feel sorry for you." She wanted to add some expletives to that statement but was able to refrain. It was the most control she could muster at this moment. She was going to get the sheriff. He had all the signs of shock; sweating, agitation, the pulse on his temple was rapid. She found his clothing and a blanket, tucking them around him to keep him warm.

For some reason, her statement and actions struck a new raw nerve for the Senator. His embarrassment caused him to lash out in whatever way possible. "You and your mother are nothing but white trash. Self-righteous idiots, spewing nonsense about honesty. I tried to get your mother to see a way to help you. I had brilliant plan. She would tell the EPA how you confided in her about your illegal environmental activities. We would have you arrested, then I could step in and help get you a lower sentence, like house arrest. But your mother was a simpleton, like you. She actually blackmailed me! She said if I did anything to you, she would reveal all my secrets from Alaska. I tried to pay her. She said no too. Then she had to have a stroke and die before I could extract my revenge. But I'll get you. You and your mother aren't going to make me suffer." The senator's head fell further to the right, and drool came weeping out the corner of his mouth.

Bernadette turned and began walking away. She felt reality slipping away and wondered if she was going to faint. Her mother had protected her! Why? Why had her mom, who hated her at every turn, why had she now protected her? Once out of view of the SUV, Bernadette fell to her knees and held her head, just breathing, deeply, for what she thought was a long time.

After some time had gone by, Bernadette became aware of horse hooves on the rock and the smooch of a wet nose. Her reinforcements had arrived. She looked up into the beautiful faces of Svalbard and Rosie. Rosie turned, walked to a stump at the edge of the clearing, and waited. Bernadette didn't even remember getting up and going to the side of the horse. The next thing she remembered, was passing the mounted police on their way to get the senator. When she got home, she crawled in bed and cried herself into the unconscious state.

Her mother had loved her.

Chapter 56
Pollution Controls

(January 7, 2000)

Even when innocently grazing goats aren't actively attempting to gain enticements on the other side of a fence, they are acutely aware of every detail just beyond the metal strands composing the inept barrier. If anyone understood the workings of a goat's mind, then they would know how the flaws within the fence system are cataloged by degree of weakness: jump-ability, scoot-under-ability, paw-down-ability, and push-over-ability. Bernadette discovered that the caprine species delighted in exploiting this information when she was dressed in formal attire, not limited to high heeled shoes, or when she was up to her eyeballs with tasks related to flooding, snow, wind, ice, or extreme heat. It was then that dormant urges within goats hatched free, from concept to action. The joy achieved in executing a release plan appeared to be proportional to the degree of miff expressed by the human. One would think that the plan was considered botched if the escapee became trapped in fencing, ditches, water, snow, or a thicket. However, in goat world, throwing in an element of distress was relished because then a human would feel more inclined to provide treats after a rescue, thinking that this would be necessary to sooth ruffled nerves and prevent illness.

It was a complicated relationship, humans and goats.

Bernadette, having only slept three hours since returning to the house, was showered and dressed before 1:00 p.m. She had just stepped outside the house to feed the goats some store-bought apples, when she discovered her most exotically tricolored doe, Mocha Poka, who had never had any prior boundary infraction, was not with the herd. Standing quietly, her head turning like an old T.V. dish picking up satellite signals, she listened for any distress call. Finally, she heard it, actually, just the echo of it. This meant Mocha Poka probably crossed the creek on a fallen tree serving as a bridge, took a munching trip in the hills, and was now unable to get back home. She was to the southeast.

Putting the bridle on Rosie, she was just getting ready to leave the barn when Peter pulled up in the yard. He got out of his car as if in pain, walking stiltedly to the picnic table and eased himself down. Riding up to him, she noticed he showed bruising and scrapes on his face. "How was last night? What happened to your face?" she asked.

Peter winked at her and a smile of satisfaction dominated his face. He said, "I'm just refreshing my fighting skills this week. We have seven criminals up at the hospital, all guarded by the police. Some in worse shape than others. A few suffered serious rat bites." Peter rubbed his hands together in glee when mentioning the rats. "You know, the police will be here later to question you. They will want to know the story from you. Also, they don't know about Carney. They know Tierney and I are involved in helping you. We have been conveniently ignoring Carney's presence."

Bernadette suddenly sat forward in the saddle, intently looking at the ground. She held up her right hand in a stop gesture to silence Peter. Peter looked at the ground by Rosie's front feet.

After a few moments he couldn't figure out what the issue was. "Can I talk now? I don't see anything on ground Bernadette. What is so important?"

"The entire mob of crows is upset. They just erupted in a flurry of caws. Here that? It is up Elmer Lane." Bernadette continued to sit with her eyes closed and head tilted to one side, listening.

Peter sighed. "Bernadette, right now we have a few issues more important than the crows. My guess is, the crows are fine, completely, totally fine. May I continue, about something really important?"

Shaking her head, she sat up in the saddle. "It isn't a sick or hurt crow, nor are they fighting, it is a disturbance to their home. Crows are fine if you are out walking in the open, most of the time. Unless there is a fledgling on the ground, but that is a completely different story. If it is a cat or something crawling through the grass, they set up the alarm big time. Something is slinking about causing them concern." Looking at Peter, she asked, "What were you saying?"

Peter continued, "I have a gut feeling that Ross is going to turn up. No one has seen him for weeks. He has to make a move."

"While you are thinking about finding Ross, I need to find Ms. Mocha Poka and extract her from some crisis. Then I am going back up on logging road 4024. I want to find the rats. This isn't the right time of year to let them go, as it will be hard for them to find food. If I can't find them, I will need to put food up there twice a week until spring."

As Peter watched Bernadette ride off toward the southeast, he wondered how she kept going. If he wanted to be honest, there were times he hated how Bernadette kept on fighting. Many people would have given up long ago. He figured he would have. After a few unsettling and nerve-racking weeks, all he wanted was a humdrum life with Janna and a better career. Somewhere in his EPA career he had gone from being a man to a yes man, from a lover to a sexually emaciated shadow, he had gone from knowing who the enemy was to not caring who was the enemy or victim. Somehow every passionate drive had been sucked out of him and replaced with a politically correct vacuum of nothingness.

Maybe humdrum wasn't fine, or was it? Sitting with his back against the picnic table, he closed his eyes, hearing the crows again. Closer, louder, more frantic. Then the awareness of sound was gone.

Peter sat for a half hour thinking about his determination, that zest for life for the last five years was shoved along by an outside force. The determination emanating from within him had evaporated as he floated along on a cloud of easy-going monotony, a weariness from too much getting; economic prosperity in a government job, nice house with veteran financing, even easy relationships where people threw around the love word. He hadn't had to fight for anything for several years. He hadn't fought for his marriage, not really. Now, in the last few weeks, he realized the fighting for what was right, for his life, made him feel alive again.

The crows' shadows cast upon him as they flew overhead startled him. The words of Bernadette floated into his consciousness. "If it is a cat or something slinking through the grass, they set up the alarm big time." *Oh no!*

Getting up, Peter headed for the car. He wanted to run but figured that would only encourage someone to shoot him. His pace was far from casual, but he whistled a tune to mask his sense of urgency. His concealed was in his jacket pocket. He had to get his jacket on, and if his guess was correct, he didn't have much time.

Peter flung the car door open, jammed one hand in a jacket sleeve, then the other, shrugging it on. Immediately he heard the crunch of gravel behind him. Peter grinned. Sometimes all you had to do was cross the finish line. He turned around and found a nicely dressed man, tailor-made navy-blue suit, only fifty feet away pointing a 2-inch snub-nose revolver at him. Peter noticed the excessive number of gold rings on his hand that flashed in the sunlight. Peter knew the man, it was Devlin Holcomb.

Janna. He thought of spending time with Janna and this idiot wasn't going to take that away from him. "Can I help you with something?" Peter's lips curled up in a snarl. He didn't think Devlin would risk shooting Peter here in the open. There was just too much at stake.

"Start walking toward the barn. And if you think I won't shoot you right now, you are sorely mistaken." Devlin's accent was heavy, for the man was filled with frustration.

Peter knew the accent but hadn't heard it in a meeting with Devlin. He was obviously good at hiding his true origins. The accent wasn't Eastern US, it was Eastern European. Peter realized Devlin had probably been put into his position as company president for reasons other than intellect and skill. Steeling of intellectual property took many forms.

"You get lost on you way from the men's room to the board room Devlin?" Peter asked.

"I don't have any patience for you. Go. You aren't worth more than one of Bernadette's castrated goats. Don't push it."

Turning, Peter wondered how long he could drag out this walk. Peter focused on his surroundings, how he could surprise Devlin. The answer was coming straight toward him, the crazy Rockin' Rooster was strutting up the gravel drive from the barn toward Peter with a look just as evil as the man behind him. Peter felt a bubble of laughter coming up, but stifled it back down.

Not wanting to startle Devlin into accidentally firing the revolver, Peter let him in on part of the plan. "This rooster is crazy. You always having to kick the thing around the barn."

Devlin's only comment was, "Shut up and keep walking."

When the rooster was only three feet away, Peter kicked a foot out, then jumped back and to the right. Peter yelled, "Get back!"

The twinkling light off the gold rings attracted Rockin' Rooster's attention and his wrath. Not taking his eyes off the threat in front of him, Rockin Rooster flared out all his feathers, took flight for as high as he could go, and swung his sharp talons out to connect with a hand holding a gun. As Devlin stumbled back, startled by the feathers in his face and the pain emanating from his hand, Peter's fist connected with Devlin's chin. Devlin remembered no more for a good fifteen minutes.

Rockin' Rooster looked at the man on the ground, stretched out his neck and crowed before turning and sauntering back to the barn. Peter pulled off Devlin's tie, binding his hands behind his back. Bernadette had always said this rooster was good at his job. Who knew how good?

The police shook their head as they picked up Devlin. They were going to have to get more funding from the voters to add more cells to the jail if this continued. But a bigger problem existed, and the situation was far from humorous. All the officers knew Devlin: he contributed heavily to any fundraising by the fire or police departments, he worked with the Boys and Girls Club including funding issues, he attended city council meetings, and when the department had lost an officer, Devlin contributed heavily to helping the family.

The police didn't like the situation, but the captain told them to bring him in and they would work on the problem at the station. When the police tried to load Devlin into the police car, he went berserk, kicking one officer in the face and another in the groin. That was the end of an understanding police force.

Chapter 57
Finding Home

(January 7, 2000)

That evening, Carney, Tierney, and Bernadette delayed dinner, waiting for Peter to finish up with the FBI, local sheriff, and the Lebanon Police. Many of the parties involved in the scandal, including the EPA and staff from EwRM2, were at the police station until very late. It was 10:30 p.m. when Peter finally arrived back at the farm and everyone sat down for dinner.

In between bites, Peter told the full story. "Here is what we have put together so far. This entire scheme began with the Rossberg and Holcomb families, who have been friends for decades and we already know how the Rossberg family likes to manipulate a company's stock for their own profit.

"Devlin Holcomb isn't a blood relation to the Holcomb family, but married in. It is postulated that his goal isn't just the monetary gain through the manipulation of stocks, but also to steal intellectual property from EwRM2, feeding it bit by bit to foreign counties for a nice price.

"Holcomb is smart. We surmise, he began by hiring a private investigator to scrutinize individuals in the company, looking for weaknesses to exploit, such as affairs, or cheating on tax returns, or drug use. He would then call that person into his office and blackmail them, getting them to agree to sabotaging the EwRM2 product at directed times. Those conversations were videotaped, thus the camera imbedded in the wall, to ensure the employee didn't have a change of heart and go to authorities. When the product was sabotaged, Devlin and Senator Rossberg would play puts and calls, depending on the stock market, making a bundle as the company announced anther failed product.

"About this time, EwRM2 was back-engineering another strange material brought to them by the FBI, much like the back-engineering they did for nitinol. Holcomb was lazy and didn't want to bother with pollution controls for the back-engineering process or one other nickel process which required expensive pollution controls. What he did was put the two processes in the same building. He succeeded in blackmailing the government employee overseeing the back-engineering when it was discovered the government employee was having an affair. As a side note, I bet that government employee is wishing he had come clean about the affair with his spouse, because his problems today are much bigger. Anyway, that government employee, who was in a bind, put pressure on DEQ and EPA though the National Security Act to make the building "exempt" from any pollution controls. There is no actual pollution control exemption through the National Security Act, but DEQ and EPA were unwilling to put the effort into challenging the situation. It would have been possible to add pollution controls, but Holcomb was becoming greedier and more overconfident of his power. He didn't think he should spend money on pollution controls because he wanted that money for his own bonus.

"What they were taking out of the building and putting in personal vehicles is unknown and will have to be investigated further by the company.

"Holcomb's biggest concern was Bernadette; that she would find out about the pollution, and he didn't believe he could manipulate or blackmail her. To get her out of the picture, he had an employee call Greg Tucker and report that Bernadette was illegally managing and shipping waste. That began the intense interest in the calcium chloride and what Holcomb hoped to be a way to get her arrested, which of course, would lead to a "clean" termination of her employment.

"Greg Tucker wasn't involved in any stock trading; he was being his normal self, egotistically out of control and therefore, pushing for Bernadette's arrest. Senator Rossberg approached Bernadette's mother for the same reason, hoping to have a method for Bernadette's arrest.

"The SEC got a tip about insider trading, which lead to their investigation. Now, the FBI hopes they can find Ed Kiel's body. Devlin and the senator were not playing around. Bernadette was lucky to survive.

"Things took a turn for the worst when Bernadette overhead the conversation about the natural gas lines and found the mysterious hidden compartment in the closet containing the tungsten tire studs. An instrument shop employee suspected Bernadette knew something and reported that to Devlin. That lead to the misadventure while skiing, as Devlin and the senator were trying to kill Bernadette, but wanted her death to be in a foreign country. The men involved in that attempt on Bernadette's life are being tracked down in Canada.

"Calvin Rossberg, our dear Ross, got involved, attempting to take Bernadette out of the picture though the enforcement action. No one knows exactly where Ross is. They had a trail on him until he got to Uruapan, Mexico, where they lost him. I don't know if Ross can survive in Mexico, but if he does, and he gets enough plastic surgery, we should expect him back in our lives within the next decade.

"Everyone is impressed with Bernadette's ability to train rats. You wouldn't believe all the jokes. They are thinking of starting a Rattus Unit for helping the police.

"Tomorrow I am heading back to Seattle for good. EPA might have to pay some money to EwRM2 for all this ridiculous enforcement mess, but then EwRM2 could be fined for the pollution problems associate with the back-engineering building. Maybe they will call it even. EwRM2 may work a deal with Cutter, to help him out. David Bernstein's professorship situation will need to be evaluated and corrected.

My boss understands that Ross hacked my purchasing account, so I will still have a job there."

Tierney chimed in, "Well, in case anyone is interested, I am staying in Oregon. I found a nice woman to date and I am looking at getting a real job with Weyerhaeuser. I can put my truck to real use that way."

Bernadette put her hand over Tierney's and said, "I am glad to hear that. It means a lot to me that you will stay here." With a sly smile, Bernadette added, "I have decided I am going to get a few more roosters and keep rats as pets." All the men groaned. "I haven't been able to find the four rats at the landing area. I decided, I am going to build them a makeshift shelter and put feed up there twice a week. Otherwise, this was just a cruel exercise for them. They helped me and if I don't help them, they won't survive in the new surroundings this time of year."

Carney said little that night and everyone noticed.

-

That evening while in bed, Carney and Bernadette discussed Bernadette's mother and that her mother, of all things possible in the world, had protected her. Bernadette said, "I have to rethink everything I knew about my mother. Perhaps none of us are all evil or all good. We are all just trying."

Carney stared at the ceiling a long time before he said, "Would you like to buy another farm with me? Have me stay in the States?"

Crawling on top of him, she said, "Of course. Why would you think otherwise?"

"You like your independence. Maybe you don't want me around after I have been absent for so long."

Bernadette gave him a kiss. "I do like my independence, and I would like to share it with you."

The End

About the Author

329

Era Lewis, born in Alaska, grew up outside of Lebanon, Oregon. She received her degree in chemistry from UCSD. In 2011, Era returned to the family farm, where she shares her life with nature.

Era is also the author of a nonfiction book:
A Woman's Guide: Cultivating Everyday Personal Magnificence

Story Summary:

Bernadette Engstrom was born with an innate strength to defend spirit and nature; a life requiring great resourcefulness should she choose to follow that path. As a young girl, she receives important tutelage which provides her with skills necessary to fight highly variable forces, both ordinary and extraordinary, which so often confront the human condition of those who stand for righteousness. Her love of animals further cements her course and by the sides of many different species, she gives and gains strength.

As an adult, Bernadette's life becomes more complicated and secretive. While on a university work-study program in Europe, Bernadette saves a man from drowning following a car accident. She is forced to marry him, as this is the only means to protect her from the people inside and outside of his secretive agency. Although they become devoted spouses, and Bernadette finds much love and courage within the relationship, they spend much of their lives on separate continents. Only a few of her husband's associates are aware of the marriage. It is within this perceived social condition of a single, lonely woman that Bernadette is stereotyped and viewed by others as a weaker and more vulnerable person, further emboldening forces against her.

In her mid-thirties, Bernadette begins working in the Environmental Department for a metal manufacturing company, a job she initially enjoys and feels compassionate about. When she accidentally discovers secrets within the company, her life is threatened. But what Bernadette has seen at her job isn't by itself a crime. Without understanding how the secrets fit into the larger picture at the company, she is unable to seek help from authorities. To compilate matters, EPA investigates the daily shipment of a particular waste for which Bernadette is responsible. EPA oddly zeros in on Bernadette, a lower-level management person, with an intense surveillance program, attempting to arrest her alone, instead of looking at other key figures in the company.

Serious issues confront Bernadette, and she gives battle in creative and often amusing ways. It is her physical, emotional, and spiritual strength which makes her a formidable opponent.

What does Bernadette know? Will she understand how her discoveries within the company fit into illegal activities before she is killed? Will she have the strength to keep on fighting? These are the questions surrounding Bernadette's life and it is within this struggle that she finds the power of nature and her immense love for nature.